CALEB'S CROSSING

Zuriel
Bethia
Makepeace } Mayfield
Solace
Caleb (Cheeshahteaumauck ("hateful one"))
Iacoomis
Peter Folger
Aunt Hannah
Goody Branch
Nahnoso · Caleb + Nanaakomin's father
Nanaakomin - Caleb's brother
Tequamauk - Caleb's uncle / healer

Also by Geraldine Brooks

FICTION

People of the Book

March

Year of Wonders: A Novel of the Plague

NONFICTION

Foreign Correspondence:
A Pen Pal's Journey from Down Under to All Over

Nine Parts of Desire:
The Hidden World of Islamic Women

Geraldine Brooks was born and raised in Sydney. As a foreign correspondent she covered crises in the Middle East, Africa and the Balkans before turning to fiction. Her novels *Year of Wonders* and *People of the Book* were international bestsellers, and her second novel, *March*, won the Pulitzer Prize. She currently lives on the island of Martha's Vineyard with her husband and two sons.

Geraldine Brooks

CALEB'S CROSSING

A Novel

FOURTH ESTATE • *London, New York, Sydney* and *Auckland*

Fourth Estate
An imprint of HarperCollins*Publishers*

First published in 2011 by Viking Penguin,
a member of Penguin Group (USA) Inc.
First published in Australia in 2011
by HarperCollins*Publishers* Australia Pty Limited
ABN 36 009 913 517
harpercollins.com.au

HarperCollins*Publishers*
25 Ryde Road, Pymble, Sydney, NSW 2073, Australia
31 View Road, Glenfield, Auckland 0627, New Zealand
A 53, Sector 57, Noida, UP, India
77–85 Fulham Palace Road, London W6 8JB, United Kingdom
2 Bloor Street East, 20th floor, Toronto, Ontario M4W 1A8, Canada
10 East 53rd Street, New York, NY 10022, USA

National Library of Australia Cataloguing-in-Publication entry

Brooks, Geraldine.
Caleb's crossing / Geraldine Brooks.
ISBN: 978 0 0073 3353 0 (hbk.: C format)
ISBN: 978 0 7322 8922 5 (pbk.: C format)
A823.3

Hardback: Original jacket design by Leo Nickolls
Jacket images: Letter from Caleb by The Royal Society; Wampum Belt by Getty Images;
    author photo by Randi Baird
Paperback: Cover design by Jaya Miceli, adapted by Darren Holt, HarperCollins Design Studio
Cover images: © William Waterway Marks; (man) © Donald Carter
Endpapers/inside cover and letter on page viii: Letter from Caleb by The Royal Society
Internal design by Francesca Belanger
Map by Laura Hartman Maestro
Typeset in 12/18pt Brioso Pro by Kirby Jones
Printed and bound in Australia by Griffin Press
60gsm Hi Bulk Book Cream used by HarperCollins*Publishers* is a natural, recyclable product
made from wood grown in sustainable forests. The manufacturing processes conform to the
environmental regulations in the country of origin, Finland.

6 5 4 3 2 1   11 12 13 14 15

For Bizuayehu,
who also made a crossing.

12

Honoratissimi benefactores

Referunt Historici, de Orpheo musico, et insigni Poeta quod ab Apolline Lyram acceperit, eaque tantum excoluerit ut dulcis cantu sylvas, saxaque moverit, & arbores ingentes post se traxerit, ferasque ferocissimas mitiores reddiderit, imo quod accepta Lyra ad inferos descenderit, et Plutonem et Proserpinam suo Carmine demulserit, et Eurydicen uxorem ab inferis ad superos evexerit: Hoc symbolum esse statuunt Philosophi Antiquissimi, ut ostendant quod tanta est vis et virtus Doctrinae et politioris literaturae ad mutandum Barbarorum ingenium: qui sunt tanquam arbores, saxa, et bruta animantia: et eorum quasi metamorphosin efficiendum eosque tanquam Tigres Cicurandos et post se trahendos.

Deus vos delegit istos Patronos nostros, et cum omni sapientia, insummaque Commiseratione vos ornavit, ut nobis paganis salutifera opem ferratis, qui vitam, progeniemque à Majoribus nostris ducebamus. tam animo, quam corporequé nudi fuimus, et ab omni humanitate alieni fuimus, in desertis here et illac variisque erroribus ducti fuimus.

Ô terque quaterque ornatissimi, amantissimique viri, quas quantasque quam maximas, immensasque gratias vobis tribuamus: eo quod omnium rerum Copiam nobis suppeditaveritis propter educationem nostram, et ad sustentationem Corporum nostrorum: immensas, maximasque expensas attulistis.

Et praecipue quas quantasque Gratias Deo opt. Max. dabimus, qui sanctas scripturas nobis revelavit, Dominumque Jesum Christum nobis demonstravit, qui est via veritatis atque vitae, praeter haec omnia, praestitia misericordiae Divinae, aliqua saepe relicta sunt, ut instrumenta fiamus, ad declarandum, et propagandum Evangelium Cognatis nostris Conterraneisque ut illi etiam Deum Cognoscant et Christum.

Quamvis non possumus par pari reddere vobis, reliquisque Benefactoribus nostris, Id tamen speramus, nos non defuturos apud Deum supplicationibus imposterum exorare pro illis piis misericordibus viris, qui supersunt in regno Angliae, qui pro nobis tantam vim auri, argentique attulerunt ad salutem animarum nostrarum procurandam, et pro vobis etiam, qui instrumenta, et quasi aquae ductus fuistis, omnia ista beneficentia nobis conferendi.

Vestrae Dignitati devotissimus: Caleb Cheeshahteaumauk

Author's Note

This is a work of imagination, inspired by the life of Caleb Cheeshahteaumauk, a member of the Wôpanâak tribe of Noepe (Martha's Vineyard), born circa 1646, and the first Native American to graduate from Harvard College.

The character of Caleb as portrayed in this novel is, in every way, a work of fiction. For the facts of Caleb's life, insofar as they are documented, please see the afterword.

I have presumed to give Caleb's name to my imagined character in the hope of honoring the struggle, sacrifice and achievement of this remarkable young scholar.

Shown opposite and on the endpapers/inside cover is the only document known to have survived from his hand: a letter, in Latin, to the England-based benefactors who funded his education. In it, Caleb discusses the myth of Orpheus as it relates to his own experience of crossing between two very different cultures.

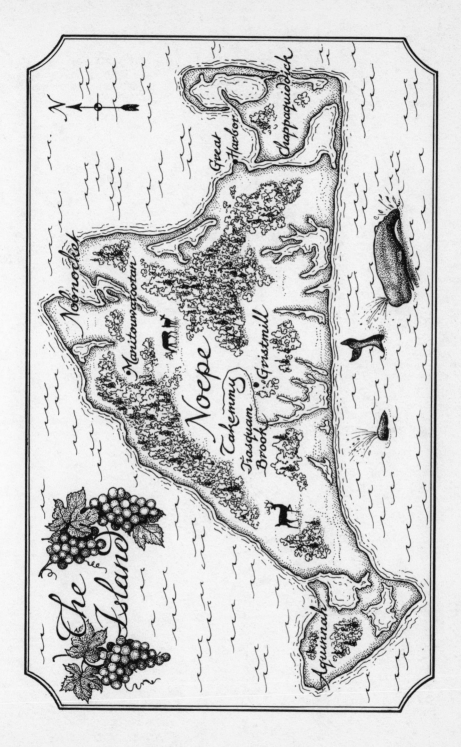

The Island

N

Chappaquidoick

Great Harbor

Nobnocket

Manitouwayootan

Noepe

Takemmy

Gristmill

Trasquam Brook

Aquinnah

Anno 1660

Aetatis Suae 15

Great Harbor

I

He is coming on the Lord's Day. Though my father has not seen fit to give me the news, I have the whole of it.

They supposed I slept, which I might have done, as I do each night, while my father and Makepeace whisper together on the far side of the blanket that divides our chamber. Most nights I take comfort in the low murmur of their voices. But last evening Makepeace's voice rose urgent and anguished before my father hushed him. I expect that was what pulled me back from sleep. My brother frowns on excessive displays of temperament. I turned on my shakedown then and wondered, in a drowsy way, what it was that exercised him so. I could not hear what my father said, but then my brother's voice rose again.

"How can you expose Bethia in this way?"

Of course, once I caught my own name that was an end to it; I was fully awake. I raised my head and strained to hear more. It was not difficult, for Makepeace could not govern his tongue, and though I could not make out my father's words at all, fragments of my brother's replies were clear.

"Of what matter that he prays? He is only—what is it?— Not yet a year?—removed from paganism, and that man who long had charge of him is Satan's thrall—the most stiff-necked and dangerous of all of them, as you have said yourself often enough. . . ."

My father cut in then, but Makepeace would not be hushed.

3

"Of course not, father. Nor do I question his ability. But because he has a facility for Latin does not mean he knows the decencies required of him in a Christian home. The risk is . . ."

At that moment, Solace cried out, so I reached for her. They perceived I was awake then, and said no more. But it was enough. I wrapped up Solace and drew her to me on the shakedown. She shaped herself against me like a nestling bird and settled easily back to sleep. I lay awake, staring into the dark, running my hand along the rough edge of the roof beam that slanted an arm's length above my head. Five days from now, the same roof will cover us both.

Caleb is coming to live in this house.

In the morning, I did not speak of what I had overheard. Listening, not speaking, has been my way. I have become most proficient in it. My mother taught me the use of silence. While she lived, I think that not above a dozen people in this settlement ever heard the sound of her voice. It was a fine voice, low and mellow, carrying the lilt of the Wiltshire village in England where she had passed her girlhood. She would laugh, and make rhymes full of the strange words of that place and tell us tales of things we had never seen: cathedrals and carriages, great rivers wide as our harbor, and streets of shops where one who had the coin might buy all manner of goods. But this was within the house, when we were a family. When she went about in the world, it was with downcast eyes and sealed lips. She was like a butterfly, full of color and vibrancy when she chose to open her wings, yet hardly visible when she closed them. Her modesty was like a cloak that she put on, and so adorned, in meekness and discretion, it seemed she passed almost hidden from people, so that betimes they would speak in front of her as if she were not there. Later, at board, if the matter was fit for childish ears, she would relate this or that important or diverting news she had gleaned about our neighbors and how they did. Oft times, what she learned was of great use to father, in his ministry, or to grandfather in his magistracy.

I copied her in this, and that was how I learned I was to loose her. Our neighbor, Goody Branch, who is midwife here, had sent me off to her cottage to fetch more groaning beer, in the hope that it would cool my mother's childbed fever. Anxious as I was to fetch it back for her, I stood by the latch for some minutes when I heard my mother speaking. What she spake concerned her death. I waited to hear Goody Branch contradict her, to tell her all would be well. But no such words came. Instead, Goody Branch answered that she would see to certain matters that troubled my mother and that she should make her mind easy on those several accounts.

Three days later, we buried her. Although it was spring according to the calendar, the ground was not yet thawed. So we set a fire on the place my father had chosen, between the graves of my twin brother Zuriel, who had died when he was nine years old, and my other infant brother who had not tarried here long enough for us to name him. We tended the fire all through the night. Even so, at dawn, when my father and Makepeace commenced to dig, the shovel rang on that iron-hard earth. The sound of it is with me, still. The labor was such that father trembled all over afterward, his limbs palsied with the work of putting her to rest. So it is, out here on this island, where we dwell with our faces to the sea and our backs to the wilderness. Like Adam's family after the fall, we have all things to do. We must be fettler, baker, apothecary, grave digger. Whatever the task, we must do it, or else do without.

It is near to a year now since my mother's death, and since then I have had charge of Solace, and of the keeping of this house. I miss my mother, as I know father does, and Makepeace too in his way, although his affections are less warmly worn than ours. His faith also seems stronger in the way he is able to accept what befalls us as the working of divine will. We have all spent many sore days and nights examining our souls and our conduct to read what lesson the Lord intended for us in taking her so soon; what failings and sins he did mean to punish in us. And though I sit in prayerful reflection with my father on this matter of our spiritual estate, I have not given to him the ground of what I know to be true.

I killed my mother. I know that some would say I was a child who Satan, trickster, toyed with. But as to soul, there is neither youth nor age. Sin stains us at our birth and shadows our every hour. As the scripture tells us: *Their foot shall slide in due time.* Loose one's footing, as I did, and age matters not. One cedes all claims to childish innocence. And my sins were not mere nursery mischief but matters etched in stone upon the tablets of mortal error. I broke the Commandments, day following day. And I did it knowingly. Minister's daughter: how could I say otherwise? Like Eve, I thirsted after forbidden knowledge and I ate forbidden fruit. For her, the apple, for me, the white hellebore—different plants, proffered from the same hand. And just as that serpent must have been lovely—I see him, his lustrous, shimmering scales, pouring liquid over Eve's shoulders, his jewel eyes luminous as they gazed into her own—so too did Satan come to me in a form of irresistible beauty.

Break God's laws and suffer ye his wrath. Well, and so I do. The Lord lays his hand sore upon me, as I bend under the toil I now have—mother's and mine, both. The tasks stretch out from the gray slough before dawn to the guttered taper of night. At fifteen, I have taken up the burdens of a woman, and have come to feel I am one. Furthermore, I am glad of it. For I now no longer have the time to fall into such sins as I committed as a girl, when hours that were my own to spend spread before me like a gift. Those hot, salt-scoured afternoons when the shore curved away in its long glistening arc toward the distant bluffs. The leaf-dappled, loamy mornings in the cool bottoms, where I picked the sky-colored berries and felt each one burst, sweet and juicy, in my mouth. I made this island mine, mile by mile, from the soft, oozing clay of the rainbow cliffs to the rough chill of the granite boulders that rise abruptly in the fields, thwarting the plough, shading the sheep. I love the fogs that wreathe us all in milky veils, and the winds that moan and keen in the chimney piece at night. Even when the wrack line is crusted with salty ice and the ways through the woods crunch under my clogs, I drink the cold air in the low blue gleam that sparkles on the snow. Every inlet and outcrop of this place, I love. We are taught early here to see Nature as a foe to be subdued. But I came, by stages, to worship it. You could say that for me, this island and her bounties became the first of my false gods, the original sin that begot so much idolatry.

Now, here, in the scant days I have left before Caleb comes to us, I have decided to set down my spiritual diary, and give an accounting for those months when my heart sat so loose from God. I have gathered what scraps of paper I could scavenge from my brother's store, and I intend to use whatever moments I can eke out before each day's weariness claims me. My hand is unlovely, since father did not school me in writing, but as this relation is for my own eyes, it makes no mind. Since I cannot say, yet, whether I will find the courage to stand in meeting some day and deliver an accounting of myself, this will have to do. In my affliction I have besought the Lord but I have had no sign that I am saved. When I look at my hands and wrists, marred by the marks of small burns from cook pots and flying embers, every red weal or white pucker brings to my mind's eye that eternal fire, and the writhing masses of the damned, among whom I must expect to spend eternity.

God alone ordains the damned and the saved and naught that I set down on these pages can change that. But since Caleb is to come here, trailing about him the smoke of those heathen fires and the scent of those wild, vision-filled hours, I need to be clear in my own mind and honest in my heart where I stand with regard to such matters, so that I can truly put them from me. I must do this for his sake, as well as for my own. I know that father sets great store in Caleb. He sees him, more than any other here, as a great hope to lead his people. Certainly Caleb seems to want this also; no one toils at his book more diligently; no one has gathered such a rich harvest of knowledge in the scant seasons he has had to study these things. But I also know this to be true: Caleb's soul is stretched like the rope in a tug o' war, between my father and his own uncle, the pawaaw. Just as my father has his hopes, so too does that sorcerer. Caleb will lead his people, I am sure of it. But in which direction? Of that, I am not in the least bit certain.

II

O nce, on a stormy night two winters since, when we had toiled through the rain and wind to pull out the boats and lash them safe, we came back to the house with water lacquered to our cloaks and frozen strands of hair clinking each against each as we moved. Our hands were numb as we crammed daub into the cracks and chinks of the house and battled to repair the oil paper that had torn loose on the windows. (We had no glass, then.) Later, as I sat by the fire, the ice melting from my person, the water pooling about my feet, Makepeace asked father the question that was even then forming in my own mind: why was it that grandfather had sought the patent to this island? Why put seven miles of confounding currents between himself and the other English, at a time when there was land and to spare on the mainland for any who wanted to hive out a new settlement?

Father said that grandfather, as a young man, had served others, putting his skills to work as factor for a wealthy nobleman who rewarded him by laying baseless charges against him. While grandfather was able to exonerate himself, the experience left him bitter, and he resolved to answer to others no more. That included John Winthrop, the governor of the Massachusetts Bay colony, a man of estimable parts, but a man increasingly willing to wield cruel punishments against those whose ideas did not accord with his own. More than one man had had his ears cut off or his nose slashed open; a dissident woman, pregnant and trailing a dozen children, had been expelled into the wilderness. And those were his Christian brothers and sisters. What he had allowed in regard to the Pequot was, my father said, not fit for our hearing.

"Your grandfather felt he could do better. So he bought these patents, which were outside the purview of Winthrop's governance, and gathered several like-minded men who were prepared to accept the light hand of his direction. Me, he sent—in 1642—to make the first crossing. It is a matter of pride to me, son, that your grandfather insisted, even though he had paid the English authorities for the patents, on paying the sonquem of this place also. Every hut and house we have built here is on land willingly sold to us through negotiations that I conducted honorably. You will hear, perhaps, that not all the sonquem's followers agreed with their chief in this matter, and some now say that he himself did not fully understand that we meant to keep the land from them forever. Be that as it may, what's done is done and it was done lawfully."

I thought, but did not say, that grandfather could hardly have expected the fine points of English property law to count for much to some three thousand people whose reputation, prior to our landing, had been ferocious. If there was pride to be taken in the matter, it could only be pride in the canniness of grandfather's plan, and of father's courage and tact in executing it. Father had been but nineteen years old when he came here. Perhaps his youth and gentle temper had persuaded the sonquem that there was no harm in the "Coatmen," as they called us. And what harm could there be to them, from just a score of families, setting down cheek by jowl along a little edge of harborfront, while their own bands ranged hundreds strong across the island wheresoever they would?

Father picked up the thread of his thought as if it were a tangled skein that he worried at. "We have been good neighbors, yes; I believe so," he said. "And why should we not? There is no reason to be otherwise, no matter what slanders the Alden family and their faction concoct. 'You may disturb and vex the devil, but you'll make no Christians there'—that's what Giles Alden said to me, when first I set out to preach at the wetus. And how wrong he is proven! For several years I drank the dust of those huts, helping in whatever practical thing I could do for them, happy to win the ears of even one or two for a few words about Christ. And now, at last, I begin to distill in their minds the pure liquor of the gospel. To take a people who were traveling apace the broadway to hell, and to be able to turn them, and set their face to God. . . . It is what we must strive for. They are an admirable people, in many ways, if you trouble to know them."

How I could have astonished him, and my brother too, even then, had I opened my mouth and ventured to say, in Wampanaontoaonk, that I *had* troubled to know them; that I knew them, in some particulars, better than father, who was their missionary and their minister. But as I have set down here, I had learned early the value of silence, and I did not lightly give away the state of myself. So I got up from the fire then, and made myself busy, wetting yeast and flour for a sponge to use in the next day's bread.

Our neighbors. As a child I did not think of them so. I suppose, like everyone, I called them salvages, pagans, barbarians, the heathen. As a young child, in fact, I barely thought of them at all. I lived with my twin brother, at our mother's hem, in those days, and their doings did not touch ours. I have heard tell that it was more than a year before any soul among them came near to our plantation, neither to hinder nor to help. If my father had business in their settlements on grandfather's behalf, he went out to this or that otan alone and I knew nothing of it.

It was somewhen later—I am not sure, exactly, the date—but after the village of Great Harbor built its meeting house, that one poor despised fellow of theirs began to lurk about on the Sabbath. Of mean descent and unpromising countenance, he was an outcast among his own, deemed unfit to be a warrior and not privileged with the common right to hunt with his sonquem or share in the gatherings at which the sonquem gave generously of food and goods to his people.

That my father ministered to this man, I knew, and thought little of it. It seemed only a common act of Christian charity such as we are commanded: *Whatsoever you do to the least of them . . .* But it was from this unpromising metal that father began to forge his Cross. Mother was fairly taken aback, one Sabbath, when father presented this man, whose name was Iacoomis, as his guest at our board. It happened that this man's unprepossessing body housed a quick mind. He learned his letters avidly and in return, commenced to teach father Wampanaontoaonk speech, to further his mission. As father struggled with the new language, so too did I learn, as a girlchild will, confined to the hearth and the dooryard as adult business ebbs and flows around her. I learned it, I suppose, as I was learning English speech, my mind supple then and ready to receive new words. As father and Iacoomis sat, repeating a phrase over and over, often it fell into my own mouth long before father had mastery of it. As father learned, he in turn strove to teach some few useful words to my grandfather's clerk, Peter Folger, who was wise enough to see its value in trading and negotiations. For a time, when we were still very small, Zuriel and I made a covert game of learning it, and spoke it privily, as a kind of secret tongue between the two of us. But as Zuriel grew bigger he was less about the hearth, tearing hither and yon as boychildren are permitted to do. So as he lost the words and I continued to gain them, the game withered. I have often wondered if what happened later had its roots in this: that the Indian tongue was bound up in my heart with these earliest memories of my brother, so that, on meeting with another of his same age who spoke it, these tender and dormant affections awoke within me. By the time I met Caleb, I already had a great store of common words and phrases. Since then, I have come to speak that tongue in my dreams.

I remember once, when I was small, and had said "the salvages" in my father's hearing, he reproved me. "Do not call them salvages. Use the name they give themselves, Wampanoag. It means Easterners."

Poor father. He was so very proud of his efforts with those difficult words; words so long one might think the roots had set and grown since the fall of the Babel tower. And yet father never mastered pronunciation, which is the chief grace of their tongue. Nor did he grasp the way the words built themselves, sound by sound, into particular meanings. "Easterners," indeed. As if they speak of east or west as we do. Nothing is so plain and ordinary in that tongue. Wop, related to their word for white, carries a sense of the first milky light that brightens the horizon before the sun appears. The ending sound refers to animate beings. So, their name for themselves, properly rendered in English, is People of the First Light.

Since I was born here, I too have come to feel that I am a person of the first light, perched at the very farthest edge of the new world, first witness to each dawn of the turning globe. I count it no strange thing that one may, in a single day, observe a sunrise out of the sea and a sunset back into it, though newcomers are quick to remark how uncommon it is. At sunset, if I am near the water—and it is hard to be very far from it here—I pause to watch the splendid disc set the brine aflame and then douse itself in its own fiery broth. As the dimmet deepens, I think of those left behind in England. They say that dawn creeps closer there even as our darkness gathers. I think of them, waking to another dawn of oppression under the boot of the reprobate king. At meeting, father read to us a poem from one of our reformed brethren there:

We are on tiptoe in this land,
Waiting to pass to the American Strand.

I was used to offer a prayer for them, that God hasten their way hither, and that he grant their morning bring not fear, but a peace such as we here are come to know, under the light hand of my grandfather's governance and the gentle ministry of my father.

As I think of it now, I haven't said that prayer in a while. I no longer feel at peace here.

III

The account of my fall must begin three years since, in that lean summer of my twelfth year. As newcomers will in a foreign place, we clung too long to the old habits and lifeways. Our barley did never seem to thrive here, yet families continued to plant it, just because they had always done so. At large expense, we had brought tegs from the mainland just a year earlier, mainly to be raised for their wool, for it was plain that we would need to make our own cloth, and linen did not answer in the foul winters here. But the promise of spring lamb at Eastertide proved very great, and so we put the ram to the ewes too early. Then we found ourselves in the grip of a stubborn winter that would not cede to milder days, no matter what the calendar might say on the matter. Though we all of us tried to keep the newborn lambs warm at the hearth, the bitter winds that howled across the salt-hay pastures, and the hard frosts that bit off the buds, carried away more than we could spare. All was common land then, and we had built no barns nor proper folds. With little store of saltmeat after so long a winter, and no promise of any fresh, fishing and daily foraging became our mainstay.

First feast, then famine. Then out on the flats a'clammin'. Such was the doggerel that year. Since clamming was a despised chore, Makepeace ensured that it fell to me. He was always quick to assert his rights, he who was both eldest, and, since Zuriel's death, the only son. If that was not enough to secure his liberty from whatever task he shirked, he would plead the heavy demands of his studies, with which, as he put it, "my sister is not burdened." This last stuck in my craw like grit, for I coveted the instruction that Makepeace found so troublesome and he well knew it.

Father permitted me to take the mare, since the best clamming flats were off to the west. I was meant to seek out my Aunt Hannah, and go in her company. It was a rule that none might walk nor ride alone more than one mile from the edge of our settlement. But my aunt was harried to a raveling by all her other chores, and was more than happy, one mild day, when a softer air had touched my cheek and I offered to do her clamming for her. That was the first time I broke the commandment of obedience, for I did not tarry for another companion as she bade me, but rode off by a new way, alone. It is no easy thing to be forever watched, and judged, as I must be as the minister's daughter. When I was out of sight of the settlement, I hitched my skirt and galloped, as fast as Speckle would consent to carry me, just to be free and gone and away.

I grew to love the fair, large heaths, the tangled woods and the wide sheets of dune-sheltered water where I had the liberty of my own company. So I would strive to get away to such places every day, excepting on the Sabbath (the which we observed strictly and prayerfully, my father adhering to the letter of the commandment—a day to be kept—not an hour or two at meeting and then on to other pursuits).

As often as I could, I would hide in my basket one of Makepeace's Latin books, either his accidence, which he was meant to have had by heart long since, or his nomenclator, or the *Sententiae Pueriles*. If I could get none of these unnoticed, then I would take one of father's texts, and hope my understanding was equal to it.

Aside from the Bible and Foxe's Martyrs, father held that it was undesirable for a young girl to be too much at her book. When my brother Zuriel was alive, he had instructed us both in reading. These were sweet hours to me, but they had come to a sudden end, the very day of Zuriel's accident. We had been at our books for some hours, and father, pleased with our progress, offered to take us for a ride on the hay wain. It was a fair evening, and Zuriel was in high spirits, plucking hay from the bales and forcing it down my collar so that it tickled me. I was squirming and laughing merrily. Reaching behind me to fetch out an itchy stalk, I did not see Zuriel overbalance on the bale and so I could not cry out to father, whose back was turned to us, driving the cart. Before we knew that Zuriel had fallen, the rear cartwheel, made of iron, had run right across his leg and severed it to the bone. Father tried with all his strength to stanch the bleeding, all the while crying out prayers to God. I held Zuriel's head in my hands and looked into his beloved face and called to him to stay with me, but it did no good. I watched as the light in his eyes drained out of him with his life's blood.

That was at harvest time. Throughout leaf fall and winter, we all did nought but mourn him. We walked through the chores that must be done, and then sat to pray, although often enough my mind was too clouded by grief and memory to do even that. It was late spring before my thoughts turned again to my lessons, and I finally felt able to ask father when they might resume. He told me then that he did not intend to instruct me further, since I already had my catechism by heart.

But he could not stop me overhearing his lessons with Makepeace. So I listened and I learned. Over time, while my father thought I was tending the cook fire or working on the loom, I shored up my little foundations of knowledge: some Latin here, some Hebrew there, some logic and some rhetoric. It was not hard to learn these things, for although Makepeace was two years my senior, he was an indifferent scholar. Past fourteen then, he might have been well begun at the college in Cambridge, yet father had determined to keep him close, in the hope of better preparing him. I think that Zuriel's death made father all the more determined in this, and I think my elder brother carried a great burden, knowing that all of father's hopes for a son who would follow him in godliness and learning now rested on him alone. There were times I worried for my brother. At Harvard College, the tutor surely would not be so forbearing as our patient father. But I must own that my envy overleaped my concern most of the time. I suppose it was pride that led me into error: I began to chime in with any answers that my brother could not give.

At first, when I gave out a Latin declension, father was amused, and laughed. But my mother, working the loom as I spun the yarn, drew a sharp breath and put a hand up to her mouth. She made no comment then, but later I understood. She had perceived what I, in my pride, had not: that father's pleasure was of a fleeting kind—the reaction one might have if a cat were to walk about upon its hind legs. You smile at the oddity but find the gait ungainly and not especially attractive. Soon, the trick is wearisome, and later, worrisome, for a cat on hind legs is not about its duty, catching mice. In time, when the cat seems minded to perform its trick, you curse at it, and kick it.

The more I allowed that I had learned what my older brother could not, the more it began to vex father. His mild countenance began to draw itself into a frown whenever I interrupted. For several months this was so, but I did not read the lesson he intended for me. In time, he took to sending me to outdoor tasks whenever he intended to instruct Makepeace. The second or third occasion, when I perceived this was to be the way of things, I gave him a look which must have revealed more than I intended. Mother saw, and shook her head at me in admonishment. Nevertheless I let the door fall heavily behind me on my way out. This caused father to follow me into the yard. He called me to him, and I came, expecting to be chastised. My cap was a little askew. He reached out a hand and straightened it, then he let his fingers brush my cheek tenderly.

"Bethia, why do you strive so hard to quit the place in which God has set you?" His voice was gentle, not angry. "Your path is not your brother's, it cannot be. Women are not made like men. You risk addling your brain by thinking on scholarly matters that need not concern you. I care only for your present health and your future happiness. It is not seemly for a wife to know more than her husband . . ."

"Wife?" I was so taken aback that I interrupted without even meaning to speak. I was but recently turned twelve years old.

"Yes, wife. It is early to speak of it, but it is what you will be, and soon enough. Daughter, you, in your proper modesty, cannot know it, but those with eyes see in you the promise of a comely womanhood. It has been spoken of." I think I blushed russet; certainly my skin burned so hot that even the ends of my hair felt as if they were alight at my scalp. "Do not concern yourself. Nothing improper has been said, and I have answered what was necessary, that the time to think about such things is still years off. But it is your destiny to be married to a good man from our small society here, and I would do you no favor if I were to send you to your husband with a mind honed to find fault in his every argument or to better his in every particular. A husband must rule his home, Bethia, as God rules his faithful. If we lived still in England, or even on the mainland, you could have your choice of educated men. But on this island, that is not the way of it. You can read well, I know, even write a little, sufficient to keep a day book, as your mother does, for the benefit of the household. But 'tis enough. Already it sets you far apart from most others of your sex. Tend to your huswifery, or look to developing some herb lore, if you must be learning something. Improve your wits usefully and honorably in such things as belong to a woman."

There were tears starting in my eyes. I looked down, so that he would not notice, and scuffed at the ground with the toe of my clog. He rested a hand on my bowed head. His voice was very gentle. "Is it such a terrible thing, to contemplate a useful life such as your mother leads? Do not belittle it, Bethia. It is no small thing to be a beloved wife, to keep a godly house, to raise sons of your own..."

"Sons?" I looked up at father, and the word caught in my throat. Sons like Zuriel—bright, sunny boy, cut down in childhood. Or like the babe who also would have carried that name, had he lived but an hour in this world. Or sons like Makepeace, slow of wit, stinting in affection.

My brother had come out from the house. He stood behind father, his brows drawn and his arms folded across his chest. Despite his frown, I sensed he was taking a vast pleasure in observing father reduce me.

Father, for his part, looked suddenly weary. "Yes. Sons. And daughters, too, as you know full well I meant. Be content, I beg you. If you must read something, read your Bible. I commend to you especially Proverbs 31: verses 10 to 31. . . ."

"You mean *Eshet chayil?*" I had learned the passage because father recited it for mother, for whom it might well have been written, she truly being a woman of valor, her long days consumed with just such unsung tasks as the lines described. Father would look into her face and chant the Hebrew, and its hard consonants brought to my mind the beating of a hot sun on the dry stone walls of David's city. Then he would say the words to her in English.

Two sins, pride and anger, overmastered me then. I could not govern myself, but spoke out petulantly. "Shall you have it in Hebrew? *Eshet chayil mi yimtza v'rachok . . .*"

Father's eyes widened as I spoke, and his lips thinned. But Makepeace erupted, loud and angry. "Enough! Pride is a sin, sister. Beware of it. Remember that a bird, too, can imitate sounds. You can recite: what of it? For at one and the same time, you reveal that you know nothing of the lessons of the very text you parrot. Your own noise is drowning out the voice of God. Quiet your mind. Open your heart. Do this. You will soon see your error."

He turned on his heel and went back into the house. Father followed him. They were both of them angry that day, but not so angry as I. I was so eaten with it that I broke the handle on the churn from thumping it so hard. I still have the scar on my palm where the splintering wood tore my flesh. Mother bound up my hand and salved it. When I looked into her kind, tired eyes I felt ashamed. I would not, for all the world, have her think that

I belittled her, in thought or word. As if she knew my mind, she smiled at me, and held my bound hand to her lips. "God does all things for a reason, Bethia. If he gave you a quick mind, be sure of it, he wants you to use it. It is your task to discern how to use it for his glory." She did not have to add the words: "and not merely for your own." I heard them in my heart.

I took my mother's words as license enough to continue to study in secret. If it had to be alone and unassisted, so much the worse. But study I would, till my eyes smarted from the effort. I could do no other.

I do not mean to say that all my stolen hours were spent at book. I learned in other ways, also. I thought upon what father had said in regard to herbs, and began to ask Goody Branch and others who were wise in such things. There was a prodigious amount to know, not just the centuries-old lore of familiar English herbs, but the uses just now being found out for the new country's unfamiliar roots and leaves. Goody Branch was pleased to have me at her side as she collected plants and made her decoctions. She told me, too, all she had learned of how a child is fashioned and grows within the womb. She said that every woman should be wise in the things that belong to her own body. Somewhen, she would take me with her to visit a goodwife who was with child. If the woman did not mind it, she would lay my hands on the swollen belly and show me where to feel for the shapeling that grew within. She taught me how to reckon, from its size, the exact number of weeks since the child was got, and to figure when she would be called upon to midwife it. I became skilled at this, judging several births to the very week. When I was older, she said, I might attend the confinements and assist her.

On days when the fishing boats put out, I would beg a place onboard, the better to learn the farther reaches of the island, where even the weather might be different from Great Harbor's, even though the miles in distance were but few. The plants, also, were various, and if we put ashore I would gather what I could and study them. Goody Branch had said that we must pray to God that he let us read his signature, written plainly for the pious, in telltale markings, such as the liver-shaped leaves of liverwort, which might hint at what ailments each was good for.

There were other days, when I did not seek out Goody Branch or any other person, but just rambled, using the island as my text, lingering to glean what lessons each plant or stone might have to teach me. On such days, I missed Zuriel most. I longed to have him by my side, to share my finds, to puzzle out answers to the questions the world posed to me.

On one bright day, when the weather had warmed and steadied, I rode Speckle to the south shore. The prospect is remarkable there, where the wide white sands run uninterrupted for many leagues. I watched the heaving waves, smooth as glass, unspooling down the rim of my known world. I dismounted, untied my boots, stripped my hose and let the seafoam froth about my toes. I led the mare along the wrack line, studying white shells shaped like angels' wings, and bleached bones, light as air, which I took to be from a seabird. I picked up scallop shells in diverse colors and sizes—warm reds and yellows; cool, stippled grays—and reflected on the diversity of God's creation, and what might be the use and meaning of his making so many varieties of a single thing. If he created scallops simply for our nourishment, why paint each shell with delicate and particular colors? And why, indeed, trouble to make so many different things to nourish us, when in the Bible we read that a simple manna fed the Hebrews day following day? It came to me then that God must desire us to use each of our senses, to take delight in the varied tastes and sights and textures of his world. Yet this seemed to go against so many of our preachments against the sumptuary and the carnal. Puzzling upon it, I had walked some good distance, head down, inattentive to all but my thoughts, when I glanced up and saw them, far off; a band of them, painted strangely as I had been told they did for war, running headlong up the beach in my direction. I grasped Speckle's bridle and urged her in all haste into the dunes, which were high and undulant and concealing. I was cursing my folly, to find myself alone, far from help, and my mare, hard ridden, fairly spent. My boots I had tied together about my neck but my hose, knit by my own hand, I lost a grip on as I struggled with the horse, and watched several hours toil and several skeins of scarce, good yarn blow away into the sea.

In the lee of the dune, protected from the wind, the voices of the band carried toward me. They were laughing and calling out one to another. The sounds were of merriment, not warfare. Taking care that Speckle remained well concealed, I fell down upon my belly and crept along to a parting between the sand hills from whence I could look back along the beach. I saw then what my first fear had obscured from me: they were unarmed, carrying neither bow nor warclub. I raised a hand to shade my eyes against the glare and could make out a small sphere of tied-up skins, which they were kicking high into the air, and I knew then that they were about some kind of game. I had to look away then, for they were clad in

Adam's livery, save that their fig leaf was a scrap of hide slung from a tie at their waists. And yet, neither could I unsee them. They were about the age of Makepeace, perhaps a little older, but their form was nothing like—they were another sort of man entirely. Makepeace, who farms as little as he must and cannot forebear from shearing the sugarloaf anytime he feels himself unobserved, is of milky complexion, slight at the shoulders, soft at the middle and pitifully tooth shaken.

These youths were all of them very tall, lean in muscle, taut at the waist and broad in the chest, their long black hair flying and whipping about their shoulders. The colored stuff they had used to decorate their bodies must have been made with grease, for they gleamed and shone in the sunlight, so that you could see the long sinews of their thighs working as they ran.

Fortunately, they were so intent on their game that they had not seen me. I led Speckle some distance to where I was sure the height of the dune would conceal me if I remounted. I urged her to a gentle canter with my bare heels. We headed away from the beach, skirting the shore of one of the salt ponds that fingers into the land from the sea. I needed to do the chore I had been sent out for, to gather sufficient clams for our chowder kettle, so when I had put some distance between myself and the beach, I tied Speckle to a great piece of driftwood, unfastened the rake from the saddle, hitched my skirt high and waded into the brine. It soon proved a poor place, and my rake was uncovering few shellfish worth placing in my basket. I was about to give up and try another spot when I felt eyes upon me. I straightened and turned, and saw him for the first time—the boy we now call Caleb.

He was standing in a thicket of tall beach grass, his bow slung over one shoulder and some kind of dead water fowl in the bag at his back. Something—perhaps the expression on my face, perhaps my frantic tugging at my skirt, which unfurled into the water to preserve my modesty at the cost of being soaked entirely—amused him, for he smiled. He was, I judged, and it later proved, a youth of my own age, some two or three years younger than the warriors at play upon the beach. Unlike them, he was clad for hunting, wearing a kind of deerskin breechclout tied with a belt fashioned of snake skins. To this was laced a pair of hide leggings. Around his upper arms were twines of beadwork, cunningly worked in purple and white. All else about him was open and naked, save for three glossy feathers tied into a sort of topknot in his thick, jetty hair, which was very long, the forelock pulled hard back from his coppery face and bound up as one might dress a horse's mane. His smile was unguarded, his teeth very fine and white, and something in his expression made it impossible to fear him. Still, I thought it prudent to retrieve my mare and get away from this place, which seemed to be teeming with salvages of one sort or another. Who could say what outlandish person might next appear?

I gathered up my soaking skirt and made for the shoreline. Unfortunately in my haste I caught my toe in a thicket of eel grass and tripped into the water, spilling the few clams I had gathered and soaking my sleeves and bodice to match my sodden skirt. He was beside me in a few long strides, a hard brown grip on my forearm as he pulled me out of the water.

In his own language, I asked him to let go. His hand dropped from my arm. I made my way, dripping, to shore. He stood where he was, fixed to the spot by his own astonishment. It was my turn, then, to struggle against a smile. I think it would not have surprised him more had my horse addressed him.

He followed me out of the water then and started to speak to me in a great rush of syllables, and I could not make out more than a word or two of it. My father had told me that they loved any person who could utter his mind in their tongue, and this boy kept exclaiming, to my discomfort, "Manitoo!" which is their word for a god, or something godlike, miraculous.

Slowly, in my simple words, I tried to make it plain that there was nothing so very extraordinary in my knowing some of his speech. I told him who I was, for all of the Wampanoag by that time had heard of the praying Indians and their minister, my father. I explained that I had learned something of his tongue by listening to the lessons of my father with Iacoomis.

He made a face at that, as if he had sucked on a gallnut. He hissed out the word they use for the product of the bowel, a vile or stinking thing, and it made me blush to hear him say such a thing of a helpful man so well beloved by my father.

He looked down then at my empty clamming basket.

"Poquauhock?" he asked. I nodded. He closed his fingers to his upturned palm, beckoning me, and turned back into the beach grass from which he had appeared.

I had a choice then, to follow or not. I wish I could say that it cost me more struggle. As I scrambled along trying to keep pace with his swift steps, I told myself that it would be a great thing to know of a better clamming place, so that I might do the chore with dispatch in future days and have more time for my own pursuits.

It was the first of many times I followed that feathered head through eel grass and over sand dune, to clay pit and to kettle pond. He showed me where the wild strawberries sweetened and fattened in the sunshine, some of them above two inches around, and so numerous that I could gather a bushel in a forenoon. He taught me to see where the blueberry bushes dapple with fruit in summer and the cranberry bogs yield crimson gems come fall.

He walked through the woods like a young Adam, naming creation. I learned to shape my mouth to the words—sasumuneash for cranberry, tunockuquas for frog. So many things grew and lived here that were strange to us, because they had not been in England. We named the things of this place in reference to things that were not of this place—cat briar for the thickets of vine whose thorns were narrow and claw-like; lambskill for the low-growing laurel that had proved poisonous to some of our hard-got tegs. But there had been no cats or lambs here until we brought them. So when he named a plant or a creature, I felt that I heard the true name of the thing for the first time.

Always, we made a great pretense that we had met by chance, and feigned amazement that our tracks had crossed each other's. And yet he was certain to let me know, in such a way as to make nothing of it, where he had a mind to be fishing or hunting at this or that phase of the moon, and such or so height of the sun. Every time, I would tell myself some falsehood as to why my day's wanderings took me in that very direction at that very hour. Once I was in the general place, it was a small matter for him to track me: he told me, later, that I left a trail plainer than a herd of running deer.

I justified the hours with him in the baskets of delicacies that

I carried home. It was my duty, was it not, to help provide for my family? As I watched the jars of preserves fill the shelf, the strings of drying cranberries crisscross the rafters, and the strips of smoked shellfish laid in against a hungry winter, I felt satisfied in my self-deception.

The truth, now, set down here, before God: I loved the hours I spent with him. In very short season he had filled the empty space that Zuriel had left in my heart. I had never had such a friend before. As a child I had not needed any, since Zuriel was always at my side, all the companion I wanted. When he died, I was without whatever knack it requires to draw someone close. In any case, the only girl of an age to have been my friend was an Alden, of the one family in the settlement with which we Mayfields were at odds. To have formed any kind of easy association with the few English boys my age would have been an unthinkable affront to modesty. But this boy was a different thing entirely. He had soon become more of a brother to me than Makepeace, whose concern for my proper bearing made him severe. I had learned to expect no word from Makepeace but to correct or to command. No playful banter, no genuine opening of our heart one to the other.

At first, I followed this wild boy hungering after his knowledge of the island—his deep understanding of everything that bloomed or swam or flew. Soon enough, a curiosity about an untamed soul had kindled, and this, too, caused me to seek him out. But it was his light temper and his easy laugh that drew me close to him, over time, until I forgot he was a half-naked, sassafras-scented heathen anointed with raccoon grease. He was, quite simply, my dearest friend.

And yet, I told no one this, not even myself. I knew that I deceived others, but the extent of my self-deception only became patent to me much later. I took pains that no one ever saw us together, forgoing meeting him if I thought there was the slightest chance that someone might come in our way. I did not take home the cuts of venison he offered, when he had killed and dressed a deer, since I could not have explained how I came by them. But I ate from a roasted haunch with him, and it was delicious. Another day, he led me to dunes rich with ripening beach plums, and as I picked them, he waded out, spear in hand, to inspect his fish traps, returning with a fine bass writhing in his hands. I heard him thank the fish for its life as he dispatched it with a quick blow. I had never thought of such a thing, and that day, I recall that it seemed to me outlandish. He said we would eat it, and I said it was not meal time. He laughed at that, and said that he had heard that the English needed a bell to tell them when they were hungry. Even as he mocked me, I realized that I was, in fact, ravenous. So we gathered some kindling and a little driftwood; he used his flint to strike a flame. We skewered the flesh on twigs and seared it, one succulent piece after another. I ate till I was sated. Later, at board, my mother commended me for my continence, and father chimed: "Son, you would do well to emulate your sister." Makepeace liked his food too well and struggled against the sin of gluttony. I colored, thinking guiltily of my full belly, and mother's eyes smiled at me, misperceiving that my pink flesh bespoke a modesty like her own; a fine quality that I did not in fact possess.

Day following day, I grew in knowledge of the island, as we foraged in one place more remarkable in prospect or abundance than the last. For him, it seemed that every plant had some use, as food or medicine, as dye or weaving matter. He would snap the heads off sumac and douse them in water to make a refreshing drink, or reach up into trees to gather rich nutmeats—white and creamy. He was forever chewing upon one or another fresh green leaf from some plant that I had thought a weed, but which, when he gave it me, proved most palatable.

As I grew to know places and plants, so also I grew to know my guide, though this came more slowly. It was many weeks before he would even give me his name, that being considered a grave intimacy among his people. And when he did finally confide it to me, I understood why it is that they feel so. For with his name came an idea of who he truly was. And with that knowledge came the venom of temptation that would inflame my blood.

IV

That summer, perhaps because of the lean winter that had preceded it, brought the first theft of a drift whale. It had been our practice to take those that washed ashore in our harbor, or those blackfish coming near inshore that our men could drive in to our own beach. Of these we generally had two or three a season. All the families would be called out, the men to do the harrying from the shallops and the butchery upon the beach, the women to set up the try pots and try out the oil. I misliked the work, and not just for the blackened, greasy air. It is one thing to butcher a deer killed with a swift arrow or blast of musket shot, or to wring a hen's neck, as I have done often enough, delivering the bird to a death sudden and unforeseen. But the whale was generally alive when they commenced to carve it, and the eye, so human like, would move from one to another of us, as if seeking for some pity. I wanted to tell the creature that pity costs dear indeed when the oil of one Leviathan could yield near eighty barrels and keep our village bright throughout a long dark winter without mess of pitch pine knots or the rancid stink of cods' liver oil.

It had been understood that whales drifting onto the other beaches belonged to the Wampanoag, who believed that a benevolent spirit being threw them upon the shore for their particular use. They made even greater employ of the creatures' every part than we did, thought the flesh a very great delicacy and cause for feasting, and had strict customs for its fair distribution. But our neighbor

Nortown, fishing offshore in his shallop, had espied a whale likely to strand down by the colored cliffs that we call the Gay Head. Nortown said he had learned that the Wampanoag of those lands were away on Nomin's island, with their sonquem Tecquanomin and their pawaaw, who dwelt there, engaged in days-long rites and pagan dancing. In such case, he argued, they would be none the wiser if we were to take the whale. He was going about from house to house, rousing enthusiasm for this venture, and had met with some success by the time he got to us. Father had gone some days earlier with Peter Folger to our sister isle, Nantucket, to transact some business there on grandfather's behalf, and mother was with Aunt Hannah, who was ill, tending to her and her babes both. I am sure father would have counseled against Nortown's plan. But Makepeace saw no flaw in it, and readily agreed to go with the other men. "Bethia, you shall come also, and do a share at the try pots, and make my meal for me," he said. All my life I had been schooled that it was not my place to argue with him, but as I hastily packed what we would need to spend a night on the open beach, and later, as our boat beat up the coast amid that small fleet of thieves, I felt a great heaviness, as one does, when one knows oneself engaged in an act of greed and sneakery.

By the time we reached the cliffs, the whale had indeed beached herself. She was huge, glistening, luminous, a pregnant shape that the surf pulled this way and that, as if she still had vigor and was not already doomed. There were many rounded rocks scattered across the shore there. As each wave receded, these stones beat against each other in a rattling tattoo. I have read that one hears such a thing at an execution.

We moored the boats in the lee of the cliff, where they could not be sighted from Nomin's island, and commenced to unload them. The cauldrons and tripods were heavy enough as I helped to drag them up the beach, but the heaviness of my mood seemed to add to their weight so that my arms ached under the strain. I helped to set them, then we rolled the butts that would receive the oil up the beach and carried the long-handled dippers that would skim it off the boiling blubber. As soon as that was done, I went off to help in the search for driftwood to feed the fires, which would not be set until nightfall, so that the Indians on Nomin's island would not descry the smoke. I was glad to leave the beach as I did not want to be witness to the cutting. As I walked away, I heard the men's voices shouting in coarse merriment even as they hewed at the whale's living flesh. I thought of the shining bass in my friend's hands, the raised rock, and his gentle words of thanks to the creature. This no longer seemed outlandish to me, but fitting and somehow decent. The idea that this heathen youth should show more refinement than we in such a matter only added to my leaden mood.

The dunes up island are very much higher than those closer by Great Harbor, and on the far side of them is a vast expanse of low, wind-sculpted moor, wrapping around damp swales and shimmering ponds filled with every kind of waterbird. There was a Wampanoag pathway leading through thickets of stunted oak, shadbush and bayberry. I followed it, until I was far enough from the beach not to hear the raucous voices of the men.

At first, I stopped from time to time to add a good-sized piece of wood to my sling, but soon I neglected this. The scent of the beach plum flowers hung in the humid air, and the drone of bees thrummed all around me. I felt heavy in limb, heavy in spirit. My head began to ache and throb. The very air seemed to push upon me. I have no idea how far I had walked, but suddenly I was aware of a deeper throbbing, a louder hum. The honey fragrance of the plants gave way to the sharp tang of woodsmoke. The path curved suddenly, and dropped away into a bowl of open grassland. I found myself on the lip of a great depression running down to a broad notch in the whitest clay cliff I had ever seen. Below me, Wampanoag were dancing in a wide circle, shaking corn-filled gourds and beating rhythmically on small skin drums.

My first thought was to drop my burden of wood and run back to the beach, to warn the others that the Wampanoag were not on distant Nomin's island, but nearby, and in numbers large enough to threaten us if they caught us red to the elbows with the blood of a whale that was rightfully their own.

But then a voice rose, high and fierce, in notes that I had not known a human throat could produce. The sounds went through to the very core of me. I could not turn away. Indeed, I felt drawn towards the maker of those sounds. I told myself that I needed to give an exact count of the band, and the number of them who might be armed. I left the path, which led down into the clearing and would have put me in plain sight, and pushed my way through the dense heath plants that gave me cover should anyone look upward. Soon, I was close enough to understand some few words of the song. The pawaaw was calling upon his gods, praising, thanking, beseeching. The drums beat in tempo to the rhythm of my heart, which seemed to be swelling at the sound. I felt my soul hum and vibrate in sympathy with his prayers. There was power here; spiritual power.

It moved me in some profound way. I had striven for this feeling, week following week, as the dutiful minister's daughter at Lord's Day meeting. But our austere worship had never stirred my soul as did this heathen's song.

Thou shalt not have strange gods before me. So I had been instructed all my life. Still, it was to those strange gods that I wanted to cry out with the same abandon as the pawaaw. Time stopped its relentless forward march as I crouched in the scrub, rocking in tempo to the drums. Finally, I threw back my head and let the breath from my body speak for me, in a sigh of surrender to some unknown thing of power and beauty, adding my breath to the prayers filling the wide sky. When it was done, I felt the day's heaviness go off me like a lifted weight.

After the pawaaw's prayer finished, I meant to leave. But songs followed, and dances, and I stayed there, to watch and to listen. For a time, the young men danced in wild leaps, brandishing polished war-clubs in a manner that seemed to mimic battle. Then came the women, old and young together, their woven blankets pulled across their shoulders. They stood for a time, their hands raised up before them so that their blanket covered them entire. They looked like a flock of roosting birds. Then, as if to some invisible signal, they all began to move with the music. All my life I had been taught that dance was the devil's business. Only whores, the daughters of Salome, danced, or so I had been instructed. But there was nothing lewd or wanton here. The women's movements were stately, dignified, entirely graceful.

Much later, when I crept back to the beach, grazed, with runs in my hose and rips in my bodice and bits of bracken clinging to my hair, Makepeace's face was thunderous with worry and rage. I concocted some lie about falling into a thicket and hitting my head.

The other women were solicitous, and bade me lie down upon the sand as dark fell and they lit the fires to try out the oil. But hours later, when the oil had been ladeled into the butts and everyone had settled wearily, I lay awake. My thoughts veered wildly. I turned on the sand, unable to find a comfortable position. I felt disgust at the behavior of those all about me, our low willingness to steal and deceive even as we preened and boasted of our godly superiority. *Subdue the earth.* So the Bible said, and so we did. But I could not believe that God meant us to be so heedless of his creation, so wanton and so cruel to those creatures over which he had given us dominion.

I knew I would not sleep. When the men's snores competed with the beating of the surf and the rattle of the stones, I got up, standing still for a moment, to make sure no one stirred, and made my way across the dunes. As soon as I was away from the camp, I turned back to the path that led to the circle cliffs, and followed it by a moon so bright it threw my shadow clear before me on the sandy ground.

Their fires had blazed up against the night sky and the music had grown wilder. The animal self inside me responded to it. Now, remembering that night, I cannot say how, or why, I felt as I did. I only know that the beat of the drumming touched me in some deep, inner, unsounded place. There, in the dark, without even knowing my own purpose, I commenced to unlace my sleeves. The warm air caressed my arms. I let fall my hose and stood, bare armed and bare legged like the Wampanoag women in their short skin shifts. My toes dug down into the sandy, cooling earth, as my heartbeat matched itself to the drumming. The soul within me, schooled in what was godly, seemed to exit my body in great gasping exhalations as I began to move to the beat. Slowly at first, my limbs found the rhythm. Thought ceased, and an animal sense drove me until, in the end, I danced with abandon. If Satan had me in his hand that night, then I confess it: I welcomed his touch.

At dawn, they had to shake me awake. For a few moments I could not recall how I had made my way back to the campsite, and a hot dread seized me lest I remained unclad. But somehow in my ecstatic trance I had found my shed garments and put them back on. I got up and made myself busy with the others to cover the signs of our theft, dragging the remains of the butchered carcass into the surf, dousing the bloodied and fire blackened sands with buckets of sea water, and hoping the rising tide would do the rest of it.

All the long journey home in the oil-laden shallop, Makepeace berated me for my carelessness, my clumsiness and my lack of consideration. I barely heard the half of what he said. My mind was still in that circle under the cliffs.

V

He was the younger son of Nahnoso, the Nobnocket sonquem, and his name was Cheeshahteaumauck. In his tongue, it means something like "hateful one." When he told me this, I thought that my limited grasp of his language was defeating me. For what manner of people would name a child so? But when I asked if his father indeed hated him, he laughed at me. Names, he said, flow into one like a drink of cool water, remain for a year or a season, and then, maybe, give way to another, more apt one. Who could tell how his present name had fallen upon him? Perhaps the giver of the name had meant to trick Cheepi, the devil-god, into thinking him unloved and therefore leaving him alone. Or perhaps it had come upon him for cause. I had found him hunting alone, he reminded me, when the practice of his clan was to hunt communally. In a band that values the common weal above all, he chose to be chuppi, the one who stands separate. When his band set out towards sun rising, he struck off towards sun setting. It had ever been thus, as long as he could remember. While most babes still nursed at the breast, he had weaned himself, left the women and set about trailing after his mother's brother, Tequamuck, who was their pawaaw. He would hide himself under mats or in thickets to hear the incantations and witness the dances. At first, he said, his elders had berated him for lacking respect, and the name might have fallen upon him out of their feelings at that time. But Tequamuck took a different view and said that such behavior presaged his destiny: to be pawaaw in his turn. So, he had gone to live in his uncle's wetu, while his elder brother Nanaakomin was like a shadow at their father's side.

Before my experience at the cliffs began to work its corruption upon my spirit, this news would have entirely dismayed me. Father called the pawaaws "murderers of souls." He said they were wizards— kinfolk of those English witches whom we burned at the stake. He said they invited trance states, in which they traveled through the spirit world, communing there with the devil through imps that came to them in animal form. From these Satanic familiars, they drew power to raise the mists and the winds, to foresee the future and to heal or sicken people as the whim led them. Cheeshahteaumauk's uncle Tequamuck was infamously powerful in these arts. When father first spoke of this, it frightened me, so that I could not look upon an Indian person without dread. But ever since the singing and dancing at the cliffs, my fear had given way to fascination, and Cheeshahteaumauk's disclosures only made him more interesting to me.

As for my name, he found it equally peculiar, once I told him that Bethia meant "servant." He said a servant was but a lowly thing—their servants being more like serfs, enemies captured in battle, who may be harassed and despised, even sometimes tortured where the enmity between tribes is most bitter. I, as granddaughter of the Coatmen's sonquem and daughter of their pawaaw, should have a higher name, as he thought. I tried to explain that my father was no pawaaw, but I did not yet have subtlety enough in his tongue to convey the very great difference between mediating God's grace and holding familiarity with Satan. I did struggle to make clear to him the nature and virtue of being a servant of God, but he would have none of it, and grew impatient. He set off down the beach with his long loping stride and I had to run to keep pace with him. Of a sudden he turned to me and announced that he had decided to name me over, in the Indian manner. He said he would call me Storm Eyes, since my eyes were the color of a thunderhead. Well and good, said I. But I will rename you, also, because to me you are not hateful. I told him I would call him Caleb, after the companion of Moses in the wilderness, who was noted for his powers of observation and his fearlessness.

"Who is Moses?" he asked. I had forgotten that he would not know. I explained that Moses was a very great sonquem, who led his tribe across the water and into a fertile land.

"You mean Moshup," he said.

No, I corrected him. "Moses. Many, many moons since. Far away from here."

"Yes, many moons since, but here. Right here." He was becoming impatient with me, as if I were a stubborn child who would not attend to her lessons. "Moshup made this island. He dragged his toe through the water and cut this land from the mainland." He went on then, with much animation, to relate a fabulous tale of giants and whales and shape-shifting spirits. I let him speak, because I did not want to vex him, but also because I liked to listen to the story as he told it, with expression and vivid gesture. Of course, I thought it all outlandish. But as I rode home that afternoon, it came to me that our story of a burning bush and a parted sea might also seem fabulous, to one not raised up knowing it was true.

One afternoon, not long after, we collected wild currents, tart and juicy, and gorged on them. I lay back on a bed of soft leaves, my hands under my head, watching a few fluffy clouds dance across the blue dome of sky. Behind me, I could hear the chink of stone on stone. He was never idle, not for a minute.

"Why do you look at the sky, Storm Eyes? Are you looking for your master up there?" I could not tell if he was mocking me, so I turned over, resting my chin in my hands, and gazed at him to better read his expression. He was looking down, concentrating on aiming the sharp, deft blows that sent tiny shards of stone flying. He had a piece of leather, like a half glove, wrapped around the hand that held the arrowhead he was making. "That is where he lives, is it not, your one God? Up there, beyond the inconstant clouds?"

I did not dignify his ridicule, for so I deemed it, with any answer. This merely emboldened him.

"Only one god. Strange, that you English, who gather about you so many things, are content with one only. And so distant, up there in the sky. I do not have to look so far. I can see my sky god clear enough, right there," he said, stretching out an arm towards the sun. "By day Keesakand. Tonight Nanpawshat, moon god, will take his place. And there will be Potanit, god of the fire . . ." He prattled on, cataloguing his pantheon of heathenish idols. Trees, fish, animals and the like vanities, all of them invested with souls, all wielding powers. I kept a count as he enumerated, the final tally of his gods reaching thirty-seven. I said nothing. At first, because I hardly knew what to say to one so lost.

But then, I remembered the singing under the cliffs. An inner voice, barely audible: the merest hiss. Satan's voice, I am sure of it now, whispering to me that I already knew Keesakand, that I had already worshipped him many times as I bathed in the radiance of a sunrise, or paused to witness the glory of his sunset. And did not Nanpawshat have power over me, governing the swelling, salty tides of my own body, which, not so very long since, had begun to ebb and flow with the moon. It was good, the voice whispered. It was right and well to know these powers, to live in a world aswirl with spirits, everywhere ablaze with divinity.

VI

Not long after, Caleb came upon me reading, before I had a chance to put the book by. He had the habit of appearing suddenly, springing up out of dune or thicket. He could move on feet silent as a stalking cat's, and walk so lightly in his thin, deer-hide shoes that he barely left a footprint in sand or leaf litter to mark where he had trod. With his instruction, and with practice, I was learning to do the same, walking softly on my heel so as to touch less of the earth. At home, I would entertain myself by stalking Makepeace, finding him resting, indolent, in the fields when he should have been about his chores. This vexed him, but he could hardly complain of it without revealing himself. I took a vast amusement from this.

On this particular day, I had made off with a new tract of my father's, *New England's Prospect*, by one William Wood, who had traveled on the mainland in 1633 and described for English readers what he had found there. I held it out and Caleb took it. This was the first book he had held in his hands. He made me smile, opening it upside down and back to front, but he touched the pages with the utmost care, as if gentling some fragile-boned wild thing. The godliest among us did not touch the Bible with such reverence as he showed to that small book. He ran a brown finger across a line of type.

"These snowshoe tracks," he said. "They speak to you?" I smiled. I could see how, to his unschooled eyes, the page might resemble a snowy field hatched by the crisscross of snowshoe sinews when the low winter sun lights up their edges. I said that they did, and pointed out to him the word for "deer," at which he scoffed, and said it looked nothing like a deer, but more like a snail. That in turn made me laugh, for he was right, and I could see that snail, its pronged head raised in the letter d, its shell curved in the double e that followed it. I explained to him that the letters were a kind of code, like the patterns worked into the wampum belts the sonquems wore, that told some kind of abbreviated history of his tribe. But unlike the belts, which were rare and each unique, there were many hundreds of copies of this book, each just the same.

"Manitoo!" he exclaimed. "So those Coatmen across the sea, they can know of the plants and animals here, so many months' journey from them?"

Yes, I said, exactly so. And men might know each other's minds, who had never met one another. "Even those who lived many, many years ago may leave behind their learning for us." I told him how we knew of great cities, such as Rome and Athens; how we read of their warriors and the wars they had fought, and how their wise men had argued with each other about how to live a goodly life. "And now, though their cities are fallen into ruins and the warriors are dust, yet they live for us still in their books."

I was enjoying this. For the most part, it was he who taught me. For once, I was able to play the instructor. I held out my hand for the Wood volume. "Would you care to hear some of what he has to say of your people?" He nodded, frowning slightly.

"So, you can make it out—all of it—from those tracks?" Indeed, I said. "Perhaps, from time to time, I might come upon an unfamiliar word, whose meaning is strange to me. But generally one can make it out from the other words about it. . . ." I was searching for the place as I spoke, and when I found the passage, pointed to the lines as I read them aloud, translating into his tongue as I went. "Here, he has set down that you are courteous and hospitable, helpful to wandering benighted coasters who are lost. He says you can do that which we cannot, such as catch the beaver, who is too cunning for the English."

I had thought he would be pleased by these and other such complimentary references, but as I read on, his frown only deepened. He tugged at his long braid. When I ceased reading, he said nothing. I asked what troubled him. "My father says that a long time ago, before those of us across the water walked with the first of the Coatmen, we had wise ones, who taught the people knowledge, but they fell dead of invisible bullets that the Coatmen used against them, and died before they could pass those wise ways on. If we had had this manit of the book, that knowing might not now be buried with them." He seemed downcast and distracted, and he kept stroking the book as if it were alive. "Give me this," he said.

I felt the ground shift uncertainly. That book was not mine to give. But I feared he would not understand this. Father had spoken often about his difficulties with Indian ideas about gift giving. For them, personal property had but little meaning. A man might easily give away every bowl or belt, canoe or spear he had and think nothing of it, knowing that soon enough he would receive goods in turn from his sonquem at a gathering or from some other person seeking a god's favor, which they held might be won by such generosity. Father and Makepeace had argued, once, when father had mused that in this, the Indians were more Christ-like than we Christians, who clung to our possessions even as we read the gospel's clear injunction to give up all we owned. Makepeace challenged father and said that the Indian generosity was nothing more than the product of a pagan superstition, not to be likened to Christian agape, or selfless love of others.

I did not know enough, then, to have an opinion. But what I have learned since tells me that neither Makepeace nor father truly grasped the root of the matter, which is that we see this world, and our place in it through entirely different eyes. When father had first come to negotiate for some land here, the sonquem had laughed at the notion that anyone thought they might "own" land. "If I have said that you might use it to hunt and fish and build your dwellings, what more do you need?" he had asked. Although father maintains to this day that he explained it, I am still not convinced in my own mind that the sonquem fully understood what we proposed to do here. To be sure, there had been enough confusion between Caleb and myself, somewhen from my inability to put my whole thought into his tongue, and somewhen simply because even when I had the words, the thing itself that they described was not in the compass of his experience.

I gazed at Caleb with the book in his hand and the asking on his lips, and did not know how to answer him without making a rift between us. There were so few books in our settlement, each of them was held to be very precious and handled only with the greatest of care. So I told him I could not give away this book, that it was not mine, and that I had erred even to have taken it from the house without father's consent. As I struggled to explain, he looked at first baffled, then, as I had feared, angry. "Since you love this thing, then love it." He thrust the book back into my hands and turned away, as if to leave.

"Wait!" I said. "I have another book. My own book. You can have that." My catechism, which I had by heart. "It is a more powerful book than this one. You would call it filled with manit. I will fetch it hither. And if you wish to learn your letters, you should know that my father teaches this to the praying Indians and to their children. I am sure he would be glad for you to join the lessons." Father had, with the help of Peter Folger, established the day school in the winter of 1652. He was talking now of building a schoolhouse, which would be the first such on the island. I had been filled with envy, when I heard him speak of it, for there was not even a dame school for the English. Parents schooled their own children or not, as they chose. "Iacoomis also teaches there. His son Joel, who is junior to you, already knows his letters. . . ."

He frowned, and made a snort of disgust. "Iacoomis has nothing to teach me, and neither will I sit down with his son who has walked with the English all his life."

"Why do you say so?"

"Iacoomis was nothing. His own people cast him out. Now, since he walked with the Coatmen and learned your God, this man who could barely pull a bowstring speaks as if he were a pawaaw. He walks tall now, and says his one God is stronger than our many, and foolish men listen, and are drawn away from their sonquems and from their families. It brings no good to us, walking with Coatmen."

"You say so, and yet you walk with me," I said quietly. He had pulled a bough from a nearby tree and was stripping the bark roughly. He lifted the bare stick and sighted along it, to see if it might make an arrow, then thrust it away.

"Why do you not ask your father, Nahnoso?" I said. "As sonquem, he might welcome it, if you told him you wished to learn your letters so as to safekeep the knowledge of your people." I swallowed hard, knowing the freight of what I was about to say. "You say you aspire to be pawaaw—does not a pawaaw seek familiarity with every god? If so, then why not the English God as well?" I was not so lost, then, that I was deaf to the heresy I had just uttered. I formed a silent prayer for forgiveness.

His brown eyes regarded me fiercely. "My father forbids it. And my uncle hates those who listen to the English. But since, as you say, I do walk with you, Storm Eyes, you might teach me this book of yours, and so get for me this manit that you say comes from your one God."

I should not have been my father's daughter if those words had failed to open to me the possibility that before me stood a brand needing to be plucked from the fire. For if I taught him to read from the pages of the catechism . . .

I might—I should—have echoed him back at once: "*My* father forbids it." It had been instilled in me often enough that preaching was not women's work. No woman was to think of giving prophecy in meeting, though any unlettered cowcatcher might exercise his gifts there, so long as he be a man. A woman might not even ask a question in meeting, if some matter was obscure to her. I had been instructed to ask at home, privily, if I needed scriptural guidance.

And yet how could I turn my back on a soul that might be saved? Had not everything in my life inclined to teach me that this, of all good works, was the highest and best of all? Perhaps, I thought, if I could teach this boy—son of a chief, apprentice to a wizard—bring him to father as a convert, versed in scripture—father might see the worth in me, and consent to instruct me again, in those higher learnings that he labored over with my dull-witted brother.

And so I commenced that very day to teach Caleb his letters:

"A," I said, tracing the shape in the wet sand. "It has two sounds. Remember them thusly: 'Adam ate the apple.'" At once there was a difficulty: he had never seen an apple. I promised to bring him one from our small orchard, which father planted when first he came here. But this snag was nought to the briars yet to ensnare us.

I commenced to introduce Adam to him, to describe the garden and the fall, and how that first sin comes down to besmirch all of us. I had then to explain sin, of which he had no ready concept. He would not concede that he had ever sinned himself, and seemed much offended when I assured him of it. His brow drew itself heavier and heavier, until he waved a hand as if sweeping away noxious smoke. "Your story is foolishness. Why should a father make a garden for his children and then forbid them its fruit? Our god of the southwest, Kiehtan, made the beans and corn, but he rejoiced for us to have them. And in any wise, even if this man Adam and his squa displeased your God, why should he be angry with me for it, who knew not of it until today?"

I had no answer. I felt rebuked for my pride. Clearly this undertaking would be harder than I had reckoned. My father must truly be a marvelous preacher if he had to answer such as this. I resolved to go with father when next he visited a Wampanoag otan. I would listen to him sermonize, to find out if his flock had so many vexing questions, and if so, how he answered them. I realized I should have to devise a pretext for this, since father was unaware I knew the Indians' language and would think I understood nothing of what passed between him and his listeners. So, at home, I began to hint that I had a curiosity to see how they arranged an otan, to visit the wetus and to meet the squas who lived in them (which was no more than the truth). After a time, I asked father if I might go with him, the next time he had a mind to it. He seemed pleased by my interest, and said he could see no harm if mother could spare me from chores. "For they hold family very dear, and count it a slight that we English do not foster more ties of affection between our families and their own."

A few days later, we went together on Speckle, and as we approached the settlement, we dismounted and walked so that father could greet everyone and tell them that he proposed to preach to them when the sun was at its highest. The praying village was for those who had been convinced by my father to embrace Christianity, and was called Manitouwatootan, or God's Town. Despite its godly name, father worried that the old ways still had a strong hold there, and that the people remained confused about the truth of Christian teaching. Some families who had removed there remained divided between the convinced and those who were not ready to yield the old ways. Some were conflicted in their own hearts, halting between two opinions. Some came only to see and hear what was done, yet though they heard the word of the one God of heaven, remained thralls to sin and darkness. "They say that their meetings and customs are much more agreeable and advantageous than ours, in which we do nothing but talk and pray, while they dance and feast and give gifts one to the other. I try, Bethia, to explain that this is the way of the Great Deluder, Satan. But I have found no words in their language to answer our English words—faith, repentance, grace, sanctification.... Well, you will see for yourself, soon enough, how it is...."

The first thing that struck me was the peace of the place. In Great Harbor, on every day except the Sabbath, there is noise from first light to last light. Someone is always splitting a shingle, hammering a nail into the latest new dwelling or enlarging an existing one. The smith's mallet rings from the forge, the pounders hammer at the fulling mill and the stone mason worries at his rocks with all manner of iron tools. There was no such English factory evident here.

The squas were in the gardens, weeding with hoes made of clamshells. In truth, they had little to weed, for the planting was contrived cunningly, with beans climbing up the cornstalks and the ground between each hillock covered in leafy squash vines that left scant room for weeds to grow. The menfolk were about the wetus, some casting jacks in a game of chance, others lying idle upon their mats. I saw father draw his brows at this. I had heard him opine that too much toil fell to the women. It was they who tilled the soil, ground the corn, foraged for wild foods, made the mats for the shelters and the baskets for the stores, and bent their backs under loads of wood for the cook fires. The men, warriors and hunters, had little to do in the way of daily drudge-work. "Of course, you should know that bow hunting is no lordly game such as an English shooting party might make of it, Bethia. It is a wearying endeavor, without beaters to drive and gamekeepers to ensure the quarry. Still, I think the men might do more to lessen the women's burdens."

To make his point, father sat down with some old women who were shelling last year's dried beans, and took a share before him, to shell himself as he talked with them. When he went to another group who were hoeing, he reached down and gathered out the weeds they had turned over.

There were some half-dozen children running in the fields or about the wetus—fewer than you would expect, given the size of the settlement, which was more than a dozen and a half families. It was just as well they were few, because those there were seemed to run entirely wild, with no check or correction, barreling through the fields in the way of the hoes, interrupting the men's talk, or snatching at their jacks so as to disrupt the game, piercing the quiet with loud hallows and curdling shrieks. An English child would have been whipped for half of what these were about. Yet I saw no elder do so much as wag a finger at them. I remarked on this to father. He nodded. "They are, as you say, remarkably indulgent. I have remonstrated with them on the matter, asking them why they do not correct their children. But they say that since adult life is full of hardship, childhood should be free of it. It is a kindly view, even if misguided."

Father had a friendly greeting for everyone, and I was impressed at how much he knew of their doings, their families and their concerns. I learned that he did a great many good turns for them, of a practical nature, and I thought it might be that these preached to them more loudly than his sermons. More than once, I had to suppress a wince when he dropped a word into the mangle of his dreadful pronunciation, so that the meaning came out quite changed from what I knew he had intended. Over time, I had come to grasp that the chief principle of their grammar is whether a thing to them is possessed of an animating soul. How they determine this is outlandish to our way of thinking, so profligate are they in giving out souls to all manner of things. A canoe paddle is animate, because it causes something else to move. Even a humble onion has, in their view, a soul, since it causes action—pulling tears from the eyes. Yet as I had begun to see this strange, incarnate world through Caleb's eyes, my grammar had much improved, and it pained me to hear father expose himself with his many errors. I blushed when he used an indecent word, quite innocently, thinking he was uttering a beautiful compliment. But these Wampanoag , who clearly loved him, kept their countenance and strove mightily to make out his meaning, so as not to shame him.

At mid-morning, a man was brought to him who was not of the settlement. He came hobbling, supported by two others. It seemed he was a fugitive from the wrath of the Narragansett, a tribe often at odds with the Wampanoag whose lands touched theirs on the mainland. This man had been captured by the Narragansett in a raid, and because one of his captors had had a brother killed in some prior skirmish, this captive had been marked for a slow death by ritual torture. He had somehow escaped when the work was only part done, stealing a mishoon and paddling to the island. The praying Indians had taken him in and now they asked father if he might treat the man's wounded foot. They described how four of his toes had been severed, one by one, then roasted and given him to eat. I felt my gorge rise at this, and turned my face away lest father divine from my expression that I understood what was being said.

Father, for his part, looked ashen. He murmured to me in English: "They *will* believe that I have healing skills, no matter what I tell them. It is because of their pawaaws, who profess to be healers.

In their minds religion and medicine mean much the same thing. Since they have given up their pawaaw in coming here, I suppose I must do what good I can...."

The injured man had been eased down onto the mat, and now father tried to remove his moccasin, dark with dried black blood. When he saw that the hide was adhered to the man's flesh, he called for some warmed water. He soaked off the moccasin and set about cleaning the pus from inflamed, swollen flesh, muttering to himself about the barbarity of such wounds. "To do such as this, not in heat of battle, but deliberately.... Bethia, it must be granted that these are a very sinful people. Iniquity does abound among them. As the scripture says, *the love of many waxeth cold.*"

I could see that he needed some clean linen cloths to bind the injured foot, but there were none here. "Should I tear some strips from my placket?" I whispered. He nodded, so I went off into the shelter of some high blueberry bushes and shredded the lower part of my undershift, and brought the cloths back to him.

He dried the mutilated foot, and was struggling with the cloth, making an awkward business of bandaging. "Shall I do it?" I said. "I have a light hand." He made way for me, and I wrapped the foot as I had seen mother do when we had cuts or burns. Father nodded his approval and the man rose awkwardly. His face, though drawn and sweaty, had betrayed no sign of discomfort even though he must have been in great pain.

As he hobbled away, father looked after him and shook his head. "God in his wisdom has not done so much for these as he has for our nation. Satan has had full charge of them. It is a blessing that God now brings us here. We are uncommonly fortunate to be able to bring that little mustard seed of the gospel, and watch it take root here."

It was getting near to the noon hour, when father was accustomed to preach. The women were setting down their hoes and the men coming out of the wetus. There were just seven or eight of these huts in the little settlement, domes of bent sapling branches covered in sheets of bark and woven mats, each housing just a family or two. But at the center of the clearing was a long house, with an English door rather than a mat for an entry way. Father said that when the weather was hard he would preach in there, amid a great press of bodies.

This day was fine, so he asked the people to meet him about a great, swaybacked rock, worn smooth through the years to a kind of curved platform. Upon this, he was accustomed to stand to give his sermon.

By noon, some twenty souls had gathered, and I stood at the edge of the group, and tried to look at my father through their eyes. He was a lean man, for unlike Makepeace he worked hard on our farm and did not scruple to chop wood or carry water or do any of the several tasks that eased mother's lot. He favored the sad colors, blacks or dark browns, as befit a minister, and wore his fair hair modestly cropped above the collars that mother kept spotless and starched for him. Though the day was warm, he did not remove his coat; since the Wampanoag set much store in their own regalia when they met in ceremony, he felt that he should retain some formality in dress, as he would if he preached in church or meetinghouse. First, he prayed, putting our familiar forms into their tongue. These he had by rote, well taught him by Iacoomis, and he uttered them without error. Next came his sermon.

"Friends, hearken to me," he began. "When we have met here before, we have agreed two truths: That God is, and that he will reward all those who diligently seek him. That the one God is the source of all manit. My friend Iacoomis has shown his heart to you, how it stands towards God, and you have seen how, when he cast off all other false worships, so he has prospered, and gained in health, he and all his family. You have asked what will happen to you when you die, and today I will answer you. Englishmen, and you and all the world, when they die, their souls go not to the southwest, as you have been taught. All that know the one God, who love and fear him, they go up to heaven. They ever live in joy. In God's own house. They that know not God, who love and fear him not—liars, thieves, idle persons, murderers, they who lie with other's wives or husbands, oppressors or the cruel, these go to hell, to the very deep. There they shall ever lament."

Beside me, two men started muttering together, thinking that I could not understand them.

"Why should we believe our English friend, when our own fathers told us that our souls go to the southwest, to the lands of Kiehtan?"

"Well, but did you ever see a soul go to the southwest? I have not."

"No, and when did he, yonder, see one go up to heaven or down to hell?"

"He says he has it from the book, which God himself has written."

"What he says may be true for English, but why should I want to go to this God's house if only English are there? If God wanted us in this house then he would have sent our ancestors such a book."

Listening to this exchange, I realized my difficulties were no different in kind to my father's, and that I should just have to persevere, and trust that in time God would give me the words that would turn Caleb's heart to him.

About midway through my father's sermon, I noticed that the people seemed restless of a sudden, their eyes glancing from father and over to the place where the clearing ended in dense oak woodland. I followed their gaze, squinting in the sunlight. Soon enough, I saw what they saw: A man, very tall, his face painted and his body decked in a great cloak of turkey feathers. He stood stock still, his arm raised, and in his hand some kind of mannekin or poppet, I couldn't clearly see. Then, from the trees beside him, another appeared. A youth, also painted garishly.

Some of the crowd started to edge away from father. The man who had remarked about Kiehtan elbowed his companion. I heard him say the name Tequamuck. I flinched, recognizing the name: Caleb's uncle. I squinted even harder, to discern the features of the wizard and his apprentice. But their faces were so fully painted over I could not tell if what I feared was true or not. Their presence clearly agitated the crowd. Father had long held that the pawaaws were the strongest cord that bound the Indians to their own way, and that breaking their spiritual power mattered far more than interfering with the ways and privileges of the sonquems.

The man who spoke Tequamuck's name was the first to leave. Soon, five or six more followed. They headed towards the woods, greeting Tequamuck with great deference. When I looked again, all of them were gone.

VII

I never did ask Caleb if he was the painted youth at the right hand of the pawaaw. I did not want to hear his answer.

As that ripe summer turned to autumn, the sunlight cooled to a slantwise gleam, bronzing the beach grass and setting the beetlebung trees afire. Caleb learned his letters faster than I could credit. Before the singing of the cider, he could read and speak a serviceable kind of English. I think that because he had learned from childhood to mimic the chirps of birds in order to lure waterfowl, his ear was uncommonly attuned to pitch and tone. Once he learned a word, he soon spoke it without accent, exactly as an Englishman would. In a short while, he would not have me speak Wampanaontoaonk to him except to explicate something he could not grasp, and before long we had switched from communicating with each other only in his language, to conversing most times in mine. But as much progress as we made in that direction, in the matter of his soul he resisted and mocked me, using wit that seemed to me devil-inspired. One day, when we had been discussing Genesis, he turned to me with a gleam in his brown eyes. "So you say that all was created in six days?"

Yes, I said.

"All?" he repeated.

So the Bible instructed us, I said.

"Heaven and hell, also, were created then?"

So it says, and so we must believe. The look on his face was the very same as when he had speared a fine bass. "Then answer me this: why did God make a hell before Adam and Eve had sinned?"

This had never occurred to me to question, but I thought quickly, and replied to him. "Because God knows all, and he knew that they would."

"Then why did he not scotch the snake before it tempted them?"

"Because he had endowed them with free will," I said.

"And so do we endow our children with free will, yet you English chide us, and say they are unruly and should be flogged."

Oftentimes, these exchanges vexed me, and I broke off and rode home struggling for self-mastery and resolving to have no further relations with this hard-headed pagan. Yet within a sennight, I would seek him out again, lingering in the places which by now were familiar haunts to both of us until he sprang up in his sudden way, materializing in the tall grasses or beech groves. And so it went on, as another year turned. We each of us grew and changed, gaining new responsibilities in our separate worlds, but always making a space where those worlds could collide and intertwine. As time passed it became harder for me to keep a bright line between my English self and that girl in the woods, whose mouth could utter the true name of every island creature, whose feet could walk trackless through leafbed, whose hands could pull a fish from a weir in a swift blur of motion and whose soul could glimpse a world animated by another kind of godliness.

I had to work ever harder to put that girl from me when I rode back into Great Harbor. I had to learn to leave her behind in the woods; her loose limbed stride, her bold gaze and her easy manners.

Lucky for me that I was so long used to considering every word before I spoke it, or I might have given myself away any number of times. Sometimes, when I came inside, mother would look up from her doughtrough or her spindle and, after admiring whatever I had plucked or gathered for the larder, would ask me what I had seen, abroad in the wide world for such hours.

I would share with her some small piece of news, such as a sighting of an otter in an unaccustomed pond, or an uncommon kind of seal I had interrupted, basking on the beach. She would nod, and smile, and pass some remark that fresh air was healthful, and she was glad I could go about so, since she as a girl had lived a town life that did not afford such rambles. One day, she reached a floury hand and touched my face, tucking in an errant hair that had come loose from my cap. Her blue eyes—much bluer than mine—regarded me gravely. "It is a good thing—for a girl," she said. "It will not be so, when you are become a young woman." She went back to her kneading then, and I set a kettle to boil the lobsters and we did not speak of it again.

It did not seem pressing then, this truth that my mother had voiced, that one day I would have to leave my other self behind forever: that it could not go on, this crossing out of one world and into another, that something was bound to happen to put an end to all of it. If I had thought clearly, and considered, and prepared my mind for it, I could not possibly have fallen so easily into the sin that brought God to smite us such a terrible blow. Looking back, it is hard to imagine how I could have been such a fool.

It was leaf fall, the third year of my friendship with Caleb. I had gone to the upland woods where huckleberries ripened late. He appeared, as usual, suddenly and unexpectedly from the shadow of a granite boulder. He had with him the catechism I had given him so long ago. He pressed it back into my hands. "After today, I will not walk with you anymore. Do not look for me," he said.

This sudden pronouncement stung me like a switch. Tears welled in my eyes.

"Why do you cry?" he demanded curtly.

"I do not cry," I lied. His people consider tears a sign of lappity character.

He took my chin in his hand and tilted my face upward. His fingers were rough as tar paper. He had grown in the two and a half years that I had known him, and was a full head and shoulders taller than I. A big tear spilled down my cheek and on to the back of his hand. He let go of my face and brought his hand to his mouth, tasting the salt upon it and considering me gravely. I looked away, ashamed.

"This is no matter for tears," he said. "It is my time to become a man."

"Why should that mean you cannot walk with me?"

"I cannot walk with you because from tomorrow my steps will choose me, not I my steps. Tomorrow will be new hunter moon. Tequamuck will take me to the deep woods, far from this place. There I will pass the long nights moon, the snow moon and the hunger moon alone." His task was to survive and endure through the harsh winter months, winnowing his soul until it could cross to the spirit world. There, he would undertake the search for his guide, a god embodied in some kind of beast or bird, who would protect him throughout his life. His spirit guide would enlighten his mind and guide his steps in myriad ways, until the end of his life. In those cold woods, he would learn his destiny. He said that if the spirit guide came to him in the form of a snake, then he would gain his heart's desire, and become pawaaw.

I thought of the quarantine of Jesus, a similar harsh and lonely trial of character and purpose. But that vigil passed in searing desert, not snowy wood. And when, at the end, the devil came with his visions of cities and offers of power, Jesus shunned him. Caleb desired to bid him welcome.

And have no fellowship with the unfruitful ways of darkness. So said the scripture. I had no choice. This marked the end of our friendship. I had to take leave of him. But before I did, I looked down at the catechism he had returned to me. No matter that he lived in a bark hut, his hands ever soiled from bloody hunts and greasy common pots, he somehow had kept the book in the exact condition I had given it him. I pressed it back into those rough hands. "Do not close your heart to Christ, Caleb," I whispered. "Perhaps he is the one awaiting you out there in the dark."

I turned away then because I knew I was about to cry in earnest, and I would not have him see me so. I mounted Speckle and threaded a careful way through the trees, but the world was a blur. I felt sick at heart. I told myself it was wounded pride, merely. I had falsely hoped to turn him from the path he was born to follow, and had failed. I told myself it was natural to regret that this pagan ceremony, whatever its nature, would set him at even greater remove from the gospel.

But this, also: I burned to know what he would know when he entered that spirit world. I recalled, too well, the alien power I had felt that long ago day and night on the cliffs. I have said that I would write only the truth here, and the truth is this: I, Bethia Mayfield, envied this salvage his idolatrous adventure.

That night, as I sat with mother at our mending, I had to use every shred of my will to keep my hands at their task. Generally, I could mend or needlepoint or embroider without the least difficulty, my fingers finding their own way over the cloth. But that night the task seemed so friggling to me that I had to concentrate on every stitch. I noticed mother glance at me from time to time as I sighed and fidgeted and tried to hide my cackhanded work. Somehow, she always sensed when something was amiss with me.

Finally, I did something most unlike myself. I asked father a question.

"Does it trouble you, father, that the people of this place are so slow to embrace the gospel?"

Father put aside his bible. "I do not see it so, Bethia. We must not be willful in this matter, but patient, as God is. Did he not abandon these people to Satan all these many ages past? We must not want a convert more than God wants him. It must not be that we, in our pride, attempt to make a convert of one who is not among the elect. We are instruments, but if there is not an influence from God, the work will not be done, nor should it be."

"But what of the satanic rites that they persist in? Is there no way to disrupt them?"

Father looked grave. "It is my chiefest concern," he said. "The devil drives on their worship so pleasantly—as he does many false worships. The gift-giving at gatherings, the feasting and the dancing—these ceremonies are, I must own it, much beloved of the people. They do not like to hear me preach against these things."

"I was thinking particularly of the trial by ordeal that I have heard their youth are subject to ... surely those rites are not so pleasant?"

"Who has told you of such things?" he said sharply. I made my face a blank mask of indifference, as though it was a small matter, and shrugged. I felt mother's eyes on me. "I do not rightly know. It is just something I overheard."

Makepeace interjected, looking up over his book. "They force the strongest and ablest of their male children to swill down poison— the white hellebore is one plant they use—and when they cast it up, they must drink it down again, and again, until what they cast is merely blood. Then, when they can barely stand, they are beaten with sticks, and thrust out into the icy night to run naked through cat briar till the devil catches them and makes covenant with them in their fainting fit."

"But why do they subject their youth to this? Surely there is danger in drinking such poison?"

"Oh, they know how to decoct so as to bring on the visions they seek to have, short of a killing dose. They do it to get power, sister. Diabolic power. Some of them learn thus to call on the force of Satan to summon the fogs and whip up the seas."

I felt the hot blood creeping up my neck. Mother placed her hand protectively on the arc of her belly. Although it had not been spoken of, we all of us knew her condition. "Enough!" she interjected. "This is not fit talk for a Christian hearth. I beg you, hold your peace." She feared to miscarry, as she had, just a year since, on a terrible afternoon of blood-soaked rags, whispers, groans, and then silence, for the lost babe, if mourned by mother, was never spoken of. Worse, perhaps, she feared that such talk of Satan might embolden that emissary of darkness to enter her womb and make a monstrous birth of that which grew there. I repented my question, and pressed no more. Although Solace was born unblemished five months later, there is no doubt: that ill-judged conversation and all that followed from it caused my mother's blighted childbed, and her death.

But I did not see that danger then. My mind was brimming with corrupt fancies. That night, I lay upon my shakedown, and though it was a night crisped by the chill of early fall, I tossed in my own heat, consumed by what Makepeace had said. I thought of that familiar chestnut-brown body, pared by ordeal, naked in the darkness. And of Satan, in his serpent form, twining about those bruised thighs, hissing out his tempting promises of potency.

VIII

W ho are we, really? Are our souls shaped, our fates written in full by God, before we draw our first breath? Do we make ourselves, by the choices we our selves make? Or are we clay merely, that is molded and pushed into the shape that our betters propose for us?

In the days following Caleb's leavetaking, I turned fifteen, and my narrow world became ever more straitened. I began to feel more and more like clay, squeezed flat under the boots of other people. I went to meeting on the Lord's Day, raised my eyes and hands to God, joined in the hymns and let the words of scripture pour into my ears. But my mind was elsewhere. What choice had I ever made that was fully my own? From birth, others had ordained my life's every detail. That I should be a colonist and an islander, a dweller on these wild shores, all this was the product of choices my grandfather had made before I was even thought of. That I might be literate but not learned was the choice of my father; the lot of a girlchild. It was around that time that I heard father and grandfather speaking together of Noah Merry, the second son of the miller who lived south of us on the island's swiftest brook, saying that he was a godly boy, a stout worker, and in time a likely husband for me. So even this choice, it seemed, would be made by others. There was a little ember of anger inside me when I thought this: a hard black coal that could be fanned into a hot flame if I chose to let my thoughts give it air. Most of the time, I did not do so. I went on, dutiful, trying to keep in mind what father preached, that all of this was God's plan, not his, not his father's, nor any man's. A small part of a grand design that we could not fathom. "Consider your mother's needlework," he said once, taking a piece from her hands. "The design is plain to us, when we examine the front, but the back of the piece does not reveal it." He turned it. "Here, you see the knots and the dangling threads. There is an outline of the pattern, but if we guess—is it a bird? Is it a flower? We might easily be mistaken. So it is with this life—we see the knots, we guess at the whole. But only God truly sees the beauty of his design."

So then, what of Caleb, or Cheeshahteaumauk, shivering out there alone, night following night? Was it part of God's beautiful design to leave him there in the winter darkness, waiting for the devil to snatch away his soul? Or did God make no designs for the heathen? If so, what was father about, in his ministry to them? Perhaps it was pride, merely, to seek these souls that God had chosen to abandon. Perhaps it was in itself a sin. . . . But no. Surely my wise father could not err so. And why had God brought Caleb into my path if I was not meant to save him? Why had he set us down here at all? I could no longer even guess at the whole, no longer even glimpse an outline amid so many dangling threads.

I was sorely troubled by these things, and did not eat or sleep well, and could give no convincing account of what distressed me. I told myself that I wanted father to go and find Caleb, wherever he was in the wild woods, and deliver him from evil. Yet where he slept that night, in all those heaths and thickets, that only God—or Satan—knew.

IX

As it happened, father did propose a journey, around that time, although not the one I longed for him to make. Grandfather was interested in acquiring a share in the Merrys' grist mill and, as ever, he looked to father to be his negotiator.

"I thought to take Bethia with me, if she cares to go," father said to mother, quite suddenly, at our breakfast board. "She is looking rather wan of late and I think a long ride in the fresh air might be good for her." He spoke lightly, but I saw the meaning glance exchanged as mother handed him a hot corn cake. "You will like to see the Merrys' farm, Bethia; I hear it has a pleasant prospect with the brook running through, which he has dammed up for a millpond, and he has built his house well, I'm told. They say, who have seen it, that he has a number of glass windows, and has installed a wainscot." Makepeace looked up at that, and made a disapproving snort. "Sumptuary affectations and an affront to plainness," he said. Me, I thought it none of my brother's affair. If a man wished to glaze his windows or line his walls, then he might face fewer drafts when the icy air of winter probed through every chink and crevice. And what harm if he have the skill to make it look well?

The appointed morning was cold, but fine and crisp. Mother touched my face before I set out, and looked at me kindly, but with searching eyes. "I rejoice that you will get out of this house for a time, into the healthful air," she said. "You have not been abroad lately, as has long been your wont. I have wondered at it." I looked down, and said nothing, but I felt the heat in my face. Mother's toil-roughened fingers caressed my cheek. "I do not ask you to account for the change in your ways. You have reached a time in your life when many things must change. You will find, perhaps, that what seemed good occupation to you one day may loose its luster the next, and seem but a child's errand. I have been glad of your help about the house; you must not think I do not rejoice to have you more often by me. But neither do I think these last weeks have agreed with you. Try to enjoy your visit to the Merrys. And whatever it is that weighs so heavy with you, try to set it by." She kissed me then, and I returned her embrace with a full heart.

I do not know if she had said aught to father about raising my spirits, but he seemed uncommonly lighthearted as we set out. In the summer, I had suggested that our tegs might do better on some higher pastures that I had found in my explorations. The sedges were lush and various there, and father, having inspected the place, had decided to try it. The ewes had thrived and put on condition and were well set now for the coming winter, when we would bring them down into the folds. Father took the opportunity of our ride to inspect them, and later to give me credit. "You will make some farmer a fine wife someday, Bethia." He meant it kindly.

As we made our way through the woods, he began to talk about Jacob Merry in a way unlike him, who did not stoop to gossip. But now, unprompted, he offered up opinions about his character, and described how he was perceived by others in the settlement. "Just as your grandfather's views were moderate by the lights of the Massachusetts Bay colonists, enough to push him to this island, so Merry's are looser still. I will be frank with you, Bethia; he struggled against adverse opinions in Great Harbor. His first wife died of consumption when his youngest children were but two and three years old and the older boys just nine and twelve, I think it was. He married again within a six month—a young girl, Sofia, who had been an indentured servant in their household. There were some who judged him for that, but I was not one of them, for those children needed mothering more than they needed mourning rites. Merry grew up a miller's son in England, so, on finding a stream fast-running enough to fill a millpond, he considered it an opportunity, and did not scruple to bring his family to a place so many miles distant from the rest of us. I do not say that he is a radical or a non-conformist as we commonly understand such things. He is a sound and godly man. But perhaps more his own man than most people find acceptable."

We saw the farm from better than a mile off: a large tract of low-slung land protected from the winds in the lee of gentle hillocks, hugging a shallow, shimmering pond. The Wampanoag, who had a settlement not far distant—from where we were we could see the curls of smoke from their fires—had gardened some of the land before Merry offered for it, so there were clearings. In between, stands of dead trees stood, girdled by the Merrys a year or more since, so as to let the light pass through to the crops. They were a forlorn sight, the tree skeletons, but as we lacked oxen or draft beasts then, to pull out stumps, there was no better way to make cropland. Merry had harvested early and the shocks were many, large and well made. As we approached, we could see three men—Jacob, Noah and his elder brother, Josiah—toiling to raise a wall from the granite stones they had wrestled out of the path of the plough. They left off readily, as soon as they saw us, and came forward with cheerful greetings.

I had not seen Noah for more than two years, since the family left Great Harbor. Because of what I had overheard regarding him, I felt conscious as he greeted me. But I also felt inclined to take more notice of him than I might have done. I observed him as we walked toward the house (which was indeed a fine one—easily the finest yet built on the island—of two full floors and an attic). He and his father and brother put off their soiled smocks and hung them on a peg rail. We sat at board in a large and sunny room with not less than four diamond-paned glass windows, and, yes, a handsome wainscot.

I decided that Noah Merry suited his name. He had a ready laugh and a mop of yellow curls that he wore rather too long, so that he tossed them back out of his eyes when he spoke. This mannerism was part of a general restless animation of his person, and as he helped himself to his young stepmother's excellent seed cake, his stream of good-humored banter was as uninterrupted as the flow of the brook that plashed and glinted outside the windows.

We were still at board when two young Wampanoag presented themselves at the door. Jacob Merry rose and welcomed them and, somewhat to my surprise, as I thought we were the only English household that did such a thing, offered them a place at board while Sofia Merry heaped their plates with seed cake and poured each a tankard of small beer.

As part of the bargain that had been struck for the farmland, the Indians were to have their corn ground at no cost and to have certain youth instructed in the ways of milling. Merry explained that these two youths had been chosen by their sonquem to learn the trade, "and likely millers they are, the pair of them." Father nodded approvingly at this. "Wisely done. This is exactly as we should be going on, as the settlement grows beyond Great Harbor. If they see a benefit in our presence, then we will have a true commonwealth of interests." He turned then to engage the youths, who seemed a little shy of him, in pleasant conversation in their own tongue. I listened to their account of themselves and their village with half an ear while pretending to be fully absorbed in talk with Sofia Merry and her stepsons.

I had a tankard, which was sweating from the coldness of the beer, raised to my lips when one of the young men, whose name was Momonequem, asked father if he happened to have any English remedies with him, for there was a sickened man in their settlement.

"He is not one of us. He is Nahnoso, sonquem of Nobnocket, come to parlay with our sonquem, and we fear if it goes ill with him his people will say our pawaaw cast a spell on him. Our pawaaw has tried to heal him, and, failing, sent for Nahnoso's own, Tequamuck, who we deem the strongest of the pawaaws. But for all he has danced and chanted, he has not been able to spear out the sickness." At that moment the wet tankard slid from my hand and clattered onto the board, slopping its contents.

I got up, in agitation, and helped to mop my spill. I heard father say to Momonequem that he had brought no medicines save some salve and bandages and that he did not think he could be of help in such a grave case.

I could not contain myself. "Do you not think you should see this man, at least?" I said. "I'm sure the Merrys have aught for a poultice, if that be what is needed. If nothing else, you could pray for him . . .

and if you can help him, where the sorcerers have failed, it surely would further the mission."

Father answered, "Perhaps I . . . ," and then he broke off and looked at me strangely. "Bethia, how is it that you . . . ?" He glanced up at the Merrys, and decided that this was not the time or place to pursue the matter.

He turned back to Momonequem and said he would go with them and do what he could. I acted as if it were natural to assume I was to go also, and asked Sofia Merry to show me what she had in her herb store that she might spare me. Even though the damage was done with father, I thought it best that I not speak Wampanaontoaonk in front of the Merrys, so I asked father to question the youths about the signs of the sonquem's illness. They said fever, a red rash and convulsing cough. So I took onions and mustard seed, willow bark, and from the garden some broad leaves of comfrey and peppermint.

Momonequem and his friend Sacochanimo each had a mishoon pulled up on the bank of the pond. These canoes were hollowed out from burned tree trunks, broad enough in the fore to carry sacks of corn to the mill. They unloaded this cargo and carried it to the mill house, then indicated that each of us should take our place where the sacks had been. Father stepped uncertainly into Momonequem's canoe and I into Sacochanimo's. The youths slipped in behind us and paddled with swift strokes across the wide pond. The water was shallow enough to reveal the bright leaves settled at the bottom. Rich colors of bronze and deep crimson layered upon each other like the intricate pattern of the Turkey carpet that warmed my grandfather's floor. The youths paddled at speed, without effort, covering the short distance between farm and settlement in no time at all. From my canoe I could see the muscles working in the arms of Momonequem as he paddled ahead with father. His oar pierced the water without a splash, sending ripples arrowing back to shore, where turtles catching afternoon sunlight slid from the banks as we approached. Momonequem turned sharply, into the river that fed the pond, and we followed his lead through the high marsh grasses towards their settlement.

There were many mishoons beached there. We stepped ashore and at once heard the unholy commotion coming from within the ring of wetus. This was the winter settlement of a large band, five or six times the size of the praying hamlet. We made our way toward the source of the noise.

They had the sick man laid out on a mat, his face painted over completely with charcoal or black clay. Set on the earth around him were all kinds of talismans of bones and fur, shell and hide and dried plants. He was a big man, powerfully built, yet his ribs seemed about to erupt from his chest as he labored to breathe in shallow, rattling gasps. The pawaaw who had stood in silent challenge to my father when he had sermonized the praying Indians was a blur of frantic motion. He cried out, leapt, beat on the ground, then shook his gourd rattles at the sky with frenzied gestures. Foam dangled from his lips as if he were a horse hard-ridden, and strands of it flew off his chin as he leapt and twirled and then fell upon the prone figure, making spearing gestures and wild, fierce faces.

It seemed impossible that any man could go on so for an extended time, but he did, seemingly tireless. He stopped only to turn aside and cast up some brownish bile, then he reached for a gourd and downed a liquid of such a sharp odor I could smell it from where I stood, many yards off. He was a very tall man, even by the lofty standards of the Indians, and though painted garishly I could see now that his nephew's features favored him. The intensity of his prayers was such that had they been to the true God, it would have been a prayer exceeding the most devoted I had ever heard.

Father had been transfixed by the spectacle but suddenly he recovered himself. "Turn your face away, Bethia. Do not gratify Satan by giving his rites your attention."

The discipline of a lifetime compelled me to do as he bade me. When had I ever, in his presence, refused a direction from his lips? But it was like tearing a nail from a board, to pull my eyes away from the ritual. Father's hand was at my back, pushing me towards the nearest wetu as he said shortly to Momonequem that we would wait within until the pawaaw was finished, after which they might fetch us to attend the sick man and see what, if anything, might yet be done.

The wetu was a well-made dome of bark with a hide drawn across its entrance to keep out the fall chill. Father lifted the hide a little, asking leave to enter. A young woman's voice civilly assented. Father signaled me to go before him, so I bent and stepped inside, waiting for my eye to adjust to the low light. It was well I entered first, for the woman within was casually shrugging a deerskin blouse over her bare breasts, in no great urgency to cover her nakedness. She was not much older than I, with long, strong legs and glossy hair tied in a single thick braid, all threaded through with turkey feathers. She gestured to us to sit, and I did so, sinking into a dense pile of fur pelts laid over timber benches. It was warm in the wetu, and the bark gave off a faint sweet smell of resin.

She offered us a mash of parched corn, which we ate with our hand from the common pot. Her cook fire was small and its smoke drew directly upward to a hole in the bark ceiling. Outside, a kind of sail could be moved this way and that to draw the smoke and keep out rain. In the dimness, I could see father staring at me with a hard, unyielding look as I fingered the mash between my lips. Knowing it was coming in any case, I thought I might as well get to it. I turned to the young woman and thanked her civilly in Wampanaontoaonk, at which she started and exclaimed. I explained to her, with my eye on father, that I had learned her speech during my father's lessons with Iacoomis. In English, I added: "Please do not be vexed with me, father. All those many winter months by the hearth when I was a babe—I could not shut my ears."

I do not know what father would have replied. He did not speak his mind to me because at that moment the sonquem of that place entered the wetu, with several of his senior men. When I looked up, the food dropped from my fingers. One of the men looked so like Caleb that I thought for a happy instant it was he, fetched back from his lonely ordeal. But a second's further scrutiny showed the likeness was inexact. This was the face of a man, not a youth, weathered and coarsened by several extra years. It came to me then that this must be the elder brother Caleb had spoken of: Nanaakomin, the dutiful son and favored heir of their father Nahnoso. Since his attention was upon my father, I was free to study his features, so like the ones that had become familiar, even beloved, to me. Nanaakomin's eyes were watchful and intelligent, like Caleb's, but darker and more opaque. His lips were thicker and more sensual.

The young woman gestured to me that she and I should go out and leave the men to conference with my father, and so we did. The settlement was quieter now. They had carried the sick man away to shelter. Only the pawaaw remained in the circle. He lay there, in the dust, spent at last, or in some kind of praying trance, I could not be sure. The people of the settlement, in any case, had given him a wide berth, and the woman at my side held her face away so as not to look at him. I sensed her fear. She walked quickly past, disappearing into some other wetu. There was no one left outside. The pawaaw lay all alone, with his sorcerer's paraphernalia—that no one else dared touch—scattered about him. Walking on silent feet as Caleb had taught me, I approached more nearly to him. His eyes were open, but glassy and unseeing. The gourd from which he had drunk his potion was set upright, just a few inches from his strange, expressionless face.

We reach, now, the place where I cannot account for my own behavior, save to say that Satan truly had his hand upon me. For I walked over to that gourd and peered in. It contained the remains of a greenish brew, the scent of which was pungent enough to burn the nostrils. I could guess what it was. A decoction from the root of white hellebore, of which Makepeace had spoken; the poisonous path to visionary power. I looked about to see if I was watched, but there was no one by me save the pawaaw, supine and insensible in his fit.

I picked up the gourd. My hand trembled. I set it down again, and went to step away. But I could not. I lifted the gourd and walked off with it, into the shelter of a concealing thicket. I set it down again and sat there, considering it. There was not a great amount of liquid left. Makepeace had said they knew well how to decoct a dose that would not poison. What matter if I tasted it? What harm? Perhaps I would gain by it. I yearned to experience, once again, that sense of holy ecstasy that had fallen upon me at the cliffs.

I raised it to my lips and took a sip. The flavor on my tongue was sweet at first, so I tipped the gourd and swallowed what was in it, down to the dregs. A moment later my mouth and throat felt seared. Then there came a bitter aftertaste. My gorge rose, wanting to cast it up. I set the gourd down on the ground and ran back to the edge of the pond, where I knelt down and quaffed water by the handful. That clean sweet liquid might have been gall ink, for all the relief it brought. Soon, I could not feel my tongue, so numb had it become. I felt my knees buckle as if someone had struck me a sharp blow from behind. I sank down by the pond side.

Time slowed. I felt the blood beat in my head. Each breath became effortful, each slower and more rasping than the last. The throb of my blood also slowed, until I felt like an age passed between each beat of my heart. I tried to raise my hand, but between the thought and the act seemed an eternity. My hand weighed heavy as an ingot. As it moved through space it seemed to leave impressions of itself behind, serried rows of hands ascending in the air. I touched my hand to my burning, swollen lips, but there was no sensation in my fingers and I could not feel my face.

The sun was low in the sky, setting the trees alight and sending their red reflections dancing across the pond like the lick of little flames. And then, all at once, the pond was on fire. The tongues of light were not reflections, but real flames, running hot across the surface of the water. Soon, they melded into great sheets of fire, leaping and roaring, taking shapes of giants whose blackened hide coruscated like gashed coals. I buried my head in my arms, but the visions forced their way behind my closed eyelids. There was a terrible noise: thunder claps and great cracking sounds as if the very earth was rending open beneath my feet. I started to pray, but the words came off my thickened tongue strangely; uncouth, guttural words whose meaning I did not know. The taste in my mouth was metallic now, warm and viscous, like clotted blood. The blood of Christ. No, not that. No sacred wine from Satan's chalice. This was the blood of some demonic sacrifice; some gentle innocent impaled upon the devil's trident, bled to desiccation. My head was about to split, so severe was the pain that wracked me.

If there was power here, it was not for me. This was forbidden fruit indeed. I did not think I could rise up off my knees, but without willing it I was on my feet and running fast as a wood sprite, leaping bushes and evading snags with an agility I had not known I possessed. I ran and leapt until my gut seized and I fell on my knees grasping at my belly. I hoped to cast up the potion and be rid of it. But instead my heaves were dry. I was wracked by cramp. I felt my belly as a spasm girded it. Something was moving there, a hard orb pushing against my soft insides. I reached down. Wet, slimy. Horned head, cloven hoof. The devil's spawn, heaving up out of my rending flesh. It thrust its way out of me, a bloodied claw gripping my shredded muscle, tugging up through glossy, throbbing entrails. Leathery pinions, dripping ordure. They flexed and extended, brushing my face. I flailed at the beast with both arms. The unholy creature beat its wings, emitting the stench of corruption and rot—the scent of death, not birth. It rose into the riven sky from which bright white arrows fell down upon me, setting me all aflame. I watched my burning flesh blister and melt, falling away from charred bone, until my eyes, withered in the heat, dropped from their sockets like dried pease. Then I saw no more.

* * *

I came back to myself lying upon the grass beside the pond. Only minutes had passed, for the sun was just fallen behind the hillock to the west of the pond. The afterglow, pink and lilac, bathed everything in a benign light. I looked at my arms, whole and healthy, and felt my belly, which was tender but most certainly not riven. There was a stench, to be sure. My cast, steaming slightly on the grass, accounted for part of it. I reached for a handful of sassafras leaves to wipe my mouth. As I rose I felt a wetness, and realized with humiliation that I had soiled my drawers. I drew them off in disgust, wrapped them around a rock and threw them far into the trees. My hands shook. I knelt down, took a deep, ragged, sobbing breath and prayed to God for forgiveness. But I did not expect his mercy.

Once, when grandfather did not think I overheard, he related to father a most terrible case that had come before the mainland magistrates. A woman had thrown her own babe down a well. When she was brought to answer for the murder, she said that one great good had come of her evil act. At last, she said, she was free of the uncertainty that had plagued her every waking thought: was she numbered among the damned or the saved? Her whole life had been bent about that question. Finally, she knew.

I thought of her, as I stumbled back to the wetus to wait for father. Now I too, seeker after strange gods, had an answer. Remarkably, rather than oppressing me, this thought made me feel oddly light, as I suppose does the reaching of any kind of certainty, no matter how bleak. I did not know then that God would not wait unto the afterlife, but move so swiftly in this world to punish my sin.

X

For over an hour, I waited while father attended upon Nahnoso. Spasms wracked my gut and my head throbbed. Pretending I was working for father, I steeped some willow bark and drank the liquid, hoping to ease my head. But it was shame that sickened me and no decoction could cure that. Finally, father sent word to me to prepare some onions for a chest poultice, and when he emerged from the wetu I asked if he thought the willow tea might lessen the fever.

"Apparently they have done this already, along with some other witch medicine prescribed by that man," he inclined his head to where Tequamuck lay, his eyes closed now, a skin cloak thrown over him, his breathing the regular breath of one deep asleep. I realized, with alarm, that I had not returned the gourd to his side, but left it in the thicket. It could not be helped; I could not fetch it now. Father was speaking to me, so I struggled to attend to him. "I propose to bleed him. You may hold the basin if you feel you can."

I followed father into the wetu where the sick sonquem lay, his son at his side, surrounded by the most notable men of the village. "What do you have for a lancet?" father asked. One of the men turned over his hand and showed an arrowhead. Father took it up. The man's arm, where father thought to open the vein, was greasy with streaks of raccoon grease and carbon black, so I washed it, to better reveal the vein, and rubbed the place with crushed mint. Father pressed the stone point into the flesh. I held the basin in my trembling hands, and tried to give myself up to the prayers that father was offering. When father believed we had let sufficient blood, I pushed healing comfrey leaves upon the wound and bound them up with a leather thong that someone passed to me.

While the onions roasted, I smashed the mustard seed into a paste to add heat to the poultice. I could hear the rattle in Nahnoso's chest as father strapped it on. Time crawled, marked by the rise and fall of that ragged breathing. By and by, I thought that the man's color began to change. It was dark in the wetu, so I thought perhaps my eyes tricked me. But in a while there could be no mistaking it, his labored breathing eased. An hour passed, and then, miracle! He opened his eyes and looked about, asking where he was and, in some agitation, who we were. His son Nanaakomin gave a great cry of joy and embraced his father. It startled me when he cried out, so like was his voice to Caleb's.

The Takemmy sonquem spoke up then, and told him the whole of it, from the time he had fallen ill: of their own pawaaw's failure to turn back the sickness, and of sending for Tequamuck and that man's day-long, fruitless efforts. Then he pointed to my father and described how heat magic (the poultice) and blood magic, partnered with spells addressed to the English God, had returned him from the brink of death.

"Manitoo!" breathed Nahnoso, and fell back on his mat. Father turned to me then and spoke in English. "I would like to stay and see to his care, but I do not want you to pass the night here."

"Why not, father?"

"Because there is no wetu in which you might lay your head without risk of witnessing some indecency. I will ask Momonequem to return us to the Merrys and then I will come back here with him."

"You need not escort me, father. I am quite prepared to go with Momonequem."

"By no means. Even if the youth is honorable, which I have no reason to doubt, I would not put your reputation at risk. What would the Merrys make of such a thing? You, alone in a boat with . . . no, it is unthinkable."

I thought of all the hours I had spent alone with Caleb. Innocent hours that would make a harlot of me in my father's reckoning, and in the eyes of our society. It was well that no one knew of them.

We rowed back to the Merry farm by rushlight. Jacob Merry insisted on ceding his place to me, so I lay down with Sofia as my bedfellow. Her featherbed was twice as wide and lofty as my straw-and-rag-filled shakedown. Though I fell straight to sleep I was awakened many times by fell dreams. I had to resort to the necessary several times throughout the night. When Sofia asked what ailed me, I blamed my bowels' distress on the corn mash I had taken from the common pot in the wetu.

In the morning I rose, weary, and gave a hand to Sofia with her chores until the men came in for bever. I felt Jacob Merry's eyes upon me as I helped Sofia serve out cider and slices of crusty bread spread thick with new-churned butter. I tried to hide the tremor in my hands.

"Noah, as Mistress Mayfield is detained here for some hours, perhaps she would like to see the farm. Why do you not show it her?"

"I will, father," said Josiah brightly.

"Not you, Josiah, I can't spare you. I want your help at the mill."

"But we already ground . . ."

Jacob Merry pushed his chair back noisily and glared at his eldest son.

"I am in want of your help."

"Very well, father." As Josiah rose obediently from his seat, I saw him wink at his brother and punch him lightly on the arm. Noah flushed.

Whatever consciousness he might have felt, he quickly shook it off as we walked the fields. I tried to attend to him, but my mind was still occupied with the prior day's madness and my thoughts were as scattered as blown chaff. Noah's zeal for farming was patent. If only I shared it, how much simpler my life would be. I let his remarks about the forage virtues of timothy and vetch flow over me, exclaimed where it seemed required at the remarkable number of twins the ewes had produced at last lambing and nodded sagely as he outlined his plans for orchards, a creamery and all manner of improvements. "Josiah's interests are with the mill, and developing that enterprise will be his main pursuit. My concern is the farm. In time, father and I hope to have the means to expand, if the sonquem will sell more land to us. There are fertile bottoms in yonder woods that would yield easily to the hoe. It does seem strange to leave them a wasteland . . ."

As he prattled, my mind was on Nahnoso. I wondered how he fared, since father's fate was now bound with his. But suddenly Noah stopped his prating and turned to me with an avid look. "It seemed yesterday that you understood the speech of the Indians at our board. Is it so, indeed?"

"Well, I—" I gazed into Noah's open countenance. His pale blue eyes looked back at me with curiosity. Was this youth really destined to be my spouse? I felt next akin to nothing in my heart that said it should be so. But if it were to be, I must not lie to him now. What manner of marriage could be built upon a foundation of untruth? The falsehood that was forming on my lips, I swallowed. "Yes," I said. "Though it is a most difficult tongue."

"I know it! I cannot retain above two or three words of it—I was never one for rote learning. Father does better, but 'tis a struggle for him also. How marvelous that you can converse with them! It would be a great thing for us if someone from our household could have easy speech with them—we could do much if we understood each other better."

Now it was my turn to color. Did he mean to say he already counted me a potential member of his household? Or did I, knowing what I should not, feel too conscious of an innocent observation? Either he was too forward, or I was too fretful. But if father had not given me a full accounting of the understanding regarding myself and the Merrys . . . At that thought, I felt the ember of anger flare suddenly and burn white hot.

"Shall we turn?" I said. "I am ready to go in."

As we walked back to the house, I kept my eyes on the ground so as not to notice the low autumn sun spangling across that extravagance of glass.

Father returned at noon time, and we set out for home soon after, in order to reach Great Harbor before dark. Although father tried to project a sober mien, I could tell he was fairly bursting with joy. Nahnoso had made a remarkable recovery, and seeing in it a sign of the English God's power, had asked to be instructed in the ways of the one true God and his son, Jesus Christ. "To convert a sonquem, Bethia . . . this will be a turning point for the mission, I know it. And such a sonquem, related so closely to that wizard, Tequamuck . . . to defeat such as he . . . if we can but break his hold on the people . . . Christ has had a great victory here, daughter. A great victory. Nahnoso has agreed to receive Iacoomis and to take instruction from him in the gospel. When he is well, he will bring his family to hear me preach at Sunday meeting in Manitouwatootan."

His family. Surely that must include Caleb, his son. What would his father's change of heart mean for him? Would his father order a stop to his heathen quest? As fallen as I felt, and heavy in my own sin-stained soul, I prayed to God to keep Satan from Caleb until his father could fetch him back out of the wilderness.

As for *my* family, we returned home that night to an evening of uncommon rejoicing. Father was full of his triumph, and I had never seen mother more radiant than she was that night, hanging upon his words. Her condition was patent by then, and it had put an uncommon bloom upon her. I overheard her confide to Goody Branch, not long after, that she had never carried easier than she did with that babe, who would become our Solace, and her mortal bane. Perhaps the joy she found in those last months was a mote of God's mercy, gifted to her, even as he shaped within her the instrument of his retribution unto me.

XI

The hour is late. It is gone past midnight, so already the Lord's Day is upon us. Once again I sin, breaking the Sabbath by sitting up to scrawl these words. On the morrow, at this hour, Caleb will be asleep in the room below.

I am bone weary, having risen early these past days and stayed too long awake to write these pages. I have not yet set down all I purposed, though I have given here the better part of it, which is the account of my own sins. My eyes are heavy, so I will add but a brief account of how we are come to the present circumstance.

I witnessed none of what follows, but rather had to prise every fact from father's talk with others when he thought he was not overheard. The short of it: father did not get his sonquem convert, nor did he break the power of the pawaaw Tequamuck.

When Iacoomis traveled out to preach the gospel to Nahnoso, as had been arranged, he was met by Tequamuck in full sorcerer's regalia. A kind of duel took place between them, Tequamuck pitting his spells and demonic familiars against Iacoomis's sacred prayers. Iacoomis stood firm, proclaiming that his God was greater than all of Tequamuck's familiar spirits. Neither man yielded. In the end, Nahnoso stood with his kinsman, and declined to hear Iacoomis that day, or any other. Whether Tequamuck worked upon Nahnoso's reason or simply bewitched him, as father believed, I cannot say. Father, much distressed by Iacoomis's account, rode out himself to see Nahnoso. He brought the sonquem a stern message, warning that God would not be slighted; that, having once resolved to accept the truth of the gospel, to turn back to the devil had become a far graver sin. But Nahnoso, returned to full vigor, would have none of it and told father to trouble his mind no further. He argued fiercely, in words given him by Tequamuck: "You come here to disturb my rest with your tales of hell and damnation, but your tales are hollow threats, meant to scare us out of our customs and make us stand in awe of you. I will not hear your words." He ordered father and Iacoomis banished from the Nobnocket lands.

Not even a month later, Nahnoso sickened again, this time with the greatest of all their scourges, the small pox. A sorer disease cannot befall them and their fear of it is very great. They that have this disease have it to a terrible extent—much worse even than we. For them, there is not the scattering of pox such as we are accustomed to suffer, but a vast clustering of pustules, breaking their skin and mattering all together.

When father first heard this report he was much grieved and made to go there, but Tequamuck persisted in refusing him to pass. We had little news of how the people fared, for the Wampanoag of Manitouwatootan were filled with dread and would not go there, not even those with family ties, no matter how father appealed to them to show Christian mercy. A sennight passed before one brave soul ventured there, and returned with a fearful report. Nahnoso had died; further, of a band numbering some hundreds, less than three score souls remained alive, and most of those were sore afflicted.

This news was too much for father. "If so many are dead there will be few to tend those that yet live," he said. He and grandfather enlisted some other good men from Great Harbor—they refused me and Makepeace, saying that elders seemed better able to withstand this disease than the young—and set out with supplies. This, even though mother neared her time. But she urged father to go, saying that she had no fears for the outcome of her confinement, but great fears for his mission to the Indians, should he forsake them in such an hour of need. The party was away several days and we feared for them. But then one among them—James Tilman—returned to gather more supplies and to bring word that father was engaged in a great struggle to save as many who yet lived as God's providence would allow.

Master Tilman was all grave looks as he asked mother to fetch what could be spared from our stores of food. When I went out with her to the buttery, we both of us overheard as he described the lamentable condition of the people to Makepeace. I could not meet mother's eyes as the words drifted through the partition, but our hands, reached out to each other and clutched tight.

"One poor man, I thought to help him as he lay in his dreadful discomfort, so I attempted to lift him..." Tilman's voice quavered and fell so low we could barely hear him. "I did not see that his poor broken skin had cleaved to the mat he lay upon, and a whole side of him flayed off as I turned him. He was all blood and gore, most terrible to look upon..." He broke off, and I heard heavy breaths as he strove to contain himself. Mother left me then and went in to warm a posset. She pressed him to drink it. As much as I felt for the general suffering, my mind was filled with thoughts of Caleb. I had wished him plucked from his quest in the woods. Now I prayed hard that he was out there still and not lying with his kinfolk, bloody and dying.

" 'Tis well your husband pressed us to go there," Tilman said to mother, when at last he recovered himself. "They have fallen down so generally of this disease that for some days they had not been able to help one another. They were without firewood and had burned their wood vessels—their mortars, their bowls, even their arrows in their extremity. Nanaakomin, the sonquem's son, was one who had done this, before the disease claimed him. Later, I came upon his mother, the sonquem's own squa, fallen dead by the wayside.... She and her babes had suffered so from thirst and none to bring water that she tried to crawl on all fours to the spring. I buried her, of course, and two of her babes with her. Your good husband has us bury them after their own fashion, tied up in deerskins. Those who survive thank him for this kindness and kiss his hands."

My insides churned as I listened to this news. I came into the room then, and asked the question that was eating me alive: "I—I heard tell the sonquem had two sons? What of the other?"

Tilman shrugged. "No one spoke to us of a second son. They counted the loss of Nanaakomin so grave I cannot think there is another."

It was Makepeace who noticed that mother was pale and sweating, and ushered her up the stairs to lie down upon the bed. It should have been me. But I was full of thoughts of Caleb, and negligent of those nearest me. I could not rid myself of the idea that Caleb was already perished. How else would his mother and kin lie dead and unattended? I plunged into a private grief at that moment, unable to unburden myself to any person as to why my heart ached so.

"Where is their wizard in all this?" Makepeace asked Tilman, once he returned from seeing to our mother. "I pray God has finally stricken him, or else how is it that you and father were permitted entry?"

"They say he yet lives. He spent himself, according to one who was able to tell of it, in all manner of sorceries, trying to turn the sickness away. And then, when his powers proved worthless, he went off, to do some other, stronger, secret rite—or so they think. For my part, I think it likely he made covenant with Satan, and left the place to save his own accursed skin."

How often do we say that *God works in mysterious ways his wonders to perform.* As God sent plagues upon the people of Egypt to free the captive Hebrews, so many here say he sent this plague upon the people of Nobnocket to free the souls of those enslaved to paganism. It is exceeding hard for me to agree that much good came from this terrible rain of death, so I say nothing when it is discussed. But the facts are these: The few who yet lived among the Nobnocket band saw the pox as a sign of God's power, a punishment of Nahnoso, and testament to the rightness of my father's preachments. All the more so since, through the marvelous providence of God, not one of the English who came to their aid was in the least measure touched by the sickness.

As they recovered, one by one, and then severally, most of those who survived defied Tequamuck, left their Nobnocket lands and joined the settlement at Manitouwatootan. Among them, at last, came Caleb. I learned much later that he had never been in Nobnocket during the season of sickness, nor even heard of it until its fury was spent and all his family killed. Tequamuck had gone to him in the woods and lived with him there through the long nights moon, performing heavy rituals, but not disclosing anything of the scourge that afflicted their kindred.

That spring, mother went to her childbed and did not rise from it. We entered our own season of mourning, all the heavier for me who knew I was to blame for mother's death. During that time, our minds were turned from the losses of others. It was only much later that I learned that Caleb had come to Nobnocket at last. While I prayed at my mother's grave, he walked the ruined remnant of his village and sought out the makeshift burying places of his family. His grief was great and his wrath at Tequamuck, for keeping the truth from his ears, waxed strong. He stayed with him only long enough to perform the death rites he deemed owed there. Then he went his own way, as he ever had, and removed to the praying town, saying he would know the English God better, before he judged whether to accept him or no.

When my father was in heart to return to his preaching, and went again to Manitouwatootan, Caleb sought him out there, to thank him for the mercy he had shown unto the sick and to ask what reward he might offer on behalf of his dead father, the sonquem. Father, much amazed by his proficiency in English, said that allowing his people to hear the gospel was reward enough. It was hard for me to prepare my face when father came home full of the miraculously wise youth who had walked out of the wilderness. Relief and joy brimmed up in me, so that I had to go out from the house and pace about before I could compose myself.

I had once yearned to take credit for Caleb's instruction; now, in guilt at what my furtive doings had brought us to, I dreaded lest the connection be discovered. I said nothing, as father speculated as to how the youth had learned his English. It had got into his head that one of the mainland Wampanoag from Mashpee or Plimoth must have come here and instructed him. I let Makepeace question, although it cost me dearly to stay mute and feign only ordinary interest in the matter. There was one moment when I almost gave myself away. When father first announced that the young adept called himself Caleb, and wondered where the son of Nahnoso might have happened upon a Hebraic name, I let out a snort, and made as if I had choked upon a piece of bread.

Father commenced at once upon a course of instruction with him, and after every encounter the talk at board would be of the young man's ready wit and remarkable progress.

And now Caleb is to quit Manitouwatootan to come here and live with us, so that father may increase his hours of instruction. He will take lessons alongside Makepeace and Joel, the young son of Iacoomis. Joel is two years the junior of Caleb, but he has been raised among the English and set to his book at an early age. Father has found him a quick study and says he is already well begun upon his Latin. Father came to me, just two days since, to give me, as he thought, the first news of our intended boarder. He had been anxious and diffident, thinking, as I suppose, that I would mislike to be in such close quarters with an Indian lad. He had prepared a long speech about how we all of us must carry our portion of the Cross, but I cut him off at the first opportunity and told him I would be very glad to help him further his mission in such a practical way, and that I looked forward to having the young man in our household. He was relieved at that, and has been giving me kind looks ever since.

It is father's intention that, if Caleb and Joel prove themselves as able to profit from his instruction as he expects, they will remove to the mainland with Makepeace, to be examined for matriculation to the Harvard College. It seems the college has built a second house there, alongside the English one, exactly for the education of Indian youths, with the aim to make them into instruments for the propagation of the gospel among the tribes.

The hour is late. My eyes are sore, and my hand cramped. I can write no more. I will place this page with the others, in a pocket I have fashioned in my shakedown. But I cannot say if I will sleep this night.

Writing this confession has put my sins plain before me, and I do repent them. Since these matters of which I have written, and most certainly since mother's death, I have kept far from all the Wampanoag save for Iacoomis and his son, who are in every significant particular just as the English. I have felt no corrupt promptings towards idolatry such as formerly ensnared me.

But Caleb is coming this day. And what will become of me thereafter, I cannot say.

Anno 1661
Aetatis Suae 17
Cambridge

I

I had not thought to take up this pen, having laid it down so long since. But my mind is afire and I feel I must make some relation of these past months and my present troublesome condition, far from home, in this unwholesome place.

I dream of mother now. For the first year after her death, this was not so. My guilt kept her from me, perhaps. But now she comes. On the coldest nights of this past winter, she would visit me, turning from the hearth and beckoning me into arms that were warm and enfolding. And then I woke, on my cold pallet in this stranger's kitchen, with ice winds from the cracked window fingering my flesh and a snowflake melting slowly on the fireless hearth.

I have longed for a visit home, but my situation does not allow for it. Those in my position may not come and go as they wish. Makepeace returns as often as he might—more often, indeed, than my master, his tutor, willingly countenances. I have seen in his face, although he strives to obscure it, a certain relief that I must be left behind, each time he has departed this place. I suppose he feared that once there I would say that which would not profit him. Makepeace judges all by the harsh yardstick of his own temperament. It does not occur to him that if I was minded to complain of my condition, or of his, I could have done so, in a letter, at any time. But I accept my lot here, and his predicament is his own affair. He must know that a word from me would have sunk this plan before its launching. But I did not choose to say that word.

My thoughts run on apace, so disordered is my mind. I mean to set down how it is we are got hither, to Master Corlett's school in Cambridge town and all the strange events since then. To this end, I must resume my relation where I last left off, on the eve of Caleb's coming to us. I have those scattered sheets and pages here assembled, having unpicked the seam of my shakedown and gathered them up in haste, before I quit the island.

The island. As I tally my losses, it figures large there. If God takes a beloved one unto himself, we feel that loss in our heart. Yet we know well enough that nowt will quicken the dead, and so we must strive to be reconciled. But the island—its briny air, its ever changing light— these things yet exist. There, the clean and glassy breakers still beat upon the sands, the clay cliffs still flare russet and purple each sunset. All of this goes on, but I am not there to rejoice in it. It is a loss I feel on my very skin. Here, I scan the flat fens and the dung-strewn pastures in vain for the beauty that once was my daily portion. In that way, my condition is like a little death; this place, a little purgatory.

One thing, at least, I have aplenty, and that is paper. While the boys scrape upon slates in the schoolroom, the master is liberal— one might even say wastrel—in his own use of paper. The better for me. I may take all the crumpled discards and part-written sheets when I clean his chamber, refresh his ink, and mend his pens each day. And so provided, I will go on. . . .

That Lord's Day when finally Caleb came to us was bright and glistering. It was one of those pet days in early March that tease the senses, promising spring when in fact much bone-cracking weather must yet be endured. But that day had brought the first sudden mellowing of the brute cold, and little rivulets of icy melt water marked the pathways and welled up through the leaf litter, seeping and trickling along their way to refresh the ponds. The hard white ice had given way in places, making a shelf for the otters, who hauled themselves out of the dark water to bask and slide in the unaccustomed brightness.

Father had fetched Caleb the day before, from Manitouwatootan, and brought him to grandfather's house to pass the night. Grandfather's manservant had been charged with bathing and grooming him fit for Sabbath meeting. Grandfather has jested that the young man must learn "the gospel of soap" before he joined us for the gospel of the Lord.

Although father related that jest to us, when he returned from delivering Caleb to grandfather, I could sense an unease in him. He had not confided to the community his intention to bring Caleb to live with us, and he could not be sure of their reaction to this news. Or perhaps I should say rather that he *could* be sure of the Aldens' reaction; that it would be unfavorable and perhaps provide cause, such as Giles Alden was ever in want of, to discredit our family and challenge grandfather's position. It became clear to me, as I considered it, that father had chosen with deliberation to introduce Caleb at meeting, where he had a measure of control over what might be done and said. But there were risks, still. An outburst from the Aldens, at meeting, on the Lord's Day, would bring grievous upset to the community, and perhaps cast a harsh and unfavorable light on father's judgment.

They say the Lord's Day is a day of rest, but those who preach this generally are not women. Even on the Sabbath, a fire must be laid, water drawn, victuals prepared, infants washed and dressed in meeting clothes. Those in purse to have a cow must see to it, for no one has preached to the cow that she must not let down the milk that stiffens her udders. So it is a great rush to get all in order and be at the meeting house in good time for the first service. None has leisure to linger and exchange greetings. All simply hasten hence, heads bent, and take our assigned benches. And so we did that day. Father went to the front and took up his book, ready to lead us. Makepeace went alone to the foremost bench to await grandfather, and I took my place with Solace in the women's seats. I tried to compose myself, but I could not forebear from turning to look who had arrived, as each new party entered.

As hard as it may be to credit this, I did not recognize Caleb when he came through the door. Even on a bright day, it is dim there at that time of year, when the sun is still low to the horizon. My first vague and half-formed thought was to wonder that an unknown young man had come to Great Harbor unremarked. Then he cast off his mantua and turned his face. The beam of light that shafted through a gap in the planking fell direct upon it, and I gasped. His chief distinguishing feature—his long, elaborately dressed hair— had been shorn away.

He was wearing a good plain doublet and jerkin that had been grandfather's, cut in at the waist and let out in the shoulders, to fit his different build. His white linen collar, starched and spotless, set off the copper of his skin and the glossy black of his short-cropped hair. His nails were clean and trimmed. Only his boots marred what was otherwise unexceptionable grooming. These were old, and hard worn, got from I know not which large-footed person among us, and no amount of buffing could conceal their defects. Caleb made to join Iacoomis and his sons, who by custom sat on a small and rickety bench at the rear of the meeting house, but grandfather signaled no, and walked him to the front, to sit between himself and Makepeace. This was a bold stroke and I caught some murmurings, for where one sat in our meeting house was fixed by age, sex, estate and dignity, and those who cared for such things were ever trying to get themselves into a better seat. Of those present that morning, only father and I and the Iacoomis family—and perhaps grandfather—recognized that Caleb, son to the sonquem of Nobnocket, had grown up as a princeling among his own people and was therefore due some precedence. Makepeace, of a certain, did not fashion it thus. From my place with the women, I watched him shift to his left, so as to leave a speaking gap between himself and Caleb. Father glared at Makepeace, and seeing this, he moved back an inch or two, but held himself stiffly.

Father commenced the service as he generally did, lining out a psalm so that the flock might sing it after him. To my surprise Caleb's voice rose with our own, clear and confident, giving the words from Ainsworth without difficulty: "Showt ye to Jahovah . . ."

It is our style to worship with our palms and eyes lifted to heaven, not bowed over clasped hands as they do in England, as the Bible often refers to the faithful lifting up their gaze to God. But this day, eyes were more upon the new occupant of the Mayfield bench than upon the celestial realm. I saw the younger Alden children nudging and whispering, while Patience Alden, who is my age, wore an expression as if something in the meeting house smelled bad. Her parents scowled through the hymn as if they were bilious.

Morning service is a lengthy business for us. As I have said, father holds that the commandment "a day to be kept" means exactly that. After many psalms came many prayers, and then readings from the scripture. I have said that father was a mild man; he was also strong at his core, and fast in his convictions. When it came time to read from scripture, he called forth his chief antagonist, Giles Alden.

My heart fluttered. Why did father call on that man, of all people? I had heard Giles Alden rant against grandfather, saying he did wrong to pay the sonquems for their land. The money would be better spent, he said, hiring musketeers "to clear the woods of these pernicious creatures, to make way for a better growth." As he walked to the front, he glared at Caleb with naked hatred, his brow drawn and his mouth twisted into an angry scowl.

As father held out the book, Alden snatched it from his hands. Then he stared down at the passage father had marked. His head dropped down between his shoulders and he looked up at father with a face distorted by suppressed rage. He reminded me of a ram about to charge. I shrank in my seat, fearing the denunciation that I felt sure was coming.

If father feared it too, he gave no sign. His face was bland and expressionless as he announced the chosen text. Giles Alden, with the book open to the place, already knew the trap that father had sprung upon him. When father announced that Alden's reading was from the Book of Ruth, I tried to keep my countenance. Truly I was tested that day, as I watched Alden choke out words of praise and welcome for the stranger, who has left a native land and come *"to a people whom you did not know before."* Giles Alden had a full, rich voice, and was a good reader, but one who had not heard him before that day would not have said so. He fumbled through the passage, stopping many times to clear his throat, I suppose because the words he was compelled to utter stuck in his craw: *"The Lord recompense you for what you have done, and a full reward be given you from the Lord, the God of Israel, under whose wings you have come to take refuge. . . ."* When he had done, he slammed the book shut. I could see the dust motes rise in the thin shaft of sunshine.

After Alden, father bade Makepeace read from the gospel of Luke concerning the ten lepers, where only one of them, the Samaritan, comes back to Jesus to give thanks: *"Was no one found to return and give praise to God except this foreigner?"* Makepeace gave out his reading with a better grace than Alden: for all his flaws he was a devout soul and strove his best to take the word of God into his heart. He also took note of the fifth commandment, and was a dutiful son.

There were several more like readings. I marveled at how father had contrived to gather so many texts to reinforce his message, so that without risk of contradiction he gave forth the spiritual ground on which Caleb's inclusion among us rested, and also let it be plain that he would brook no dissent over the matter. Well and good; father had a tight hand over what transpired in morning service, when we read the texts and prayers he had selected. Afternoon devotions were another gate's business, for there we gave confession and prophecy. Those who wished to speak were obliged to come before father or grandfather, our elders, ahead of meeting, so that their thoughts might be properly shaped into what was fitting for all to hear. But it was always possible that someone might flout this custom.

Father did not seem in the least concerned. With the morning service safely negotiated, he stood in the dooryard, greeting everyone and introducing Caleb as he would any other newcomer amongst us. I stood with him, and noted that most people, if not warm, were at least civil. The Aldens of course did not tarry to be introduced, but gave us their backs as quickly as they might, hurrying off to their own cottage, where I am sure the iniquity of my family was much discussed.

Father was in a merry mood as we walked the short distance home to take our meal. I had made a hearty chowder and some cornbread with a browned crust; I also set out some dried fruits and nuts from the last season's gathering. As I put a dish of huckleberries and hazels before Caleb, he glanced up at me. I knew that he recalled the day he had shown me where to find them. He smiled, and said a mannerly thank you, and I turned away, blushing.

Father engaged Caleb right away in conversation, asking him what he thought of the service compared with those he had attended at Manitouwatootan. Caleb said that he enjoyed the hymn singing with English voices all in unison, "for at Manitouwatootan, there is always some newcomer who *will* sing, even if he knows not the words or tune . . ." and then he commenced to give a parody that made father laugh with recognition. Makepeace passed the dishes in silence, and took no part in the conversation unless father addressed him directly.

For myself, I had even less to say than usual, the strangeness of having Caleb so close at hand in this unfamiliar setting rendering me dumbstruck. I had to think about even the most ordinary task, willing my hands to do the normal business of setting down dishes and taking them up, for my head was full of his presence, and I felt all light and a-tingle. But no one seemed to mark this. If any noted my silence and my oddity, I expect they felt it only natural before—as they thought—one who was a stranger to me. I did attempt to study him, as best I could. He had changed a great deal, in the months since I had taken tearful leave of him in the woods. He seemed older, certainly, but also somehow winnowed, whether by the magical and diabolic rites demanded of him during his ordeal, or by the simple human matters of loss and death. He had exchanged the restless, flaring energy of his boyhood for a mannerly restraint. But the sense was of fires banked, not extinguished. One thing hadn't changed: even in the unfamiliar English garb, he glowed.

Just before we were to return to meeting, I drew father aside, and did ask him who he expected to speak. He named two men, each of whom had come to him regarding certain texts they felt inspired to explicate, and another whom he said intended to confess corrupt promptings towards the theft of a neighbor's unearmarked tegs. "As to the Alden faction, no one has approached me. I do not expect anything from them today. I think they will bide their time and take the sense of the settlement regarding the inclusion of our hopeful young prophet here."

"Does Caleb—I mean, does the young scholar—know about the Aldens and their hostile views towards his people?"

"I have enlightened him. Why do you ask?"

"I just—I know that their views are very harsh and I—"

Father reached out a hand and patted my shoulder. "You are a kind girl, Bethia. Considerate of the feelings of others, just as your beloved mother was. But do not distress yourself on Caleb's account.

He knows that harsh words pass between the Wampanoag and the English, and not all one way either. His uncle Tequamuck has that to say about *me* that would flay me to the bone, if words were whips. Luckily, they are not, and we must toughen our hides and withstand adverse comments, just as did our blessed Lord when he was subject to slander."

Father, as ever, proved himself a shrewd reader of men, for the afternoon service passed unremarkably. At supper I served small beer and the rest of the cornbread smeared with honey from my own hives, in which I must confess I took a little pride. Makepeace, who loved sweetmeats, had consumed his in a few bites and rose, excusing himself to go to his rest. Caleb, however, chewed his food thoughtfully, refused the beer in favor of water, which he rose and fetched for himself, although father told him that in future he must just ask, since it was my place to serve the men at board.

I cleared the board as the others rose to retire. I had looked out the spare shakedown for Caleb, one I had pieced from burlap grain bags. As I shook it out before the hearth, I thought of the furs layered upon the plank benches in the Takemmy wetu, and how my hands had sunk deep into that buttery softness. As sonquem's son, Caleb would have been used to wrap himself in the finest of such furs—even those we did not generally see here on the island, like bear and beaver, which the Indians traded across from tribes on the mainland. Well, I thought, he had to sleep hard upon the plain ground often enough these past months: he would be able to make shift with burlap.

It did set me to wondering in what things Caleb might feel a lack, living here with us. Those English who have never been within a wetu fashion them squalid, inferior to their own habitations in every way. They would naturally assume that Caleb would be grateful for the chance to live with us. But I was not so sure that he would find his lot materially improved here. For one thing, the winter otans are generally set in well-drained, sheltered places. By changing these sites each season, the freshets run untainted and the grasses regrow. But the land on which we had chosen to set ourselves down is in the path of maritime gales, and already constant use has fouled the nearest springs. So have the years of our habitation worn well-trodden ways down to bare rock and claypan—slick in winter, dusty in summer. I feared that Caleb would feel himself in a reduced condition here.

When I had made Caleb's place, I gave a general good night and carried Solace up to my own bed. I heard Caleb ask father if he might sit up a while. "For I see here many of the books of which you have often spoken to us, at Manitouwatootan. . . ."

There was a sputter and hiss as father lit a stick of pine tar. "Take care not to tire yourself. We rise early here and are to chores until dinner. After the dinner hour, we will commence your course of study. I intend to bring you along as fast as may be, so you will need your wits tomorrow. Do not stint your rest."

When father and Makepeace had settled, I noted no low murmurs from the other side of the blanket. They did not engage in their usual quiet conference that night. There was a constraint between them, clearly caused by Caleb's presence. I lay there, considering my brother. I knew that Makepeace cast his concern about taking in Caleb as a wish to safeguard me from the arrows of slanderous tongues. It was no hollow pretense; his desire to protect me was well meant. *"A good name is as a precious ointment,"* he would say, and I knew it to be true. It is a great favor to have an unblemished reputation, and no small matter for one of my sex in a close community such as ours. But his vigilance, however motivated, also was vexing; like having a dog that *will* snarl at whomever approaches, whether the person be friend or foe. And truth to tell, it was also offensive to me, that my brother should think I cared so little, or so lacked wit, that I would fail in the standard of conduct required of me. Then, as I lay there, it came to me that I had no business to be either vexed or offended. Had I not, these past several years, taken the gravest risks with my reputation, and that with the very person whose presence in our home now troubled him?

In any case, Makepeace's concern did not prove so great as to keep him long awake. Soon enough, I heard him snoring quietly. Solace's hot little head lay, heavy and damp, against my breast, her arms flung out in the deep, abandoned sleep of infants. But I lay open-eyed in the dim glow of the pine tar, smelling the resinous scent and listening for the rustle of pages turning softly in the room below.

II

I woke in the blueblack predawn, and got right about my chores. Since mother's death I had reformed myself. I no longer roamed the wilderness evading English glances, nor crept off to lay myself to books. And neither did I lurk about, listening an ear to my brother's lessons, hoping to steal wisdom like a cur dog after scraps from the midden. For one thing, my duties were become too onerous. But even had I time and space in my day, I had decided that the best way to honor mother and atone for my sin was to try to follow her in her acceptance of humble duties. I strove to see each simple task, whether the making of barley malt, gathering herbs or brining of meat, as she had. She believed that each humble thing, if done worthily, might be touched by grace. I hoped it might be so, for it would require an abundance of grace to clean me of my sin.

So, before sunup I left Solace asleep on the shakedown, pausing for a moment to stroke her warm head and tuck the coverlet around her. As the sky lightened I was at the hearth, raking over the coals and setting a new fire. Father's concern, that Caleb might not be equal to the hours we kept, seemed to have been misplaced. He had evidently risen while it was still dark out, since his shakedown was folded and placed neatly in a corner. For a moment I thought he might have left us and returned to the woods, but then I saw the grass basket that contained his few possessions hanging up upon the peg rail.

I went out to draw water. As I straightened from lifting the full bucket, I saw Caleb, the dawn breaking fair behind him, walking back from the low dunes by the shore. The frosty grass crunched under his feet. When he approached the garth I gave him a good morning, which he returned civilly, laying a hand to the bucket. "No need," I said. "I can manage it." He smiled, but did not let go, and rather than grapple I released the handle and let him take it.

"You are abroad early."

"Always," he replied. "Not a morning has passed, for as long as I can remember, that I did not sing a greeting to Keesakand upon his rising."

I stopped sharply in my tracks. Was he then, as my brother held, an idolator still? I was glad I no longer had charge of the water. I might have spilled it.

He smiled. "Do not look at me so, Storm Eyes. Did not God create the sun? Mayn't I make a hymn of gladness upon it? Your father has never taught me that the only one place to pray is in the dim confines of your meeting house. God's spirit shines out in every goodly thing. Do not wonder that I stretch up my hands and reach out for his grace."

We were at the door by then. I lifted the latch for him. The others were stirring. Makepeace had Solace, who had wakened, in his arms. I took her from him and fed her some clabber, wondering what father would make of our exchange. All morning, as I went about my tasks, I thought about braiding together two beliefs that seemed at first so much at odds, and how so doing might sit with our precisian faith. How easily Caleb had taken the teachings of his youth—the many gods, the animate spirit world—and simply recast them in terms of our teaching. And father, so it seemed, was satisfied.

Later that day, when the men came in from morning chores, I served them dinner and cleared the board as father instructed, to make space for the lesson. I was then obliged to go out from the house for my field tasks, which began as soon as the ground had thawed and the soil dried out a little. As all know full well, one must plant pease on the New Moon, so I was bent backed, turning clods of chill earth, and was not there to witness the encounter when Iacoomis brought Joel to join my father's afternoon classroom. I hoped that Caleb would be able to o'ermaster his oft-stated distaste for Iacoomis and his son, and that his own change of mind had caused him to look at them in a different light. It was a strange thing, that we, who had spoken easily and for so long on this and every other matter would not now be able to converse beyond the most hasty exchange in a rare unobserved moment, or mere commonplaces when in company. Even though we shared a single roof, the distance between us was become as great as if the years of our friendship had never been.

When the light faded and the cold seeped through my clogs and set my chilblains a-throbbing, I returned to the house and found Solace, who had wakened from her nap, mewling softly and waving her fists about before her face. When she saw me, she smiled a joyous grin and reached out her arms. I lifted her from her crib, all warm and heavy limbed, and nuzzled my face into her soft neck, blowing gently till she laughed aloud. I took up a posset I had made for her earlier, and carried her with me to the lean-to that we called the buttery, though tool store and henhouse also would describe the place, for we had staked out a small indoor roost for the fowl when the outdoor coop grew too cold. I put an old flour bag down on the dirt floor and set Solace there, with a peg doll that Makepeace had fashioned for her, and got about draining the whey off the cheese curds.

Even as I sang softly to Solace, it was impossible to shut my ears to the business under way on the other side of the thin wall. Makepeace was lumbering through a translation of Gaius Mucius Scaevola, butchering his fourth conjugations. I noted that father was even more forbearing than usual with his corrections, letting several errors pass unremarked, not wishing to reduce Makepeace before Joel and Caleb. When Makepeace reached the end of his short passage, father called upon the boys to recite the first declensions of *vita* and *mensa*, which he had set them to conning, and each managed well enough. I heard father contrasting the Latin form with the English: "We say 'I strike him' not 'I strike he,' because the person who strikes we put in the nominative case, but very few words in English as it is spoken and written nowadays have an accusative case different from the nominative. In Latin, on the other hand, . . ." and I thought to myself what a vast thing it was that these boys were being put to—having, in Caleb's case, no formal grasp of English grammar, and yet being called upon to master the peculiarities of Latin, with Greek and Hebrew to follow.

Since I did not wish to intrude, I went out again to draw water. I lifted the well cover, as usual, and dropped the bucket down. When I brought it up, I could tell, even in the twilight, that something dark and unwholesome floated there. I plunged a hand into the icy water and pulled it back at once, having touched the fur of a dead rat that had contrived to fall in and perish, though how, with the cover in place, I could not think. Then I realized that I had left it off, in the morning, distracted when Caleb had appeared. Someone else must have replaced it later in the day. It was impossible to see much in the gathering dark, so I put back the cover, tipped out the tainted water and left the investigation of the small wet corpse till the morrow. Fortunately I had a little water left in the kettle in which we might wash before supper.

The class had ended, but Caleb was still bent to his book when I came back in and announced the sorry news about the well. Father shrugged. "We are fortunate that we do not have to dig any great depth to strike fresh water in Great Harbor. We will see at first light if there is a risk it has been befouled. We may dig another with no significant effort, and fetch from our neighbors' meantime."

I set out the curds and some bread for supper. Father and Makepeace went out to the buttery where I had set the basin with warmed water, leaving Caleb, still seated with the Latin accidence, whispering to himself the words he had just learned. He glanced up, following my hands as I arranged the board. He flicked through the accidence, and closed it with a smile of accomplishment. *"Puella . . ."* Here he pointed at me. *"Mensam . . ."* Then at the board. *"Ornate-* arranges," he said softly. I stopped, struck anew with the agility of his mind. He glanced up. We exchanged smiles with the ease of an earlier season. "I have missed our lessons, Storm Eyes," he whispered. Then he too went out to the basin to wash.

III

So it went on, day following day, as the weather steadied and the early seeds stirred beneath the soil. At first, Caleb held himself aloof from Joel. He reminded me of a powerful dog, who will stand back, hackles raised, if he sees another approaching. Joel had always been a silent boy, coming and going with his father but saying little. In truth I had not passed above a dozen sentences with him through the years, and had formed no opinion of his character. His handling of Caleb's wary manner revealed that he had a measure of his father's self-possession and courage. He neither cowered before Caleb nor did he fawn upon him. But in diverse subtle ways he made it plain that he was a ready ally, helping Caleb betimes to the proper English phrase, correcting with a meaning look should Caleb seem likely to err in some matter of English manners. Because Caleb was quick and perceptive, oftentimes these subtle intercessions thwarted Makepeace, who stood ready to censure or mock any misstep.

Before very many weeks passed, Caleb and Joel were on easy terms with each other. This blossomed, before long, into a fast friendship, which was no strange thing for two boys who shared much with each other and so little with the others closest about them. Caleb's confident spirit seemed to draw Joel forth, so that he spoke up more in company, and thus I grew to know him more fully, and to admire his gentle, generous spirit. They were, the pair of them, quite unalike, feature for feature. Caleb, product of the wilderness, had the long-legged, lean muscularity of a boy born to running after game and hastening through the woods beside long-striding warriors. His eyes were avid and his gaze intense. Joel was in all ways softer—heavier in build, his long-lidded eyes dreamy and contemplative. He was short of stature, like his father; an uncommon thing among that people, and one of the reasons Iacoomis had been shunned by their warrior class. But like his father, he had an agile mind and a determined spirit. Caleb and Joel were, the two of them, quick studies, and father was more than pleased at the profit they took from their lessons. As the weather softened, I would see them walking out together, two dark, cropped heads bent over some book or smiling at some private jest, and I felt a stab of envy for a lost intimacy that could not be mine again.

Truly, there was no place in my life for such a thing, even had propriety allowed it. I struggled with the many demands of the turning season, up much of the night to help a ewe with a difficult lambing, then up again before first light to work through the blur of daily tasks. Always tending to Solace, who needed an eye upon her at every minute lest she pick up some bright, sharp-edged tool thinking it a fine plaything, or pull a boiling kettle down upon herself—as Aunt Hannah's seventh babe had done, and was scalded to death, the poor chuck. I looked forward to the day, not so very far distant, when Solace would become a helpmate, rather than a charge, able herself to feed hens and fetch eggs and the like small chores which I had done for mother with a high heart when I was barely more than a babe.

Oft times, as I bathed her or rocked her in my arms, I would look into her sky-blue eyes and wonder what her character might prove, in time, to be. I would let a finger stroke the line of her rounded cheek and tickle the folds of soft, creamy flesh beneath her chin. She would stare back at me with an intense, knowing gaze, and I would imagine her, a year or so hence, at my hem, as I had been at mother's. I was, after all, the only mother she had ever known. I was determined to be worthy of the charge God had set for me. I let my mind run on ahead, seeing us together as she grew into her girlhood. She would be always at my side, and I would open to her the world and all that I had learned of it. If she wished to study her book, she would not be obliged to go to it alone. I would see to that. I would carve out the time to instruct her, no matter what father or Makepeace had to say of it. And I would not marry any man without wit and heart to understand that Solace was my sacred charge and the first of all my duties.

She played beside me as I thinned out the seedlings, picking up clods and mashing them in her tiny mittened fingers, then smearing her face with the mud. I had come to think that the Wampanoag, who dealt so kindly with their babes, were wiser than we in this. What profit was there in requiring little ones to behave like adults? Why bridle their spirits and struggle to break their God-given nature before they had the least understanding of what was wanted of them? So I smiled at her, and made faces, although I knew I would have to clean the muck from her clothing, and from her silky hair, and that there would be howls of protest when I did so. It was a small price to pay for the sound of her merry laughter.

That night, at board, I stole a look at Caleb, considering him. As I had learned from him, and changed my views about the discipline I should mete out to Solace, so he must have changed his views on so many matters. I recalled how he had vexed me with his hard questioning about the scriptures and I wondered what it was among the many things father might have said or done that had won him so fully. In every outward particular, he was now a Christian. But who could see into his heart?

I was wandering along this line of thought when father turned to me. "Do you not think so, Bethia?"

Since I had not been attending to the conversation in the least degree, I had no idea how to answer. But Makepeace broke in, and said, "Perhaps better we ask Caleb for his views. His people have age-old experience in this place and must know when the danger of frost is generally past. I am sure he will like to help Bethia in the planting of corn and beans when that time comes."

It was the first time Makepeace had directed such an amiable remark to Caleb. Having been the target of my brother's wit often enough, I felt sure there was some barb to it. And to hear him proposing that Caleb and I do something together seemed odd, given his supposed reservation concerning the enforced intimacy of our situation.

Father saw the trap before I did. "Surely not," he interjected, turning his face to Caleb. "Planting is women's work, is it not, among Wampanoag? The menfolk shun such tasks, I think?"

Caleb smiled, sensible of father's kindness. "True. But since I eat at your board, how not help raise the food set down upon it? *Cum Roma es, fac qualiter Romani facit.*"

Father laughed so he had to wipe a tear from his eye. "*Faciunt,* dear boy, *faciunt,*" he said at last. " 'Do as the Romans do,' plural, you see: do as they do. *Facit* would be 'as the Roman does.' . . . But very well said, I am sure. We are each, in a sense, in Rome, are we not?

You must learn the ways of our family, and we must learn the ways of your island. It would be a kindness if you would teach us."

I glanced at Makepeace. The arrow of his wit has missed its mark and his expression revealed vexation. "I'll not favor making our tidy English field into an unruly salvages' hillock and an object for our neighbors' jests."

"Makepeace," said father sternly. "I might be more inclined to note what you favor if you were more inclined to do your share of field work." Father rarely rebuked Makepeace. But rudeness was a thing he never could countenance. "We will hear the advice of our young friend, and if our neighbors care to laugh, well then. We will see who laughs when the bushel baskets are counted."

So it was that instead of ploughing up the whole field into straight rows and hauling hods of manure—all of which was back-breaking work—we left the earth be. We made small mounds and buried a herring in each, digging in handfuls of sea wrack that had the salt washed off it. When the soil was warm enough, we planted a corn kernel in each mound, and when it sprouted, we placed our beans all around to climb upon the stalks, saving the trouble of staking out air rows. We followed that with the squash as the heat increased, and presently the vines covered all the unploughed ground, smothering unwanted growth. If neighbors raised their eyebrows, I did not care. Their opprobrium was a small price for the many hours I no longer had to spend with a hoe, fighting back the weeds.

The one person who did not raise his eyebrow at our tousled field was young Noah Merry, who walked all around the plantings, praising the work and the robust growth and declaring that he had thought of adopting like practices, and our experiment emboldened him. Suddenly, it seemed, we saw a good deal of Noah Merry in Great Harbor. Whenever his family was in want of supplies or due to pay grandfather his share of receipts from the grist mill, it was no longer Jacob or Josiah who could best be spared from the farm, but always Noah. Whatever business brought him, he generally contrived to drive his cart past our dooryard just as I was setting board for dinner. Each time, father would tell me to make another place.

I do not say it was a hardship to have his company, such a lighthearted young man. On other nights, talk at board might go on in Latin, as practice for the boys, who sorely needed it, since they would be allowed to speak nowt else at college. Though I had ceased to try to advance myself in that language, I could follow well enough, and I liked to try to construe father's questions and form answers in my mind, matching them against those my brother and Caleb brought forth. Even when they spoke in English the talk must be of scholarly things. But since Noah was clearly no square cap, conversation in his presence went on differently. The chatter might be of village matters: comings and goings to the mainland, a new family making the crossing to join us, a birth or a death, who had published their names to marry, who had bought a cow, and such small, pleasant bits of news. When Noah asked how someone did, he actually listened with attention to the reply. For his part, he spoke with greatest animation about his farm.

And this, also, was different: father and Makepeace were grown used to me sitting in silence, letting the talk pass around me. They rarely pressed me for an opinion or turned to me for comment, and Caleb had taken the lead from them in this. But Noah was another gate's business. He was forever turning to me with a "Do you not think...?" or a "What do you say...?" and in courtesy I would stammer out something so as not to seem cold. He must have noted that I grew more animated once, when talk turned to the Takemmy otan that neighbored his farm, for the next visit he came supplied with information. He was full of a description of a mishoon he had observed in the making, praising the patient industry whereby a great log would be part-burned, day following day, the coals scraped out until the exact shape for a swift canoe was accomplished. He questioned Caleb closely as to how it had gone on in Nobnocket, whether the trees were chosen in like ways or whether each otan had singular practices. Caleb seemed out of sorts, and answered tersely. I thought this odd, until I reflected that talk of his old life might bring unwelcome memories. But then it came to me that he often was reserved when Noah joined us, no matter what the subject. I concluded that he had not yet learned to be at ease with any English person outside of our family. I could not see any other reason for his coldness.

IV

Yester eve, when I wrote of the ordinary daily doings of those early summer months, a feeling of peace brimmed up within me. I dreamed of that time last night, and woke to disappointment. It is true that I was tired to the bone then. I often woke in the half-light wishing for more sleep above all things, my arms aching from the last day's toil, so that it was all I could do to gather up Solace and carry her downstairs. Oft times during the day I would straighten up from the kneading trough or rest on my hoe and think how, a year earlier, I had been running free and wild with Caleb in the soft air, still innocent of the sin that had brought such affliction. For I was foolish, and thought my life a sad business that summer, and did not value the gifts of that season. I had not foreseen the loss and the hardship yet to come.

The wearisome chores of those days are as nought to my present labors here in Cambridge. This morning, letting down the bucket to draw water for the wash, I caught a glimpse of my face in the well. I did not at first recognize the gaunt, frowning drab gazing up at me. On the island I could revive myself with sweet air. There was never lack of clean water or of wood to warm the house. My tasks, though numerous, were various. Here, I am cold and clemmed, and all is drudgery. The late mistress of this house was elderly, and with poor eyesight. She had not maintained a godly cleanliness, so it took me some time to scour the floors, rid the corners and recesses of mouse droppings, and restore the dingy linens with blue starch and boiling kettle. It falls to me to launder all the scholars' clothes and the threadbare linens, mending them as needed. Daily, I sweep the floors, scrubbing and sanding them every sennight as we did at home, though here, with the muddy boots of so many lads, the task is much the heavier. The master sets the boys to chop the wood, such as we have, but I am left to split bavins. We rely on gifts to build our woodpile and most times the supply is short. I cook the poor dinner and set out the scraps for bever and supper. I bake loaves, I boil a thin broth. I can do no more with such a frugal providence—a sack each of rye and Indian corn, a little yeast, some gristly cuts of meat and a turnip or two. When one of the pupil's families comes with an offering—a neck of mutton or a brace of hens—it is a blessing, and I make the most of it, boiling the goodness out of the bare bones till not even a starving cur dog would trouble to carry them off. But times are hard for the planters, and such gifts have been uncommon this season.

The school faces on to Crooked Street, with a neighbor house pressed upon the other side. There is room for a garden on our small patch of earth, whose produce, even if just roots and herbs, might keep the boys in better health. I was much astonished, when I came, to find that nothing of the kind had yet been put in hand. There was space enough to keep a few hens at the door, and I thought to hatch some chicks once the weather warmed. Through the fall season I had walked the Cow Common and clipped sprigs of wild dill or gathered leaves for a salat, falling upon any berries other gleaners had missed and sprinkling them through a hasty pudding. But come winter there was no chance for even these small measures, and every one of us now is hollow-cheeked, with running nose or a wetness in the chest.

Cambridge is an unlovely town. Those who settled here in the '30s decreed that the first sixty houses be pressed tight together, for fear, I suppose, of assault by European rivals—the native inhabitants of the place having been laid waste long since by some earlier plague of which there is no record. The house lots, along a gridiron, are narrow, and the low ridge on which they were built has formed a barrier to the drainage of the land behind, so that in foul weather all turns swamp and mire. There is factory here, enough to rob the peace—tanner, brick maker, smith and shipbuilder fill the daylight hours with their clamor—yet not enough to bring prosperity. The roads remain too rough for carriages. Since the townsfolk do not trouble where they tip their slops, the air reeks, and everywhere the middens rise, rotting in steaming piles of clutter and muck. The creek is brackish, but even were it not, its waters would be unwholesome, since the township uses it as a drain. One must, in consequence, drink only the small beer, which makes my head ache and I cannot think helps the boys, especially the youngest, two of whom are not yet nine years old. Since there is no wood to spare for warming bathing water, the master expects the boys to wash in an outdoor trough from which they have to crack the ice each morning. Of course they do a poor job of it. I had to badger him for a little fat and lye to mix with ash for soap. I cannot think how it was before I came here. Even now, with soap in hand, the boys' bodies are rank when pressed side by side on their benches in the schoolroom, and I can barely take a breath of the foetid air when I am obliged to clean their crowded sleeping loft.

It has all of it been sore trial for Makepeace, the oldest pupil here, a full two years senior to the next closest him in age. It may be why he traveled to the island at any excuse, to dine at a good board and sleep a few nights warmed by a decent fire, and to get some peace and solitude away from the rackety boys. Yet these absences did not prosper him in his studies, where the younger pupils all too often overpeered him. Whenever we walked out together, I saw his gaze travel the short distance from the school to the Harvard College. His gaze would follow the gowned scholars. He had a hungry look at such times, but a small frown played about his brow. I knew then that doubt ate at him as to whether he would ever take his place among them.

For Caleb and Joel, there is no such respite as Makepeace takes for himself. The island is barred to them by lack of means for the journey. I can only think it is insupportable for them here, in this world so strange, and in many ways so inferior, to the one they knew. For Caleb, especially, who lived most of his life as a natural man, to be cloistered up in this way is a vast change of condition, and I know full well how he struggles to fit himself to it. Several times, in the first weeks after we came here, something would disturb my sleep in the dark hour before dawn. I would turn on my pallet as a shadow passed across me. It was Caleb, stalking on silent feet, out the door and through the kitchen garth. He was looking, as I suppose, for a place to greet Keesakand. He does not do this now. I have not spoken to him of it, not wanting to rub upon a wound, so I do not know his reasons. I suppose that he looked for a place such as he was used to, from which to greet the sun, a place unsullied by the smear and stench of English industry. If so, he looked in vain, for upon every rod of nearby ground, man's mark is already darkly etched.

It galls me, when I catch a stray remark from the master, or between the older English pupils, to the effect that the Indians are uncommonly fortunate to be here. I have come to think it is a fault in us, to credit what we give in such a case, and never to consider what must be given up in order to receive it. And yet, it is not for me to weigh this balance: Christ, and knowledge against a pagan pantheon and an unaccomodated wilderness existence. I must suppose that Caleb and Joel believe the scale weighs fair. For they keep faith with my father's ambition for them and work diligently at their lessons. They are each of them determined to matriculate to Harvard next leaf fall. They have taken to heart father's belief that they are destined to lead their people out of darkness, and to do so they must endure hunger and cold as they press their understanding to its limits.

I will say this for Master Corlett: he will extend himself to an extraordinary degree for those who wish to learn, instructing them late into the evening hours. I pray only that Caleb and Joel do not founder under the burden and that their health proves equal to the unwholesomeness of this place. They are strong, but even so, I see a change in them.

Joel has taken on something of the hungry looks his father once wore, in those days when first he haunted the edges of the English settlement, before he and father became friends. Sometimes, when I round a corner and see Joel unexpectedly, the resemblance strikes me. Iacoomis had prospered well amongst us in Great Harbor, rising from his outcast's lot to become a skilled provider, who fed his brood good meat. But nowadays Joel has lost his well-fed fleshiness and is on the way to being scrawny. Caleb fares better, his body seasoned to yearly cycles of plentiful summers and leaner winters. How he will do, in time, with the constant and continuing privations of this place, I cannot say. Yet each day he gains another graceful turn of phrase or gentlemanly gesture, and his height and natural bearing give him a great distinction. He brims like a stream in spate, gathering all the knowledge that floods in upon him, whatever its nature. I note that he watches the other pupils, even the younger ones, if they are the more gently bred. From the first, he had an excellent ear for English, and now he speaks fluently and entirely without accent. So naturally does he carry himself, even with the highest among us, that very soon, I think, those who do not know his history will be hard put to guess it, and might take him for a Spaniard or Frank, or another among the darker of the civilized races.

Not so long ago, as I passed through the hallway by the schoolroom, I overheard the master ask him to read aloud a passage from the Hebrew bible. Since they had only recently commenced upon the study of that language, putting sounds to the strange, firey letters, I stopped there, my arms full of linens, to listen how he did. Master Corlett had asked him to choose a passage, and he had taken some verses from Jeremiah. I heard his voice, strong, confident with the guttural sounds that so closely resembled those of his own mother tongue. Since I came here I have heard that some learned men think that the Indians are the lost tribe of the ancient Hebrews, because of this similarity in the tongues. He went carefully, sounding each word in his head before he spake it aloud. At first, my heart lifted, to hear him get on so well with such difficult work. But there was that in his voice more foreign than the speaking of strange Hebrew words. His voice, in the ancient tongue, took on a different pitch and tone. It went through me that he chanted the words in the voice of a pawaaw ... and, with that thought, I was under the gaily-colored headland again, the wild, fierce prayers rising into a flame-lapped sky.

My arms became slack. Some pieces of linen fell to the floor. As I bent to retrieve them, the master commenced to translate the Hebrew into English, and the full meaning of the passage fell into my heart: *"Let us go into the fortified cities and perish there; for the Lord our God has doomed us to perish, and has given us poisoned water to drink, because we have sinned against the Lord. We looked for peace, but no good came, for a time of healing, but behold, terror."*

At that, I caught another echo—of Tequamuck and his fearful prophecies. If it is indeed so, that the Indians of this place are lost Jews, perhaps such as Tequamuck are the Jeremiahs of their race. Not for the first time, my mind ran on what had happened to Caleb in those wilderness months. Was he, as Makepeace held, a vessel through which darkness yet trickled, a conduit that might carry the taint of evil into God's own churches ... ?

Of course it was not so. These morbid imaginings sprang from exhaustion, merely. Yet tears filled my eyes. They come all too easily now. They come now, again, even as I write this. It seems I could weep forever, and yet not empty the reservoir of my grief.

V

This night, I read over what I have set down here, and resolved to be more clear in my account going forward. I must not jump hither and yon, as I did in my writing yester eve. And this, also: I must refrain from indulging in excesses of sensibility and flights of morbid imagination. The last of the lines I wrote are smeared because I gave way to myself. Despair is a sin, and I had best not add it to my ledger. I will strive therefore, not only to maintain an exact diligence in my place, but to set out in plain words what passed that season on the island and try withal to see God's hand in it:

Whatever joy there might have been in the summer that followed Caleb's coming to us, it ended on a day so sweet and still that I moved through it as if floating in a bath of honey. It had rained hard the night before; that kind of heavy, sharp-scented summer rain that lays the dust and washes the pollen from the air, leaving everything rinsed and bright. The fragrance of ripeness and bloom grew more pungent as the morning waxed fair. The harbor sparkled, and when the lightest of breezes rippled through the sea grass, each blade shimmered like a filament of beaten silver.

On a day so Godsent, your mind is untroubled, the entire world seems well. You gird for tragedy on a different sort of day—a day of bleak gray sky, blowing mists and bitter, howling winds. You pray to avert ill fate on such a day. This I know. But on that day, my thoughts were all of fruitfulness and promise. Even when a rough-footed hen crossed my path in early morning, which all know for a token of fell tidings, I discounted the omen. It was not possible to imagine that anything should go awry on such a day.

I went out to pick the ripened beans and squash. They were coming in so plentiful I had to take two whiskets to carry home the yield. I liked to pick at first light, if I could slide from the shakedown without wakening Solace. It was lovely to do the chore in the cool, dew-moistened field. But if she waked, as she did that morn, I had to set the task aside till after dinner, in the full heat of the day, while she napped. I would see her settled in her crib as father commenced the lessons. If she stirred before my return, Makepeace would gather her up and jostle and coo at her for the short time necessary. He never shirked or complained of this: Solace was the one being with whom he did not feel constrained in expressing his true affections. Also, as I now think, it gave him some relief during the lesson; some cover for his slowness. This is how we went on every day, and I had no reason to question the arrangement.

Because the day was so fair, I did not hurry through the picking, as I did when heat thickened the air. I dawdled about, sampling the young filet beans, crisp and juicy, right off the stem. Then I ambled home at a leisurely pace. I sang a psalm as I walked, and barely thought to hush myself until my hand was upon the door latch. Father was reading aloud the Polyphemus episode from Homer, and you could have heard a needle drawn through cloth, so quiet were his listeners. Since there was no stirring from Solace's crib, I conceived that she napped still. I untied my hat, flicked it playfully up onto the peg rail and busied myself in the buttery unloading the whiskets, setting out some of the tenderest beans to eat fresh, laying the fatter ones upon racks to dry and shell for winter store. I will own it: I too listened to father read the familiar tale, waiting for my pet lines, where Odysseus in his pride discloses his identity and brings on the wrath of Poseidon that will cost him and all his men so dearly. It is a stirring passage. I was struck, as always, that a heathen poet from long ago should know so much of the human heart, and how little that heart changes, though great cities fall and new dispensations sweep away the old and pagan creeds.

I pondered this for a good while even after father left off his reading and set the boys to translation. Finally, I was minded to see to Solace. I went in, and found the crib empty. I looked under the board and in the corners and all about the room, feeling no misboding, thinking only to discover her playing quietly in some unlikely place.

But finding her not, I interrupted father to ask where she might be.

He looked at me, startled, and then glanced all about him in confusion.

"She was here just now presently. She woke, and was making a fret, so I told Makepeace to set her down here, by me. . . ."

Caleb and Makepeace were already on their feet, followed by Joel. Makepeace did as I had already done, and searched round and about him. We all of us moved in confusion, increasingly frantic, calling her name. But Caleb went straight as an arrow to the place, covering the short way in a few long strides.

She was facedown in the shallow hole, not yet three feet deep, that was to have been our new well. There was rainwater from the night's shower puddled there, inches merely. Yet somehow enough to steal breath from a babe who crawled to the edge, tottered on her unsteady little feet, and tumbled in.

Caleb snatched up her limp, muddy little body and ran back to where I stood with father in the garth. He was crying out in Wampanaontoaonk. Makepeace, coming from the house, saw, and howled like a wounded beast.

As Caleb handed her into father's outstretched arms, I remember the water, dripping off her hem and sluicing from her silky hair. I remember that the droplets sparkled in the sunlight, as if an angel scattered gems in the way of her ascending soul.

VI

It was like Zuriel's death, lived a second time. Father had blamed himself then—I think, groundlessly—for running the wain over Zuriel, and now he blamed himself for lack of attention to Solace when she was in his care. His pain was all the greater, perhaps, because Mother was not at his side, requiring his strength to help her bear it. Indeed, the loss of the babe stripped the scab that had formed over the wound of losing mother. It had been just a little more than a year since her death, and now we found our grief for her ran fresh, feeding this new anguish.

Makepeace, too, felt the weight of responsibility. His faith, as ever, instructed him to bear God's will without complaint. When we wept, he prayed. But this time his body proved less mighty than his will, so that his very skin broke into canker sores and his hair commenced to fall out in small clumps.

Joel and Caleb also mourned. Although they prayed our Christian prayers with us, I am certain that the two of them went to the woods, after her funeral, and daubed their faces with charcoal as they would for a child who died among their own kin. On the day following her burial, upon her grave I found evergreen sprigs, which surely was no English doing. I feel sure Caleb was behind this, for Joel was not raised in the heathen traditions of his people, which say that their god made man and woman from a pine tree, and even if he did know of them in a general way, I do not think he would have felt moved to perform such things unprompted. If father was aware that they had done pagan rites, he said nothing of it in my presence. But it was plain enough to me, who emptied the washtub and laundered their sleeves and collars.

And this too I will set down: father was sitting up with Solace, the night before we buried her. I had washed her tiny body for the last time, my tears mingling with the bathing water. I had made a simple dress for her, and trimmed it with the lace from our baptisimal gown. Mother had made it for me, and Solace had worn it on that day when, still grieving for mother, we took her to the meeting house to wet her head. While I sewed, father and Makepeace together had fashioned her tiny box, and the scent of planed pine filled the room. We had laid her in it, but had not yet found the heart to nail up the lid. So we sat in prayer until finally, as the hour drew late, father sent us all to our shakedowns. My arms were so empty, I could not sleep. In the small hours I heard a stirring in the room below, and thought that father must be restless and troubled. I threw my shawl about my shoulders and was going to descend when I saw that the person moving about was Caleb. Father, exhausted, had fallen asleep with his head upon the table. Caleb was standing by Solace. I saw him lift her tiny hand and slip something into her fingers.

In the morning, I went privily to Caleb and asked what he had done, fearing that whatever he had put into her hand might be an un-Christian thing. He told me that it was a scrap of parchment on which he had made a fair copy of the scripture of our Lord, *Suffer the little children* . . . He had tied it up with his own wampum-beaded thong of deer hide, around the peg doll that Makepeace had fashioned for her and that had been her chief plaything in her last month among the living.

"A medicine bundle, such as the pawaaws use?" I said, troubled.

"No," he replied calmly. "Not quite."

"But surely something very like . . . ," I said, wringing my hands.

He reached out and put his hands on mine, unclenching them gently. His own hands had grown less rough in the months since he had come to us.

"Why send her into the earth without some token of the love we all of us bear her? Your father preaches that not all the old beliefs are evil. If, as he fashions it, Kiehtan our creator god is Jehovah by another name, then why shun the customs we have that come from him, to give the departing a small gift of comfort from this world as they pass into the next? A piece of gospel scripture, a few beads, and her doll. What harm is in it?"

I could not say. But my mind remained uneasy, weighing the matter like a scale that cannot find a balance point.

After her burial, we embarked once more upon a time of hard soul-searching, seeking to know where each of us had failed in the eyes of God. I saw more punishment for my idolatry, the truth of which I still could not bring myself to confess. Makepeace, for his part, went to meeting and accused himself in public of an inventory of offenses, from gluttony to sloth—flaws of character of which I had been aware—but then also lust, which did surprise me, until I looked at him with something other than a sister's eyes, and reflected that he was in truth a boy no longer. I found myself wondering if his lust had an object, and if so, who it might be. I followed his gaze after with greater attention, but did not learn anything by it. He made strenuous efforts to reform himself of the first two categories of sin, becoming quite abstemious at board and applying himself in an uncommon way to his chores. I do not know how he fared with regard to the other, and if his affections were engaged somewhere, I was not sharp-eyed enough to discern it.

It was father whose season of reflection led to the greatest change in our condition. His conscience prompted him to conclude that he had been insufficiently zealous regarding the pawaaws and the breaking of their hold on the people. "They are the strongest cord that binds these people in darkness," he said. "I must sever it. There is no other way." He decided to stop waiting for converts to come in, and to take his message beyond Manitouwatootan. He began traveling to the non-Christian settlements, begging the sonquems for permission to preach. One or other, Makepeace, Joel or Caleb, was always at his side during these ventures, and from their talk at board I conceived a picture of the encounters. What I learned troubled my mind.

Father, it seemed, had become fierce, abandoning a gentle gospel of love and forgiveness in favor of fire-and-brimstone threats, promising hell and damnation and bloody vengeance to nonbelievers.

One day, he arrived home after preaching to the stiff-necked sonquem of Chappaquiddick. He was spattered in sand and muck and wet through from the crossing to the smaller island, and as I warmed water for his wash, I saw that he could not move his right arm, and when I asked, he told me that indeed he had been dealt a blow from the sonquem's warclub, but that the arm, though sorely bruised, was not broken.

"Do not concern yourself, daughter," he said. "I have one arm for receiving injuries and another arm to lift up in praise of God. While

I received wrong to one, I raised the other higher to heaven, and truly, when the sonquem saw that I did not fear him, but stood firm, he consented to listen to my words in full, and bade his pawaaw do so, which he has never countenanced heretofore."

Father's preaching became ever more firey as the summer reached its height. This was so even in the staid confines of our own meeting house. He would work himself up to a pitch of passion, the sweat flying from his brow as he gesticulated wildly, declaring at the last that he would put all of the island's pawaaws under his heel. This drew approving looks and cries of "Amen!" from the Aldens, but when I ventured a glance back toward the Iacoomis bench, the family looked pained, and, in the seat by Makepeace, Caleb's brow was drawn.

In mid-August, father consented to meet a challenge from the pawaaws, to confront five of them, who said they would jointly try their power against his. I overheard Joel and Caleb speaking of this, their voices low and troubled. I passed the news to Makepeace and asked him to persuade father against this venture, which I thought fraught with danger, for himself and for the gospel also. Anything might thwart him on the given day. He might be served some tainted bever or by chance develop an ague, and everyone would take it as a sign that the pawaaws had o'ermastered him.

Makepeace took my point, I must say, most civilly, and thanked me for my counsel. I overheard as he and father talked late into the night, Makepeace urging him to caution, but to no effect. That night, it was father who could not command his tongue. I could hear him quite clearly through the blanket that divided us, his voice growing louder in his ardor: "Makepeace, you must see that if I do not go, then they will conclude that I quailed. I will not have them think that of me, or of the message of the Lord."

Father rose on the appointed morning and set off for the meeting place. He had told Makepeace he was not to accompany him; he wanted to face the pawaaws quite alone, so that it would be clear that he did not fear them. But Caleb and Joel went, privily, taking secret ways that Caleb knew. They returned, much excited, and in the brief moment we had alone told me that father had prevailed mightily, and this before a large crowd of Wampanoag who had gathered to witness the confrontation.

At board, Makepeace pressed father into an accounting. Father said he had stood in a circle formed by the painted sorcerers, and for some hours all, together and severally, had tried their most malign spells, cursing and execrating, dancing and chanting, drumming and shaking their gourds. Father had only laughed, which enraged them, and never ceased to raise his voice, preaching the power of the one true God. At the end of it, he had gone untroubled on his way.

Converts flocked to him in the weeks that followed, as news of the encounter spread from one end of the island to the other. When one of the five pawaaws fell ill with spotted fever, and then another, the remaining three came into Manitouwatootan and accepted the gospel of Christ.

But there was one who remained beyond father's reach: Caleb's uncle, Tequamuck. Father did not speak ill of him before Caleb, but when I overheard him in conversation with grandfather, he fretted and railed at the reports which reached him of that pawaaw's teachings. Tequamuck continued to put fear into the people, spreading outlandish and dreadful prophecies about the

English that he claimed had come to him in visions, the gift of his familiar spirit. Tequamuck hated father's prayers, saying they were spells crafted to lead the people away from their own gods. He warned that once father had contrived to strip them of their protecting spirits, the English would destroy them utterly. I do not know if Tequamuck truly thought my father so malign. I do think he hated him, as one man will hate another who draws off the affections of a beloved. Tequamuck burned with a jealous rage that Caleb studied with father to serve the English God. Word came to us from time to time of terrible threats against my father's life. But if these troubled father, he gave no sign of it.

Instead, he set about even more diligently to win converts. He began to correspond more regularly with John Eliot, who conducted a mission on the mainland and was, as far as we had heard, the only one among the elect of the entire colony who laid himself sincerely to this sacred duty. From this correspondence, father took great heart, and conceived a desire to bring a second missionary to the island. Particularly, he talked of what more he could do if he was in purse to employ a schoolmaster for the Indian children. Yet we could offer no such salary as would invite either a trained minister or master to embrace such a troublesome employ.

It was grandfather who said that father must consider making a voyage to England to solicit funds for the effort from the Society for the Propagation of the Gospel of Jesus Christ to the Indians. That group had been most openhanded with John Eliot. The English— wealthy folk and ordinary yeomen alike—who banded together under the name of that society were ardent to win converts and impatient of New England's lack of success in this.

Grandfather had ever been shrewd when it came to funds. But as I look back upon it now, I think that he also feared for father's state of mind. He had seen the change in his mild son since Solace's death, and perhaps felt he had embarked on a dangerous course with regard to his preaching, for all its early successes. I think he wanted to divert my father by setting a new task before him.

At first, father would not hear of such a journey, saying that he had undertaken to prepare Makepeace, Caleb and Joel for their matriculation and could not leave them at the midpoint of the endeavor. We had gone to grandfather's to take dinner between our Lord's Day meetings, and were walking back to the meeting house. Makepeace had gone on before, and Caleb walked with the Iacoomis family. I was a few paces behind father and grandfather, and I am sure they had forgot that I was there.

"Think on it, my son," said grandfather. "You are putting the needs of three above the souls of three thousand. If you wait until these boys are prepared, a year or more will be lost. Go soon, and you return in good time to put the final touches to the edifice of learning that you have built together. Surely Makepeace is advanced enough to continue the two hopeful young prophets in their Latin."

"Maybe, in Latin, he might manage something, but the younger boys are well set to outpace him in no great length of time. As to Greek, he struggles. Makepeace has a plain mind, moved from the pages of the Bible. There is nothing wrong in that; such a man can make a useful minister. But I fear he is too apt to feel that all other letters are a vanity and a snare for the soul." Father laid out his concern that without diligent guidance and constant instruction

Makepeace might easily fall short of what would be required of him. "And who will instruct him, if I do not?"

"If he cannot get on for a few short months, then it hardly seems likely he will profit from an education at the college," grandfather replied. "Better to face that truth sooner than later. The Lord makes all kinds of clay, does he not? Some may be shaped into delicate porcelains, others a serviceable slipware. There is a use for each, but not even the most skillful potter can make the one do the work of the other. . . ."

They turned into the meeting house then, and I was obliged to go and sit with the women, so I did not hear how the conference concluded. But by that evening it was decided that father would indeed set sail for England as soon as it was practicable to go. Father solicited letters of introduction from John Eliot and received back such encomiums as were hard for a modest man to read. For propriety's sake—meaning mine—Caleb was to board with Joel during father's absence, and Makepeace would oversee lessons, with grandfather reviewing the work as and when his heavy obligations allowed. I was left to keep house for Makepeace. It would be but light huswifery, tending to the needs of one other only. I hoped we would do tolerably together, and resolved to help him in whatever manner I could and to give him no cause for complaint.

VII

On the morning of the day he was to sail, father rode out to Manitouwatootan to preach a last sermon and make his farewell. I begged to go with him, wanting to keep by him as long as I might. When we came into the clearing father pulled up Speckle and gazed out, full of amazement. The clearing was crowded with Wampanoag from every part of the island, convinced Christians and heathen all alike. Some in English dress, others in deer hides. Men, women and children, some whom he had helped through a sickness, others he had never set an eye upon. Hundreds had gathered. He dismounted and moved through the throng, speaking a word to as many as he could.

His sermon that day was gentle in spirit, more like his preaching of old. He talked of the love of Christ and likened the bonds of affection between people with those between God and his faithful. That love, he said, endured, and was no less real and fervent, no matter that the parties did not see each other face-to-face. So it would be with the great love he bore them, he said. Although he would be gone from their sight across the seas through several moons, his love would be with them and they would be ever in his thoughts.

When it was time for him to mount up and go, it became clear that the men intended to follow him, on foot, all the long way to the hole in which a sloop lay that would bring him to Plimouth on the first stage of his voyage. And so we proceeded. I remember looking back over the mass of gleaming heads, traveling with one purpose through the trees, and being moved to tears that my father was so well beloved.

Makepeace, Caleb, Joel and his family, and grandfather, all were at the hole to make their last farewells to father. I saw their faces register amazement at the procession that swarmed the beach in our wake. We stood on the shore and waved as he took his place in the gig and oared out to where the sloop lay at anchor between the chops. It was only when the sails were set and the anchor weighed that I turned to go and saw Tequamuck, on the bluff above the hole, his feather cloak billowing in the summer breeze, his arms outstretched in an invocation. Although he was too far off for me to make out the words he chanted, I knew that they were not benign. Soon the Wampanoag on the beach saw him, too. They began murmuring among themselves. Some cried out against him in their own tongue. Others knelt in the sand and threw their hands up to heaven. But most of the crowd melted away faster than I would have thought possible for so large a gathering.

It took Makepeace a little time to register the cause of the sudden disarray, but once he knew its source he turned towards the bluff and cried out: "Cease your foul and clamorous noise! You offend the ears of the holy God! Cast yourself down upon the Earth before God and beg he would humble you!" The remaining Wampanoag were staring at Makepeace now with dismay upon their faces. Grandfather tugged at his sleeve and whispered urgently into his ear. I hoped that he was counseling what I felt—that a better course would be to ignore the wizard rather than give stature to his magic. Makepeace looked fierce, but he would not disobey grandfather. So they handed me up onto Speckle and we all turned for home.

Tequamuck remained on the bluff, the sound of his chanting loud at our backs.

A fog rolled in that night, shreds of swirling mist that gathered and thickened and settled heavy on the island. We did not think anything of it; dense summer fogs are common enough here. Generally, the sun burns them off by mid-morning, and days that start so often are among the fairest. But by midday the fog had not lifted, and I moved through my chores in a cool veil of milky white, barely able to see the hand stretched out in front of me. The whole day passed so, the sunset a pale rumor on a pearly horizon.

That night, a light wind rose. Well, I thought: it shall blow the fogs away. But this wind was like no other we had ever had, and certainly not of a summer eve. In the dark of night it grew up into a fierce thing that howled and groaned. I woke to hear it driving sheets of rain in hard lashing blows against the house. I threw my cloak over my nightgown and went out with Makepeace into the wild dark. Speckle, hobbled in the dooryard, was white-eyed and haggering with cold. I held her head and spoke to her as Makepeace secured her blanket and tethered her securely beneath the eaves on the lee side of the house. Then we battled to close the outer shutters. The wind blew me flat against the shingles and I had to cling to them to remain upright. Makepeace had to give me his hand to bring me safe indoors. Even with all the shutters secured, still the house was shroudly shaken. The timbers complained under every thrashing blow and I feared that the roof beams might shiver. So strange was this wind in its unpredictable eddies that I could barely keep the fire lit. At times, the howling took on the form of human voices, keening in an unknown tongue. Other times it was a loud, rhythmic beating, like the bellows feeding Vulcan's furnace. I heard more than one tree crack and split, and the crashing fall of mighty limbs. Every so often a gust would swirl down the chimney and scatter gray ash across the floor.

I looked at Makepeace, who was pale in the uncertain firelight.

"Do you think we ought to pray?"

"I do," he said. And so we knelt together, side by side, and at the end of it, he reached for my hand.

The storm lasted through the following day, and only began to ease during the second night. At first light we walked out into a scarred world. The sea was pewter, and the wrack line stood high upon the strand, even to where the first low scrub oaks struggled for their spindly lives like aged and bent-backed crones. The branches of torn trees lay all about, as did ripped shingles and bundles of sodden thatch. There were other sights, most strange. A coracle had been lifted off the beach and blown atop the roof of our neighbor's house, while a shutter of another dwelling had been torn away and impaled upon a pine bough. The fields were all of them ruined, as if reaped by a Bedlamite. Stalks had been hauled up out of the furrows, clods still clinging to the root. Our corn had come in early and been picked and cribbed, which was our good fortune. Those who had not yet harvested were left to glean what they could among the broken and disheveled plants.

While Makepeace gathered and replaced our torn shingles, I went to check on our tegs. As I expected, they were not in the open meadow, which was in the upland and exposed to the full force of the storm. As I walked the surrounding woods, searching for them, I wondered at what the storm had wrought. Full-grown trees were wound all around, as if they were mere withes of willow twig, very strange to behold. Nearby, a thicket of young maples had been pulled out of the soil entirely, the base of their tangled roots like a great disk set on end, affording an earthworm's view of that world generally hidden beneath our feet. I reflected that the signs and marks of this storm would be written on this island for many years. Finally I came upon our sodden ewes. By God's providence they had weathered the storm well enough, wedged all together in the lee of a pair of great boulders. None were missing. Other neighbors were not so lucky. Their flocks had scattered, and it was the work of several days to gather them. Some few were never found, a sore loss, their wool so valuable and the numbers here still so few. Makepeace and I busied ourselves lending a hand where it was needed, and were glad to be thus occupied. At dusk, we ate our bread in a pregnant silence, afraid to speak our minds.

Word that father's ship had gone down came to us a fortnight later. It had broken up entirely. Scraps of wreckage had been sighted, so far off course that at first we fanned a hope that it was another unfortunate vessel, and that word would come to say father's ship had weathered the storm in some safe harbor. But that slight candle of hope was snuffed soon enough. By chance the sloop's figurehead was recovered among the jetsam, and that made identification certain.

Death by water is an abiding fear for an island-dwelling people. But to loose two souls so, father and Solace both, and in such short season, was a sore trial. Father gone down into the fathomless deep, and my Solace, poor tiny one, drowned in a mere puddle just paces from our door. Although father was a very precious man and the loss of him is very great to me, as it is to all honest folk who knew him, it is Solace's death that is the harder for me to bear. All the world mourns father, whose labors God blessed while he lived. Many will remember him. Not so my Solace, who made no mark upon the world. Nights I can barely sleep for the loss of her weight against my body. In dark of night, I hear her cry, and start awake. But it is a voice of my dream only, and it wakes me to an aching loneliness. Now, all these months since her death, I think of her, and how she would have grown and changed. I see her walking beside me with a rolling gait, reaching out a plump hand to clasp my fingers. I see her hair lengthened and curling about her face. I imagine the sound of her voice as she says her first words, the small frown at her brow as she puzzles at something, a glimpse of her milk teeth as she smiles. It will be so, always. As the years pass, she will live and grow in my mind's eye, from infancy through sweet girlhood, and when I am old I will see her still, coming herself into womanhood, her sky-blue eyes expressing a kindly wisdom, her laugh as she lifts up her own babe . . .

Yet all that time, she will lie in the ground, an infant always, her life ended just a little after the world had turned a full year. In my dreams, she comes to me. But always, in the end, frightfully. For I see her in her grave. Frail little finger bones, bleached white, curl around a crumbling parchment, a rotting peg doll, and a scatter of wampum beads fallen loose from a decaying shred of deer hide . . .

God is pleased to dispense himself variously. But while I fill up my mouth with prayers, they bring no comfort. My words rattle against each other like the last beech leaves on a winter branch, and though a hard wind scours the forest, it cannot free them from the bough; it will not lift them upward into the wide white sky.

VIII

In the days that followed the discovery of the wreck, the sea spewed up the bodies of several perished souls, casting them ashore in diverse coves upon the mainland. None of them was father's. Although we felt ourselves orphans, we were not yet so: without a body, under the terms of the law, father could not be considered dead until the court ruled upon it. But whatever the letter of the law said, we and all the island knew that father was gone, and we did not wait for a magistrate's permission to mourn him. Some very considerable persons marked his passing. The commissioners of the United Colonies referred to his loss, "which at present seemth to be almost irreparable." The Apostle Eliot wrote a letter expressing his hope that the Lord would help us bear "this amazing blow, to take away my Brother Mayfield."

His flock, too, mourned for its lost shepherd. I say "all the island," for his death was not grieved in Great Harbor only. The Wampanoag, in ways which are not plain to me, in concert decided upon their own observance of father's passing. They marked it in a most singular manner. As soon as father's loss became known to them, each one, when traveling up or down the island, would fetch from the shore a smooth white stone such as can oft be found there. These they carried until they passed the place where father had taken farewell of them. There they deposited them. Within days, there was a cairn. In the weeks that followed, you could say, a monument, each stone of it placed with the care of an artisan. The last I saw, it had grown higher than a man, and still the Wampanoag came, one by one, placing a stone upon a stone. I cannot say if they do this still, or what by this time it might look like, but I picture it, white snow fallen upon white stones, the meltwater slicked into curtains of shining ice that catch the flares of the setting sun.

In the early weeks, after we heard of this thing, Makepeace and I made a habit to ride out there, to see how it went on. We each of us felt called to the place, and would linger. The stones had a kind of inner radiance that answered to the sun's changing light at different times of the day. It seemed a speaking sort of monument, unlike the mute gray headstones in the English burying ground. We were, I think, taken aback by its power to touch our deeper feelings, every time we went to it.

Something had changed between my brother and me, since Solace's death. I knew how he suffered, even in his accustomed silence. He, for his part, had thrown over his habit of constantly passing judgment on me. I believe he allowed himself to see that I was engaged in a great struggle against the prideful, independent nature he had deplored, and I think that at last he began to give me credit for my effort.

We sat before the stones in silence. In time, we began to speak about father. I did not say a great deal at first, confining myself to pious platitudes such as I thought my brother would find consoling. But one day he turned to me, raking his hand through his poor hair. (The tufts that had fallen out had started to regrow, but the short ends stuck out strangely.)

"Do you think that pawaaw killed our father?"

I looked at my hands and tried to still a slight tremor.

"I think . . . I believe he meant to. But surely we must hold that it is the Lord who dispenses tragical providences. Father is not the first of his faithful servants to be the subject of a dismal dispensation. To concede unto the pawaaw such a prodigious mastery . . ."

"I think he did," Makepeace interrupted. "I think he killed him as surely as if he had raised a warclub and stove in his skull."

"But Makepeace, think what you say. If the mist and gale rose to his order, it means Satan's diabolical designs o'ermaster those of God. Can that be? You surely cannot believe so. . . ."

"I think he should be brought to account for these awful works of wizardry. I have said as much to grandfather. As magistrate, he should act. . . ."

"But Makepeace, grandfather is magistrate to the English only. His writ does not run among the people who answer to their sonquems."

"So he said to me. His exact words, in fact. But if he will not act, I am of a mind to solicit the help of Giles Alden."

"Brother, no!" I jumped up from my mossy stone seat and paced the ground. "It would be just the opening he craves. Why, he would do it, with a high heart, and bring war upon us if he could. Do you think he would stop with Tequamuck? And even if he did, do you think Tequamuck's followers would leave such a thing unanswered? Some one or more English would be killed, then Alden would have the pretext he has long sought to dispeople this island. He would have his musket-wielding fanfarroons from the mainland cross here. It would be a slaughter—"

I caught Makepeace's hands up in my own. I stared into his face. "You must see. It is the last thing our father would wish for. . . ."

"What, then? Just let him live on, wallowing in his wickedness, having conference with Satan and doing his bidding, murdering not only heathen souls, but also the most godly among our living saints?"

"No. By no means. But fight him with faith, as father did. Think, brother: *Resist not evil*—are those not Christ's own words? How can we preach this hard teaching to them if we do not live by it in our own time of sorest trial? And how to expect Caleb to keep his feet on our path if we become the instrument of bloodshed, the slayer of his nearest living kinsman?" I saw then that Makepeace's countenance was hardening against me, as I became more strident. Struggling for self-mastery, I lowered my voice and softened my expression. "Do as father intended for you. Get yourself to Harvard's college, prepare for the ministry. Help Joel, help Caleb, to stand with you in this work. Why, there is no limit to what great things might be done, what Caleb, highborn among them, might—"

"Caleb!" He spat out the name, kicking up a clod of turf with the toe of his boot. "I am weary of hearing about Caleb and his greatness. This same Caleb, who is of such brutish stock that his own uncle consorts with Satan daily. Oh yes: blood will tell, sister. But it is not princely blood that runs strong in his veins. It is wizard blood. His own people knew well enough, when they sent him out to live with that servant of darkness who is his uncle. I can hardly tolerate to sit at board and take a vessel from his hands. It is like being pricked all over with thorns, I tell you, to have him by me in meeting, mouthing God's word, he, who was not so long ago in the wilderness, calling forth Satan. And yet all about me all I hear are paeans to his pregnant wit: 'Caleb can construe Virgil ... Caleb's grasp of the gospel ... Caleb's fair hand ...'"

He turned then and looked at me strangely, his eyes narrowing. "That day, when Solace drowned. Did it never occur to you it was Caleb who found her? That he went straight as an arrow to the well pit, without the slightest hesitation? Who is to say that he did not witch her to her death?"

I gaped at him. I could not believe he truly harbored such vile fancies. What other corrupt, lunatic thoughts might he be entertaining?

"Brother," I said, striving for patience. "The well pit was the place of gravest hazard close by to us. He went there directly because he, clear witted, recalled as much when the rest of us were too addled to—"

"There it is again! Caleb's accursed wit!" He threw himself down upon a fallen log and pulled out a spike of goldenrod that grew there, stripping the bloom from the stalk with a violent energy. "I know what you think. Do not trouble to deny it. You think I am blinded by envy. I tell you this: it is you who is blind. You and father both. Father was bedazzled by that boy. I could see it in his face, day following day. How he would smile with pleasure as Caleb mastered some difficult piece of scholarship, and then his glance would shift to me, and the smile would fade. I could see him, tallying up how long it had taken me to meet the same mark. I could read the disappointment in his eyes." He looked askance at me. "Truly, I had thought God tested me when he sent a sister who outshone me in learning, but at least father had the propriety to put a stop to that indignity. Now, to have this stranger, this savage heathen, this, this sorcerer-to-be plucked from the wilderness—to have him come and to have to sit there and watch him usurp father's regard, and to see father bestow on him the loving looks that should have come to me . . ."

"Makepeace, you are mistaken. Father never—"

"Hold your peace, Bethia," he hissed. "You, of all people, are no one to speak."

"I do not know what you—"

"Do you think me entirely witless? I know where your affections are engaged. Oh yes, I see that you struggle to obscure it, because you know that such unlawful feelings are begat of an abominable animal lust."

"That is false!" I said, the blood scalding my face. "There is nothing in the least degree of that nature in my feelings for Caleb."

His eyes held mine. I willed myself to gaze right back at him. His jaw worked and his skin became blotchy but still I would not look away.

"So then," he said coldly. "You deceive yourself, where I believed you meant merely to deceive others. You are in even more danger than I supposed."

"Makepeace, I tell you, you are mistaken."

"Sister, it is you who are mistaken, in word, in deed and even, it seems, in thought. I see how you look at him, when you think yourself unobserved. I hear the intimate tone in your voice when you snatch a word with him, taking yourselves to be alone. You do not look that way, you do not speak so, when your object is Joel Iacoomis. Not even when young Merry, that love-sick calf, moons about you. No. These fond looks are for Caleb only. Admit it. He has bewitched you. You are besotted with him."

"Not so!" My heart was thundering and I could barely draw

breath to speak. But when I saw him opening his mouth to continue, I mastered myself and held up a hand to stop him. "No, brother. You have said quite enough. At meeting, you confessed to gluttony and sloth—you had best return there and add envy to your list. For clearly your jealousy of Caleb's God-given wit is overweening your reason. Further, you confessed to lust. I can only think that being wanton in your own longings you imagine the like sin in the hearts of others. I am innocent of your foul accusations. Entirely innocent. My feelings towards Caleb are unexceptionable, and your allegations as to my deportment are unfounded and ridiculous." Since I could not tell him, in truth, what the nature of my feelings was—that I did love Caleb, as the brother that he, Makepeace, had never been to me—I turned my back on him and went to untie Speckle. My wrists were weak with anger and my hand shook as I worried at the knot. As I struggled to work it free, I lowered my voice with some effort, and spoke again without meeting his eyes.

"You know full well you would never have presumed to speak to me in these terms had father been here to upbraid you. Now you strut and swagger over me like some barnyard rooster, thinking you may insult and slander me without consequence. Do I need to recall to you that grandfather is my guardian? Not you. If you believe the truth of what you say, then go to grandfather and make your report of it. I dare you to do so." I put my boot in the stirrup. Makepeace reached out a hand. I batted it away. I glimpsed his shocked expression for just an instant as I set myself astride the horse, hitched up my skirt and leaned forward. Then I dug in my heels. Speckle answered me with a burst of speed that left Makepeace eating dust.

It took him a long time to walk home. I expected a tongue lashing, or worse. But all he said was, "Be sure, grandfather will hear of it, if any other saw you riding in that indecent, manlike manner." I maintained an icy silence, set out his supper, and took my own bread to eat in the garth. When I went to my shakedown, I did not give him a good night, and the next morning I rose early, made the fire and set a pot of water upon it, and then set out for the field, leaving him to break his fast alone.

IX

Not long after, the court formally pronounced the death of John Mayfield, aged thirty-eight years, minister to the Christian people of Great Harbor and Manitouwatootan, by misadventure upon the high seas.

Grandfather summoned Makepeace and myself to hear the will, which he had sat down to revise with father just before that deadly voyage. There was nothing very surprising contained therein: the house, woodlot, beach lot and field lot went to Makepeace, with all the furniture and livestock. I would have the right to live in the house and receive my keep and care until my marriage. On that occasion, Makepeace was to provide my portion "according to the state of himself at the time." I was also to have a small, silver-framed pen-and-ink drawing of mother, made when she was a girl in Wiltshire, England. "Your father also wills to you his Homer and his Hebrew bible. . . ." Grandfather muttered on to himself, seeming distracted, his hand playing with the parchment. "Strange bequest, as I said to him. Makepeace, to my mind, might have better profit from. . . . But there it is . . . as he directed. . . ."

He let that sentence trail away, smoothed the paper and put aside his glass, folding his long hands together on the desk before him. I had thought the meeting over, and was about to rise from my chair, when he spoke again.

"Now, I fear, we are come to a difficulty," he said, turning to Makepeace. "You know, I expect, that your father gave out in charity inamost every penneth he earned, as soon as it came into his hands. Seeing this, I had set aside, over the years, funds for your college board and tuition. I am afraid I advanced him from those funds to pay for a first-class passage to England. I also sent with him a tidy sum in cash so that he might present himself in a gentleman-like manner upon arrival. Those monies, of course, have been lost. All my doing, I must own. His own modesty and prudence inclined him to travel steerage and rely on God's providence on his arrival. I overruled him. I had large expectations for him in England; the Society must have been impressed by the scope of his work, must have showered funds upon him to make good such expenditure and much, much more. I did not wish him to come before them as a threadbare mendicant. But—"

Grandfather broke off and gazed down at his desk. "In any case, the point is, we now have a large deficit as regards provision for your college, but one that, given time, it is in my power to mend."

Makepeace let out a relieved breath. He looked very pale but did not say anything. I sat forward in my chair as grandfather spoke again. "Alas, an additional difficulty presents itself in that—it is my understanding and please correct me if you think differently—you are not quite prepared to take the matriculation examinations for the college?" Makepeace said nothing, but gave his head a barely perceptible shake. "As you know, I have not time enough, nor, in truth, skill enough, to undertake your preparation. So there is a need for funds for a preparatory school for—what would you estimate? A year? Not more than, at your age, I hope?"

Makepeace, his face blotched red with mortification, gave his head another tiny shake.

"I am glad to hear it," said grandfather. "Uncommonly glad. However, how to put this? One year, two years—whatever the term, I am not in purse to pay for it just presently. Weld's school at Roxbury demands a substantial annual donation, and an allowance for wood that is not inconsiderable. Corlett's school at Cambridge also sets high fees. All my funds are sunk into enterprises on this island or invested elsewhere at fixed terms. If I have to raise funds on such little notice it will be most disadvantageous, most imprudent. Are you sure, boy, that the scholar's life is really for you? You know that I went not to any college, and neither did your father, though 'tis true that he as good as, since I had him well tutored by Trinity men. Would you not rather stay here, tend your fields, perhaps open a chandlery or some other profitable enterprise?"

Makepeace jumped to his feet. "I am to be a minister! It is all I have ever thought of.... Please, grandfather, you cannot mean to ..."

"Very well, do not upset yourself. I simply felt it my duty to enquire. I am no mucker—I hope you know me well enough. I do not grudge the expense. It is only that I know you have struggled as a scholar from time to time. That is the whole of it. I wished to be certain, before we take great pains, that this is truly your desire and not some duty you feel obliged to shoulder for your father's sake...."

"By no means. It is all I have ever wished for."

"Then there is nothing for it. We shall have to do our best. Sit down, sit down, boy, and do not distress yourself. I have written to both the schools and have had an interesting reply from Elijah Corlett, the master of Cambridge Latin. Through John Eliot's offices, we have secured places for Caleb and Joel there, as Master

Corlett has some experience in instructing Indian youth, and the Society funds that work. Although you are above the usual age, he writes that he is prepared to accept you there when they come to him. And though, as I have said, I am sadly not in purse to provide the usual fees, Master Corlett confides that there may be a way to waive them, if . . ."

And here grandfather's gaze shifted, unexpectedly, to me. "If you, Bethia, agree to be indentured to Mr. Corlett, as housekeeper at the school."

"Indentured?"

My face must have been a study in astonishment. Indentures were for the children of the indigent. Grandfather, who liked to fashion himself after a feudal lord, attempting to get those about him to call his wild tract of island land "the manor"—and this to the point where the Aldens made jest of his pretensions—this same gentleman could not mean for me, his granddaughter, to be sold away as a bondswoman. It would shame him, surely, to do such a thing. A glance at Makepeace revealed that he, too, felt great discomfort. He squirmed upon his chair. Grandfather could not meet my eye but looked down and fiddled once again with the paper upon his desk.

"It would not be a common kind of indenture. For one thing, the term would be short—just four years, not the more customary eight. Also, it would address the problem of where you are to live, for you cannot keep house alone if your brother is gone to Cambridge, and as you know, I do not have room in my household to accommodate you in any degree of comfort. Aunt Hannah's house—well, we all of us know you cannot set one foot in there as it is without stepping upon a sleeping child. If you were but a little older . . . but no, we must not think of that. I myself would be willing, since you will be seventeen come leaf fall, and at such an age it is not unheard of . . . but no. Your father was quite firm when this was last broached and I will not flout his wishes in that regard."

I wanted to say, does no one think to enquire as to my wishes? But since I took him to refer to Noah Merry, it seemed better to keep silent. I was relieved that he did not seem inclined to follow that line of thought to its inevitable conclusion. I had nothing against young Merry. Indeed, I liked him well enough. But he was a boy yet; it was not possible to say with certainty what manner of man he might become. And I had no wish at all to be his wife, or any man's wife. For one thing, I was in mourning. Each death, coming so swift on the heels of the last, had left me adrift. I had looked, in each case, for a new direction in which to steer my life. When mother died I thought I was meant to raise Solace—that this would be the larger part of my life's work. When Solace died I thought that I was meant to support father, to keep his house so that he could pursue his mission untroubled by daily concerns. His death had left me utterly rudderless. Perhaps this service with Master Corlett, unwelcome as it seemed to me now, was meant to give me some new bearing. Since I was banned, by my sex, from the work of ministry, perhaps God meant to use me as the instrument by which my brother might follow that path.

"Mr. Corlett writes that he is but recently widowed and is in want of a gentlewoman to assist him in the running of the school. He has a number of boys boarding with him, English and Indian both, and is sensible of the fact that such boys, especially those of tender years, need a steady feminine presence. It seems there has been a difficulty obtaining a locally hired servant adequate to the situation, on account of the Indians, you know. I have assured him that you are a most capable girl, despite your youth, and quite accustomed to our tawny brethren." He paused there, with such a look upon his face that signaled he expected me to be conscious of a compliment. I gave him back no sign of it.

"Consider, Bethia. You would be doing a service, not just for your brother, but for the other boys resident there, including young Joel and Caleb, in whose fortunes I know you take an interest."

Makepeace shot me a look at that. I answered his glance with a withering glare. I saw the thought dawn on his countenance: it was in his interest now to do or say nothing that would anger me. His future seemed to rest, quite suddenly, in my hands.

"May I have some time to think on this, grandfather?"

"Yes, yes, of course you may. Consider well. But keep in mind that it is only four years that are asked of you. And we do not need to announce the nature of your service. You go there as companion and helpmeet to your brother, merely. Not that the arrangement is anything to be shamed by, I do not suggest that it is. . . . I would not have you think so. The school is highly thought of. Why, Corlett writes that he has charge, presently, of the late governor Dudley's own son, so do not think I ask you to be handmaid to just any gaggle of snot-nosed urchins. And after, you may return here, of an age to marry and have a family and a household of your own. But you will have seen the mainland, tasted town life. The school neighbors the Harvard College, did I tell you so? Master Corlett's son serves as a fellow and tutor there. And I have heard that the Corletts are intimate friends of the college president. Who knows? You may catch the eye of some square cap who suits your fancy better than a farmer lad. In any case, it is not an opportunity that presents itself to island girls very often, Bethia. Bear that in mind as you consider."

We took dinner with grandfather, during which he talked of everything but the subject that burned in my mind like a brand. Caleb joined us at board and I felt his gaze on me. I was not sure how long he had been within the house. I wondered if he had overheard the conversation and knew what was proposed. I supposed that he and Joel would be glad to have me nearby—a familiar face, a helpful hand. But when our eyes met, his expression surprised me. His brow was creased and his looks cold.

Before we left the house, I took grandfather's sleeve and drew him a little aside as Makepeace searched out his hat.

"Grandfather, may I ask you—you say Master Corlett is but recently widowed. I wonder what you might know of him, his character?"

Grandfather, grasping what was behind my question, reddened slightly. "My dear, be easy. Master Corlett is an elderly gentleman. He has grown children—a daughter, married and settled with a large family of her own, at Salem; another son, as I said, a tutor at Harvard. I'm sure Master Corlett will treat you as he would his own granddaughter."

I wanted to say, "I hope he would not indenture his own granddaughter because he is too thrifty to bear a slight financial loss." But I thought of mother, held my peace and walked home at a fast pace, in silence, aware that my brother's stare was boring into my back.

X

I decided that night to give my assent to grandfather's plan, because I discerned God's hand in it. But I thought to keep my own council regarding this choice for reasons that were not so godly. I had Makepeace upon a pin, and I intended to let him squirm there. For three days, I took a vast amusement in the small courtesies that came my way. Of a sudden he was splitting bavins unasked or at my elbow at the well, offering to carry my water.

Each night, I took up the Homer that father had bequeathed to me and I gave myself the luxury of a candle by which to read it. The first night, Makepeace looked askance, but then quickly arranged his features and went up to his shakedown with nowt but a civil good night.

On the third day, I asked Makepeace if he might spare me for some hours, and though he talked around the point of what might be my purpose, when I showed that I was disinclined to give it, he did not interrogate me further. Had he pressed me, I do not know what I would have answered, for my purpose was obscure even to myself. I just knew that I wanted to be free and alone for a time, as I used to be, as I had not been in such a while, and as I could not be again once we left the island.

I rode first to father's cairn and sat on my accustomed mossy stone. It was shaded by an old beech, and the light, filtering through the swaying leaves, cast shadows like lacework across my folded hands. Speckle walked to the pond's edge and set her great head down to drink. It always made me smile to watch her. Even if she had been hard ridden, she drank with a delicate restraint, her muzzle barely breaking the surface, her lips closed, sipping as daintily as a duchess. When she had her fill, she turned and cropped the grass, twitching her rump to shift the flies that lit there. I listened to the sound of her teeth ripping at the sedge, the wet champ of her jaws, the buzz of the discommoded flies in wait of a chance to resettle on her sweaty flank. The sun was warm and buttery. I tilted my face towards it. After a time, the tears ran, and the mare turned her liquid gaze on me, laying back her ears as if struggling to understand what was amiss. She left off her cropping and walked over to stand by me, as if to bring me comfort. I stood, wiped my palms over my face, passed a reassuring hand down her neck and remounted, turning her for the south shore.

When we reached that long expanse of sand it was low tide. I walked her down to where the strand hardened and the waves broke about her hocks. She lifted her head, her nostrils widening. I took off my cap and tucked it into my bodice. I leaned close to her ear, and urged her to a gallop. The salt spray winged high on either side as we pounded down that beach. I felt the wind and the spray, the thud of her hooves, the counterpoint of the hammering surf.

When she began, finally, to tire, I eased the reins and let her slow as she would. When she brought herself to a stop, I turned her up the beach, slid off her back, loosened her bit, and threw myself down upon the hot sand. I felt my skin tighten as the spume dried into a white crust on my hands and forearms. Speckle dropped her soft muzzle and nudged my ear. I smelled her grassy breath. She licked the side of my cheek, tasting salt. A long, glistening thread of drool detached itself and fell onto me. I sat up, laughing, and pushed her off, wiping my face with the wet hem of my skirt. She walked away a few desultory paces and stood, slack hipped, blowing great, soft snorts.

I lay down again and closed my eyes against the glare, listening to the sound of the surf as it arced all around me, the thrumming fall of the breakers, the shush of the receding waves. Every now and then I felt my skin cool slightly as a cloud passed across the sun. From time to time a gull would voice a rich cry, high and urgent.

I lay there for a long while, drifting, letting thoughts pass like the clouds. Then Speckle neighed softly and tossed her mane. I looked across to see what had startled her. There was a shadow on the sand. Even before I turned my head, I knew that it was Caleb.

In that shimmering, golden light I saw the wild boy I had met here four summers past, no longer wild, nor boy. The hair was cut short and plain, the fringed deer hide leggings replaced with sensible black serge. The wampum ornaments were gone, the bare mahogany arms sheathed now in billowing linen. Yet neither was the youth who stood before me some replica of a young Englishman. He was hatless, shoeless, and without his hose, so his long calves were bare. He had no doublet, and his shirt, sweat soaked, clung to his chest.

"I saw you ride out of the settlement. I knew you would come here—." He was straining to contain some strong emotion. He seemed to almost vibrate with the effort.

I scrambled to my feet. "You don't mean to say you ran here, all the way from Great Harbor?"

He turned an open palm as if to say, How not?

"But why would you follow me"—I lifted a hand to indicate his undress—"in this state?"

"I had to speak to you privily before you assent—it is true, I hope, that you have not yet assented—to this shameful plan of your grandfather's. And there is never a moment . . . you come not in my way." His effort at restraint failed him at this point, and he almost shouted. "Do not let them make a slave of you, Storm Eyes."

I stepped back, surprised by his sudden wrath.

"I have no idea what you—"

"I thought your grandfather honorable." He turned and spat on the sand. I winced.

"He is honorable, Caleb. You must not—"

"'Must not!' I am full up to my throat with 'must not.' You English palisade yourselves up behind 'must nots,' and I commence to think it is a barren fortress in which you wall yourselves."

His anger sparked my own. "Is that so? Then may I ask what you are doing, taking our bread and our instruction? Laying yourself to our books as if your very breath depended upon uttering a phrase in Latin? Mouthing our prayers so piously at meeting?"

"I do not come here to speak of myself," he said. "I know what I am about. I am come here for you, because I see now you have no family worth the name. Your father was a good man. He would never have countenanced this. But your grandfather loves his gold more than he loves you. As for your brother . . ." He lifted his chin sharply, his mouth drawn into a scowl. He thumped a fist against his chest. "We make slaves of our defeated enemies whom we hate, to avenge a death or the like grave wrong. How comes he to think it right that you, a sister, should be enslaved for his profit?"

"As if you did not work every woman in your otan to a raveling, day following day! I have seen how it is among you. You do not find hard toil dishonorable when you set your own women to do it."

"Shared and necessary toil is one thing. Slavery is another. If I were your brother, I would not sell you into base servitude just to buy myself a future."

The easy tears of that season welled. "You *are* my brother, Caleb. My heart tells me this more clearly than any ink mark on a document." I reached out as if to take his hand, but some constraint stopped me in mid-gesture. "The law may say what it will, but you and I know what is true. And father—he loved you as a son. Look to Makepeace, if you do not credit what I say. You will see that he eats himself hollow with envy of the love our father bore you."

I watched the anger leave his face, the muscles of his jaw relaxing under the high broad bones of his cheeks. He reached for the hand I had half extended, lifted it and bent his head to it—a gentleman's gesture: I could not think where he might have seen it done. I felt the heat of his breath, the hint of his lips, and then he let the hand go, reaching for a strand of my hair. The pins had fallen, and it hung, loose and damp, almost to my waist.

He spoke softly, almost as if to himself: "When we first met here, my hair was longer even than this." He fingered the strand and let it fall, raising his hand and running the palm across his own close-polled head. A thought came to him then, and he gave a sudden, dazzling smile. "It may be that your father loved me, as you say. But not until I cut my hair. He had a boiling zeal to see it gone. My 'barbarous deformity,' he called it." The smile faded. "Truly, I did not know I was such a sinner until he taught me to hate my hair." His face was grave now, his brow creased. "So many things I loved, I have had to learn to hate. And it all started in this place, with you, Storm Eyes."

He turned from me then and looked back across the dunes that hid the pond where we had first encountered each other. Then, with his easy grace, he folded his legs under him and sat down upon the sand, his back very straight, his eyes upon the horizon. Without looking at me, he beckoned—the same brisk gesture he had always used when he wanted me to follow him. So I settled myself on the sand beside him and stared out at the waves. Often, in the past, when we had looked together at a common thing, I had learned that we saw it in quite different ways. He had taught me, long ago, how to see a school of fish moving through the water deep below the surface—how a certain change of light and dark could disclose them and reveal where one must throw out a net. Because of him, the sea to me was no longer an opaque mystery, but a most useful lens.

He lifted a fistful of sand and let it fall through his fingers. "You ask why I eat with you, learn your prayers. Why I study to hate all that I once loved. Put your ear to the sand. You will hear my reason."

I tilted my head, puzzled.

"Can you not hear? Boots, boots, and more boots. The shore groans under the weight, and yet more come. They crush the life from us."

"But Caleb," I said. "This land—I mean, the mainland—they say it is a vast wilderness—there is room and to spare even when we come many thousands. . . ."

He had scooped up another handful of sand and stared at each grain as it fell through his fingers. "You are like these. Each a trifling speck. A hundred, many hundreds—what matter? Cast them into the air. You cannot even find them when they land upon the ground. But there are more grains than you can count. There is no end to them. You will pour across this land, and we will be smothered. Your stone walls, your dead trees, the hooves of your strange beasts trampling the clam beds. My uncle sees these things, here and now. And in his trance, he sees that worse is coming. Your walls will rise everywhere until they shut us out. You will turn the land upside down with your ploughs until all the hunting grounds are gone. This, and more, my uncle sees." Caleb slapped his hand down upon the sand, then he drew it into a fist. "And yet he refuses to see that God prospers you, and protects you, and keeps from you the sicknesses against which his powers are as nothing. So, this do I see: We must find favor with your God, or die. That, Storm Eyes, is why I came to your father." His expression was grim. I wanted to reach for his hand, offer some comfort. But I did not. I just sat there, wordless, until he spoke again.

"Life is better than death. I know this. Tequamuck says it is the coward's talk. I say it is braver, sometimes, to bend."

He turned to me. "That is why I will go now to this Latin school, and the college after, and if your God prospers me there, I will be of use to my people, and they will live. But you. There is nothing for you in that place. Why should you go? You know full well your brother is a dullard. He will not profit from this schooling, even though you give your freedom to buy it."

"Caleb," I said. "I do not go to save grandfather his precious few guineas. Neither do I go for the love of my brother, and although I will rejoice in his success, I am not so blind as to conceive that my efforts for him will in any way assure it. If I am enslaved, as you call it, it is not to any but God. I go to Cambridge for the same reason you do. Because I believe God wants it."

"I do not understand you, Storm Eyes."

"Caleb, please. Do not call me by that name. We are neither of us children who may run hither and yon, as if this isle were another Eden. If it were so, once, then those gates are closed behind us now. That life is over and done." He looked at me, and then away. I could not tell if he was puzzled by my words or hurt by them. I softened my voice, and touched his arm lightly. "You taught me once that names might serve for a season or two, then pass away. The season of Storm Eyes has passed. It is time we both of us stopped looking behind us and set our faces to the toil ahead. I told you once, long ago, that Bethia means God's Servant. It is what I am striving to be, Caleb; it is the right name for me now. Call me so, as befits one who is my brother." He said nothing but kept his gaze upon the sea. I felt a strong desire to make everything plain and open between us, for as he had said, such opportunities to speak one to the other had become so very few.

"There will be a time," I said, "perhaps soon, when our paths will go separately onward. But for a little while yet, it seems, we will walk forward together. I, for one, can say that I am glad of it. As for understanding me, I think that you do, better than any other now alive, whatever name I go by. As I would understand you." I plucked up my courage then, and asked what I yearned to know.

"Caleb, will you tell me what happened to you, when you went alone into the wilderness? Did the serpent come to you, in the end?"

His chin went up as I put the question. He did not look at me, nor did he answer. There had been a light, warm breeze, all morning, from the southwest. But while we sat in speech, the wind had turned around, and freshened. Now a sudden, sustained gust blew from the north. You could see its shadow passing across the face of the ocean, pushing up flecks of white foam. The beach grass, bending to its force, sent up a whispering, and the oaks behind the dunes answered with a low roar. Sand grains stung my face.

"He came." He had switched into Wampanaontoaonk. Even though the glare upon the beach was intense, his eyes had darkened, the black of the pupils swallowing the brown. "The night was cold. So clear. The stars were so bright you could count the trees by their light. . . . I had fasted many days. . . . I drank the white hellebore, and cast it up, many times. . . . I passed between this world and the other world. And then he came, and I took him up, into my hands, and the power flowed into me." He had raised his hands in front of him, the palms curled to grasp the muscled, twining form as he remembered it. "I took it, Storm Ey—Bethia. I took it." His voice had deepened, finding the resonance of his native tongue. "Pawaaw."

The word hung there. I thought of Tequamuck. I do not know if the wizard had the power to reach into my mind, whether my thought of him called upon some dark art that he had, or whether he, by some demonic rite, had formed up visions out of sage-scented smoke and breathed them into me across all the distance between us.

The sky cracked open and I was in a storm, wreathed in fog. I turned away from the lacerating sheets of rain, but all at once the wind lifted and blew me off my feet, into the swirling air. Then I was falling like a plummet, deep into roiling waves. When I came to rest, on the ocean bottom, there was a great silence. Father's body floated, an arm's length from me. Seaweed-shrouded, bloated, tugged this way and that by unseen tides moving deep beneath the waves. I reached for him, but even as I willed myself forward, I was tugged backward, speeding through water and into air. I was in our garth, the sunlight so dazzling I could not see. I blinked, and when I opened my eyes, Caleb stood there, Solace limp in his hands. He held her up to me, but as I reached out she turned into a snake, writhing, head rearing to strike. . . .

I felt my gorge rise. Caleb grasped my hands then and shook me. The vision crumbled into bright shards and fell away.

"What is it? Are you ill?" His eyes were once again their normal color, treacle brown. He stared at me, full of concern. I swallowed, and gulped the clean salt air, fighting down the sickness. I could taste the bitterness of hellebore in my mouth. I closed my eyes and drove my fists against them, hard, as if I could push the monstrous visions out of my sight. I wanted to confess to him what I had done at Takemmy, tell him what my sin had caused, warn him that this so-called power he had reached out for was a devil's snare. But all that came out of my mouth was the one word: "Pawaaw."

"Remember what it means, Bethia: I taught you, long since. . . ."

"Healer," I whispered.

"Just so. That is all my intention. To use this power to heal the sicknesses that beset my people."

"But Caleb, the power comes from Satan. . . ."

"And from whence did Satan get it? Was it not from God, who created him a great angel? So your Bible says." The wind had eased again; the trees behind the dunes quieted to a low rustling. He had switched back to English, his voice low and weary. "I am a man, Bethia. A man must take power where he finds it. If I find it in your books, I will take it. If I find it in visions brought to me by my familiar, then I will take that, too. It is what the times demand of me."

"Power? Does not a lightning bolt have power? Reach for it, and become a blackened husk. . . ." My voice cracked. I drank the cold air again in greedy gasps. Caleb's eyes regarded me.

"Maybe," he said at last. "That may indeed prove to be the cost."

I did not have the courage to look at him. I just shook my head and tried to swallow away the bitter taste that lingered in my mouth, and the salty tang of suppressed tears. When Caleb spoke again, his voice was calm and steady.

"Not long ago, Bethia, when your father yet lived and taught us every day, your brother was struggling, as is his wont, with the Greek. When he could not get it, he became very agitated, and at the last he turned to your father, and demanded to know why we, as would-be ministers, must needs learn these things." I have set down before that Caleb was a natural mimic, and here he pitched his voice higher and gave it a hectoring edge, becoming, to the life, the mouthpiece of my brother. "'What has Apollo to do with Christ? Is not the study of these pagans akin to Eve and Adam's prideful seeking after forbidden knowledge?'"

As Caleb spoke, I could easily imagine the scene in my mind's eye. Despite my agitation, my lips twitched with amusement. "And what did father say?"

"He said that of course all learning must have Christ in the bottom, as the only foundation. But since God had seen fit to give us Christ's gospel in Greek, there was surely a sign for us in that. And then he told us the Greeks' story, of how Prometheus stole fire from the gods. He said that fire represented the lamp of learning that had been lit by the ancient Greeks and passed to us, to keep alight. So am I a thief of fire, Bethia. And since it seems that knowledge is no respecter of boundaries, I will take it wheresoever I can. By light of day, in your schoolrooms. By candlelight, from your books. And if necessary, I will go into the dark to get it."

We were kindred indeed, Caleb and I. I cast my hands over my face, but Caleb reached out and pulled them away. "Tell no one, Bethia. You must never speak of this. There is not another soul alive who would understand it. Not even Joel." His eyes bored into me. "I am not even certain that you do."

"Oh, I understand. Perhaps more than you think." My voice was as weak as a mewling kitten. I stood then, unsteadily. I could not speak anymore. I felt wrung out. The shadows had begun to lengthen on the other side of the noon hour. Makepeace would be looking for his dinner.

"I must go," I said, still shaken, struggling for self-command. "Caleb, you should know that I mean to accept this indenture, and if my reason remains obscure to you, all I ask is that you believe it is my willing choice. As I try to accept what you say, even though it scalds my heart." I brushed the sand from my skirt, pulled out my crumpled cap, and tried to knot up my hair. Caleb made to walk back to Great Harbor, but I would not have him do so. He climbed up behind me on Speckle, and we rode by a slow way, through the woods, so as to be unobserved. When Speckle foundered slightly on an uneven tussock, his hands grasped my waist for a moment, and I was conscious that however much I might feel him to be my brother, it was not so in fact. In the town, we would need to be even more wary of our manners one unto the other.

A half mile short of the plantation, he dismounted. As he turned to go, I reached down and touched him lightly on the shoulder. "One thing further: hold some charity in your heart to grandfather and Makepeace. Even if they do not always do well, they mean well. I truly believe so. And it is what father would want of you." He lifted his chin in a gesture that might have been assent, might have been dismissal. I rode on then, alone. When I glanced back, my hand raised in farewell, he had melted into the trees, invisible. He had not lost the art.

A good thing I had been prudent, because Makepeace was in the dooryard when I rode up, and when he saw my state, he turned a bilious shade. He barely held in his wrath, even though I could see it cost him. I tried to imagine what would have happened had I added a half-clad Caleb to the spectacle. The thought of it caused a smile to break across my face, and at that, Makepeace snatched his hat and staff and stalked off, needing to put some distance between us or else loose what remained of his composure.

By the time he arrived back, I had seen to the mare, dressed my hair decently, donned a fresh cap and set a hearty board. When he saw the plate of roasted cod and green beans, he made an eloquent and heartfelt grace, including in it a blessing upon the hands that had prepared the food. I let him eat a slice of treacle pudding and a dish of raspberries. As he scraped up the last of it, I told him I meant to accept the indenture. I would dearly have liked to keep him on my pin a few days longer, but we all of us needed to plan for the journey, and time was short.

I had never seen a set of indentures, and had surely never thought to see my own. In as much as I had given my mind to such a thing, I had thought perhaps that I would, as a wife, one day in charity assent to take into service some poor young person in need of a roof and sustenance.

Grandfather, sensible of the awkwardness of the moment, paced his chamber as I read over both copies of the paper. I could tell that it irked him when I insisted to read them, just as he was about to set his name and seal. But willing or no, he handed them to me. It was a short form of words, but since it bore so heavily upon my future I read it over slowly.

This indenture, made the 25th day of August one thousand six hundred and sixty between Elijah Corlett of Cambridge on the one part and Thomas Mayfield of Great Harbor on the other part, that the said Thomas Mayfield has bound and does hereby bind minor child Bethia Mayfield his granddaughter and ward by law to any lawful work for and to reside with the said Elijah Corlett until the 25th day of August one thousand six hundred and sixty four. During which time Elijah Corlett covenants to use all means in his power to provide for said Bethia Mayfield boarding and lodging and such attendance as is necessary to her keep and care in health and sickness and further covenants to afford her brother, Makepeace Mayfield, full scholar's privileges, board and lodging at the Cambridge Latin School and to educate him in Literature as he is capable.

The papers already bore Corlett's sign and seal, and both had been laid together and cut around the edges with a set of indentations so that the one paper exactly matched the other. When I had read and compared them, I handed both silently to grandfather and watched as he dipped his pen and made his usual flourishing signature.

"So, that is done," he said. "I will send the one copy with you to Master Corlett and keep the other safely here, not that I expect for one moment that Corlett would transgress any particular of the agreement . . . but . . . just to be prudent . . ."

I watched him place the paper in the box where he kept wills and deeds and debtors' bonds. He locked it with a key that he kept on a fob. I thought how glad I would be, four years hence, on the day I could retrieve that paper, tear it into small pieces and feed it into the fire.

From Great Harbor to Cambridge as the crow flies is no great distance. But alas, we are not crows. The choice lay between a short sail across seven miles to the nearest point on the mainland, and then a long and difficult trek west and north upon narrow Indian paths through wilderness; or else a longer sail, up and around the arcing arm of the cape and onward to Boston, which takes the better part of a day and night to accomplish, in fair weather. From there, one must arrange a barge up the river to the town landing at Cambridge—an hour with a fair wind and a flood tide, but an impossible journey should an easterly prevail. As we needed to fetch books and clothing with us, we decided to go by the longer sea route—despite great misgivings.

There was much to do. I had to instruct the neighbor's young boy, who was good with the tegs, on the special care of my ewes, and show him how to make my earmark on the lambs in due season. I saw Speckle into the hands of grandfather's manservant, and, before I left her, spent some time stroking her long nose, telling her not to become too spoiled while we were gone. The day before we were to sail, I conceived an errand to the Iacoomis cabin, telling Makepeace that I thought it would be charitable to let that family have the last of the season's unspun wool, since I was not about to fetch it with me to Cambridge. He raised an eyebrow, saying that a nearer neighbor would be just as glad of that kindness, but in the end assented. I walked out to what had once been the extreme edge of Great Harbor. When I was small, and Iacoomis had first settled down there, he had built a rude sort of a hut, made of poles and timber sheets in the native manner. Over the years he had enlarged and amended it to a sound wattle-and-daub dwelling, not much different to its English neighbors. The cabin had once been set off at a distance from the nearest English house. But now the town had grown out and past it, and no one save the Aldens thought anything about it any more, the Iacoomis family living just exactly as we did in every particular.

By great good fortune, I found Caleb in the dooryard, playing at jacks with Joel's young brothers. After I told Iacoomis's wife, who went by the English name of Grace, about the wool, I tarried for a few minutes and joined in the game. Under cover of the children's merry voices, I asked Caleb, in Latin, if his uncle Tequamuck knew we were to sail on the next morning's tide. Caleb's head lifted sharply, his dark eyes regarding me gravely. "I know what you fear," he said, also in Latin. "I, too, fear it. I have said nothing to him. We have not exchanged words together since Worm Moon. But Tequamuck hears and knows much."

"Will he do to us as he did to father?"

"My heart says no. He loves me, Bethia, even now. He was always more to me than father or mother. I think he feeds a hope that I will yet abandon the English God. That hope is therefore our hope. . . ."

We had to stop then, for Iacoomis himself came out of the cabin to thank me for my gift, and for my attentions to Joel's welfare in Cambridge, and to wish me Godspeed.

The next day dawned bright and fair and almost windless. We had to sit at anchor until the breezes picked up late in the afternoon. All that time, I scanned the shoreline with a tightness in my throat, trying to make out that feathered cloak upon the bluffs. I saw Caleb's glance turn that way also. But his uncle did not come, and as the canvas bellied out and the timbers creaked we beat away from the island. I watched from the stern until the last low nob of land flattened to a dark line, then a hazy disturbance on the horizon. Finally it merged into the edge of the world and vanished from my sight. At that moment, fear gave way to a grief for home that has not left me since.

To be sure, the journey hence is hard enough even without devilment, and since others have written of its rigors I will not trouble to set them down, except to say I was able to get no sleep aboard the sloop, which pitched and yawed to an alarming degree for almost every hour of our voyage. In Boston's harbor the next morning all was delay and frustration in finding a barge, and then an easterly blew that kept us from setting out till sunset. The wide river wound through fens and marshes, all bronzed in the failing light. It was full dark when the bargeman sighted the rushlight that marked the turn into a canal dredged from the Cambridge town creek. He disembarked us at the landing and hallowed for the carter who lived in a rude hut nearby. I could see nothing beyond the narrow circle of the carter's lamp. I could, however, smell my new home. There was a reek of beasts from the Ox-Pasture and the Cow Common, a rich tidal stink of rot and decay, and a stench such as comes from people pressed in close habitation. When finally we arrived, exhausted, at Master Corlett's door, the hour was late. Although the paths around the college were lit by cressets full of burning rushlights, I couldn't tell much about the town. The lamplighter himself showed us the way to Master Corlett's school. The master greeted us civilly, roused a pair of bleary-eyed boys to help fetch our boxes off the cart, and after a few words to Makepeace, sent him with Caleb and Joel to find their places in the attic dormitory among the other pupils. As their boots clumped up the narrow stair, he ushered me into his own chamber.

"You brought the document, I suppose?"

I handed his copy of the indenture across his desk.

He barely glanced at grandfather's signature, and then pushed the paper away as if it were as distasteful to him as it was to me. He gazed at me with a pair of watery blue eyes. "Uncommonly obliging of you to join us here. I trust you will not find the duties too onerous, and if you do, you must come to me at once and we will see what can be done to adjust them. I told your grandfather that I was in want of a gentlewoman, and you shall be treated as one, within the limits of our means here. I will not ask of you anything that my own dear wife Barbara did not do, full willingly, to keep these boys in health and heart. But here I am, speaking of my fine intentions and I do not even offer you a chair—do sit." I looked about the sparsely furnished little chamber, which contained a hand-hewn desk, a bookshelf, a single ladder-backed chair, a bedstead, and little else. Then I spied a rush-seated stool tucked under the bedstead and pulled it out. I was glad to sit, even on so low and rickety a perch.

"I had the pleasure of meeting your father, did you know, when he was a stripling in Watertown. Never did meet your grandfather, though saw him at meeting. Interesting venture of his, the island. We all of us thought it a bold and reckless plan, at the time. But they say the settlement prospers. And your poor late father. Such miracles they say he wrought, bringing the gospel. Cut down untimely there, to be sure. Always an excellent scholar, and godly, so his master said, when he was but a youth. Privilege for me to teach his son, your brother, as I said to him just now. Uncommonly fortunate that you are easy in company with the young Indian pupils—we have two others enrolled, younger than the brace of islanders come hither with you, and the prospect of at least one other, perhaps, from the Nipmuc people. . . . Most interesting case, though not without challenges. . . . I will tell you of it, perhaps, another time. I expect your grandfather shared with you the catalogue of my difficulties here. The Cambridge women, most reluctant to bide with the Red Man. Even, it seems, with the Red *Boy*. . . ." He gave a little wheezy laugh at that. "Any rate, one went about with a switch in her hand, and used it, any time the poor mites came near her, whether they erred or no. The next had such a case of the vapors if she was obliged to be in the same room with them that she could barely get her work done."

I was swaying on the stool, my fatigue so great. I longed for my pallet. I began to wonder if he would ever think to show me to it. I envied Makepeace and the others, able to put their heads down. But Master Corlett seemed oblivious to the hour, and my state. He was speaking now of Master Eliot, and his great hopes for education in the colony, so as to ensure the ministry and professions endured beyond the talents that immigrant generation had brought with them from their English colleges. "He was ardent for it, yes. Fervent. I heard him once pray: 'Lord, for schools everywhere amongst us! Before we die, may we be so happy as to see a good school encouraged in every plantation of this country.' And so we have, now, in all places with one hundred families or more. His own town, Roxbury, boasts an illustrious school, having fitted more scholars for the college than any town of its bigness, or even twice its bigness. . . . But we are hard upon its heels, here. Indeed we are. We may be poor in material goods—you will see that we get on hand to mouth here— but we are rich in the things of the mind. . . ."

I felt my eyelids droop and strove to prop them open, as good manners demanded. But my body defied my will. I must have dropped to sleep for an instant, for my head lolled onto my breast and I came awake with a start, lifting my chin with a sudden spasm.

". . . and I am sure you will find the boys conscious of the good fortune that brings them here." Master Corlett rambled along, undaunted by, or oblivious to, my stifled yawns. The boys might very well be conscious of their good fortune, but I was near to *unconscious*, and I realized I would have to speak up or fall down. So I stood.

"I am sorry, Master Corlett. I would be very glad to hear more of the school tomorrow. But I have had a trying journey and a very long day, and I would be most grateful..."

"Of course, of course. Must forgive me." He rose and came around the desk, offering me his arm. "Too much on my own of an evening, that is the trouble. Used to sit up till all hours, talking with my son Samuel, when he... Thoughtless of me. My son still, sometimes... but generally his evenings are bespoke by his duties—at the college— you know.... I fear you will find your accommodations rather Spartan. I have no chamber to offer you. There is only this one, then the schoolroom, which doubles as refectory, and the dormitory, which is in the attic... eight boys up there now. Your brother the only one won't have a bedfellow, the rest all go two-a-pallet. There are another six boys come as day pupils, families live here in town, you know. You'll need to give them bever, but they don't take commons with us—home to their families for dinner. Any case, as I was saying, no chamber for yourself, but I thought, a pallet in the kitchen... private from the boys, and the cook fire, warmest place when the weather hardens. We haven't the luxury, generally, of a fire in any other room, unless a boy's people gift us extra wood." He directed me along a short hall, and then we stepped down into the dark kitchen. There was a scent of old fat, damp rags and mouse piss. A pallet with a thin shakedown was wedged against the wall. Half of it extended underneath a worn deal table, very stained, greasy and unwholesome-looking. Scrubbing it white and clean would be my first chore. He set the candle down and took a taper to light his own way. "We follow the college schedule here, get the boys used it, do you know. Prayers at six, first class at seven. You will please serve them their morning bever at nine. That will be a pint pot of small beer and a slice of bread for each boy. I will instruct you on the rest of your duties at that time. Good night to you now. God keep you till morning."

I murmured a good night. As soon as he closed the kitchen door, I snuffed the candle and fell upon the pallet. I barely had the strength to unlace my boots. For the rest, I fell asleep fully clad.

XII

I woke to a clatter of feet above my head, followed thereafter by a bustle of young bodies jostling each other down the narrow stairs. When the last pupil had crammed himself into Master Corlett's chamber, I heard the door close and the master's quavering voice rise to lead the prayer.

I got up, stiff and weary still, to take the measure of my new surroundings. Throwing a shawl over my shoulders, I stepped out into the garth. It was true, what grandfather had reported; the college was not a stone's throw away. The older building was a large clapboard structure, which must have seemed very fine when they first built it on these wild coasts, almost twenty years earlier. It was a full three floors, with three wings set off at right angles to the main structure. In the center was a tall turret with a bell tower. It seemed a remarkable thing, to have raised such a place as this, at the very dawn of settlement, when material cares and the very business of survival pressed so hard upon the colony. I had heard that some had deemed the college building too gorgeous for a wilderness. But the grace of its design cannot have been matched by skill in its construction, for its shingle roof sagged woefully in several places and the sills showed signs of well-advanced rot. The neat new brick building beside it— which I guessed must be the Indian College—only emphasized the decayed condition of the larger and more venerable structure.

I turned back into the kitchen, to assess the place that was my more immediate concern. A single large kettle and small selection of pans hung above the pot well. There were eating utensils on the dresser—pots of chipped slipware and three good pewter tankards which, upon examination, proved to have pupils' initials scratched crudely on the base. Likewise the trenchers were of worn wood, except for three pewter plates, also etched with initials. So there were some better off pupils, who had brought their own things— Makepeace would be mortified when he learned of this, as I knew he had not thought to pack anything of that nature.

I soon enough learned the names of the "pewter platers," as that trio tended to give the most trouble and make most demands upon my time. One set of initials, JD, belonged to Joseph Dudley, the former governor's son and the most difficult. He was one of the elder scholars, who would also attempt the matriculation examination. He was a well-favored youth with an unlovely manner, haughty and cocksure. During my first days at the school he treated me in a most peremptory way. While the other boys folded their soiled linens and set them on their pallets for me to collect on washday, he dropped his upon the floor. At board, when the other boys carried their dishes to the trough after meals, he rose from the table and left his as they lay.

The second week, when he once again left his linens scattered, I did not trouble to pick them up. It was a fine day, and I was able to get all dry and the collars pressed by sunset. Most of the boys returned to the attic to find their clothes folded neatly on their beds. Dudley found his as he had left them, and commenced to curse the "slattern" that Master Corlett had employed. I would like to say that it was Makepeace who leapt to my defense, but I learned later, from Joel, that it was Caleb. Makepeace, ardent to curry favor with the highest born of his fellows, had been ashamed to speak for me. But Caleb stepped up to the young man and enlightened him, in strong terms, as to my family's position, and said that he would take personally any further insults upon me or my work. Dudley was a well-built young man, and I am sure he knew how to use his fists. But he was also an intelligent boy and no hothead, and could readily calculate that in a bout with Caleb he might not show to advantage.

I knew nothing of this exchange the next day, when young Dudley came to me in the kitchen and begged my pardon, saying he had been uninformed as to my connections and had taken me for a common servant, and now he repented his incivility to me.

"I thank you for that, young master," I said, rather coolly. "You study here in hope of taking orders, I understand?"

He nodded his fair head. "I do, if I am equal to that high calling."

"Then I hope you will not take it amiss if I, as you now know, the daughter of a minister, recommend to you some verses: Matthew, 21:26–28. You will note that Jesus does not enquire as to connections before he extends civility to those of a servile condition."

I turned then and went back to my scrubbing. The next thing I knew, he was beside me, clout in hand, rubbing at the deal with great energy, his fine skin tinted a mottled pink.

"I think you have not done this work before?" The pink of his cheeks became a little bit more intense.

"Am I doing it poorly?"

"By no means. You are doing well." I sprinkled some more sand on his side of the table. "I enquire only as I assume you come from a household with servants?" I knew very well that Governor Dudley's house was the finest in the colony. At the time it was built, Winthrop had made a scandal of it, decrying its sumptuary excesses.

"We have one, an indentured person. When I was a child, of course—but perhaps you are not aware—my father was in his seventieth year when I was born. I was his Benjamin, indeed. He died when I was but four years old and my mother remarried soon after and removed to Duxbury. My stepfather is the Reverend Allen. He mostly had the raising of me. Although I did bide for a time with my elder sister, Anne Bradstreet, and she of course has a larger household, with several servants."

I stopped scrubbing and straightened. "Anne Bradstreet? Our poet?"

"You know her work?"

"Of course. I find it remarkable."

He looked at me with greater interest. "I shall tell her, when next I write. She will be glad to know of one of her own sex who reads and appreciates her. Few can. You know Latin? The classics?"

I nodded.

"Extraordinary. I had thought my sister unique in this."

I went back to scrubbing the table. The scrape of clout on deal was an odd accompaniment to the rich lines of verse, dense with scholarly allusion, that now filled my head. When I had first come upon the poems I had taken great heart from them. If she, like me, a woman of the wilderness, had studied and mastered these things, then so might I. Since then I had got several of her poems by heart.

His young face was scrutinizing me closely. "I expect you find the privations here difficult to bear with?"

"I admit, I do. It is difficult, in many ways. As it must be for you."

"Well, yes, although I would not like to own it. May I speak frankly, Mistress Mayfield?"

Conscious of his courtesy in addressing me so, I nodded.

"To be quite honest, I do not think well of being required to room with salvages, such as those I understand are known to you. I cannot think how you and your brother abide being in such close quarters with them. I imagine it tries your patience, as it does my own. I would be glad of some counsel as to how you manage to bear it." I gave him no reply other than a cold glare. He barely glanced at me, then went on scrubbing. "I wrote to my stepfather and asked that I be allowed to board upon the town, when the first of them came here. He wrote me back and said he was not in purse to board me out. I do not see why *they* cannot be boarded elsewhere, as the funds for their education are limitless, seemingly. You know, I suppose, that it comes, all of it, from England, where the cause of Christianizing the salvages is well supported. I have heard that the new building, the Indian College as they call it, over yonder in the Harvard yard, cost in excess of four hundred pounds of English money. Can you credit such a sum? For salvages. While English scholars crowd into a leaking, drafty ruin. Of course, no sooner was it up than President Chauncy was canny enough to see its uses. He has filled its rooms with English students, who had been in such cramped quarters. A cunning ruse, do you not think? To get so fine a building in such a way . . ."

I wondered if what he said was true. If so, it seemed an injustice to those religious persons that their money be employed contrary to their mind. Perhaps, though, it was simple prudence of Master Chauncy to put the building to use while he awaited the matriculation of its intended occupants, all of whom were either undertaking preparatory instruction here or with Master Weld at his school in Roxbury.

But young Dudley had not had done with the subject. "My stepfather wrote that I must be patient, and console myself with the thought that I would not long be inconvenienced by the salvages, their nature not fitting them for the rigors, you know, of a Christian education." He paused his sanding then, and leaned on his clout, considering. "I am not sure that I agree with his reasoning on this latter point. Those here, at least, seem uncommonly well suited. One or two of the newcomers, indeed... But these are the ones instructed by your late father, I think?"

I inclined my head.

"I suppose they were with you for some time, plucked out of the wilderness at a tender age?"

The heat had been rising under my skin for some time. I clenched the clout in my fist, to conceal the tremor in my hand. "By no means," I replied, as evenly as I could. "One, in particular, had the benefit of my father's instruction for a very little time before God saw fit to..." I had no wish to say more. "I thank you," I said, relieving him of his clout. "But I do believe Master Corlett would prefer to find you laying yourself to your book."

Dudley's words prickled me like a hair shirt all that day. After, I resolved, for my peace of mind, to avoid any such intimate exchanges. I would simply tend to the boys' physical needs and leave their moral state to Corlett. And so my days passed by in a dull blur of toil. The Lord's Day would arrive and I would lie upon my pallet and try vainly to recall something that had occurred, of note, to distinguish the week just passed from the one before it. Then I would get myself reluctantly to meeting, to sit through preaching whose narrowness sat ill upon the broad foundations of faith that my father had set down. Somewhen during those tedious weeks, as the weather hardened, the day dawned on which I turned seventeen, but it passed and no one made note of it, not even myself.

And then, one chill evening, Master Corlett first spoke to me of Anne. It had become a habit in him to invite me to his chamber for a conference at day's end. He would enquire of the small matters of the household, always apologizing for the many wants we faced and complimenting me on this or that shift I had made to do more with less. Then he would turn to the matter of the boys, and each one's character, and how he did. Although he was forbearing in his words regarding Makepeace, I knew well enough he was troubled in mind to find my brother so behind hand with his studies. Of Caleb and Joel, he was laudatory, but always, when he spoke of them, it was with an eyebrow raised, as if he doubted his own judgment of their progress. Often, as on the first night, he would ramble off into reminiscences of earlier times, or into his philosophy of education and its necessary place in the success of the colonies. His thoughts seemed to run ahead of his words, and if I was very tired it was quite hard, sometimes, to sift together the fragments of his sentences. So these conferences, although interesting to me, were also often quite trying, and I would be thinking of my pallet long before he was willing to let me go to it.

This night, he was quite agitated. "I mentioned to you, I think, my expectation of a Nipmuc pupil who might soon be joining us?" I had a vague memory that he might have said something of the sort.

"I think I hinted to you that this was an exceptional case. So it is, most exceptional. And I must allow that I am at a loss as to how ... in any case ... quite an odd request ... but from such a source, one must...."

I sat there, studying the new blister on my hand, my mind drifting, until suddenly he said that which got my full attention.

"... an Indian maid, Anne. The governor, generally speaking no lover of the native people, as I am sure you know—he did lead the militia against the Pequot in that lamentable business—has taken a fancy to this girl, whom he found already an abecedarian. He took her into his own household some months since and sent her to a dame school nearby to his residence, in Boston, where it seems that, at age twelve, she has outstripped the mistress in learning. He says she is quite a curiosity, and it is his whim that I have her here for one year and see of what more she might be capable. He then intends to take her into service in his household as governess or something of that kind and show off her abilities to his diverse guests, in order to wring more funds from our English benefactors. She comes already with a generous stipend from the Society's funds, but even were this not the happy case, how to refuse a request of the governor? Still, I am troubled in mind, sorely troubled, as to how to accommodate this girl...." He leaned forward. "I have never instructed a girl— even my own daughter had a governess—I suggested the same to the governor, but he would have her here. He wants to be sure, he says, that her wits are taxed just as the other pupils, so that there can be no question as to her abilities. All very well, indeed, for him to indulge his fancies. But what am I to do with an Indian girl? I can hardly include her in the same classroom.... The disruption would . . . no. It cannot be. I am, truly, at a loss as to how to go on, and she comes here within the sennight."

"Cannot she be boarded upon the town and come to you for private instruction?"

"I had thought of that. But then we should loose the benefit of most of her stipend. As you know as well as I, our wants here are many, and the stipend, as I said, is uncommonly generous. . . . I do not like to ask you . . . who live so far beneath your station as it is . . . to take a bedfellow, . . . but I do not see another way. . . ."

I felt a pang of dismay at that. My only peace was when I lay my head down at night and I was loath to surrender that shred of solitude for an enforced intimacy with a stranger. And yet my interest to know more about this girl was much inflamed.

She arrived a few days later, fetched hither in the governor's own carriage. She was a tall girl for her stated age, slender, with thick black hair drawn into a tight braid that was not pinned up, but fell from beneath her cap and reached nearly to her waist. She was dressed in a good gray worsted—imported, not homespun—such as the governor's own daughter might have worn. She had arranged her cap with the fold far forward, so that it hid much of her face, and she walked into the house with bent head and downcast gaze, which she did not raise as Master Corlettt showed her into his study, gesturing for me to come in also. I closed the door, aware of a great and uncommon stillness in the schoolroom across the passage, where every eye had been trained upon the doorway to catch a glimpse of the curious new pupil.

It wasn't until the master introduced her to me that the shadowy, heavily lashed eyelids flickered, and she raised her head and looked at me for just an instant, before dropping her chin again. Her skin was very dark brown and smooth, like a chestnut, drawn tight over the high cheekbones common to her kind. But her eyes were another thing—a deep, luminous green like moss refreshed by rainfall. I had never seen anyone of her people with eyes of such a color. She had her hands clasped before her, and I noticed that the knuckles were white against the dark brown of her skin. She was making a great effort to still a tremor. The poor girl was afraid. I spoke a kindly greeting in a low voice. Then I glanced at Master Corlett with a meaning look. "Perhaps your interview might wait? Let me take Anne with me to the kitchen for a bever." Master Corlett mopped his brow, which was sweating, despite the cold. "Very good, very good," he said and, greatly relieved, returned to the classroom full of boys, where he knew very well how to get on.

I ushered her to the kitchen and explained that she was to share my pallet there. A sigh passed through her thin frame. At first, I took it that the idea repelled her, she having been lodged in what I assumed must have been far superior quarters at the governor's house. But then I saw that her face had relaxed its drawn, tense expression. She stood, waiting for instruction, so I invited her to sit and asked if she wished to eat something. She shook her head. She perched rigid upon the chair, as if staked to it. I poured her a pot of small beer, but she made no move to drink it.

"I hear tell you are an outstanding scholar," I said. She did not look at me. The green eyes were fixed on a burn mark in the surface of the table, her thick brows drawn into a frown, as though the blackened wood was displeasing to her.

"Might I know how you began upon your course of study?"

She drew in a breath, as if she were about to speak, but uttered no word.

"What are you afraid of?" I asked her suddenly, in Wampanaontoaonk. Her head lifted sharply, the green eyes wide with astonishment. For a moment, I was back on the island, a girl her own age once again, dripping pond water, as the same look of wonderment lit the face of a wild heathen boy in deerskins. It seemed she understood me, but I could not be sure, as I did not know how closely Wampanaontoaonk might relate to the Nipmuc's speech.

"How come you to know that tongue?" She spoke in barely accented English, her voice low.

"My father was a missionary, and he spoke it. But I truly learned from a friend who is Wampanoag. We grew up together. . . . I should say . . . we spent some time, when children, in each other's . . ." This was more information than I had meant to offer, and I trailed off. But since she did not offer anything in return, I tried to come at my earlier question again. "And you? How did you come to learn English?"

"I was raised to it."

"Did your parents—?"

"My parents died. Spotted fever. All the village lay ill with it. I was taken away by an English fur trader who passed by at that time."

"What town did he bring you to?"

"No town."

"You lived in the wilderness?" She nodded. "Was it he who taught you your letters, or his wife?"

She looked up for an instant and then down again, rubbing her fingertip over the scorch mark.

"There was no wife."

"You lived alone with this Englishman, in the wild?"

"Until he died, a half year since."

"Who has cared for you since then?"

"I tried to walk back to my country, to see if any of my family yet lived. But the constables caught me upon the road."

I suppose that they took her for an indentured runaway. "Did they lock you up?" She nodded. "Did they mistreat you?" Her only answer was a shrug.

"How came the governor, then, to hear of your case?"

"I wrote to him."

In terse sentences, she explained how she had asked to be allowed to return to the western woodlands from whence she had been plucked years since, and the flurry of attention that had followed the governor's receipt of her letter. He denied her request to return to the remnant of her people. Instead he had taken her into his household and sent her to the dame school.

"When I spoke to the mistress in Latin, they said I must come here."

"*Latine loqueris?*" I asked, surprised. The master had seemed to think he was meant to be starting her on that language.

"Some," she replied. "But I do not know that I pronounce correctly, having got it from an accidence."

"The master will be very glad to know you have made a start, I am sure of it. Shall I fetch him? Do you feel ready to speak with him now?"

Her hand shot out across the table and grasped my wrist. It was a soft hand. A lady's hand. I had not seen, in my time, a hand so unblemished as hers. Certainly not my own. Not my mother's. So this man, whosoever he was, had not set her to hard chores in their wilderness redoubt. The green eyes scanned my face avidly for a moment. "Please. No." She was trembling again.

"My dear. I know this must be a very big change of circumstance for you. But you must not fear Master Corlett. He is a kindly gentleman. No one here means you any harm."

Her only reply was to look down and keep on shaking her head, so I let the matter lie. No profit to rush her, shy and frightened as she was. I needed to get to my chores, in any case, so I started peeling turnips for the pot, thinking of this child, snatched from her people into such an improper arrangement. Clearly the trader had fed and educated her. Perhaps he had been a godly person, saving a child from a disease-ravaged town, raising her with a kindly fatherliness. But her fearfulness implied something other than fatherly affection.

She rose and made to help me, but I laid a hand on hers, removing the knife she had taken up. I put the knife down upon the table. "No, Anne. You are a scholar here, not a servant. You must be clear about your place from the first, and insist upon what is due to it, because you can be sure there will be some always more than happy to reduce you." I went into the master's study and fetched Tully from his shelf. I set it before her. "Can you read it?" She nodded. "If you like, read aloud to me, and where I hear that your pronunciation errs, I will correct it, as far as I am able, although I, like you, have got my learning from books. I must confess I have had no formal Latin instruction myself, only what I have gathered from listening an ear to my brother's lessons."

She read with very little hesitation, the slight remnant of her Nipmuc accent making the words sound well in her mouth. That was how Master Corlett came upon her, some time later. She did not at first observe him, standing just back from the doorway, and she read on, until, when she reached the end of a sentence he gave her a hearty "Well done, indeed! Remarkable."

She started, glanced at him, and then away, and commenced to tremble again.

"Very well then," he said, washing his hands together uncertainly. "You seem to have made a good start. Carry on there, and I shall see you in my study after commons, and we shall make some determination as to how we shall go on." He turned, and then he hesitated. "Bethia, I think it best if Anne takes her commons here, with you. We can make introductions to the others in due course. No need to hurry these matters."

"Very good, Master Corlett. I shall see to it."

Anne barely touched her broth and bread as I bustled about fetching the pupils' meals and scouring their dishes. When it was time for her conference with the master, she pushed herself up from the table with what seemed to be an immense effort of will. "Would you like me to come with you?" I said. She reached for my hand. "Very well," I said. "But just for today. I have work I should be about at this hour, and as I said, you have nothing at all to fear from Master Corlett."

It was difficult to say who, of the two of them, was the more shy and awkward. The master's stumbling manner of speech was worse than I had ever heard it, and her voice, as she construed the passages he set before her, was barely audible. Each time he corrected her, she started as if she had been struck. I burned to know what had put this child into such a state, beyond anything that mere shyness, or the novelty of the situation, could account for. On the other hand, if the answer was as I feared, then I preferred not to know it.

I felt this even more strongly after I passed the first night sleeping beside her. I should say, rather, attempting to sleep beside her. Hers was the wracked slumber of the tormented. I had set us head to toe, as is the usual way with a bedfellow, but I soon had to revise my position as her long legs thrashed about so, I thought she might blacken my eye with her violent kicking. Despite the difference in our ages, she was fully as tall as me, and despite her slenderness, there was a sinewy strength to her. As I laid my head down beside hers, I caught a sharp fragrance from her long braid—a clean scent of wintergreen and sassafras that made me ache for home. I had just managed to drift to sleep when her hand locked about my forearm and tightened there like a noose. She was still asleep, but whimpering and pleading withal. She did not waken even as I peeled her fingers away. I got up then, realizing that I could not share her pallet and expect to close my eyes. I took a threadbare quilt to wrap about me and lay down on the stone hearth with a grain sack as my pillow, feeling cold seep into my bones until weariness claimed me.

She was standing over me when I waked. "This night you have the pallet." I started to say of course not, since she was the pupil and I the servant, but she interrupted me.

"Did I say aught in my sleep?" The beautiful eyes slanted away from me as she spoke.

"Nothing I could make out," I said. "Though it seemed you had troubled dreams."

"Always." She turned then to go out to the necessary. "I am sorry I disturbed your rest." I stood up stiffly, with aching limbs, and looked after her. The long braid swung as she walked down the flagstones.

XIII

Some weeks later, Makepeace sought me out for a private conference, which was not usual. He had been reserved since the morning after our arrival; civil enough, but never more than that. We would walk out together on the Lord's Day, after meeting, if the weather happened to be good, but during the rest of the week he was no more to me than any of the other pupils. I could not tell which galled him more: my menial status in the house, or my conversations with the master of an evening, when he was obliged to keep dormitory hours with the younger boys.

"I would be glad if you would walk with me. I have that which I need to say to you."

I sighed inwardly, thinking of the chores that would pile up in my absence, but I was anxious to hear him out, so we fixed upon a time, and in the afternoon I left Anne in the kitchen, at her book, and fetched my cloak.

Generally we walked down Crooked Street in the direction of the meeting house and town square, but this time Makepeace stepped off the other way, toward the college and the Cow Common beyond. We made our way between the Indian College and the sagging clapboard hall that housed the English scholars. From the common, the cows turned their slow heads and regarded us. We walked on in silence through the apple orchard. The mud had iced over so that the path, although slippery, was not the usual boot-sucking wallow. Even so, I did not like to risk my one pair of stout footwear to it.

"Why must we go this way?" I said.

"I do not wish to be overheard," he replied.

The trees were glossy with ice, but the first buds had begun to form and snowdrops bloomed about the base of the trunks. Makepeace reached out a hand and worked off a curved wafer of ice. He raised it, like a glass, and gazed through at the wavy vision it afforded. He let it fall and shatter, and looked up into the dark squiggle of branches. "These trees," he mused. "Almost as old as the colony. A quarter century, they must be, now. Do you know, Bethia, that these were planted by the sweat of the scholars of the very first Harvard class? They say Master Eaton billed as if he had paid local workers and pocketed the cash himself."

I did recall something about those long ago scandals, for it was a favorite jest of grandfather's, at board, to remark that he was glad that Mistress Eaton was not his cook. She had been accused, in the General Court, of feeding the scholars a hasty pudding made with goat dung, and mackerel with the guts still in. He liked to read over the cases that came before the court, and that was ever one of his favorites.

"Such a flawed man," my brother went on. "Yet chosen for a post deemed essential by the living saints of the colony. So may we learn that none but God has perfect judgment regarding the true state of a man's soul."

I was sure he had not brought me here for spiritual musings, yet he seemed downcast, so I tried to cheer him. "Perhaps you will make a sermon upon that theme, one day." I could not, it seems, have said anything less apt to the purpose. His eyes filled, and he turned from me and pressed his brow into the icy tree trunk. I laid a mittened hand upon his back. "What is it, brother? What troubles you so?"

"I cannot do it, Bethia. It is plain to me now. On the island, with father, alone, I could tell myself that my abilities, though less than I wished, would serve. Even when you found so easy what cost me such struggle, even when that heathen lad...still...I deluded myself. I thought that with steady work I could o'ercome my deficiencies and get on, as everyone about me seems to do. I said to myself, Makepeace, in Cambridge you will not be found wanting. Others there will be, whose wits work more slowly. But it is not so. Though I am oldest, yet am I generally the least able pupil in the room."

He raised his head, his brow all cratered from the impression of the rough bark. "And now comes this squa, and I hear her, reading to you, and even she, a self-schooled salvage, does with ease what I cannot do with utmost effort." He gave a dry and humorless laugh. "I tell you, I am fortunate that Master Corlett is no Master Eaton, or I would be thrashed thoroughly every day, so behind hand am I with my lessons."

"But Makepeace," I said, feeling an unaccustomed tenderness, reaching up to smooth his brow. "Surely Master Corlett does not despair of you? Has he spoken to you?" He shook his head. "No? Then neither must you despair of yourself. You have struggled, yes, but through that struggle you have come far—" I knew this to be true; I was not just speaking words to ease his feelings—"You must know this. You must feel your progress. It is plain to me, who has watched you through these months and years."

"It will not serve! If someone says a thing to me, it is plain enough, and with effort I can con it by rote and repeat it back to them. But when I turn to books the writing there makes no good sense to me. English books and Latin—these are trial enough. But Hebrew, Greek—the characters swim all about and I cannot...I will never..." He reached up, snapping a budding twig and brandishing it at me. "You see? Spring is almost upon us. Summer brings the examination. I will not pass it."

"Makepeace. They will test your Latin knowledge and a very little Greek. Surely you might—"

"I cannot! And what is more, I will not! I will not set myself up to be reduced. Caleb and Joel will matriculate with colors flying, and I will be shamed before everyone who knows me: Makepeace Mayfield, more stupid than a salvage. I cannot bear it, Bethia. I... I... want to go home." He sounded now as plaintive as a small child, and my sympathy that had waxed so strong waned of a sudden.

"So. You cannot bear it." My tone was mocking, insolent. "*You* cannot bear it. You are a man, Makepeace, with all the privileges and rights that come with the title. Why then do you not act like one? You want to go home. Do you trouble to think, for one instant, how sorely I might want to go home? And how is *that* to be accomplished, since, on your behalf, I am indentured here, deprived of my right to go and come for three and one half years more? You will go back to the island, to warmth and friendship and a certain station in society, and I am to stay here, in this vile town, scrubbing and mending, deprived now even of a pallet on which to lay my head in peace and solitude? No, Makepeace. You will stay. And you will study and endure, and earn this sacrifice which I have made for you. And if, when you meet Master Chauncy at yonder college, you are found unequal to the challenge, then you will strive to see God's will in it, and to find what it is he intends for you. If you do other, then I tell you, Makepeace, from the day you quit this place I will not call you my brother."

Even as I said this, I knew I did not mean it. But the words rode out of my mouth mounted upon an anger I could not bridle.

Makepeace looked stunned. In seventeen years, this was but the second time I had spoken my mind to him, and on the first occasion I had been defending myself from his attack. Now I was attacking him. His face hardened. He drew himself up and folded his arms across his chest in the gamecock pose I had always despised.

"'Tis well our mother did not live to hear what a hectoring fishwife you are become, sister. You do not even give me space to say my piece. Do you not think that your condition daily rebukes me? It is the chief cause of my despair, that I have brought you to this. I lie awake at night, thinking how to redress it." I felt the sting of his words, and lowered my gaze. "If you were not so quick to abuse and to condemn me, you would have heard what I propose. I have written to Jacob Merry regarding his son Noah and his suit for your hand in marriage. I have said we will accept it, if he is in purse to buy out your indenture, the which sum I will work to pay off in whatever employ I am able to obtain."

"Makepeace!" If I had been angry before, my new condition was of so violent a nature that I do not know what word to put upon it. "Please, tell me you have not sent this letter?" His look told me the answer. "Then you will write another, this night, retracting it."

"That is not possible. . . ."

"Not possible! What is not possible is that you should usurp the right to sell me off into a marriage that I have not agreed to, a match that father himself deemed untimely, that grandfather, who—must

I again remind you?—is my guardian, also felt unsuitable at this time...."

"But grandfather has reversed himself."

"He ... what?"

"I unburdened myself to him, when last I was on island, one month since. He told me to consider well, and make no decision, and work my hardest, and if after one month had passed I still felt the same way, then he thought my plan a good one, and said he would carry my letter to Jacob Merry in person, and stand surety for the debt."

I could hardly breathe. I felt all the blood drain out of my face and a great coldness rise. For the first time in my life, I thought I might faint. I leaned my weight against a tree and grasped at a low-curved branch to support me.

"Why look you so? Why such a violent reaction? Any one would think I—" He stared at me, frowning. His face darkened. "It is your unlawful affection for that half-tamed salvage that brings this about, is it not? There is no cause otherwise for you to have such a revulsion to so suitable an alliance as Merry." His mouth twisted then, into a mirthless smile of triumph. "I knew it! All your protestations to the contrary, just feints and falsehoods. Know this, sister: you will put that attachment behind you today. You shall do my will in this, and that is an end of it."

I had never in my life uttered an oath to God but I did so then. "God damn you, Makepeace," I said, and turned, and made an unsteady way back towards Mr. Corlett's house, with Makepeace's voice calling after me that I was the one at risk of damnation.

XIV

I entered the kitchen only to find the room crowded, just when I most needed some time and space alone. Anne was seated where I had left her, her book open upon the table. Master Corlett had joined her, and Caleb and Joel one on either side of him. A lively seminar of some kind seemed to be under way. Anne's face, no longer hidden and shadowed, seemed lit with a sharp intelligence as she listened to Caleb and Joel, who were engaged in a disputation on whether beauty implied godliness. She had just asked a question, and Caleb had his face turned to her, answering. His voice, as he addressed her, was soft and solicitous. As distracted as I was, it struck me how different this was to our rough and tumble arguments, our many seminars held upon sand dunes or under oak boughs. He had shown no care for proper manners then but spoke his mind in a carefree, brotherly way.

Brotherly. Now, of all times in my life, did I wish Caleb truly was my brother, rather than that selfish, imperious, weak-willed soul to whom fate had shackled me. If it were so, I could turn to him now, and he would surely help me change the fate being thrust upon me.

I had my hand on the door latch, hesitating. There was supper to prepare, and yet I did not want to interrupt the teaching, nor could I get about the kitchen with so many bodies in my way. I was struggling to keep my composure, and felt I might give way at any moment. I turned, to go back out, but the master called my name and bade me sit. "I—I do not think—I need to be about my duties,"

I said, trying to speak in a normal voice. Caleb, whose back was to me, caught the agitation in my tone and turned. I have no idea how much of what I felt was disclosed in my face, but Caleb's gaze informed me that I did not look myself. He stood up and grasped my elbow, and steered me down upon the bench.

"Are you quite well?" said Master Corlett, all concern. "You look flushed—are you fevered?"

"It is nothing," I said. "A headache merely."

"My dear, please, go into my chamber and lie down upon the bed. I shall send a boy to the apothecary for a draught. . . ."

"No, master, do not trouble a boy, there is no need of a draught." The apothecary charged a chouser's prices for draughts any goodwife could distill. I knew the master was not in purse to pay for such things. "But I will lie down for a brief while, if you can spare me."

I was never so pleased to be alone. When the master closed the door I turned my face into his pillow and wept without restraint. After, I lay there, depleted, unable to summon the will to rise. Before long, the exhaustion of the previous night lay hold of me and I fell into an unintended sleep.

When I woke it was full dark. I jumped up, poured some cold water from the master's pitcher into his washbowl and splashed my face, straightened my cap and went to the kitchen. There was no one there, just a pile of trenchers piled into the sink. It seemed the boys had fetched their own bread and cheese and I had not even heard the racket they usually made in the dining hall. They were all now at evening prayers, where I should have joined them. Instead, I pulled out a stool and sat quietly, trying to think. I decided that if the master called me to his chamber after prayers I should unburden myself to him, and seek his counsel. He was a kind man, wise and godly. He would know how to advise me.

Not long after that, one of the younger pupils came to say that the master indeed wished to see me. I knocked upon his door and entered, expecting his usual kindly good evening, and perhaps a solicitous enquiry as to my headache. Instead, he looked up at me with a face stern and filled with displeasure.

"Your brother reports that you have subjected him to most grievous execration, even unto uttering an oath to God. What say you?"

"Well, yes, master, I did, but—"

"There are no buts in this matter, Bethia Mayfield." He stood. "Here in Cambridge, in the absence of your grandfather, your elder brother is your head and guide, to whom you should submit yourself. And yet you cast aside his guidance as if you have more wit and care than he. Since you confess your sin freely, and in light of your unexceptionable behavior until this day, I see no need to involve the court in the matter."

"The court?" I had been stunned into silence by the severity of the master's tone and his unaccustomed harshness toward me, but at this I could hold my peace no longer. "Why should the court care about what I said to my brother in a private conference?"

"Leave aside for a moment your abusive carriage towards your brother and your hectoring and unbecoming speeches. As a minister's daughter you must know that uttering an oath to God is a grave sin. As a magistrate's granddaughter, I expected you also to be fully aware that it is a crime against the laws of this colony. I do not know what may be your grandfather's pleasure should such cases come in his way, but here the General Court exacts stern penalties upon it, even unto driving an awl through the offending tongue."

My hand flew unbidden to my mouth. "That very kind of zealotry is the reason my grandfather quit this colony and took ship for the island," I said. My head really was aching now: a sharp, stabbing pain that felt as if the torturer's awl had been driven between my eyes. Even so, I should have known better. Had I laid a finger upon a red-hot iron, I would have had wit enough to snatch it back, not reach forth and grasp the thing. Where was my self-mastery, my long self-schooling in discretion? I seemed of a sudden compelled to speak my every inner thought, to puke them out, like bile.

He gave me over to Makepeace for beating, and I shall not write of it, only to say that, when I turned, between blows, to look at my brother, I saw that his eyes were glazed, his lips moist and his face slack with pleasure. I did not look at him again, even as I lowered my skirt and thanked him, as I was obliged to do, for correcting me.

There was no private place to look to my weeping stripes, so I neglected them, and a day or two later they commenced to fester. I had noticed, with the boys' various cuts and scrapes, that nothing in this place healed speedily, as young flesh should. There were of course no salves or anything of the kind. I had had it in mind to compound some, later in the spring, when I could find the right plants, so as to have store on hand for the younger boys' scrapes and bruises, and for the rare occasions when the master laid the switch to them. I had not thought to need such a product for myself. Anne saw me struggling awkwardly to wrap a linen piece around my angry sores. She drew from her own box a bottle of some sharp-scented, cooling lotion and applied it with a gentle and practiced hand.

I told no one of the beating. But Anne must have disclosed something about it to Caleb. When I passed by him in the hall, he bent his head close to mine and whispered, "I will see to your brother."

"By no means!" I hissed. "You must not think of it!" But he had already gone by me, his attention seemingly engaged by the spine of the book he held in his hand. The next day, Makepeace could not rise from his bed. A gripe had seized him, so severe that he lay moaning in pain as each spasm wracked his belly. That, when he was not wobbling, wan and weak, to the necessary, which he was obliged to do more than a dozen times in as many hours. I confess it; I am no saint. I took some pleasure in his suffering, though I did ask Caleb's advice as to how his people might compound a binding draught should such a condition beset them, and sent, in due course, to the apothecary for the remedies he named.

As for me, my punishment was not done with. It continued the following Lord's Day, when I was required to make public amends. To do so, I had to stand forth in afternoon meeting and declare my remorse for having inadvisedly and blasphemously expressed myself. For the week thereafter I was obliged to wear a paper pinned to my breast which bore the words of the psalm: *I will take heed unto my ways that I sin not with my tongue; I will keep my mouth with a bridle.* This was unfortunate, as the younger pupils felt licensed to make sport of me by poking out tongues or neighing like a horse every time my back was to them.

When the sennight had passed I tore the paper from my bodice and cast it into the fire that warmed the oven for the morning's loaves. As I watched it burn, I told myself that I must root out from my heart the bitterness that had set its seed there. I tried my best to pluck up the anger, the mortification and, yes, even hatred. It had come at last to this, that I felt actual hatred towards my closest living kinsman. I found myself, at prayer, chiding God for taking Zuriel and Solace, and leaving Makepeace. This was a wickedness. I knew it. So I tried to vision these ill thoughts as something written on a parchment that could be balled up and burned away to wither in the flame and be carried off like smoke. But the passions are not corporeal things that can be unmade so easily. The stripes from my beating had scabbed over, at last. I could not say the same of my injured spirit.

That night, the master called me to his chamber. I went, heavyhearted, and sat upon the rush stool, my hands folded in my lap and my gaze upon the pattern in the turkey carpet. If, as the minister at meeting had proclaimed: "It is the whore that is clamorous," then I would school myself, once again, to be silent.

"The maid Anne tells me you do not eat." I felt the master's watery blue eyes upon me. "Indeed, you have a pinched, spare look. It will not do. This unfortunate business is done now, and over. I feel confident that you have seen your error and have repented it. There is no cause for you to continue to mortify yourself through fasting."

I did not make him any reply.

"You cannot hope to manage your work if you do not eat."

Without raising my eyes, I whispered: "Does the master have cause to be dissatisfied by my work?"

"No, no, no. That is not at all what I meant. Your work is quite satisfactory—indeed, exemplary—as always. I do not like to see you so woebegone, that is all. Can you not put this thing behind you?"

I continued to stare at the floor. When he saw that I would not be drawn on the matter, he changed the subject.

"How do you think she gets on, the Indian maid?"

I lifted my shoulders in a shrug.

"The two lads, Caleb and Joel, have taken it upon themselves to befriend her. I see no harm in it. You know them well: you have found them to be entirely honorable?"

I nodded. He waited for me to add something, but I did not.

"She seems less shy with them, at least. Do you think she is content here?" I replied by opening my hands in my lap. I might have said a great deal on the subject, at another time. It seemed to me that Anne had bloomed under the tutelage of Joel and Caleb. She no longer trembled at the slightest cause, and even seemed to sleep more restfully at night. But I pressed my lips together stubbornly. If silence was what they required from a woman, then silence they should have.

The master stood up suddenly and walked the few steps to the small diamond-paned casement that gave onto Crooked Street. "This will not do, you know. Will not do at all. I have come to rely on you, you see, and now, because of this business with your brother . . . you'll not speak to me. You'll not even look at me. And you are putting yourself in the way of becoming ill. How am I to get on?" He turned around then, wringing hands that were ropey with prominent blue veins. "Am I to take it that you do not want to marry this fellow—this islander—Merry, is it?"

I looked up then, and met his eye for the first time. "No," I whispered. "I do not."

"Is there something wrong with the man?" I shook my head.

"Then what, exactly, is it that you object to? Surely there must be something wrong with him for you to take on so?"

"Nothing is wrong with Master Merry," I said in a low voice. "There is a great deal wrong, in my view, with Makepeace Mayfield, who would buy and sell his sister as if she were a sow."

"Well. Quite. I see. Though you do know, you must surely realize, that you mayn't usurp authority from those who have been made head of you." He sat down again at his desk and commenced to finger the pens I had mended for him. "Whole of it, most unfortunate. Your guardian, your very esteemed grandfather, he stands behind your brother in this. So, even if one were to raise, as I might, as his schoolmaster, raise—the matter of your brother's judgment, raise a question as to his maturity, as it were—there is still your grandfather to be managed. Thing of it is this; I do not want to release you from the indenture, and you, seemingly, do not wish to be released. Not if it means marrying this man, albeit you say you find him unexceptionable. It seems a strange business to me, that you would rather toil here as a servant than make what your brother represents as a most advantageous match. But what do I know of women and their fancies . . . ?"

A coughing spasm wracked him. Like so many in the school, he had a wetness in the chest that seemed to last all winter long. I wished, again, that I had at hand the proper herbs for a good expectorant. He dabbed at his mouth with a square of linen. I had hemmed some for him, finding his own stained and threadbare. I saw him run his finger over the place where I had embroidered his initials. His eyes, as he looked up at me, were tired and rheumy, and very sad.

"Your brother confides he intends to leave the school, so you will be here, serving in payment of a debt beyond the which he owes. I know full well that legally you are bound to me, whether he completes his year or not. And neither am I obliged in law to agree to sell the indenture to any person. I don't wish to be uncivil to your grandfather. But neither do I wish to let you go, all the more so since I see you so very unhappy."

He was clearly distressed, and not only at the thought of losing a capable housekeeper. He got up again and came toward me. "Dear to me, yes. You are. In a very short while, I have come to feel . . . our talks, they bring me . . . I don't suppose you would consider . . . that is, I wonder if you have any . . ." He had turned a pale, putty color. He reached out a liver-spotted hand. He lifted my chin. "That is to say . . ." The pads of his fingers were shrunken and fleshless, the loose skin cool and dry. "I do not know . . . I cannot tell . . . what your views might be on the prospect of a different marriage . . . to . . . to . . ."

I shot up off the stool, toppling it beneath me. He was not a tall man and suddenly we stood, eye to eye.

"You?" I blurted.

He looked startled by my violent reaction. He ran a hand over his crown, raking the thin, sand-colored hairs across the mottled flesh of his balding pate.

"Me? Of course not! My dear Bethia. You misapprehend me. I was going to say, to my son. To my son, Samuel. You have seen Samuel at meeting. Indeed, I introduced you, when first you came to us."

He had righted the stool, and gestured for me to sit down upon it. I did so, in a state of some distraction. I did not hear the half of what next he said. My mind was busy conjuring Samuel Corlett, probationer fellow at Harvard, whom I knew only as an austere presence beside his father in meeting, and a rather less austere, more animated figure when I had glimpsed him, gown billowing, walking in the college yard with one or another of the scholars he served as tutor. He did not visit the school, his duties requiring him to be at the college of an evening. But I knew that the master passed a good part of the Lord's Day visiting his son in his college rooms.

The master was asking my age. I gathered my wandering wits and made him an answer. "I will be eighteen in October, master."

"He is twenty-six. No yearling, but neither by any means a graybeard. A considerable difference in age is no bad thing, if the parties . . . But I put the stern before the bow here. Samuel expressed himself to me of an interest in being acquainted when first you came to me. But when I broached this with your brother, he led me to believe that your affections were engaged by this island lad, Merry. The way he framed it, you came here all but handfasted. So I told Samuel. But now, you say that the business with Merry is by no means as your brother presented it . . . and my son still . . . the short of it is, I told him today I would speak to you. He was impressed by your eloquence, in meeting . . . that unfortunate matter. . . ."

How odd. At the very moment I had been called upon to reduce myself before the community, I had, apparently, elevated someone's estimation of me. It had crossed my mind, as I stood to speak my confession, what a remarkable thing it was that the rare time a woman's voice might be heard in our church was when she was execrating herself.

"He is a serious man, excellent scholar, high in the regard of President Chauncy. And when I told him you knew Latin ... I will let him press his own suit of course, but I think you will find ..."

The picture of Samuel Corlett was becoming clearer in my mind as the master spoke. I was thinking to myself that he must have favored his late mother, for he looked nothing like his father. For one thing, he was very dark, the opposite of the freckled, fair-haired Master Corlett, and a good head and shoulders taller. He was a plain man, not handsome—his nose had been broken, perhaps in some childhood mishap, and no one of any skill had seen to it. It splayed across his face, giving him, at first glance, the cast of a ruffian rather than the look of a refined scholar. But his eyes belied that first impression. These were deep-set, quite black, watchful and intelligent. Thinking on it, I now realized that I had often looked up, at meeting or while passing near him upon the common, and noticed those eyes upon me. What harm could there be in agreeing to meet with him? I turned the matter over in my mind.

The master had stopped rambling. The silence lengthened.

"Forgive me, Master, for my earlier misunderstanding," I said at last. He gave a dry little laugh. His hands were folded on the desk in front of him. He let them fall open and raised his brows, questioning.

I looked down, and fiddled with my cuff. "I would not, that is, I have no objection...." Of the two of us, of a sudden, I was the addlepated, tongue-tied one. I took a deep breath.

"What I mean to say is, I would be pleased to receive your son, Samuel Corlett."

XV

In the event, it was Samuel Corlett who received me. The master
and I had reached the same conclusion, though we never voiced
it one to the other. Since it was probable that nothing would come
of this conference, there could be no profit in alerting Makepeace
that the master and I together plotted to flout his will. Better, then,
to meet Samuel Corlett in his college rooms, where we would be
neither watched nor eavesdropped upon.

My brother had made known his desire to quit the school, and
waited only on word from the mariner on whose sloop he had
previously traveled of a shipment of goods headed for the island. He
did not attend the classroom. This made it easier for me to avoid all
but the most perfunctory contact with him. When the Lord's Day
came, I walked to the meeting house with Master Corlett and set
out after also in his company. What then could seem more natural
than to join the master in an afternoon visit upon his son. The
weather was unsteady, in the way the townsfolk said was typical
of a Cambridge spring: a sudden rise in temperature that roused
the senses, then, just as sudden, snow again. Even as a warm day
brought relief from the long winter, each thaw uncovered the town's
ugly middens, awakening their stench and setting it in competition
with the sudden, elusive fragrance of an early blossom.

Samuel Corlett had moved into vacant rooms in the Indian
College, which had housed no native scholars so far. It presently had
in residence five or six English scholars, and a young Nipmuc man,

John Printer, who tended to the college press. This press—the only one of its kind in the colony—had formerly occupied space in the college president's house, but Master Chauncy had a large household and was very glad to have it removed to the Indian College hall.

I was curious to see where Caleb and Joel would be housed, should they matriculate. It was a good building—showing every penny of the four hundred pounds young Dudley said it had cost—although the brick walls held the cold air inside them and some parts of it remained unfinished. As we passed by the chambers and studies, I saw that some of the interior walls were bare, not yet plastered, and several windows were oilpapered and unglazed.

We climbed the central staircase, and Samuel Corlett showed us into his own study, which was a large room with a diamond-paned window looking back across the yard towards the northern end of the dilapidated college hall he had recently vacated. "I could not have received you with any degree of comfort, over yonder," he said. "Of course, I must not get too settled in this place." His father smiled. "Indeed you should not. You will be ousted soon enough by my brace of likely young prophets, Caleb and Joel. When they matriculate, you will be obliged to give up these rooms to whomever Chauncy selects as their tutor."

"And then I shall have to wedge myself back into the cabinets that pass for chambers at the old hall," his son replied. "But I shall welcome the privation, if it advances the cause for which this building was made."

There was a good fire in the study grate and I was glad to give up my cloak and mittens. There were two large bookshelves, full, with several more volumes piled in small stacks upon the floor.

There was also a cabinet of curiosities which drew my eye, filled as it was by skeletons of diverse small creatures and jars of organs in preservative. Samuel Corlett saw my eyes upon these things. "These do not disgust you, I hope?"

"By no means," I said. "I am much interested in the natural sciences, although I have never been able to study them in a formal way. Forgive me for asking so directly, but I understood you were taking a higher degree in theology, not physiology?"

He smiled. "You understand correctly. But sometimes, I allow myself to be distracted. Reading is the mind's good provender, but one wishes, at times, to engage the hands, with the mind, in learning. A botanic garden, a mechanical workshop, an anatomy laboratory such as they have, in the universities of Europe—one day, perhaps, Harvard too might boast of such things. I would study physiology and theology both, were it in my power."

"Like the pawaaws . . ." The words were out before I could snatch them back.

Samuel laughed. "You are too long out upon your island amidst the salvages, if you think those warlocks know aught worthwhile of physic. Even so, I think they are wise who say that the soul has its part to play in the health of the body."

His rebuke was made in the most amiable manner; still, I felt I had stepped into a mire, and did not wish to plod further on such uncertain footing. In some areas I might not show myself to advantage. I changed the subject as naturally as I could, shifting my gaze to the bookshelves and remarking upon the great number of volumes. His face became animated. "It is my personal library—my one extravagance." He had seemed pleasant enough, but as soon as I showed an interest in his books, he came fully alive, taking down his pet volumes, expounding on when he had first read them, or where he had acquired them. "Do you admire poetry, Mistress Mayfield? Then you may like to see this—by our colony's first poet—the sister of one of my father's pupils." He thrust a slim volume into my hands. It was "The Tenth Muse," by Anne Bradstreet. I exclaimed, and said how much I admired her.

"How came her work in your way, out there upon your island?"

"You may well ask," I said, smiling. "The merchants who ply the channel are not apt to include poetry in their cargoes of necessities. Though I think one might soon come to deem it a necessity, who has the good fortune to be able to read it often."

I had been looking down at the book in my hands, and when I glanced up I was startled by the transformation in his face. His expression had softened, yet his gaze seemed more intense. "In any case, I came upon her poems by merest chance. Someone had used a page of a broadside to wrap a bottle. It was my habit, always, to look over any such scrap that might come our way—news, as you can imagine, is scarce and valuable to us—and this one rewarded me most richly. One of Mistress Bradstreet's poems, upon the late Queen Elizabeth, was printed there. You cannot know, Mister Corlett, how it thrilled me to learn that a woman might write and publish poetry, and such poetry! And such a woman—a faithful, blameless daughter, an esteemed wife and mother. My own dear mother shared my admiration for the work, when I showed it her, and she petitioned my father to seek out others of her poems for me." I closed my eyes, and words I had committed to memory came easily:

"Now say, have women worth? Or have they none?

"Or had they some, but with our Queen, is't gone?

"Let such as say our sex is void of reason,

"Know 'tis a slander now but once was treason."

That line always brought a smile to my lips, and when I opened my eyes, both the Corletts were staring at me. I colored slightly. But then Samuel smiled too. His teeth were as crooked as his nose, but the effect was not unpleasant, for his eyes came alight in their deep recesses. "That has always been among the poems of hers that I most admire," he said. "She is courageous, is she not? She goes right to the heart of it: A woman as exemplar for men." He held out his hand for the book, and came easily upon the page he sought. "Here, she has it—Elizabeth is a 'pattern of kings.'" A rare inversion of our present, lived reality. But one I think you would favor?"

He had a serious look now, and I did not want to give the wrong answer. I felt like one of the scholars he tutored, and I found the notion agreeable. How would it be, to have a husband who strove to elicit one's ideas, with whom one could, over months and years of companionship, hone and refine them? Such a life would be something, indeed. I thought of Caleb's reference, on the beach—it seemed an age since—to Prometheus, stealing fire. So might I steal learning, with such a husband. I thought of the alternative: arranging my face into an expression of interest while my spouse expounded on the conditions of pasture or the virtues of an undershot millstone, the struggle to access a book—any book—and the loneliness of longing to explore its weighty ideas and having no one with whom to share them.

"I do not ask for an inversion, Master Corlett. But perhaps the very volume in my hands bears witness to the fact that women might sometimes be fit to stand beside men, and not always and in every case behind them."

The elder Corlett raised his eyebrows at that, but his son nodded, considering. "Well put, though a body may only have one head, is that not so?"

"True. But if you speak of marriage and the management of a household—" and here I felt the color rise again—"perhaps two heads offer twice the wit when dealing with the challenges of raising and sustaining a godly family."

He laughed at that. "Your own wit makes the case most clearly, Mistress Mayfield."

Wanting to get onto safer ground, I turned the subject then, to the college and Samuel's role as fellow. He explained the course of study, speaking warmly of the scholars he tutored. "Master Chauncy of course gives all the lectures. My role is to discourse with my scholars and examine their understanding of what has been taught them." A tutor was assigned to a freshman class, and rose with them. Master Corlett's class were junior sophisters, who would enter their senior year in leaf fall. It was a class of some distinction, having in its number three of President Chauncy's boys—a pair of twins and an elder brother, all having matriculated together. There was also John Bellingham, the governor's son, a Weld from the Roxbury schoolmaster's family and several ministers' boys. But Samuel Corlett spoke most warmly of two others in his charge. One, young John Parker, was the son of a butcher, and had paid his tuition in sides of beeve and flitches of bacon. "He may not have been born a 'son of the prophets,' as the lads here like to style themselves," Corlett said, "but he has made a prodigious effort at learning." The other was John Whiting, a dreamy youth "so abstracted from temporal concerns" that he had oft times arrived for lectures with his shoes upon the wrong feet.

And in such discourse so we passed a pleasant hour. As we rose to leave, the father proceeded a little ahead of me, while the son helped me with my cloak.

"You will like, I am sure, to visit the college library—John Harvard's books, you know, form the spine of the collection, but there have been many interesting additions since his most generous bequest. I am sure President Chauncy would not object to me showing it you, at a convenient time."

I said, of course, that I would like that above all things, any time that I might be spared from my duties. As soon as those words were out I regretted them. I did not wish to remind Samuel Corlett that I was a lowly indentured servant. He seemed to sense my discomfort. As he passed me my mittens, he took my hand between his own.

"What an odd course fate charts for us, does it not? Bereavement is the unwelcome current that forced you to an unintended harbor. But here, perhaps, the vessel lies that will carry you onward to the place where you were always meant to go."

I had been looking up into his black eyes, but now I looked away. This stilted little speech had a stale air about it, as if he had fashioned it in advance of our meeting. He was moving swiftly. Too swiftly, perhaps. Could any man know his mind, as this man seemed to imply that he did, on so slight an acquaintance?

On the short walk home, and then, as I set out the supper things, I pondered this, and tried to sort my own feelings: intense pleasure in the conversation, an undeniable attraction of mind, an unfamiliar sense of being admired in a very particular way. Makepeace had liked to claim that Noah Merry mooned over me, and certainly he had sought me out and seemed pleased to be in my company. But I had never felt anything from him quite like the sense of decided attention that had emanated from Samuel Corlett. There was an entirely different quality to their regard. Noah Merry was like a pup, full of zest, ready to lick a friendly hand. Samuel Corlett was more like a wise old collie, head on paws, eyes following his one master's every move.

Like that collie, he proved set on his task. The next morning, when the boys were bent-headed over their slates in the schoolroom, there was the lightest of taps on the kitchen door. I lifted the latch, and there he stood, dark and tall, the scholar's gown falling from his shoulders like the cloak of the Black Knight in the old tale. His arms were laden with boughs of apple blossom. He lifted a branch, high over my head, and shook it, so that the petals showered me, releasing a heady scent that promised spring. As I laughed with pleasure, he thrust the boughs into my arms, and then, from the folds of his gown he drew forth the Bradstreet volume. "'Tis for you," he said. "Mistress Bradstreet belongs with you—a kindred spirit among her own sex."

"But I cannot—it is too much. . . ."

He raised a hand to hush me. He was already stepping back from the door. He smiled—that crooked, crinkled smile. "It is not entirely generous, my gift to you. I entertain the hope that the book might, soon enough, find its way back under my roof." And then he turned on his heel and strode in long swift steps towards the college.

I closed the door and leaned against it. Anne sat with her back to me, eyes down, feigning great interest in Tully. But as I came around the table to place the blossoms in the trough, I saw that she was struggling to suppress a smile.

She must have said something to Caleb—she spent a good deal of time with him, and with Joel. The master, unwilling to have her in the general classes, sanctioned the three of them to meet in a small seminar to practice disputations. All day, I noticed Caleb's eyes upon me, his expression questioning. I longed to speak with him. He was the one person to whom I might unfold the turmoil of my heart and expect in return some sound counsel. This did not seem possible, however, as there was no one moment of the day when we found ourselves alone. But then I heard him begging permission from the master that the three be allowed to hold their seminar out of doors, the weather being fair. He made the case that all could do with air and exercise, and could quite well dispute together as they walked. When the master assented, Caleb turned, as if in afterthought, and asked if I might be pressed to go too, by way of chaperone for Anne.

"Yes, quite. That would be proper—" he looked at me. "If you, Bethia, will not mind giving up some time to it?"

And so we set out. As soon as we turned off Crooked Street, Joel and Anne increased their pace, as if by arrangement, so that Caleb and I could fall just far enough behind to have private speech. Caleb, as ever, was direct. "Anne says you have a suitor. She said he as good as proposed marriage to you this morning."

I turned my face to him. "It is true. I believe he will ask me, formally, at the first opportunity. I don't know how I should answer him."

"Marriage is a heavy choice for an English woman."

"Why do you fashion it thus? Surely for any woman?"

"Not so, for ours. A squa does not cease to be a person, in our law, just because she has got herself a husband. In most cases, he will go to live with her family, not she with his, so her daily state changes little. And if, at some later time, she wants to leave him and be married to another one, then that can be settled through parley."

"Perhaps so," I said, bridling a little. "But neither will the husband I choose take a second wife, or third, as I have heard tell happens among your heathen kin."

He tossed his head and shrugged at that, and we walked on a little way. Then he asked me: "What does your heart say, about this son of Corlett's?"

"It seems to say yes. But I cannot tell if it truly is yes to Samuel Corlett or no to a fate forced on me by others. Caleb, I have not had a vast experience in choosing for myself. Yes, I did choose to come here, but that was an act of duty, and I thought that God's will was clear in it. It seemed the godly thing. This marriage . . . it is not so clear what God wants of me in it."

"It is—what did we just now learn that the Greeks say of it? Hubris?—to think we can know God's will. The better question— the one question, in this matter—is, what do you, Bethia, want?"

No one had ever asked me that before. What did I want? I wanted my old life, before all of its losses. I wanted mother, to guide me through this time as only a loving mother can guide a daughter in such things. I wanted to be Storm Eyes again, leaving dutiful Bethia carelessly behind me, shrugging her off, like a cloak left crumpled on the sand.

What I truly wanted—Zuriel at my side, Solace in my arms—I could not have. But I did not share these thoughts with Caleb.

Instead, I opened my heart to him, in rambling fragments, on the choice that now seemed set before me. My thoughts were all confusion, unformed shards. These Caleb drew from me piecemeal, prompting, with a question here and an observation there. When it was all of it out, he reordered and said my own thoughts back to me with greater clarity, the very way the master guided the pupils to muster their arguments in a disputation. Only then could I fashion it thus:

The choice before me, it seemed, was a marriage to Noah Merry or to Samuel Corlett. With one came the island: its beauties, all of its abundance. I would live a plain life in a place where every step I took was sweet to me. Unless the years worked unwonted changes upon him, I would have in Merry a husband of easy temper, pleasant manner. It would be a life free from want: fine house, rich farm, prosperous mill. I could be useful there—that woman of valor from *eshet chayil*—useful to my household, useful also, perhaps, to the Takemmy people. In time, I might start a dame school for their children, even introduce the gospel, if the sonquem allowed it. The choice of Merry would be smiled upon by grandfather, and would not cause a rupture with Makepeace. This latter consideration was—I learned, somewhat to my surprise as I set it forth—not nothing to me, even after the way he had ill used me.

If, on the other hand, I chose Samuel Corlett, I would be obliged to follow him and settle wheresoever his work took him, even if that were back across the seas to some England college or to a university in an outlandish foreign place such as Padua, where Harvard's graduates had found their way from time to time. Most likely, it would be a life by the unlovely fens in the tight-pressed town of

Cambridge, under the heel of the Massachusetts Bay Colony, part of a communion more harsh and zealous than the one in which I had been raised. To feed a family on a scholar's scant pay would mean a life of thrift and want. But I would be married to a man whose mind I could admire. I would live among books and thinkers and conversations that engaged me, with every day the gift of learning some new thing. In such a life, I might be of some use to the young scholars—a female presence for boys like Caleb and Joel, torn away from family and familiars. I would be able to stay beside Caleb, to help him through what surely would be hardships in the college years to come. Perhaps, in time, I might even interest Samuel in tutoring the Indians—to help to build up the reputation of the Indian College would be a worthy achievement, sending forth, year by year, our newly minted prophets into the wilderness. Instead of helping one small Indian settlement, in such a way I might help many. Or perhaps Samuel himself might take a pulpit among the Indians—perhaps he might—there was no harm in dreaming, after all—agree to further my father's work, back on the island. And while to choose him might at first seem less dutiful, more headstrong, I felt sure that grandfather would see the merits of the match, and in time bring Makepeace to accept it.

When Caleb had helped me to marshal my thoughts as I have now set them down here, he turned to me. "You say this and so, this and so, all of the points important, in their way. But you say a great deal more of the life you will have and little of the man you will have it with. One important point you have not disclosed to me. I do not ask you to speak it, but only to ask it of yourself: Which man quickens your blood?"

I gave him no answer, but even as he posed the question, the truth of the matter fell into my heart. The flush crept up my neck and prickled my scalp. There are some questions that can be answered, and some that cannot. And some questions that should never be asked, even of one's self.

I reached up and fumbled with my cap, pulling the fold forward to hide my scarlet face. Then I increased my pace so as to catch up with Anne and Joel.

And now, I sit here, at the deal table, as Anne tosses in her sleep. The house creaks and shifts. A floorboard complains as a boy rises, in the attic, to make his water in a chamber pot. Outside, a tomcat howls. The master told me this evening that Samuel Corlett intends to call upon me tomorrow, and that I should be prepared to receive him alone.

The candle end gutters. I reach out a hand, and touch a finger to the puddle of wax. It hardens on my fingertip and I peel it off, looking at the whorls impressed there. They say that each person's finger bears a unique pattern upon it, although how they can say such a thing, without having made an impression of every person's finger, I know not. The sorcerers and consorts of the devil say further that they can read one's fate in the marks upon a hand. Truly, tonight, I wish it were so. I would know my fate.

Bethia Merry. Bethia Corlett. I, Bethia Mayfield, must make this choice. Probably the last choice that will ever be entirely my own. The wick dips into the clear molten wax and the flame falters.

I will have to make the decision in the dark.

XVI

To say I did not sleep that night would be a falsehood. I slept well. I was so tired that season, not the most severe mental disquiet could keep me wakeful.

In the morning, I gazed at my face in the trough and wondered that I had been kept up even as long as I had by such speculations. That any man would want to marry me, such a haggard, hollow-eyed drab as I had become, strained all reason. I did, I confess it, take more than usual pains about my person that morning, pinning on a fresh cap and collar and doing what I could to trim and clean my ragged nails.

As expected, Samuel Corlett presented himself while his scholars were attending President Chauncy's morning lecture. He had, he said, secured permission from the president to show me John Harvard's library, if I should care to see it, while the students were occupied in the great hall.

He helped me into my cloak and we walked the short distance to the old college, which I had never yet entered. It was, as I have set down, a most handsome building in its design, if not in its state of repair. We entered a wide oaken door in the central of its three bays. In front of us, a broad stair ascended, and Samuel indicated that we should go up, for the library was housed upon the second floor, towards the rear of the building. To reach it, we had to pass by the scholars' chambers. He pushed open the door to show me one. It was a large room, with four beds and truckles under. Light poured in through the diamond-paned casements, and little cabinets that served as private studies gave off each angle of the room. "The boys are eight to a chamber," he explained. "We try to place a senior sophister or a tutor in each room, to keep the younger ones in order." He gave a smile. "Not that we always succeed to do so, as you'll see, in here." He ushered me then into a second, long chamber that sat above the great hall below. "This is the freshman dormitory." A glazier was at work replacing some shattered panes. "Good morning to you, cousin Ephriam," Samuel called.

"Good morning to you, cousin. It's always a good morn, for me, when your lads are unruly!"

"My cousin, Goodman Cutter, gets much work from this college, I regret to say. The boys *will* take out their high spirits on the glazing, for all that they know it will cost them stripes when they are caught at it. Sons of the prophets indeed!" He shook his head as he closed the door.

"But how can you be sure," I said, playfully, "that the sons of Amos and Elijah were above high-spirited frolics of such a kind? Not every boy in the Bible is of spotless character, after all. Look at Cain, or the brothers of Joseph. . . . What is a broken window or two, in comparison?"

"Well said," he answered. "They are boys, after all, before they are scholars. And some of them do come here very young. Aside from skating the ponds in winter I fear they get little activity for their bodies. It is always the mind we exercise. They are too cloistered and confined to suit their natures, spending such a vast amount of every day bent over their books. And speaking of books . . ."

He pushed open another door—heavy, oaken—to reveal the library. It was the most beautiful room I had ever seen. There was a row of lecterns, their polished wood gleaming dully in the good light. Each held a shelf, snug with volumes. There were half-lecterns on each endwall, these, too, filled to brimming with books. I had never in my life seen that number of books all together. "They have fashioned it after the libraries of Cambridge's colleges, from whence our two presidents have come. As I told you, John Harvard's original bequest accounts for some four hundred of the books you see here," he said. "There are now twice or three times that number." His sentences came out all in a tumble. He seemed suddenly all on edge, filling the air with this rush of words and facts that were clearly far from the thoughts at the forefront of his mind. I commented as aptly as I could, though my thoughts too were elsewhere.

"John Harvard must be pleased," I said, "could he know how his gift is now enlarged." The air in the room had a pleasant biscuit tang, like a hard-baked crust just drawn from the oven. I ran a hand along the tooled leather spines. Cicero, Isocrates, Virgil, Ovid. Luther, Aquinas, Bacon, Calvin. Just to have the liberty of such a room would be an education in itself. "The scholars must happily spend their hours here," I said.

"Oh, we do not generally open the library to *them*. They are expected to purchase those books required for their course of study. These are for the use of the fellows, such as myself—for those, like me, in pursuit of the higher degrees. The collection is rich, as you see, in the works of theology and philosophy, poorer in books on medicine, and on the law. President Dunster had no success in obtaining money for such, our benefactors being most interested in minting divines. I do not think that President Chauncy will fare any better. Yet I believe strongly these studies should be counted among the professions, and taught with greater rigor here."

"Whatever deficiencies you might see, to me it seems that one could profitably spend a lifetime here. I feel sorry the younger scholars are restricted, as you say. Why must they wait four years to access these treasures?"

He shrugged his shoulders and gave no answer. He seemed suddenly to have tired of playing the role of guide and interlocutor. He had walked to the window and was looking out, as though something below in the college yard required his full attention. A silence lengthened in the room. To cover my awkwardness, I drew out a fine edition of Plutarch. Sounds drifted up from the stairwell: someone was banging insistently upon the college door. But here, in the library, only the flutter of turning pages broke the hush.

He stood with his back to me. His hands, clasped behind his back, gripped and released each other. I set the book down on the lectern. It was a heavy volume and it landed with a dull thud. He did not turn.

"I think you must have formed some idea," he said at last, "of the great regard in which I hold you."

So we came to it. I took a deep breath. The silence in the room lengthened. Since he said nothing, I was obliged to.

"I am not sure . . . ," I began, but my voice broke. I coughed a little, to clear my throat, and tried again. "That is, while I welcome your good opinion, I do not see how it is I that I have earned it. Until this past sennight, the only one time you had heard my voice was in meeting, execrating myself."

He turned then, a slight smile playing on his lips. "But you did it with such eloquence. Who could be unmoved?"

"I do not think your minister would be glad to know of it. Confession as a rite of courtship. No, I do not think that would gratify him at all."

"I do not give a fig about my minister! It is you, Bethia, that I seek to gratify. Can I do that? Will you have me?"

Prepared as I was, this was too quick. I sat down upon the lectern bench and struggled for composure.

"I know this is abrupt. I would not have rushed this courtship in such a way if necessity did not compel it. And I must tell you, in all fairness, that I have nothing in my hands to offer you. My salary is a beggarly twelve pounds a year, and I have managed to put nothing by. My father is a poor man. The school is all he has, and he barely ekes a living from it, as you know better than most. You met, just now, the glazier, son to the brother of my late mother. So you see with what humble stock I ask you to connect."

He was pacing now, restlessly, up and down between the rows of books. The room was very quiet, except for the squeak of his boots. But from downstairs, I caught the sound of voices, raised. "I must tell you one thing further," Samuel said. "Even were you to agree to make me the most fortunate of men, we could not marry at once. I offer an engagement only, since if any tutor shall enter into the marriage state his place at the college shall be ipso facto void. I must serve my charges, the boys over whom I have had supervision these last three years, until they complete their senior year. At that time, I will take my master's degree. After, I would go to Padua, if I could, for the study of medicine, but I cannot yet see how I will be in purse to do it. Likely, I will hope for the offer of a schoolroom, if not yet a pulpit."

He knelt down then, so that his eyes were level with mine as I sat on the bench. He reached for my hand. "Will you take me, Bethia, on such terms as these?"

While he spoke, the blood hammered in my temples. As I struggled to form an answer, the voices drifting up from the hall below us grew louder. Then there was a great tattoo of boots, pounding up the stairs. The latch rattled, the door opened. Samuel Corlett dropped my hand and jumped to his feet. A scholar, ruddy and gasping, almost fell into the room. Caleb stood behind him, his face, generally schooled to an inscrutable stillness, twisted up by uncontained emotion.

"Excuse me, tutor," the boy stuttered, "but this lad here burst in, demanding . . ."

Caleb extended an arm and firmly pushed the stammering scholar out of his way and addressed Samuel. "Your father sent me to fetch you." He looked then at me. "Both of you. The matter is pressing. Will you come?"

We hurried behind him, out of the library and down the stairs. Caleb's long stride meant he was soon ahead of us, so I gathered up my skirt and ran, not caring what Samuel thought of it. We entered through the kitchen door. There was blood, a glossy pool of it, upon the floor. A dark trail led away from the kitchen, into the hall. The master's voice, high, cracking with emotion, called out to us from his chamber. "Son? Bethia? Are you come? In here, quickly."

I could see a blur of faces in the schoolroom, every eye trained on the closed door to the master's chamber. Samuel opened the door and pushed me in ahead of him, pulling the door shut behind. I glanced back as the door closed and saw Caleb. For the first time since I had known him, I saw tears pooling in his eyes.

Anne was upon the bed, writhing, her face, sweat-misted and clenched in pain. Her skirt was blood soaked.

"Have you sent for the midwife?" I demanded.

"Midwife?"

"Yes. Midwife. The girl is plainly miscarrying."

"But she . . . that would . . ."

"Master Corlett, send a boy to fetch the midwife, before this child bleeds . . ." I was about to say "to death" but I bit back the words, seeing the fear in Anne's face. I knew the scene before me. I had witnessed it through terrified girlish eyes: mother, crying out, grasping at the table for support, staggering to her pallet, trailing blood. The arrival of Goody Branch, the low groans and muffled voices and the carrying away of a bloodied bundle. It was long ago, that afternoon, when mother lost an unformed womb-infant that was never mourned nor even mentioned in our prayers. But I had not forgot one detail of it: what was said and what was done.

"Get another boy to the apothecary's for some ergot, in case the midwife has none on hand. . . . Bring me some linens, bring some warmed water from the kettle upon the fire and some cool water in a basin, and, if you please, leave me to tend the girl. . . ."

I was aware of figures moving behind me, and of murmured commands in the hall. I stripped off Anne's sodden skirt and her undergarments, and elevated her legs with a bolster. When the linens and basins of water arrived, I wadded cloths into a pad to stanch the hemorrhage as best I could, then I held Anne's hand as another spasm wracked her. I made a cool compress for her forehead, and bathed her blood-streaked thighs with the warm water. Then I prayed.

XVII

By the time the boy located the midwife and fetched her back, the worst of the spasms had passed. I wrapped up the expelled contents of Anne's womb as she lay, limp and panting. Her dark complexion had turned pale as plaster. The midwife, whose name was Goody Marsden, was a thin, wiry woman, quite elderly. Her manner was terse, unlike kindly Goody Branch. As she drew off her gloves, I noted that her fingernails were unclean. I proffered her a basin of warm water, of which she barely made use. She made no spare of Anne, but examined her untenderly, without speaking a kindly word. When the girl cried out, in pain from the prodding of her claw-like hands, she barked a harsh, "Be silent. You have caused quite enough unseemly clamor."

Then she turned to me, asking if I could assize how much blood had been lost. I told her it looked to be a woundy amount. "She will need broth—a good strong one, be sure to prepare it so—and some watered wine, and rest. She has not sustained any lasting hurt." I let out a sigh of relief at that, and she looked at me sharply and added, tight-lipped: "To her body."

I was about to go to the kitchen to see what I could fetch when she laid a bony hand on my arm and tilted her head towards the bundle in the corner. I picked it up and turned, so that my back was to the bed and Anne could not see. Goody Marsden opened the towel and examined the bloody, waxy contents for a few moments, then threw the cover back over. "Burn it," she said. She peered at me, her eyes a pair of hard, shiny brown pebbles. "Do you so. Directly. That is for the best."

By late afternoon, I repented that I had followed her instructions so swiftly. For by then the whispers were already rife, and the evidence that might have silenced them nought but smoke and cold ashes. Words like "wild fornicators" and "lustful heathen" passed from mouth to ear until the muttering grew to a babble and any faint hope that the matter might be kept in hidels and smothered up was gone and done with.

When it came to my ears that Caleb and Joel were severally suspected of performing this corruption upon the girl, I went straight to the master and gave him the ground of what I knew to be true. The interview on this indelicate matter was the most awkward exchange I had yet had in my life, all the more so since Samuel Corlett was there at his father's side. It took place in the schoolroom, since Anne still occupied the master's bed. The master had asked Makepeace, who was still in residence at the school, to take the boys to the meeting house and supervise them at their books there while I had dealt with the bloody linens and bedclothes as best I could.

I sat upon the bench, fidgeting under their gaze like an errant schoolboy. I stared at the hands in my lap, wrinkled up from the effort at the wash trough, as I spoke my piece.

"You are sure of it?" Master Corlett said. I felt his eyes, and his son's, regarding me gravely. "I know these boys are dear to you. You would protect them, to shield your father's legacy as their patron and first preceptor, perhaps . . ."

I cut him off, perhaps uncivilly, but there was a great deal at stake.

"Master, the state of what came from that girl allows of no doubt. She was with child when she came here. I am certain of it." Yet I thought of the willowy waist, swaying as she walked away from me down the path that first morning. Others too might remember that, and wonder. If she had thickened a little around the middle since, I had thought only that she was taking more nourishment, being easier in her mind. Yet the shapeling I had consigned to the fire that afternoon had been larger than the size of my fist, and fully formed. I had spent enough hours with Goody Branch to know that a womb-infant did not come into so humanlike a form unless it had been got at the least four, or even five months earlier.

"There is no way Caleb or Joel—or any other male person at this school"—and I said this last plain and slow, so that he would understand that the shadow of suspicion might fall not upon the two Indian youths only—"could possibly have committed this debauchery. Furthermore, master, we cannot lay it upon her English foster father, nor upon the police or militia or whosoever it was who held her incarcerated several months ago. It is my belief—no, certainty—that the girl was defiled somewhen between a month or two months before she arrived here, while she was in attendance at the dame school."

"But that cannot be. She was biding then with the governor—in his own household. . . ."

"Exactly so."

"Bethia, have a care what you do." It was Samuel who spoke. "This is a grave charge."

"Do you think I do not know it? I do not say this lightly, but say it I must. Even though her state was not yet patent, she was bastard-bellied when she came here. Do you not see that your father's reputation—and his school's—also are at stake in this, if it comes to be falsely believed that the sin took place under this roof?"

"Well," said Master Corlett querulously, "no one would blame me if the lusts of wanton young salvages proved too much for my powers of oversight."

I leapt to my feet. "Master Corlett!"

The wrath and disgust I felt must have showed in my face, for he recoiled. His son put out a hand and laid it protectively upon his father's shoulder. He regarded me coldly, not liking that I had addressed his father, my master, in such a way. The black eyes glinted.

"Will Goody Marsden second this opinion?" he asked. "It must be hoped she will, since you are no midwife, nor even yet a . . ." He colored, and left off.

"As she saw what I saw, I do not see how she could do otherwise," I said.

"What of the girl? Surely her testimony counts in this matter more than any other evidence. What says she of who harlotized her?"

"I do not know. I have not spoken to her. I thought it better to let her have her rest, rather than trouble her in her grief with such a distressful subject."

"If it is as you say, she will not own it." Samuel's voice was as cold as his eyes.

"Why think you so?"

"You say she is intelligent. Well then. She will know better than to lay scandal upon such a powerful doorstep."

His judgment proved correct. Anne would not name the man who had forwhored her, to me or to any other person, even when the master, his hands a-tremble and his head shaking, told her that if she did not do so, the matter surely would come to the attention of the General Court, and that as soon as she could stand upright she would be called there to be pressed by those hard men. "Be sure, they will have the truth, even if they find it necessary to whip it out of you. They will not scruple, if your obstinacy drives them to do it. They will lay you open to the bone." At this, she simply turned her head into the pillow and sobbed so hard that the bed shook.

Samuel Corlett returned to his duties at the college while I was yet with Anne, trying in vain to comfort the fit brought upon her by the master's ill-judged threats. Instead of taking the broth she had such need of, she had puked up the better part of what I had already given her. I was therefore in no mood to see Samuel and I was relieved that we had had no opportunity to resume our interrupted conference. Still, I was struck that he left without giving me so much as a good night.

When finally I managed to pacify the distraught girl, I went to the kitchen to warm over the broth, which had gone quite cold. I was ladling some into her bowl when Caleb and Joel entered the room. Caleb laid a hand upon my arm.

"You know what they are saying?" he whispered. His face was haggard.

I nodded. "I told them it is not possible, this scandalous charge."

"But the midwife and yourself are the only ones who can speak to it. She—" and he tilted his head in the direction of the master's room, his face suddenly softened by a tender concern "—will not give it out."

"Perhaps she would, to you, if you counseled her so."

Caleb turned to Joel.

"How can I counsel her on this matter?" Joel whispered.

Their expressions told me then more than I had guessed as to how things stood between them. I felt a pang of envy at this, which shamed me. Why should they not feel a bond of affection with this poor girl? I looked away, attending to the soup kettle. It suddenly seemed indelicate to look into their faces, when they revealed so much.

"They will give her no peace." It was Caleb who spoke.

"I know it."

"We cannot allow it, Bethia."

"But what power have we in this?"

"We have to get her from here. If we could bring her to the island, she could disappear among our people and be safe from their questions and their scorn and their brutishness." His voice was rising. I turned to him then, and put a finger to my lips, to remind him where we were.

The island had always been a place of refuge for Wampanoag in flight from trouble on the mainland. Indeed, my own grandfather had brought his English followers there seeking sanctuary of a sort. The heat of the broth had made its way through the bowl I held, and brought my mind back to the chore at hand.

"I have to bring this to her now. If she does not take some nourishment she will not live to need our rescue. Let me think. We can do nothing this night. We will try to talk more on this matter come the morrow."

XVIII

But come morning, the school was still on end, roiling like a smote anthill. Tempers were frayed and nerves raw on all sides. It had not helped when, in the small hours, Anne, crying out in night terrors, brought the whole place awake and astir all over again. It was as much as Master Corlett could do to marshal the boys to their books, and more than he could do to have them attend to them. They were rowdy and unsettled when a heavy knock upon the door further disturbed them. My heart flipped, thinking that it might be an officer of the court, come for Anne already. Instead, into all the upset suddenly stepped the person I least expected to encounter.

I was with Anne at the time—I had slept in the room with her, or tried to, at the least—the master consigning himself to my pallet in the kitchen. He sent a pupil to answer the knock.

When I heard the familiar voice, I could not credit it, so I stepped out into the hall. Noah Merry, wild curls caught back into a tidy queue, barn frock laid aside for sober town apparel, and standing a good head taller than when I had last seen him, was asking for the master. When our eyes met, we both of us colored. He made me a slight bow, but we did not speak, as the master came from the schoolroom then and the two of them retired to the kitchen, where they were shut up together in private conference for what seemed to me to be a long time. When they emerged, the master called for me and told me he had consented to spare me for an hour, after I served the boys' bever, so that I could walk with Noah Merry.

At first, I was dismayed at this. But as I served the boys, I had a moment to reflect. Better to give him, face-to-face, my grounds for refusing his suit, and not send them on a cold sheet of parchment carried to the island by Makepeace along with I knew not what slanders about my character.

We walked out, side by side, past the tight-pressed houses on their narrow lots. I stole glances at Merry, when I could. He wore his new height well, and although his looks were still softened by a boyish smoothness, a comely man had begun to show in a certain line of cheek and jaw. He seemed agitated as we made our way past the meeting house and turned north, along the narrow path that followed the meanders of the town creek. I burned to know if the master had said aught to him as to how things stood between myself and his son. In all the alarms of the recent hours, nothing had been resolved. Samuel Corlett's proposal still hung in the air, unanswered.

For a good while he gave me news such as any islander might speak of, and which, in the usual run of things, I should have been avid for, since it closely concerned those nearest to me. It seemed that challenges to grandfather's leadership were on the rise, led by the Aldens and their followers, who clamored for a say in the plantation's management and law making. They were ever on the lookout for excuses to stir up the settlement, the matter of drift whales being one rub, chousing in certain land sales another. Because grandfather, as magistrate, took the Indians' part when justice demanded it, the Aldens had used this in their agitation against his leadership. Merry reassured me that their cause as yet had attracted few followers. "Most remain content enough to leave your grandfather in charge of affairs. We do not share Giles Alden's appetite for sitting in meetings to dispose upon every rod of fence post or peck of corn."

But the talk was stilted, our minds severally running on the matter that stood at the bottom of our joint concern. We had reached to the burying field, which marked the northern edge of the settlement. Beyond were only cattle yards, giving way to marsh meadow and the tangled pine swamp that passed for forest. We turned, and were almost to the watch house, when Merry stopped in mid-sentence and dashed a hand across his forehead, which was sweating, even though the day was cool.

"I had to come here in person," he blurted. "My conscience would not allow me to do otherwise."

"Your conscience?" I asked, puzzled.

"Bethia—if I may address you so—as you well know, it was long our fathers' wish that we—that you and I—should one day marry, and you must know, or I think you must know—that for a long time it was my most ardent wish also. . . ."

"Noah, I—"

"Please. This is difficult. Let me say my piece. The short of it is, since you left the island, my affections have become engaged elsewhere. Father did not know of it, and I now see it was very wrong in me to keep my own counsel in this matter—I should have made a clean thing of it and told him from the beginning—but in the event, I did not do so, the lady in the case being even younger than yourself and not of an age for handfasting. And so when your grandfather of late came to father—well, father liked your brother's proposal, and he accepted it without consulting me, thinking I would be glad to have sooner what I had schooled myself to wait upon. You can imagine how low I felt myself when he told me. It was only then that I made plain to him that there was a bond of affection sprung up between myself and another and—oh, Bethia, I am sorry—but after you left, and even before, to be quite frank, I had allowed myself to entertain doubts, you see, that you returned my regard in any degree. I had never been sure if you had any particular attachment, or feelings, for me, except those of a friendly neighbor, and so when Tobia, I should say, the young daughter Talbot—"

"Tobia Talbot? But that is wonderful, Noah! I do wish you both the greatest joy." The Talbots had come to the island just a year before I quit the place and I did not know them well. But I had formed an impression of a cheerful and capable girl, a year my junior, with easy, open manners and a lovely singing voice, which rang out in meeting, but also might be heard in snatches as she went about her chores, if she thought herself alone.

He stopped in midstride and looked at me, his forehead creased. "So you are not . . . you do not . . . ?"

"Dear friend," I said. "I am not anything other than delighted for you, and I do nothing but wish you joy of each other."

His face, which had been pinched with strain, eased itself back into its familiar pleasant amiability. He swept his hat off his head, threw it up into the air and caught it, making me a cavalier's bow. "I cannot tell you what this means to me," he said. "I have lain awake, waiting for a ship to bring me here, dreading this day, and how I must, as I thought, cause you pain." He reached inside his jacket then, and produced a roll of parchment. "Now, at least, I can give you this as a gift outright, and not, as I had thought, in payment of an obligation."

"Obligation? You owe me no debt. . . ." He put the roll into my hands. I felt a ragged edge. My heart fluttered. I opened the roll, and my eyes confirmed what my hands had already told me. It was my document of indenture. Corlett's copy, and grandfather's, both.

"I—I don't understand. What does this mean?"

"It means you are free. We have bought you out. The master's only condition in releasing you was that you stay on at the school during preparation for the matriculation. After, you will be free to go, or stay, on whatever terms you agree between you."

I felt the old anger rising. "Did grandfather force you to this? Did he accuse you—falsely—of breach of promise? There was no ground—"

"Not at all. Be easy, I beg you. It was my own idea, and my father seconded it at once. It took a vast amount of persuasion before your grandfather acceded."

I stifled a snort of derision. Merry read my face. "No, I speak the truth. I was there, in the room. Your grandfather was at the first most unwilling for us to undertake this expense. But we made our argument, and he consented, on the condition that he will reimburse us when a certain venture of his matures. You know we are business partners, after all. His investment in our mill has allowed us to bespeak some ingenious new equipment that is to be manufactured for us in England." He went on then, into some detail about gears and flumes and things that I could not picture nor had any interest in. I was staring at the parchments in my hand. Suddenly, I was free. Free to come and go as I would. To choose Samuel Corlett or not choose him. Free to make no choice at all, for the moment. I suddenly felt so light that I thought I might lift off the ground and float away like the seeds of a blowball.

* * *

I entered Master Corlett's house still elated, but I was brought swiftly back to ground by the brooding silence of the place—an unnatural absence of sound in a house that usually wore out my nerves with its clangor. It was clear that the pupils were gone. My footfalls were loud in the hall. Hearing me come in, Master Corlett stepped out of the empty schoolroom. His face was gray. "I asked your brother to take the pupils out. Bethia, this matter of the girl has taken a grave turn. I have had conference with Goody Marsden. She does not support you as to the . . . to the . . ."

I did not leave him groping for a delicate word. I knew well enough what he meant. "What says she?"

"She says three months. She says it is a common thing, to miscarry at that time."

"So it is." I tried to speak calmly but my voice shook. "On that at least she is correct. But master, on the other, she is entirely wrong. I cannot think why she is saying this. A shapeling of three months is hard even to descry from among the clots with which it is expelled. . . . Master, this was no three-monthling. I held it. I burned it, as she bade me, but it was difficult, so humanlike—" My voice was quavering. I took a breath. "Master, it was a formed infant. He was a boy."

He sank down onto the boot bench in the hall. He looked old and spent as he buried his face in trembling hands.

"I will go and see her myself," I said. "I will know the basis for why she makes this untrue claim."

I turned and went back out into the street. I was angry and upset, and I strode on swiftly, eager to confront the woman. But on my way to Goody Marsden's rooms I slowed, and then stopped, as it dawned on me that my errand was quite futile. I thought of Goody Marsden's hard looks, her rough and dirty hands, the discourtesy, even cruelty, with which she had dealt with Anne. It came to me plainly that whatever lay at the bottom of her wrong opinion—failing eyesight, incompetence, malice—or even, perhaps, the corrupt influence of some powerful interest—she would not recant it. And my word would not count against hers. Not with anyone. It was unclear whether even the master put store in it. Better, then, to get Anne away, out of reach of lies and slander. I retraced my steps back to Crooked Street and made towards the nearest tavern. There were three in the town; Noah Merry had to have taken rooms in one of them.

I came first to the Blue Anchor, plucked up my courage and walked in, ignoring the stares of the low kinds of men and the dissolute youths taking the hot waters sold there. Luck was with me, for just as I was about to apply to the tavern keeper, Noah Merry came upon the stair, and seemed much struck to see me in such a place. I suppose he read the distress in my face, for he gave me an arm and led me into the street, and once again we walked.

Quickly, and with as much self-command as I could muster, I related the flagitious history to him. His kindly, open face closed in upon itself, and when he spoke, it was with a depth of anger I had not credited him capable. It came to me then that the very openness of his character and his frank, unstudied manner would feel revulsion at the kind of Janus-faced behavior Anne's plight evidenced. It clearly disgusted him, that those very ones who set themselves highest—those "living saints," as they styled themselves—were in fact but whited sepulchers, the stench of their true baseness deeply offensive to him. While he did not fashion it in those words, that was the import of his reaction, and when I begged for his help, he offered it readily.

"I think that there is no need to involve Iacoomis," he said, when I mentioned that my plan was to send the girl to him. "They would think of him, first, if suspicion arises that she has fled to the island, and if there is any appetite to pursue her there. There may very well not be. As you say, those most responsible in this might well be those who have it in their power to let the matter drop. In any case, do not write to Iacoomis regarding the girl. Better he not know her whereabouts, and then he cannot be pressed to tell them. Neither do I think Manitouwatootan is a good place for her. There are too many in that town who now have dealings with the English, and her presence would be remarked upon, perhaps, in some loose exchange."

I was struck by Merry's good sense and cool head as he continued. "Better, I think, to bring her home with me, and from thence to the Takemmy sonquem. His family will shelter her, I have no doubt of it, and the people of that otan have little contact with Great Harbor but through my family. We are on good terms, Bethia. It is as your father always wished it—we each of us profit fairly from the other. If they cede land to us, we are at pains to see that they get a fair return, in corn milled, or iron goods, or skills shared—whatsoever kind we can repay them."

"If only all the families dealt so," I said. But I had little interest, at that moment, in the broad matter of relations on the island. My mind was all on the Takemmy sonquem, and his large village in its handsome setting: the ponds, sparkling expanses of sky water catching every golden-red gleam of sunlight, and the clear, dancing rills and brooks that fed them. I could see Anne there, living the life she might have had, before disease robbed her of parents and clan. Then I thought of that young woman—not so many years older than Anne, whose fire-warmed wetu had sheltered us the night Caleb's father lay close to death. Anne was not that woman, and never could be. She could not peel off the life she had lived like a shed skin. She would bring her Englishness with her, for better and for worse. It was hard to see what use she would find, in such a life, for her extraordinary gifts. Instead of a life as scholar and then governess, she would be consigned to the lot of any squa—the backbreaking toil of the field and the common pot. Yet there surely was no better choice for her, or none that we had in hand to offer.

"But if we are to attempt this thing," Merry was saying, "we must do it soon. I have a shipment of goods due to sail when the tides and winds are fair. Will the maid be fit for such a journey within the next two or three days?"

"She will have to be," I said. "She is young, with the healing powers of the young. The chiefest enemy to her recovery is, I believe, the fear of what will follow it. There is little to promote a return to wellness when she knows that if she rises from her bed she will be hauled to court and bound up to a whipping post. But to leave all of that behind—well, I will be unsurprised if that prospect does not speed her to her feet."

When we reached to the schoolhouse, Merry offered his hand, and I took it with a high heart, knowing that I had a true friend there. He said I should look for him an hour before rush lighting the following day, or at first light the next. He would come with a cart;

he would not risk a barge where concealment of the girl would be impossible.

What neither of us had factored upon was Makepeace. Now, in the midst of our leave taking, he came walking towards us from the meeting house, the younger pupils, whom he had taken in charge, following behind him like a line of ducklings; Caleb, Joel and Dudley bringing up the rear. Merry then drew off Makepeace, to give him the ground of how things now stood regarding the matter of our supposed betrothal. I helped to shepherd the boys indoors and tried to keep them in order as I gave them bever.

Makepeace sought me out while they were still at board. He could not meet my eyes as he enquired, with as much delicacy as he possessed, whether Merry had given him a true account as to my feelings. I assured him that he had. "I had gathered," he said dryly, "from your behavior some weeks since, that your heart was untouched by Merry. But I wonder that you are not made a little aggrieved by the loss of material prospects. It is by no means certain that the offer of such another establishment will come your way."

"As to that," I said, "I am content to trust to the providence of God."

"Well said, I am sure. So, that's an end of it then. The whole thing has been most unfortunate, I must say." His face took on a blotchy hue. There was some strong emotion working there. He could barely meet my eye. It came to me then that he felt ashamed. "I am sure it is all for the best," he sputtered. "Those that marry where they affect not will affect where they marry not, and that is an occasion for sin, as all know. And I hope you will forgive me if I forgot that, for a time." He looked down, and picked at an invisible speck upon his cuff. "I miss father, you see. I am not the man he was. He would not have misjudged the matter so. He would not have spoken, or acted, as I did. I will strive—I will pray—to do better.... And I will see to it that Merry and grandfather are swiftly repaid the monies outlayed upon your—forgive me—I should say, upon my behalf."

I thought the interview concluded with that almost apology. But then Makepeace surprised me. "You will not mind, I trust, finishing out your month and a half with Master Corlett here alone? I should have liked you to have come away home with me directly. But it just came to me now that I might apply to Merry for a place on his sloop, rather than continue to wait here, week following week, for that tardy ship on which I have bespoke a passage."

At once I was alarmed for Anne. It would be impossible to transport her secretly with my brother in tow. "Does Noah Merry have room for you?" I said, trying to keep my voice level. "It is likely that the passenger list is already subscribed."

"I am sure I do not know why you should assume so." He looked at me oddly. "In any case, I go forthwith to ask him."

I misdirected him then, saying that Merry had planned to go directly to the town landing. In fact, I knew full well he was returned to the Blue Anchor. As soon as Makepeace had left, I went myself in search of him, once again braving the stares of the alehouse haunters.

"I can hardly prevent him from taking ship with me," Merry said. "But if he does so, we shall have to tell him about the girl. I see no other way," he said.

"It is not in his nature to flout authority. I doubt he has the temperament for this business. I foresee a great difficulty in it."

But there I was wrong. I had become so accustomed to look at my brother through the one, clouded lens of our own fraught relations that sometimes I could not see him as he truly was. When he returned from his fruitless walk to the landing, I screwed up my courage and drew him off for a private conference. I told him I had a grave favor to ask of him. He listened calmly to what I had to say, his brow cleaving itself into a deepening frown as I spoke. I had girded for any reaction—doubt, wrath, chastisement—any reaction other than the one I got.

"As I see it, this child has suffered quite enough at English hands," he said. "If what you say is true—and I do not question it, I know you made a study of these things with Goody Branch, though I must tell you at the time I thought it most ill judged, a girl of your age— but that is neither here nor there at the present. The fact is, this child has been used most infamously. As to what the midwife's motive might be, I cannot imagine, but it is clear that you will be exposed to grave censure if you voice an opposite opinion. And another matter, of which you do not seem to be sensible: the girl was with you, was she not, all night and most of every day? If you make the matter hot with your claims, they might claim in turn that you acted as her bawdress."

This had not even occurred to me. As repellant as it was, I could see how my brother might be right in this. It would be hard to imagine a way that the girl could have been forwhored while she was at Corlett's school without my being party to it.

Makepeace let that prospect play upon my mind for a moment, then said, "I know you better than to suppose you might let the matter drop?"

Since he had answered his own query, I gave no reply. He nodded to himself. "As I thought. And I do not ask you to do so. Do not conceive that I do so. This girl has suffered, at the very least, from a reprehensible degree of neglect at the hands of those who would now sit in judgment over her and try to compel her to give testimony. And at the worst—no, I cannot even give it voice—depravity in such a degree. Whosoever did this—a sinner of that stripe—will go to any length to hide his fault. If Merry has already consented to this scheme, then I will do nothing to sink it. Let us by all means deliver her to people who might be able to provide her a measure of protection. Even a band of salvages could hardly do worse than our own have done."

And thus, with Makepeace as the most unlikely of conspirators, the plan went forward. Anne, pale and weak, grasped my hand when I told her what was afoot. At first, the thought of a clandestine escape and a sea journey with my stern brother and a strange man only added to her terrors. But I spoke to her of the island that lay at the end of the journey: of the rainbow bluffs and the cool sweet brooks; the verdant woods and gentle, watery light. I told her of good people and ample providence and at the end of what I had to say the tears of longing for my home were upon my cheek, and her dulled eyes were lit again with a spark of hopefulness.

Her only grief was in parting from her friends, Joel and Caleb. I contrived a brief, secret leave taking, and since I had to remain in the room, for propriety's sake, I could not help but overhear what passed. It was clear that a definite bond of affection existed, though if there was some special understanding with one more than the other, I could not make it out. I heard them reassure her about the journey. The two of them also waxed fair about the island, and how it would gladden them to know she was safe there, where they promised faithfully that they would find her when their circumstances allowed.

Two days later, Makepeace took his leave of Master Corlett privily, and what words of thanks or regret passed between them I do not know. In the deepening dimmet, I walked out with my brother and kissed him, the hatred I had felt melted all away by the warmth of his concern for Anne. He climbed up to ride beside Merry. I raised my hand, and bade them a fond farewell. I put my whole heart into my good wishes for their safe and easy journey, knowing my words carried to that other passenger, hidden under a burlap in the cart.

XIX

"You might have consulted me." Samuel Corlett's countenance was severe. "You put my father in a most difficult position. The governor's protégée, a runaway . . ."

"I do not know that I have given you cause to think I was in any way involved in Anne's departure from this place. In any case, I hardly think the governor will like to consider her his protégée, still, given his signal failure to protect her."

"Have a care. That wit of yours mayn't always prove a blessing."

"So I have been reminded, all my life."

We were walking in the apple garth, where the fruits were beginning to swell on the boughs. Samuel gave a great sigh and turned to me. "All my life, I have waited, hoping to encounter someone like you. . . ." His face was at odds with his words, his expression haunted and joyless. An impish spirit seized me, and I decided to try to lighten his mood.

"What do the sages say? Be careful what it is you wish for, lest your wish be granted you."

He did not answer my smile, but only sighed again. "My mother was an excellent woman. Pious, virtuous. Kind. But she was not the intellectual equal of my father. Not by any means."

"It would have been strange if she had been," I said, "seeing that your father had the benefit of two degrees at Oxford and she was the unlettered daughter of a yeoman."

"I do not speak of book learning," he said. "I speak of a certain innate quality of mind, a superior understanding. Because she had it not, their companionship was—diminished. Father looked to his books, rather than to his wife. She tried, oh how hard she tried. . . ." His face clouded, as if at some particular memory. "It was pitiful, sometimes, to observe how she would struggle to form a remark to the purpose of some study that engaged him. You know him. You know he is not an unkind man. He has patience enough with these mewling schoolboys, because he sees their promise. But he never had that degree of patience with her. He would dismiss her attempts in a most painful and belittling way. I observed this, even as a lad, and even before I could have given the ground for it, I swore to myself that I should not make such a marriage. So I have reached the age that I must now own in a single state." He pulled a bough of apples down and stared at the beginning fruits, but l did not think he was seeing them.

"Bethia, when father first spoke of you, when you came to him, he was loud in praise of your understanding. He told me how he looked forward to converse with you each evening. At first I did not credit it. Knowing how he had been with my mother, leaving her to a lonely silence, night following night. He is become old, I thought, and fond. He would not be the first, in his dotage, to find pleasure in gazing at a fair young face. But I took note of you, thereafter. I admired what I saw. I felt regret, when father allowed me to know that you already had a suitor. Then, when father confided that you were minded to refuse that suit, I began to fan a hope. And of course, there was the trouble with your brother, and there you were, at meeting, in the sinner's box, standing under accusing eyes, confessing to weighty faults. And yet there was a luminance about you as you spoke. You admitted your sin, but even as you did, it was with such eloquence and dignity that those with ears to hear must know it was no true evil, what you did, but necessary and justified."

He fell silent. I said nothing. I had no such fond recollection of myself in that hour. Luminance, indeed. I had never in my life felt so extinguished.

We continued walking. His eyes regarded me, slantwise. "Three days ago, I asked you a question. We were interrupted before you could give me an answer."

"Quite a lot has happened, since."

"Exactly so."

"And I think it troubles you?"

"Indeed."

"May I ask in what—?"

He had cracked a switch from a low-hanging branch, and was picking the young leaves off one by one. He tossed it aside, turned suddenly and grasped my shoulders.

"It had not occurred to me that strong-minded also meant headstrong!" His voice was raised. I took a step back, detaching myself from his grip. Although the trees were in full leaf, I was not sure what might be seen from the college windows, and I had no wish to be the object of boyish gossip. Nor could I afford to be.

My wisk was creased where he had gripped it. I raised a hand and tried to smooth the marks upon the linen. He grabbed my wrist mid-gesture, to force my attention.

"Bethia, why must you involve yourself so intimately with the affairs of these salvages? What are those boys to you, that you take up such cudgels in defense of their reputation? You sat there in my father's schoolroom, and I saw that you were prepared, if necessary, to blacken the name of the highest in the colony in order to defend them. A defense, I might add, that would have put you at great risk. I see, dimly, how they might represent your father's work to you, which you would not have besmirched by the evidence of so great a moral lapse, and I begin to grasp an edge of it. But then I think of that girl—whom you have not known above three months. What can she possibly be to you, that you would abet her flight? Oh, do not trouble to deny it"—I had opened my mouth to protest—"She was in no state to affect such a thing without assistance and you are the only one person she trusted in the least degree. Nor do I think the act wrong in and of itself. She faced harsh treatment, which she likely did not deserve—"

"Likely?" I spat the word back at him and pulled my wrist away from his encircling fingers. I could contain myself no longer. "How say you so? That child did nothing to 'deserve' any of this. It is calumny to suggest...."

He threw up a hand and shook his head impatiently. "Hear me!" His voice was quite loud. I, unaccustomed to being addressed so, was briefly surprised into silence.

"You risk bringing down the ire of the General Court upon yourself, for obstructing the functions of justice." His complexion had darkened beyond its usual olive cast. He began to look like a Moor.

"You really think the General Court will be anything other than grateful that she is gone? You have an exalted view of their dedication...."

"And you have an exalted view of your own opinion!"

I considered for a moment before replying. I could see the blood beating in a vein at his temple. It had become engorged in a most uncomely fashion, and writhed there like a worm.

"You are right. I do. Since God has seen fit to take my parents from me, I see no one left above me whose views on my conduct matter more to me than my own."

"You see? That is the very—What sort of speech is that? No dutiful wife should utter such—"

"You forget yourself. You may have asked me to wife. I have not accepted you. And from what you now say, it seems that such a match would be most ill-advised. I think it best for all concerned if we wind the clock back and forget that the question was ever put."

I turned then, and made off quickly in the direction of the school.

"Bethia!" he called. I did not turn, but quickened my step. He was running after, and with one or two long strides drew close enough to reach out and lay a hand on me. His grip was hard, and this time I could not pull free. His ruffian's face was close to mine. I turned my head away from him. He reached out with his other hand and dragged off my cap and dug his fingers into my hair, pulling my head back so that I had to look up at him, right into the deep of those ink-black eyes. His voice, when he spoke, was low and urgent. "I love you," he said, and kissed me.

XX

I do not pretend to know what would have happened to me had I in fact been wrong in my predictions about the General Court. But in the event, I was not wrong. With the girl out of sight, so vanished the scandal. There had been no appetite on the part of the governor to investigate her whereabouts with any degree of vigor. I was not even questioned in the matter. If Master Corlett shared his son's conviction as to my role in Anne's departure, he elected not to raise the subject with me. He had never wished to have her under his roof, and all that had followed her coming had justified his view of the thing. Having her there in the midst of his male pupils had been as unsettling as a snake set loose in a stable. Master Corlett, more than anyone, seemed relieved that the matter was behind him. The whole sorry affair had been let fall like a plummet down a well shaft and forgotten, by all except those three of us who cared for her.

Caleb, particularly, pined after justice in the matter. "It beggars belief, that this goes unpunished," he said one evening, as he carried in bavins for me from the yard. "If she were an English maid, raped by an Indian, that man would have been swinging from the Common's gallows long since."

Since what he said was true, I did not attempt to contradict it.

"Caleb, you know well what the price of such justice would have been. I do not think Anne could have withstood that court and its cruelties. And had they flogged a name out of her, do you think

264

such a devil as would forwhore a child would thereafter scruple to traduce her? She would have stood there, tarred a liar. And even in the unlikely event his part in the act was somehow proven, he would cry off the charge of rapist and make her out a jade and a Delilah who seduced him. Truly, a man so pressed might say anything...."

"I would discover him, if I could...."

"Caleb, no. You must put it behind you. I do not say forget it. Who could forget so horrible a crime? But set it by, for now, and get you to your books. That is the best thing you can do for her. Distinguish yourself, and then, one day, you might take your place among those whose word shapes justice here."

He looked up at me as he bent to the hearth, stacking the wood. I could see him, entertaining some dim notion of such a future. But his face remained drawn, his looks entirely sorrowful.

"God knows who did this thing," I said. "Leave it now in his hands, and trust to him for justice."

"I will pray for it," he said. There was a dull, rote quality to his response. He stood up, and walked out into the garth. I saw him, standing there, gazing up at the waxing moon.

Two nights later, the moon was full. I turned on my pallet, stirred from sleep by a shadow passing over me in the dark.

"Caleb?" I whispered.

"Hush! Go back to sleep."

I sat up. The moon was so bright, I should have been able to make him out, but I could not descry his features. Then I knew why. He had taken a coal and blackened his face below the line of his cheekbones. He was wearing the master's long black gown.

"Caleb!"

"Quiet!" he hissed. "This is not your affair, Bethia." He passed through the door, silent and invisible, into the dark. Even if I had summoned the courage to follow him, I could not have done so. He had vanished entirely, as if conjured away.

I lay there, fretful, sweating with anxiety and oppressed by a sense of doom and helplessness. My first thought was that Anne had indeed confided the name to him and that he had set forth thinking to administer some rough justice, an exploit that likely would cost him his life. Then, as clouds scudded across the luminous disc, riding high now in an inky sky, the truth of the thing fell into my heart. I had told him to pray, and he was doing so. But not necessarily to a just and loving God.

He was back within the hour, his face scrubbed clean and the master's purloined gown folded neatly in his arms. I did not speak to him as he passed by my pallet, nor for the next sennight. I could not look him in the eye without the greatest agitation of heart. But to the extent that my spirit was roiled, so his seemed calmed. The heaviness about his brow had lifted, and he applied himself to preparing for the coming examination with a renewed diligence.

Then came the morning when Master Corlett was obliged to suspend instruction at the school while he attended the burial of the governor's second son, who had served as his father's clerk. As I helped the master prepare his mourning dress, he reflected that the loss was a heavy providence, since the young man left a widow and two babes. He had been carried off quite suddenly, after an uncommonly violent bout of flux.

I do not know if it was my ungoverned fancy, but later that day, when I passed by Caleb in the hall, it seemed to me that his face was lit by an expression of ardent satisfaction. By coincidence, the next day I heard from Makepeace, in a letter, containing the news that the "gift" for the Takemmy sonquem had been well received, and that "the squa in his household in whom I had once taken interest" was in good health.

It was the first time I had spoken to Caleb beyond a few required words since the night of the full moon. As I gave him the news, I had thought he would be pleased, but I soon sensed that he set little store in it. "I wish we had some authority, other than your brother's word, that she is indeed well set. He is not a man renowned for his fellow feeling. I will be glad, Bethia, when you are safely returned to the island and can see to her welfare."

"Caleb, I should tell you that I might not—" I began, but I could not continue, for we were interrupted then, by one of the smaller boys, crying out for my help with a splinter driven deep into the fleshy part of his palm. I turned to the boy. Caleb sighed, and went off to give the news to Joel.

As the candidates for the college examination sat late at their book and the master heard their sundry recitations, I went about my work, but my mind was unquiet. With the approach of matriculation day, the matter of my own future was in the balance as much as theirs. I had to consider what to do with Noah Merry's gift of my unexpected liberty. At one time, the choice would have been plain. I would have scuffed the stinking mud of Cambridge town from my boots, packed my box and booked a passage on the first boat heading for the island.

The island cried out to me. I longed to feast my senses on its light and air, and restore my spirit with its peace. If I answered its call, soon enough I would live again in the familiar rhythms of its seasons—the wincing winters and dappled summers, its shy, reluctant springtide and gleaming, bronzed leaf fall. I would be cradled by the known world of kine and crop, the heaviness of each day's familiar chores lightened by love of the very place in which I did perform them. I knew that life; I knew my place in it. If I threw my thoughts forward I could see myself at every age. To be sure, parts of the picture were wreathed in fog—the goodman beside me did not turn his face to show me who he was; the number of children at my board ebbed and flowed—but the woman at the center of the vision was clear; in bud, in blossom, and blown. I did not fear even the last of these visions: the frail old crone, hands gnarled and claw-like from a lifetime's toil, cheeks, etched and hollow, billowing forth a final breath. I knew that even as her petals withered, a good fruit ripened: the fruit of a life lived for family and faith and the rich harvests of a fertile place.

But there was another vision, less welcome, that went with this one: a single image in my mind of a door—heavy, solid, oaken—closing forever in front of me. It was the door to a library. The door that had opened for me, just a chink, in this place of learned men. I did not have an exact vision of what my future life would be if I married Samuel Corlett. I only knew what would not be, if I did not. There would be no more Latin phrases drifting down hallways, no works of poetry gifted me by tall men in scholars' gowns, no high rhetoric or witty disputations.

And this, also, I could conjure, for better and for worse: the press of lips and urgent hands. These had not made fertile furrow for lucid thought about my future. Instead, the memory of a moment under the apple boughs would come to me unbidden. I would have to stop what I was doing and try to gather myself. I learned then that girlish yearnings are one thing and womanly desire quite another. One might feel the light brush of Eros's wing and entertain forbidden fancies when one knows full well that what is longed for lies far beyond reach. It is another thing to burn with lust and be sure that a turn of your finger will bring the object to his knees before you. I had a struggle now that threatened my peace and looked set to pull me in the direction of all manner of vanities and follies if I did not take the most stringent pains to discipline myself. Had a speedy marriage to Samuel Corlett been on offer, I believe I would have consented to it, whatever my misgivings about the suitability of the match. But I was saved by the certain knowledge that even if I accepted him, we stood a year off the safe harbor of a marriage bed. An engagement, I reasoned, would create more, not less, temptation.

No further words had passed between us, that day in the apple garth. I had been in no state to speak, or even to think, so completely governed was I by the animal passions he had awakened. I had run off, mute as a beast, and he, perhaps as startled as I by his lack of restraint, had let me go. It was many days before we next had opportunity to speak, and I had had time to consider my answer. The interview began awkwardly, once again in the college library. It was the Lord's Day, and we were meant to be returned to the meeting house, for afternoon devotion. But Samuel had asked his father to go on ahead of us, and the master, divining our need for a private moment, had done so.

The college, at that hour, was deserted. So the impropriety was just as great, alone together in the library, as it would have been in his chamber. But I could not sit in his chamber with any composure, so we walked out and made our way, as if sleepwalking, to the library. He closed the heavy door and leaned against it.

"Better to leave it open, do you not think?"

"Wherefore? There is no one here."

I breathed again the biscuit tang of the books and struggled for calm.

"When last we were here, I asked you a question. Here we are again. And so I await your answer."

It was clear that he was not in the least degree pleased when I gave it, and less so when he grasped that he could not sway me. But I was able to quoth his own words back to him: "You yourself said you would have preferred an unhurried courtship, and that only the press of events drove you to make your offer when you did. And you told me quite frankly that aspects of my character are displeasing to you. . . ."

He would have cut me off then, but I continued to speak right across his words of protest. "My circumstances have, happily, changed. Let us take full advantage of the change. Let us have the courtship that you, yourself, spoke of so favorably. Let us come to know each other more fully. That way you will see, in time, if my 'headstrong' nature really is supportable to you."

"Bethia, I misspoke. I was not myself that day. I do not—"

"Samuel, I am asking for a small investment of patience. Let us use the time we have been given, by the exigencies of your present employment. I am speaking of a few months, only. I will undertake to remain here, in Cambridge, during that time, so that we may probe this thing, without tie of obligation on either side. Let a half a year pass, at the least. If—and only if—please be clear that I expect nothing from you and hold you unbound in every particular—after that time, you still wish to enter into an engagement, ask me again for my hand. By then I will be able to answer you with reason, and with my whole heart."

"I cannot like this plan, even though I realize I brought it upon myself, by my boorish manner to you over the matter of that salva— that maid, Anne."

"That is not so." I took a breath. We had not troubled even to sit upon the bench, but stood, just as we had entered the library. I turned a little aside and let my hand run across the spines of the nearest volumes. "You force me to say what I would not. But I must begin with you on a ground of complete honesty. A marriage that has not got such a bottom is like a building with its sill laid down upon sand. You might not wish to hear this, but it is the truth. There was no way in which you could have expressed yourself to me, no silken poesy with which you might have glossed your offer, that would have induced a different answer, once I had my indenture papers in hand."

"Is that so?" He had stiffened. "Honesty is certainly a fine quality between a man and wife. A little tact, perhaps, also might be considered an asset."

I colored. He studied his nails. "As my feelings seem to be a matter of indifference in this plan, I suppose I must consent to it."

"Is that what you think? Then I must think you have not been attending to me closely. Let me be even more plain. If I had no concern for your feelings, and, indeed, did not in some degree return them, then I should be on the first boat south the day following the matriculation examination, and I should not care if I set foot in this reeking midden of a town ever again. I stay here for the life I believe we might be able to make together—" I swallowed. "I stay here for you, Samuel."

His face changed then. The strain went out of his brow and his eyes—his expressive eyes—gazed at me with a look that combined ardour and tenderness. A line from Anne Bradstreet's poem came to me: "If ever two were one, then surely we." She must have known it, too: this same maddening desire. Was it wrong to give way to it? At that moment, all my mental reservations burned away. I was consumed with the urge to make two one, then and there, no matter what commandment I might break to do it. I had broken commandments before, after all: the very highest of them. All my efforts at reformation seemed nought but vain folly to me at that moment. I felt the reckless freedom of one who knows she stands already among the damned. Why not, then, another sin? One that stood much lower upon Sinai's list of Shalt Nots?

This time, it was my fingers that dug into his hair. Then his hands were on my waist, lifting me up to him.

XXI

Master Corlett called me into his study as the matriculation day neared, and asked if I had formed an idea of what I wished to do thereafter. "Much as I rely upon you, I do not ask you to stay here now that your brother is gone. This situation is beneath you. It has ever been so, and I know you took it on only out of sisterly duty and warm affection."

I tried to suppress a smirk at that last. I did not want to offend or shock the master. But he was off on one of his meandering tracks and did not notice my unseemly reaction. "Unfortunate, that your brother felt as he did. I do think he might have . . . but there it is. He is gone, and you still here. Entirely unsuitable . . . And then, of course, quite unexpectedly, that unfortunate girl, Anne, is also gone, although—" He was looking at me queerly as he said her name, but a spasm of coughing seized him, and when it quieted he did not complete the interrupted thought but passed over Anne entirely. "Next week, of course, the other two, Caleb and Joel, will matriculate—"

He must have noticed my start of surprise at the certainty of his expression, for he did glance at me then. "Oh yes—I have no doubt of it. No scholars of mine have ever gone before the college president better prepared than they. They will matriculate, and move, forthwith, to rooms in the Indian College. I have told the steward he would do well to see that a place is furnished ready to receive them, and I have told President Chauncy that they will need a tutor. He of course remains a skeptic as to their capacities and has done nothing in that regard, no matter how I prod him. Do you know what he said, Bethia? You, particularly, will not credit it. He said he had written to the Society for the Propagation of the Gospel, to tease out yet more funds. He is claiming that he will have to pay such a tutor a higher salary than the tutors of the English scholars. When I asked him wherefore, he said it would be necessary 'to encourage them in the work, wherein they have to deal with such nasty salvages, and for whom they are to have a greater care and more diligent inspection.' Nasty salvages indeed!"

"How did you answer him?"

"I told him what he seemed incapable of hearing: that these youths were some of the ablest I ever had, and if anything would require less inspection. Do you know, Bethia, I think at bottom he cannot be so deaf as he seems to be. But since he came here and perceived the flow of funds that had already been got from the Society—and that with no likely Indian scholars yet in sight—he has come to think of the entire venture as a kind of milch cow. His mind is ever on what he might extract from these youths and not what he must impart to them. But I feel sure that must change, once he comes to know them. . . .

"In any case, what I was getting to is that once Caleb and Joel are gone from here, I will be left with only the very young Nipmuc boys resident, and encountering them should not prove too fearsome, even for a timid Canterbridgian goodwife. With the money young Merry paid for your indenture—most generous, I must say—I am in purse to offer a good wage to a daily woman who'll not need to lodge here . . . the short of it is, you must feel free, my dear, to return to keep house for your dear brother on that beloved island of yours."

I shifted on my stool. "Master, I do not plan to do so. Not just presently."

His watery eyes gazed at me from beneath brows that had grown as unruly as an unmown hayfield. "What says your grandfather to that?"

"He is indifferent." It was true. I had written to grandfather seeking his permission to remain in Cambridge, and the letter I had back from him dealt with the matter in half a sentence, before devolving into a catalogue of his own squabbles with the Aldens and their faction, who continued to press for popular governance on the island and to mock his manorial ambitions. "He said I should do what suits me."

"Is that so?" His eyes traveled to the ceiling. "Do I dare to entertain a hope that it suits you to stay because there is some sort of . . . some manner of . . . understanding . . . between yourself and my son?"

"Perhaps better you should apply to him on that matter," I said, but the sudden heat in my face had given him the answer. The pale eyes twinkled with pleasure.

"I am glad of it. Though I wish it were a clear and settled engagement. When the two of you came in so late to afternoon meeting on Lord's Day last, and looking rather ill, the both of you, I thought you must between you have decided against. . . . I do not press you to say more than you feel is right. No. I do not. But I at least will speak it plain: I look forward to the day when I might call you daughter. And I am sure I do not know what Samuel is about, a man of his age. Then again, a man of his age may keep his own counsel and need not seek the light of his father's countenance on his every step. But you, Bethia: whatever lies between the two of you, it does not change the fact that you should not stay on here. And I speak unselfishly, for you have been a boon to me this year, and I will sorely miss your service, and your company. I would help you to a better situation. There must be something more suited, in the town, a position as a governess—"

"Master, I do have a situation in sight. I had hoped you might recommend me for it, though it would mean that I left your service a little before matriculation day. I heard of a place just now come vacant at the college—a young woman who served in the buttery. She is to marry next month and will leave in a few days to her new home, with her husband's family in Ipswich. I have enquired for it."

"But Bethia, that is but a menial post. Lighter work than here, perhaps, but still lowly. You are a learned girl; you have every quality that good families seek in a preceptress for their daughters. You should not toil as a scullery maid, it is beneath you—"

I looked at the kindly old man, his face creased up with concern for me. I decided to open my heart to him.

"Master, there is a reason I desire this situation—"

He smiled knowingly, and interrupted me. "It is evident. You wish to be near to my son."

I hardly knew what to say to that, since being near his son burned me like a brand. "I could not of course expect his attentions while he is engaged with his students. I was speaking of something else."

"Well then?"

"Master, all my life, the one thing I have yearned after is an education of the kind that is closed to me by my sex. My father stopped instructing me when I was nine years old. He did not wish me to learn Latin or Hebrew, and yet, as I think you know, I am a fair way upon the path with both those ancient tongues. I have done this by listening an ear to the lessons of others. Makepeace's. The boys here, with you. . . ."

"Did you so? I was not aware of it. You seemed fully occupied by your work."

"I did not mean to deceive anyone, and I listened only when the work allowed of it. But as to the college: you recall how the rooms are arranged—the great hall, how the buttery hatch opens right into it?" I leaned forward, warming to my subject. "Master, it is where the scholars take their meals, but it is also where they gather every morning, after prayers, to hear President Chauncy lecture to them. Do you see? I will have the benefit of those lectures—I cannot help but hear them, as I go about preparing the dinner. My hands will be engaged in menial tasks—but my mind . . . my mind will be free. Three hours—every morning. And in the afternoon, while the freshmen are with their tutors, I might overhear the sophisters' disputations in the hall, as the president moderates them." I felt my face glowing, anticipating how it might be. But the master's face was stern. He shook his head.

"This is most unwise, my dear. Most imprudent. These lectures are not fashioned for the unfurnished mind of the fairer sex. What need has a wife and mother to cudgel her faculties with the seven arts and the three philosophies? Have a care, or you will torment yourself into a malformed, misguided wretch. . . ."

"But you have taught young Dudley here; you are acquainted with his sister, Mistress Bradstreet. Surely you would not call her intellect malformed, for all its learning . . . ?"

"Well, she—" he spluttered, and coughed again. "I had in mind another Anne, one whose fate you would not want to call down upon yourself. The infamous Mistress Hutchinson. I expect you know what judgments God heaped upon her. Exile, monstrous birth, scalping at the hands of salvages . . ."

I leaned forward, ardent to win my point. "Master Corlett, you make, I fear, the case opposite to the one you intend. Mistress Hutchinson preached against the very learning I seek. Her heresy was that knowledge came to her as the direct revelation of God. She scorned the good men of letters who were her ministers; she denigrated the very kind of hard-won book knowledge that the Harvard College was set up to impart. There are some who say there would have been no college founded here, had her faction prevailed. . . ."

Master Corlett was suddenly sitting upright in his chair. "How can you possibly be so familiar with her case? The woman was surely dead and gone to her ultimate judgment before you were even born."

"But her words live," I said. I was flustered now. I saw, too late, that I should not have opened my heart to him. He did not understand, any more than father had. My father had loved me dearly; Master Corlett, I believed, felt true affection for me. Both were learned men who devoted their lives to teaching others. Then why not me? Why did they want to confine me in the prison of my own ignorance? Why was it so wrong, in their eyes, that I should love what they loved? Would Samuel prove the same, in the end? Would he, too, strive to put a bridle on my mind and a branks upon my tongue? Once again, I had spoken too freely. I seemed too dense witted to learn the simple lesson: silence was a woman's sole safe harbor.

"Words? What words? I never heard that Mistress Hutchinson committed her heresies to the page." I did not answer him. Belatedly, I recognized that the last thing I should be speaking about was an infamous instance of female outspokenness.

But he was pressing me now. To maintain a surly silence would be worse. "What words do you speak about? Tell me!"

"Her words to the General Court, master." Grandfather had oft cited her case as one of the chief pricks that drove him to the island, to be free of such a harsh governance as would send a pregnant woman into a howling wilderness in midwinter, with nine children trailing after.

"Do you mean to tell me you have read her testimony to the court?"

I nodded.

"How came you to do so?" He had a stricken look. I could not think that what I had done was so extraordinary as to provoke such a reaction in him.

"They are kept at our meeting house, where she was tried," I said. "It just—came to me—one day—that the records must lie there, where we come and go so often. And I thought I should like to know what she said. Since so many were convinced by her. At that time."

"And our minister let you read heretical testimony?"

My cheeks were on fire now. "I did not apply to the minister." My voice had shrunk to a bat squeak, almost inaudible.

"How, then?"

"I asked the sexton." That poor man, simple and frail, had hardly understood what I required. But he had been glad to give me his broom when I offered to sweep the floors for him. He had fallen into a doze in the corner, and so I had ample time to search out the old record and page through it, to marvel at how she had parried every thrust of Winthrop and the others, shielding herself with both wit and prodigious knowledge of scripture so that they could not land a blow. And then, just at the end, when they would have been forced to let her walk free, exonerated, she offers to set forth to them her heretical beliefs. Offers. And so indicts herself. Exactly as I had just done.

Master Corlett shook his head and wagged a crooked finger at me. "It was very wrong in you, Bethia. These things are not fit for eyes such as yours. You would not, I hope, drink from a spring that was befouled by a rotting corpse. Why then foul your mind with the rantings of a heretic?"

There were many ways in which I could have answered him. I could have said that Hutchinson's words, though clearly contrary to accepted doctrine, were by no means rantings. I could have said that one must study even incorrect opinions in order to learn how to discern their flaws. I could have said that I ached to read the words of a learned woman, because such women lived and died in silence while men alone set down their thoughts. But I had said too much already. So I answered him thus:

"I am sorry, master. I see now it was very wrong in me. I thank you for correcting me in this matter."

"Very well said." He looked relieved. "As for this situation at the college: you say you have applied for it already?" I nodded. He shook his head. "I will not cry you up for it. I cannot think I would do you any kindness to expose you in that way. Indeed, if I could, I would sink your chances there. But if I speak against your employment, it might be misapprehended, casting a shadow on your character. I would not have aught come to President Chauncy's ears that might make him think ill of my son's future wife, if such you are to be. But if the situation is offered, I beg you not accept it. And if you refuse to heed that counsel, then I advise you most ardently to accept this one: Keep the buttery hatch closed."

XXII

"Name?"

"Caleb."

"Caleb? Caleb what?"

"Caleb . . . Cheeshahteaumauk."

"Cheshchamog?"

"Cheeshahteaumauk."

"Outlandish name. I suppose you insist upon it? You will not like to take another? What was your father's name?"

"Nahnoso."

"No better. Sounds like a donkey's bray. The other will have to serve. Caleb Chis-car-." President Chauncy's pen scraped across the parchment: "-ruimac. So be it." He set down his pen and bridged his fingertips together upon the desk. He gazed at Caleb with an air of slight puzzlement, blinking a number of times, as if to clear the rheum from his eyes and get a better look at the specimen placed before him.

I set down the tankards I was carrying for Chauncy and his clerk and backed up against the wall, guessing that my presence would not be noticed. Although I was but two days employed in this service, I had already learned that it was easy to be overlooked here. The scholars and their tutors lived in their own world, walled off from ordinary folk by their black cloaks, their Latin speech and their high thoughts. Samuel had told me that there was much talk, in the early days of the settlement, against the expense of building a college such as this one. It would have been easier, and cheaper, in that straightened time, to have the scholars boarded among the townsfolk, meeting together for classes, as the universities of Europe generally fashioned it. But the English who visioned this place had graduated from the colleges at Cambridge in England, and they aspired to what they had themselves known: a gated sanctuary where the boys and their tutors lived together, at a lofty remove from the town, with its miserable distractions and ungirt life. Scholars were not to leave the college yard, except by express permission of their tutors. In that way, it was supposed, they would eat, sleep and breathe their studies, encountering nothing that was not to the purpose of learning.

It fell to the steward and his minions, such as myself, to deal with the world, to do what was necessary to keep the scholars fed and watered, shod and clad. There were five of us who served so: the steward, Goodman Whitby, his wife Maude, who was the cook, their lad George, who cleaned the scholars' quarters, a laundress who came weekly, and myself, the scullery maid. We scuttled about our chores, as unremarked as ants.

President Chauncy took a swallow of the small beer I had set down for him and dabbed at his lips with a crumpled handkin, still peering at Caleb. Caleb returned his gaze, sitting very straight in his chair. He was dressed in the plain, sober style that befit a scholar. I had sewed his collar myself, and taken some pains with it. It had a narrow border of drawn threadwork, and I had starched and ironed it perfectly. The white of it contrasted with the glossy black fall of his cropped hair. The year since our crossing had wrought a marked change in him. He had always been lean, but in the muscular way of an outdoorsman. Now he commenced to look thin, pared down by poor diet and indoor life. He was become, I would say, too spare for his tall frame, and his skin, a paler shade than seemed natural to him, had lost its luster.

But he had gained something, too. I studied him, as he sat there, and tried to discern what it was. It came to me that there was a rigid discipline at work in him, a stern self-control. If his physical fires seemed dimmed, perhaps it was because they had been directed to the service of a bright hot flame of mental will and purpose. He meant to succeed here, in this cold and alien place, no matter what it cost him. His dark, golden-brown eyes met the president's pale gaze without faltering.

"Your age?"

"I have seen sixteen summers."

Chauncy put a hand to his brow, as if a sudden pain stabbed him. He shook his silver head, frowning. "No, no, no. You should have rid yourself of these barbarian expressions long since. You are sixteen years old. Fashion it thus." He turned to his clerk and muttered under his breath: "A salvage, still, in the vulgate tongue, and yet Corlett wants me to believe him fitted for high study of the classics. . . ." He gave a great sigh that turned into a yawn, which he did not trouble to conceal. He riffled through the pages on his desk and pulled out a sheet, looked it over perfunctorily and handed it across the desk to Caleb.

"Here is a page of English sentences. Give them me in Latin . . . *suo ut aiunt marte.*"

Caleb pushed his lexicon to the side of the table as the president had instructed. Chauncy raised an eyebrow, as if surprised that

Caleb had understood even that little shard of Latin. I saw Caleb's face lighten as he scanned the page that Chauncy had given him. Then he bent his head and his hand moved fluidly across the parchment. I raised myself up onto my toes so that I could look over his work. He had developed a fine hand, elegant, yet legible even to me, who struggled to read most men's script. I soon saw why he had smiled. I could make out that the sentences were from a passage he knew well, on Caesar's crossing the Rhine. It was one he had studied with father, thoroughly, long since.

Caleb passed back the completed page. Chauncy pursed his lips and tilted the paper in the direction of the clerk. "He writes a fair hand—I will say that much." Then he brought it close and began to read over the lines. His mouth slackened a little as his eyes traveled down the page. "I see but one error—here." He struck out the offending verb and scrawled a correction. "Most surprising. Most unexpected . . . My brother Corlett did say, but I thought him wishful and deluded." The clerk nodded agreement. Chauncy looked at Caleb more searchingly. "Be so good as to give me the several terminations of the futures in the different conjugations?"

Caleb answered without hesitation. Chauncy then embarked upon an interrogation in Latin that was, most of it, too swift for me to follow, unpracticed as I had become. Occasionally, Chauncy had to repeat a question, and from time to time he raised a hand to halt Caleb's answer and to correct an error, but then the exchange would resume. As the conversation continued, Chauncy began to lean forward in his chair, increasing the difficulty of his questions.

"So," said Chauncy, switching back to English at last. "It seems your Latin is grounded solidly. You are on the way to mastery of correct speaking. At this college, we go further. One of the seven arts we teach here is fine speaking. I assume you know the name we give to that study?"

"Rhetoric," answered Caleb.

"So you have heard of it. . . ."

"Heard of it, and heard the thing itself, long before I knew that there was a name for it. Where I grew up, that man was prized who could deliver himself of a well-fashioned and persuasive speech."

Chauncy smiled indulgently. "Is that so? I think you will find, in the course of your studies here, that the best efforts of unlettered salvages ill compare. . . . Some half-clad pagan warrior, after all, could hardly be said to employ the rhetoric of Athens."

Caleb returned the president's smile. "Yet they say that Homer was unlettered, and did he not give us Achilles, a half-clad pagan warrior, who was both 'doer of deeds' and 'speaker of words'?"

Chauncy sat back in his chair and peered at Caleb. Then he nodded approvingly. "Well argued. Indeed. And since I am now made aware that you have read Homer, let us turn to your Greek."

I tensed. Samuel had told me that the study of Greek was Chauncy's great passion. He had lectured upon it at Trinity College in Cambridge, before a dispute as to whether or not a church erred that erected a communion rail for the service of the Lord's Supper. He had been briefly imprisoned for his views—such were the desperate straits, for reform-minded persons, under Charles I. When he was released, he took ship for the Plimouth colony, to serve as minister there. Before long, he had fallen out with his flock upon another dispute, this one of more practical import. He had insisted on total immersion of infants at their baptism. The parents, rightfully fearing that this might not be so convenient for their babes in the chill of a frigid Plimouth winter, had refused to allow it. He had been about to take a passage back to England when Harvard's overseers offered him the college presidency. There was to be one condition, since they had just rid themselves of the former president, Dunster, over his Anabaptist tendency: Chauncy would be required to keep his immersion ideas to himself. Since college presidents are not generally called upon to perform the baptisimal rite, he had managed, so far, to do so.

"What cases do the verbs of admiring and despising govern?"

"Genitive and dative."

"Well. Give me then the formation of the first and second aorists...."

And so it went on, Chauncy nodding approvingly at each of Caleb's assured responses.

"I must say, my brother Corlett has fitted you for our college most soundly. Most soundly indeed. I must tell you that despite your master's lofty claims, I had my doubts that one from your ... station ... could readily join this particular freshman class. You will study here beside the scions of some of our most distinguished families. We have already admitted in your year Benjamin Eliot, the youngest son of our beloved apostle, and another youngest, Joseph Dudley, son of our late governor—but you already are acquainted with Dudley from Corlett's school, of course—and then there is Edward Mitchelson, son of the marshal, and Hope Atherton, whose father is a major general.... *Liberi liberaliter educati*. I suppose I must assume now that you know what that means?"

"Gentlemen, educated like gentlemen," Caleb replied.

"Very good. It remains to be seen if such stuff as you can be fashioned into a gentleman. . . ."

"*Hic labor, hoc opus est.*"

I felt the blood beat in my head and wondered at Caleb's composure. His face, as he had said this last, was a picture of sincerity. But something in the tone of his voice told me he was playing with the pompous president. Sitting there erect, in the grace of his natural bearing, Caleb looked more the gentleman than the lardy, stoop-shouldered old Chauncy, with his dingy collar and threadbare, rumpled gown. I had not met the college laundress, but it came to me that she could benefit from some instruction in the use of a bluing wash and a flat iron. Samuel Corlett had told me that Charles Chauncy was, in fact, a gentleman born, from an ancient landed family in Hertfordshire. He had finished near the head of his class in both degrees at the Trinity College in Cambridge. But you would not guess these things by looking at him.

The old man's mottled hand trembled as he held out a parchment. "I give you here a signed copy of my *admitatur,* and a copy, in Latin, of course, of the laws of the college. Your first work of scholarship in this place is to transcribe these. Keep your copy by you always, and refer to it often. The steward will help you fetch your things across to the Indian College, and will fit you up with a gown and bonnet. Take care that you wear the bonnet to your first commons." He turned to the clerk. "The junior sophisters will have their sport with the freshmen, and send them in uncovered." He glanced back at Caleb. "Do not let them persuade you. Only those sit bareheaded at board who are in disgrace and under punishment. I hope never to see you so, if indeed you can raise yourself up to the opportunities and responsibilities that you now assume."

Caleb stood, gave a slight bow, and turned. Chauncy raised a hand. "A moment, if you please. I should say, lest you be in any doubt, that we are glad to have you here. I am sure there will be difficulties, small and large, as you go forward. But you must not think you are unwelcome. Truly, you are more than welcome. You are necessary. I had begun to think this day would never come. I rejoice in it—it will give satisfaction to our honored benefactors in London. Now send in the other salv—the other lad, and we will know if he is as well fitted as you are."

As Caleb turned, he saw me, standing against the wall. He glanced down at the *admitatur* in his hand, and we exchanged a smile of triumph. Chauncy caught the looks passing between us. His brow creased with displeasure. "You. You are dismissed." I nodded obediently and withdrew, regretting that I would not be able to witness Joel's examination and see how he did. I passed by him, waiting in the hall. Caleb and I murmured words of encouragement. He was dressed as fine and plain as Caleb—I had seen to it—but he lacked his older friend's composure. His usual dreamy gaze was gone, replaced with the desperate look of a beast at bay, and his skin was misted all over with sweat. As he rose to enter the hall, I could see that his hands trembled. Suddenly, he looked very young. Caleb placed a hand on his shoulder, and whispered to him. I could not hear the words, but I know they were Wampanaontoaonk.

Perhaps Joel was one of those who require an agitation of spirit to elevate his abilities. I heard later that he acquitted himself even more nobly than Caleb.

XXIII

If I had thought to find a more ample providence at the college than we had enjoyed at Master Corlett's school, the steward's complaining, as he tallied up the tuition payments, soon set me to rights on that score. The college was kept all year, without closure or recess, but the main part of the fees was paid in early fall, when the freshman class entered.

"Short commons again, this leaf fall, by the looks of what's acoming in." Roger Whitby was a masty Yorkshireman, florid of face, with an easy temper, quick to laughter. I soon learned that his chief amusement was to prick the self-important manners of the tutors and their charges. "If these lads be the sons of the prophets, then they sires ought to seek out another line of work, one that yields up better wages."

I had been tasked to help him sort and store the various goods in which families paid their college bills. When he learned I could count, he set me to tally sacks of Indian corn and rye that had just come off a dray. He looked over my reckoning—"Brussen lass, who can cipher, and knows her letters; the last lass could do none of that, willing worker though she was; I'll speak no ill of her. I see here it's two to one, corn to rye, coming in this term. That's as well. Wife says thee can make a good brown bread so. Some years, it's all corn we get, and then the pones might as well be made on sawdust, since we've nary enough eggs to bind 'em." I took note of that: perhaps establishing a henhouse would be a project I could undertake to better the lot of the scholars.

Someone had sent a milk cow, so I tagged her ear with the college mark and set her out to pasture on the common. There were hogsheads of molasses and sack, the former welcome, the latter sealed with wax and set aside. "That'll not be wanted before the next commencement, and then 'twill be drunk dry in an hour's revels." There were cords of wood, but too few: "Whittlings, merely. Scarce enough to warm a workhouse." A barrel of saltcod, which garnered a rare nod of approval: "Saturday dinners there, for a month or more." A cobbler had paid his sophister son's tuition in shoes—a score pair. Whitby fingered the well-stitched leather but scratched his head. "We can get a good coin for these, upon the town, but who accounts for the time it will take me to sell them?"

I was curious to know how many scholars I would be serving, and Whitby was pleased to enumerate the classes. I knew already of the senior sophisters, for they were Samuel's charges, and he spoke of them with the tender interest of one who had lived with them and tutored them the past three years. There were twelve of that class who had advanced through the rigors of the college program. The class was unusually enlarged by three sons of the president who had all matriculated together: the twins, Elnathan and Nathaniel Chauncy, and their brother Israel. There were only half as many junior sophisters and just seven sophomores. So with the eight freshmen, I calculated that college body came to thirty-three, plus the four fellows who resided with their charges. "But that doesn't reckon on thy commoner fellows," Whitby remarked. These, he said, were generally older students who paid double tuition to attend lectures. Their higher fees earned them the right to be addressed as "mister" while the younger scholars were called by their unadorned surnames. The commoner fellows dined at the high table. But few if any of them were serious candidates for a degree, and it was rare for one to attend at college the full four years.

Whitby was most interested in the incoming freshmen, hoping for one or two scions of wealth whose families might be liberal provisioners. He had been given a list of names of the youths who had matriculated and who would need to be accommodated. He scanned it carefully, jabbing a fat finger against each name as he read down the list. "Atherton. Had several of that brood here before. Big family, the Athertons. Father some kind of military man. Not a chouser, but not as thee'd call liberal either. Samuel Bishop—I don't know his people. Dudley. That one would have been rich pickings, had the father, our late governor, not gone to his rest. I'll not expect much from the stepfather, being as how he's a minister. Ministers are the last to be paid, in hard times such as these uns. Always in arrears, they be, waiting on flock to pay thine coin. Though I expect this one"—he jabbed the name Eliot—"will do what he can by his only son. Apostle Eliot's funds come to him from England, not from the poor planters hereabouts. Jabez Fox— that's another preacher's boy. So's young Samuel Man. Edward Mitchelson—that'd be the marshal-general's boy. Might be good for summat. I tell thee, it's these two outlandish Indian names I'm most chuffed to see upon the list. Thank God's providence for 'em. The class'll be feeding off of 'em. The Society for the Propagation of the Gospel—all them godly English—they'll pay coin for the tuition, and a good coin too—Chauncy will see to that. Not that we'll get more than tuppence here or there of it, I'll be bound. The president'll like as not feather his own bed with that money. He takes a goodly salary off the college—a hundred pounds a year is the whisper. Most of it, he's obliged to take in kind, so he's glad to have the coin if he can get it."

It had been decided that I was to board with the Whitbys, sharing their quarters at the college just as the former maid had done. The family lived all together in one long, narrow room that ran behind the buttery. Half the space was crowded out with extra stores of one kind or another that Whitby wanted to keep a close eye upon, such as the sack and the mulled cider and a barrel of rum.

"The devil gets into ye boys, he does, ministers' sons or nay. We've had our share of drunken revels end in riot, oh aye, and don't let any prune-faced tutor tell thee different, lass. Boys who prate Latin are nay better than any other boys, with a bellyful of hot waters in 'em. I wager there will be more than one flogging, thy time here, to be sure. If such mayhem breaks out, get thyself back here and use ye door bar. My goodwife would wash my mouth for saying it, but the older lads are not above whore hunting for hackney wenches upon the town, and betimes, if they get soused, they'll touse honest girls. Have a care, lass, is all I'm saying. Ye'll be safe enough in our quarters, me lad and meself will see to it."

I was to have a slim featherbed, set into the inglenook beside the fireplace, with a curtain around it for privacy, which was a vast improvement upon my last accommodations, and I drifted to sleep there the first night easily, for all that Goodman Whitby and his boy both snored like a bellows.

Since I was the underling, it fell to me to rise earliest, draw water, kindle the cook fire, and prepare the morning bever. It made no mind to me; I had always risen before the sun. I was to start my morning chores on the first day that the new freshman class took up their residence in the college. The kitchen and the buttery were very fair rooms, of good size, scrubbed soundly, every nook and cranny, and the wood waxed gleaming. The girl I replaced had clearly been diligent. She had hung branches of herbs from the rafters, so the scent of the cook fire mingled with the clean tang of beeswax, sage and rosemary. It was peaceful there, in the predawn hour. Then, at four-thirty, the college began to stir. Soon, the first of the scholars came rapping upon the buttery hatch. I opened it with a creak and saw young Joseph Dudley. I was glad to see him, familiar as he was to me, but he did not return my smile. His sleepy face wore a disgruntled expression.

"Good morning, Dudley," I said. I handed him his portion.

"Nought good about it." He snatched the tankard and hunk of bread and was backing away at double time towards the stairs. "I surely didn't come to this place for this purpose."

"What purpose is that?"

"To serf for the sophisters." He was upon the stairs, taking them two at a time. "Pynchon's my man, and he has threatened to pickle me if I don't bring his bever at a run."

A half dozen more freshmen already crowded the hatch, grabbing for bread and beer as quickly as I could lay it up.

"That will do!" I said sternly. "This isn't a pig's trough. Line up like gentlemen!" There was jostling and grumbling, but the boys fell into some kind of rough order. When it was Joel Iacoomis's turn, he gave me a civil good morning.

"Thank you, Jo—I mean, Iacoomis," I said, passing him a bever. "And who are you serving?"

"Brackenbery."

As soon as Joel moved aside the others continued to push and shove, so I stood back with my hands upon my hips, refusing to put up any more tankards. "I said, behave like gentlemen. I will serve no one of you until all act more civily."

"Hard to feel the gentleman when the first thing they do is make a serf of you." The speaker was a thin, frowning boy, with very dark hair and pallid skin.

A taller boy punched him playfully upon the shoulder. "There now, Eliot, surely your elder brothers told you how it would be. Did they not?" I supposed that the pallid boy must be Benjamin Eliot, son of the famed apostle. Eliot frowned. The taller boy just laughed at him.

"Well, I have five brothers—Rest, Thankful, Watching, Patience, Consider—and each one of them the very opposite of their name. But they all went through this, and they all survived it. And you will too, if you follow Atherton family advice: Have Patience, keep Watching, and soon you can Rest, Consider and be Thankful. Or so I Hope."

I smiled at Hope Atherton as he grabbed his sophister's bever. He was the only one to offer a thank you before he turned and hurried across the hall, slopping beer on the boards as he ran.

Only as the last of the freshmen darted up the stairs did I see Caleb, sauntering towards the hatch in no apparent hurry.

"Good morning," I said. "And who do you serve, that you dare to keep him waiting so long?"

He smiled, and took the bread and beer I held out with a civil thank you. "Who do I serve? Who should I serve? I serve myself, of course." He wandered out into the yard then, and from the buttery window I saw him standing pensively in the garth as the sky slowly grayed and brightened. When he came in, to return his tankard, I cast an eye to see that we were unobserved, and then I placed a restraining hand on his sleeve before he could turn away.

"Have a care," I whispered. "It is one thing to go your own way in the woods, among your own people—another thing in this place, where there are those aching to see you falter. . . ." Gently, he put his hand atop mine. He gave a slight smile. "Thank you for your concern for me," he said. "There is no need for it."

I watched his retreating back, and called out softly after him: "I hope that you may be right."

I closed the buttery hatch after I had taken back the last of the tankards, and set to sanding and scrubbing them. Even above my own clatter, I could hear the racket as the college assembled for morning prayers. Maude Whitby had come in and commenced to cook, but now she wiped her hands upon her pinafore, for we were expected to set aside our tasks and join the reverence. Chauncy led us all in a psalm, which he did not line out as was our custom, but expected all to sing with him in unison. Then he read and expounded some verses from Leviticus, and closed with a blessing. At seven, from the cupola above our heads, the bell tolled, and I turned back to my work as the students dispersed to their tutors' chambers for a study hour. I knew Joel and Caleb would be meeting their tutor for the first time; I wondered how they would get on together. I had not seen the man, and had not learned his name or had opportunity to ask Samuel what he might know of Chauncy's choice for the role.

Goody Whitby was of a mind to chatter through her work, and while I did not wish to seem cold or uncivil, neither did I wish to encourage her in this overmuch, as I hoped fervently to listen to the lessons, which I could not do very well if Latin in one ear had to compete with gossipy Yorkshire dialect in the other. When the bell tolled again, at eight, I could hear, through the closed buttery hatch, forms scraping across boards as the scholars assembled for the morning lecture. I felt a great rise of excitement at this: here was I, at college, as I had always longed to be. That I had my hands up to my wrists in a doughtrough made no matter: my mind was free to drink in wisdom as much as I could imbibe. I wondered if Caleb shared my high heart at this moment, and could only think that he must.

The buttery hatch was not three yards from where President Chauncy's lectern was set up. I could keep faith with Master Corlett, and leave it closed, as he bade me, and yet still hear the lectures quite plain. Goody Whitby fell mum as soon as the president commenced to speak. I guessed it was a rule of the kitchen to make as little stir as possible, and I was glad of it. I had thought I might find the Latin difficult, but that first morning Chauncy addressed himself mainly to the freshmen, and expressed himself with simplicity. I could follow along with but little effort. His lecture that morning was a justification for an education in the liberal arts, and its relevance to the life of a minister, which, he said, "I expect, with the grace of God, will be the destiny of more than half of you now in this hall. The founders of this college sacrificed to build this place because they dreaded to depart this new world and leave but an illiterate clergy in the pulpits of its churches. So what need has such a minister for the poetry of Ovid, the rhetoric of Cicero and the philosophy of Aristotle?

Were not these men pagans, living in the stews of anti-Christ and the devil's house of lies? Perhaps so. One may say it, in the knowledge of their time and place.

"Yet all knowledge comes from God, who creates and governs all things. You will find many excellent divine moral truths in the works we will study together in this place—in Plato, in Plutarch and in Seneca. These pagans treated of the works of God most excellently. So does God use them to prepare the ground for the perfect teachings of Jesus Christ.

"The liberal arts that you will study here all inform us of the divine mind. They derive from it. They reflect it. We study no art for its own sake but to help us restore our connection with the divine mind. God's reason is perfect, human reason no more than pale shadows.

"The Greeks had a goddess whom they named Eupraxia. For them, she was the spirit"—here he switched out of Latin and gave the Greek word, *diamona*—of right conduct. "I want you to develop a great fondness for that name, Eupraxia. We will invoke her here in this place many times. The whole object of your studies is summed in it—right action, right conduct, doing the right thing at the right time. All your works here are aimed to help you learn to discern the right—to winnow the chaff, to smelt off the dross. . . ."

I had formed a rather unfavorable impression of Chauncy based on very slight observations of him. But now, as I listened, I perceived that the unkempt exterior and peremptory manners were only the unfortunate gown thrown atop a great intellect. Further, he had a wonderful way of taking high matters and bringing them down to the capacities of the scholars. I found as I listened an ear that I had not the least difficulty in following the line of his thought, even as I bustled about, helping Maude to prepare a hasty pudding of cornmeal, molasses and milk.

Chauncy was outlining how he proposed to divide the hours of study throughout the week. The Lord's Day would be spent at meeting and at rest, but the scholars would be examined by their tutors upon the content of the sermons during the following week, to make sure they had attended to and profited from them. On the second and third days—Mondays and Tuesdays—freshmen would gather at eight and hear him lecture on logic and metaphysics. Sophomores, at nine, would hear ethics and natural science. Sophisters, at ten, would hear arithmetic, geometry and astronomy. I smiled. Listening from the buttery, I would have the profit of all of these lectures. In the afternoons, students would practice disputations upon the topics covered in the lectures, which the president would moderate. The fourth day of each week would be given over completely to the study of Greek. On Friday, scholars would toil upon Hebrew, until they had a grounding in that language, at which point they might add the study of Aramaic and Syriac. In the afternoon they would study the Bible. The sixth day, Saturday, was to be devoted to the practice of rhetoric and declamations.

When Chauncy concluded, Goodman Whitby herded the scholars out into the yard to stretch their legs while we all of us bustled to convert lecture hall into dining hall, setting up trestles and rearranging forms and stools. Promptly at eleven, the scholars filed in and took seats at their assigned tables. Then Chauncy, the fellows and the fellow commoners entered, in procession, and mounted the dais to the high table. As soon as they were seated,

Whitby took up the Great Salt, and carried it with stiff formality through the hall, placing it before Chauncy.

The undergraduates ate off wooden trenchers and drank from pewter tankards or slipware mugs. Each carried his own knife and spoon. The high table dined off the college silverware. For all the stir and fiddle-faddle, the fare was plain and, I must say, insufficient. The service might have been plate, but the small dollop of pudding set down upon it was less ample than any but the poorest board might boast.

Perhaps it was the excitement of finally being in this place, but by afternoon I was tired and addled. As I cleaned the dinner things, I could not take much profit from the doings on the other side of the buttery hatch. The senior sophisters were disputing, and since their Latin was of a much higher level than mine, I could not follow the wit in their arguments. From time to time, I heard Samuel's voice, as he joined with the president in moderating the debate. That was an added trial upon my powers of concentration.

At half past the hour of four, the Whitbys' boy George tolled the bell for afternoon bever. I scanned the faces as they came to the hatch, waiting to see Joel and Caleb and get some sense of how they liked their new tutor. When they presented themselves, I could not read their expressions. I had thought to see them lit up with the delights of their first day in this place, but instead the spirits of both seemed sadly quenched, sober and withdrawn. I did not read too much into this, as we could hardly speak in the press of bodies all reaching hungrily for their bread and beer, which had to be consumed before evening prayers commenced at five.

At half past seven, we served a frugal supper—if the dinner fare was sparse, this could only be termed paltry—after which the scholars had a recreation hour to use as they would. I could tell that many of them gathered about the hall fire. I could hear them, talking and laughing together, as I cleaned and set the kitchen to rights for the next day. As much as I would have liked to stay and listen to their chatter, I was spent, and went away to my pallet long before the nine o'clock bell sounded to send the lingerers to their chambers.

I am writing these final words by the light of a tallow dip, both the Whitbys having made plain to me that they like it not. They fear the flame, in my curtained nook, lest I fall into a drowse and set the college all afire. I see that to keep the peace, I shall have to end this account here. It matters not. Now that I am got here, and my fate, for the nonce, is a settled matter, I do not feel so pressed to scrive my daily thoughts. The Whitbys are abed, and the son has commenced his bellows snore. The father, I suppose, stays for me, waiting wakeful to see my tallow safely snuffed. I will do so now, and let him have his hard-earned rest.

Anno 1715
Aetatis Suae 70
Great Harbor

I

This morning, light lapped the water as if God had spilt a goblet of molten gold upon a ground of darkest velvet.

I was awake to see it, as I generally am at sunrise. I do not know when it was I last lay down my head and slept through the night. I doze merely, night or day without distinction, in the brief intervals when pain ebbs and I can steal some rest. The deepest featherbed may as well be a gibbet for all the comfort I can find upon it. I gave up the idea of lying down to sleep some weeks since, because I cannot turn myself from that position and I will not trouble the others to be in constant attendance upon me. I have a chair and a footstool, quilts and pillows, and these I can arrange as I need, to ease an ache here or a teasing pain there.

I will die soon. I do not need the funeral looks in others' eyes to tell me this. I have seen enough of death to know its signs. I can read my failing body in the laceration of every labored breath. When one of the children comes in, to see how I do, I no longer open my arms to invite an embrace. They are kind children, and would, if I signed to them, come and rest their sweet heads on my breast for a polite moment or two, but I will not subject them to the stench of my decay. In any case, these days, even a well-meaning caress leaves purple bruises on my skin.

God is gathering me, little by little. He has already taken much, but he has left me my sight, and for that I am thankful. I can still see the glory of his sunrise through the wavy panes of my chamber window. I can still watch the wind riffle across the water, the osprey's sudden plunge from the sky, the thunderheads gathering in billowing, wine-dark blooms. I sit here, propped up like a poppet, and I watch. I watch, and I remember. Now, when everything else has gone, this is what remains: vision and memories.

Yester eve I asked them to bring me my inlaid box, the one I got in Padua the year of my marriage to Samuel. It had been an age since I had thought to look inside it. The sea air had rusted the clasps and the hinges, and my stiff hands fumbled for a while before I could prise it open. But the pages were there. The earliest, mere scraps, crumpled and stained, some with a few Latin sentences from Makepeace's boyish hand, errors struck out with furious pen strokes before the spoiled sheet was tossed aside. Then the later pages with a few words in Elijah Corlett's fair script, discarded perhaps for a small ink blot or an imperfect pen stroke. And on every sheet, my own scrawls, writ dense front and back.

My hand aches now, as I write these spidery lines. With each press of the pen, pain grinds the bones in my wrist. But I must write. Now, near the end, I feel an urge to finish the story I began, so many years since, when this new world and I were young and all things still seemed possible. I need, I suppose, to account for my life, and for my part in Caleb's crossing from his world into mine, and what flowed on from it. Time is short, but I pray that he in whose hand my life rests will grant me days enough to make this accounting.

It took me the better part of this day to read over the faded dispatches from my girlish self. I had to stop many times, as memories crowded upon me and tears blurred my sight. Once, though, I came to a place where I laughed out loud—and paid for the mirth in the stinging spasm that followed. The lines that provoked me were those that my seventeen-year-old self had set down, foreseeing my old age and death.

Oh the self-weening certainty of the young! *Frail old crone*— she wrote. Well and good—she foresaw *that* fairly enough, but this next: . . . *good fruit ripened* . . . I smile again, as I copy down the words. I could tell that fatuous girl a thing or two about ripe fruit. Maggots and rot. Putrefaction and waste. A sour taste that lingers in the mouth.

Is it ever thus, at the end of things? Does any woman ever count the grains of her harvest and say: Good enough? Or does one always think of what more one might have laid in, had the labor been harder, the ambition more vast, the choices more sage? I read on, and I find myself smiling at that sound-fleshed young girl, her daring and her folly and her many fears.

Now, when perhaps I should be most afraid, I find that there is very little left that can put me in dread. Not my death, surely; though a lifetime's sermons tell me I have earned the hard judgment of an angry God. I do believe that God appointed the moment of my birth and the instant of my death and all the circumstances of my life in between. I wish I could say, as the elect among us are wont to say, that I would not turn a finger to alter his dispositions. But I cannot say so, for there is much I would change, were it within my power. Perhaps this is why God has not spoken to me. I do not expect that my salvation will be revealed to me in what little time remains. As I sit here, awake and aching, I am aware that this pain may be but a foretaste of what awaits me in eternity. Still, I do not choose to fear what I cannot know.

This I do know, for the surfeit of loss in my life has convinced me: it will be easier to be grieved for than to grieve.

II

I worked for one year in the buttery of Harvard College. Through those thin walls drifted every kind of knowledge. I learned with freshmen and with seniors, imbibing the work of their four years in one, as Chauncy stood and gave his morning lectures to each successive class. I do not say that I understood all that I heard; how could I? One cannot place a pediment when one has not yet laid the foundation. Much of what was given out to the senior sophisters remained obscure to me. But I hoarded a sherd here and there, as I could, and as the year wore on some kind of odd edifice assembled itself. While I did not have the benefit of the scholars' daily tutorials in which to interrogate what had been said, when I could snatch an hour with Samuel and his father, I plied them with questions. From them I was able to borrow books, and I would read till the Whitbys snuffed their candle. So was I able to make my way in several subjects.

For Hesiod, that ancient poet-farmer, I conceived a particular affection. Like me, he loved the natural world, and strove to find the words to set down what he saw. I could say that I learned my Greek memorizing the lines of his "Works and Days," because they lodged in my mind so naturally it was as if he gave word to my own thoughts. It is his night sky that I see now, through the seasons: Arcturus rising brilliant from the ocean stream at dusk, Pleiades like a swarm of fireflies, Sirius parching the hayfields on hot late-summer nights, and Orion striding across the winter sky.

I had much to be thankful for that year. My toil was undemanding compared with what I had been used to do, and the Whitbys so agreeable and good-humored that I soon felt as at home with them as if they had been kinfolk. Of course, I missed the island, but I felt that what I gained each day, in learning, somehow compensated for that loss. Only two circumstances marred that time for me.

The most troubling concerned Caleb and Joel. Their first months at the college were harsh and bitter. The other students spurned them. It was not an overt shunning, such as one could have described and chastised and thereby put an end to. Rather it was that their fellow scholars did nothing to make them welcome, and instead contrived an array of small slights, such as leaving no place for them to sit upon the forms in the hall and never addressing a remark to either one at dinner or during the brief recreations in the yard. Somehow—I do not know what means were used—it was made plain that they were not welcome to join in the hour of fellowship around the fire after supper, but were expected to retreat to their cheerless room in the Indian College, where the large printing press occupied what might have been a pleasant hall. Later they would be obliged to hear the English students who shared the building— some five or six of them there were, in two chambers that flanked theirs—amble in, still wreathed about with the warm wood smoke, carrying on some congenial conversation from which they had been excluded.

So Caleb and Joel took comfort one in the other, becoming, each for each, an indispensable support. They walked in each other's shadow by day, finished each other's sentences in conversation, and would retire together to their room at night, watching by the light of tallow dips and helping each other to further their understanding of the days' texts. If I was watching late myself, I would see the pale light flicker in their chamber window until the college rule required it be extinguished, at eleven o'clock.

These social hardships transcended the mere lack of fellowship. They had a practical consequence. It was common for the better off scholars to receive from their families gifts of food—a round of cheese, a sausage or the like. These they would share out during the evening fireside revels. It was a rare night when someone did not have some kind of victual to add some heft to the scant supper fare. Caleb and Joel, deprived of this fellowship and meat, went hungry to their bed each night. And cold too—since the ration of wood for the Indian College was paltry. I feared for their health and their spirits. So I began to slip some extra food to them, whenever I could do so: an egg here, a dried fish there, a smear of sweet butter upon their portion of bread. If Maude Whitby knew of it, she was kind, and did not say.

At this same time, Caleb suffered persecution for his intransigent refusal to take part in the custom by which freshmen served as errand boys for the older scholars. The sophisters exacted retribution upon him in sundry ways, blotting his copybook or making away with his pens. Once, they hid his bonnet, thinking he would have to appear for commons uncovered and so be humiliated. But they underestimated him there. He simply found some dried grasses in the yard and deftly wove them into a passable cap. When it became clear that none of their pranks had succeeded in humbling him in the least degree, the older scholars eventually wearied of oppressing him, and went on, as youths of that stripe will, to search out an easier victim.

I was not the only one to note that this was the way of things. Young Dudley, the proudest of all the freshmen, and Benjamin Eliot, who also was somewhat jealous of his own station, soon took in the fact that Caleb was neither in thrall to a sophister nor suffering greatly for his failure to be so. They, in their turn, began to rail against the custom, until you could say a general rebellion was afoot. In time, a group of them, led by Dudley, screwed up their courage and brought their grievances to Chauncy. He listened, considered, and ordered the practice done away with.

This outcome had the effect of raising Caleb's stature with some among the freshmen, especially when Dudley made a point of publicly thanking him for his example. Slowly, one scholar, and then another, began to look past Caleb's skin to the man within it. And as they accepted Caleb, so Joel also won acceptance, since the two were by then so close that one was like a side to the other. Amity did not come in a day, but, by slow stages, it came at last.

And all this while they had another, graver struggle. This concerned the tutor that Chauncy had given inspection over them, a recently arrived Trinity graduate named Seward Milford. The man was a drunken reprobate who misliked Indians and had taken the position only because it paid better than any other tutorship. Caleb and Joel had to make shift to learn what they could while he pursued every gaiety and dissipation the town allowed. When they came to his rooms after morning lecture, he would still be abed, often insensible from previous evening's revels upon the town, and would call down curses at them for troubling his sleep. Instead of educating them as he was charged to do, he tried instead to seduce them to his own dissolute state. He would smuggle hot waters into the Indian College and then mock them as mewling infants when they refused to join in his drunken excesses.

I was dismayed and heartsick when, one night, making my way back from the necessary, I saw a figure stumbling in the dark, and recognized Caleb. He made a weaving way from tree to tree, until he stopped, and propped himself up against a young oak. He bent over and cast up, noisily. I hurried to aid him, hoping to get him back to his room before anyone caught him violating a half dozen college rules for which the punishment was a flogging.

I gave him my arm and tried to hush him. He was babbling, and loudly. His words were slurred—Wampanaontoaonk one sentence, Latin the next, and I could make no sense of his rambles. He was almost shouting. I recoiled from his breath, so hot with spirits I could have lit a torch from it.

"Hush!" I said. "Don't speak now." He staggered, and I thought we would both fall. Then I heard a twig crack behind me and turned, afraid. By great good fortune it was Joel, come to the aid of his friend. Somehow he managed to get him up the stairs, the sick and spittle cleaned off his face, and into bed without waking any other student who might have been glad to carry a damaging report to the monitors. The next day, a pale, bloodshot-eyed Caleb crept to class, wincing at the scraping of forms across the floor and the thud of books dropping upon tables.

He apologized to me, some days later.

"But why did you do it?" I asked. "You see your tutor often enough, unmanned by strong drink."

"I needed to know," he said. "I needed to know what it was, and if it brought any vision. I thought that perhaps the outer signs might mask some inner effect that was not apparent to any but the imbiber. I thought there must be some good in it, since so many seem enslaved to it."

"And did it bring you anything?"

"Nothing." He smiled. "Nothing but a loss of my dignity and a cloven head." To my knowledge, neither he nor Joel ever touched any form of hot waters again.

The absence of capable guidance stalled their advancement, no matter how they plied their books by night. I knew what the lack of a tutorial meant and how it hindered understanding. I spoke to Samuel, to see if he could influence the situation, but he begged off, saying Chauncy had tender family ties to Milford's people and had long since proven deaf to any ill word of him. Meantime, those in the college, student and master, who had set their faces against the Indian project thought to see their views confirmed by the boys' seeming failure to advance in their studies.

It might have gone on so, had not Milford overreached himself and pilfered a butt of sack from Goodman Whitby's closely held stores. Whitby did not concern himself with dissolute conduct in the college. If it came to his notice, he turned a blind eye, believing that a man or boy's behavior was a matter for his maker, his minister and the appointed college monitors. But the supplies were another gate's business. It was a point of pride to him that he managed to husband an insufficiency and stretch meager rations further than any other might do. This made pilfering a particular affront to him. He laid the suspected theft before Chauncy, and the president, who set great store in the steward, went at once to confront Milford in his rooms. By happy chance, he came upon the scoundrel tutor in the drink, and abed with a hackney wench from the Blue Anchor.

I expect that Chauncy heard, that day, the groans of the sinking college if word of such a scandal should come to the Society for the Propagation of the Gospel, and their funds be withdrawn. He resolved to take no further risks with these, his long-awaited Indian scholars. He dismissed Milford and took charge of Joel and Caleb personally at that time. This brought about a remarkable change in their condition. From barely tolerable obligations, the youths in time became Chauncy's proud obsessions. He schooled them as carefully as he had his own sons. By year's end he had remedied the defects in their instruction, so that when the examination results were posted, they overpeered not a few of their classmates.

III

The second, and lesser, shadow upon my life that year was my own struggle with ungirt desire. After that Lord's Day assignation in the library, Samuel and I took care never again to meet, the two of us alone, but only when others were present. It was necessary that it be so; we both of us knew our own weakness in this matter. After that day in the library I had several sleepless nights, awaiting the onset of my courses, and knowing if they did not come I would have ruined not myself only, but Samuel's life and the babe's as well, on the shoals of a moment's unrestrained appetite. As decayed as I am now, and as long as that carnal life has been over and done with, I can still recall, with the greatest vividness, what it felt like that year, to flail and struggle against tides of wanting that would tug at me, sweeping away lucid thought, judgment and propriety. It did me one good, at least, and that was to strip away from me, then and thereafter, all sanctimony regarding sins of the flesh.

Samuel waited, as I had asked, a full six months before he renewed his suit for my hand. During that time his behavior made clear that he accepted my character as it was, and did not hope to somehow refashion me as a more compliant bride. My fear, that he would seek to stifle my mind, proved to have little foundation. Although we saw each other in passing every day, we had speech together only on the Lord's Day, when we sat together after meeting with his father present as chaperone. If I asked for explication of some matter from the week's lectures, his father would draw a brow, but Samuel would smile, and gladly lead me in discussion of whatever topic I had raised. Soon enough, his father would forget his disapproval and join in the debate, until such informal seminars became a settled thing.

So it was that we married during the festive commencement week, with Samuel's merry young graduates as our witnesses. My brother and my grandfather made the crossing and joined in the revels. Even Makepeace suspended his dour judgments for once, and smiled on the carousing afoot in the town. Grandfather and Makepeace gave me to understand they were well content in my choice of husband, and the three of them fell easily into civil discourse on a range of topics.

Makepeace brought news that Caleb and Joel were glad to hear, of how Anne had settled with the Takemmy people and was loved by them. I was pleased to know that she had found a use for her studious mind as tutor to the younger Merry girls, who otherwise would have gone without instruction. (Their stepmother, Sofia, was unlettered and their father barely so; what learning Noah and his brother could boast had come from their natural mother, product of a Herefordshire dame school, and had ended with her untimely death.)

I found Makepeace much changed—lighter in his looks and altogether less stern in his manner. I set this down to the fact that he no longer was required to scale the mount of academe each day and face his own insufficiencies. Instead, he worked the farm and read his Bible and was minister to the settlement in all important ways. Although he was not qualified to be ordained, most island folk were happy to have him take father's place upon the pulpit, where he preached a plain and unadorned gospel.

The need had been great for some other who spoke Wampanaontoaonk to help Iacoomis and grandfather continue father's missionary works, Makepeace being disinclined and ill-fitted to make any headway in that difficult tongue. Peter Folger, grandfather's agent, was persuaded to take the post. He had removed himself to our sister island some years since, after falling out with grandfather on a difference regarding the thorny issue of baptism. But somehow the thorns were clipped, and he returned, so that father's work of catechizing and teaching school in Manitouwatootan continued in due season.

The reason for Makepeace's softened manner had another ground beyond his satisfaction at being liberated from arduous studies. This became patent when he confided that he was to be married soon himself, to the widow Gaze. I knew her only slightly as a quiet, devout, older woman, two years senior to Makepeace. Her short marriage to the mariner Eliahu Gaze had left her with an infant son. As Makepeace waxed on about this babe, it became clear that he doted on the child and the mother in equal parts. I wished them joy with all my heart, and all the more so because Dorcas Gaze's widow's thirds had come to a tidy estate. Makepeace, showing himself fair and principled to a high degree, was most liberal in figuring my marriage portion, allowing me a larger share than I had expected.

This mattered more than it might have done. Quite unlooked for, Samuel had been furnished with the means to realize his long desire: he had been offered a place in the chirurgical school at the University of Padua, along with a modest bursary towards his expenses. With certain shifts and dispositions, we calculated that we were just in purse to accept the offer. So we set sail in December. I took leave of Joel and Caleb with few misgivings: they seemed well embarked upon their sophomore year, and well set, both in their studies and in their place as members in good standing of the college community. With the president himself so invested in their success, the fact of it seemed to me to be assured.

It was a long journey, and difficult. But on a winter morning, wreathed in mists, a muscular boatman poled our craft across a milky lagoon. He spoke neither English nor Latin, but when he raised his arm and pointed, I could descry, in the distance, a squiggly horizon. At first, my mind could not reason out what my eyes beheld. When I had looked out from water towards land, it had generally been toward wooded bluffs or lightly settled harbors. Then suddenly I knew what I saw: a horizon entirely fashioned by the hand of man. And such a horizon: the spires and cupolas of Venice, luminous in the pale sun. We stepped ashore near St. Marco's plaza, just as that great square erupted with noise. It was noon, and the bells of a hundred churches were pealing. The sound seemed to rise up everywhere around us. It was as if the very stones were singing.

For a girl raised on the rim of a wilderness, it was strange to be in a place where every inch of ground had been settled for hundreds upon hundreds of years. I felt the press of people, and the press of ghosts— great hordes of those who had lived and walked before me. That time in the Old World—its different light, strange scents, foreign sounds— comes back to me now in bright memories: a summer day in Padua. Samuel returns from the Anatomy Theater. The words tumble from him as he tells me all he has learned that morning, of the circulation of the blood through ropey artery and slender vein. We sit in the courtyard as the hot sun beats down on the crumbling roseate walls and the fragrance of lavender rises from the herb pots. There are bees, their legs heavy with pollen, fumbling the tiny blooms. I tear a chunk of good bread and smear ripe cheese upon it. I take up a tiny piece of nobbly root. The landlord had handed it to me that morning with great ceremony, as if it were a gemstone. I grate it, as he has shown me, atop the oozing cheese. There is a sudden wonderful aroma—strange, rich, earthy. I feed the luscious bread to Samuel as if he were a child. We laugh, and he takes my hand and draws me inside, to lie upon the cool sheets in our shuttered chamber.

We were two years in Padua. In the mornings, while Samuel attended the Anatomy Theater, I earned a good coin teaching English to a pair of charming little *contessas* and their boisterous younger brother. They were papists, of course. In that city, whose university has been famous for four hundred years, we lived cheek by jowl with all manner of outlandish persons who had been drawn to study there—wandering Jews, dark-skinned Musalmans, tonsured monks in roped-belted robes. On Fridays, at sunset, we would hear the haunting Hebrew melodies drift from the nearby synagogue and see the men issue hence in their striped silk coats and flat fur hats. On feast days we would marvel at the processions of the papists, carrying their gilded, flower-bedecked statues through the streets. In time, even Samuel came to wonder if our austere form of worship was the only one way to be godly.

We returned to Cambridge in 1664. Samuel's father beckoned us home. His strength was failing and he required his son to keep the school until a suitable master could be established in his place. I was ill all the voyage. We docked in Boston harbor in a driving rain and I wanted to kneel in the mud and kiss the ground—not because Boston was dear to me, but because it *was* ground—terra firma—and not a roiling ocean. The next morning, I was ill again. Samuel looked at me strangely, and asked the question that I should have asked myself, weeks since, had I not been too ill to think clearly. We had, after more than two years, begun to resign ourselves to the possibility that God would not bless us with issue. But that day I realized that I carried our child. I will not write of the birth, except to say that I barely survived it. He would be our only child, for though Samuel and the midwife together saved my life, they gave me to understand there would be no other. So we chose the name from the bible verse: *Call your son ammi* (my people) *and your daughter ruhama* (beloved), because this child would be both son and daughter to us. And so he has proved: a strong man, yet a tender one. He lives with us now—or perhaps I should say, we with him—for even though Samuel still has vigor and answers occasional calls for his chirurgical skills, it is Ammi Ruhama and his Elizabeth who order the life of this household now. They have made it a haven for all of us, frail elderly and boisterous grandbabes alike.

But I run ahead of myself. I was not long risen from my troubled childbed, and Ammi Ruhama was an infant in my arms on the warm June morning in 1665 when we entered the college hall to hear Caleb and Joel, at the end of their senior year, sit solstices with their classmates. For six days, the candidates for graduation were required to be in the hall until the dinner hour, ready to match wits with any who held a master's degree, or with such members of the college's Board of Overseers who cared to quiz them. One by one, the good and the great men of the colony came, as they did every year at that time, to try the knowledge of the graduating class.

Caleb's looks troubled me. He had become rail thin. A persistent cough wracked him. In the years of my absence he had grown out of his health by reason of poor diet and too close an application to his studies. Yet his face was handsome, still, in a drawn and spare way, and as he argued in Latin with one of the college overseers I noted that it lost its haggard cast. Even though he had far surpassed my skills in that tongue, I knew enough to judge that he spoke with eloquence, buttressing his argument with useful epigrams and citations from Ramus and Aristotle. His own gifts were the ore, and now that ore had been refined and forged by years of effort under the preeminent scholar in the colony.

As impressive as Caleb's disputations seemed to me, the whispers about the hall that day concerned Joel. The rumor was that come commencement, Joel would be named valedictorian of his class, ranked above the scions of Eliot and Dudley and all the other high-born English scholars. I flushed with pleasure to hear this: I could imagine his aged father, who had risen up from spurned outcast, watching his son lead the class to commencement. I resolved to see to it that plans were made to fetch him hence from the island when the time came.

I had been made aware, on my return to Cambridge, that Caleb's future also was assured. He had become protégé of Thomas Danforth, the esteemed magistrate and assistant to the governor. As treasurer of Harvard, Danforth had been much about the college and had noticed Caleb, encouraging him in his studies and speaking often with him about issues in law, such as natural and chartered rights. Caleb was to go to live in his house at Charlestown, directly from Harvard, and study the law under his inspection. I rejoiced to learn this, and felt sure his health would mend itself once he was free of the privations and restrictions of college life.

I was even more convinced of this when Samuel and I dined with Thomas Danforth and shared his ample board, soon after our return from Padua. Danforth had heard that I had been acquainted with Caleb from his early youth, and he plied me with questions about the style of life for native peoples on the island, and about Caleb's family, the role of his father the sonquem, and how it might be like or different to the role of our English lawgivers.

He was most interested when I told him what I knew of how my father had first negotiated for land. The sonquem at the time thought the sale a good thing, but not all of his band had agreed with him. Instead of proceeding as an English Lord would do, disregarding his subjects, the sonquem had ceded some territory to the dissenters and sold to us only from his own remnant holdings. Danforth found this idea of government most arresting. Through the entire meal, he cried up Caleb's abilities, saying there was nothing he might not do, given time and chance. It gave me such joy to hear him talk of his high ambitions for my friend, whom he already cast as a coming man of affairs. He speculated that we would see Caleb one day take his place upon the bench of justice, representing the native peoples in the colony's good governance.

Joel, for his part, told me that he was resolved to follow his father in the ministry. He planned to return to the island to see how his people stood in regard to their spiritual estate, and how he might further his father's work of bringing them to Christ. He hoped, if funds were forthcoming from the society, to pursue a second degree, and become ordained. During the sitting of solstices, he drew us apart. Diffidently, his eyes upon the ground, he asked if Samuel and I would travel with him to the island before the summer's commencement exercises, to witness his marriage to Anne. It seemed the two young people had corresponded through the years, in secret from all save Caleb, ever since her clandestine escape from Cambridge. They had been handfast for a year and were impatient for the sanctification of their union.

Samuel and I each congratulated him most sincerely, and when I looked a question at Samuel he said he was sure he could arrange a tutor for the school so that we could make the voyage. I grasped his hand when he said this, and gave him a look which I hoped conveyed my full heart. I had not seen the island in five years, and I longed for it. Joel seemed pleased, and went to sit again in his place, which was, as ever, beside Caleb.

He was soon engrossed in a disputation with an elderly divine, but all the while, apparently, managing to lend an ear to Caleb's argument as well. At one point, he turned and offered Caleb a point of logic to use against his opponent. It was a witty point, and all who heard it laughed in appreciation.

At that moment, Ammi Ruhama started a thin, catlike mewling, which I knew from experience would soon turn to a piercing howl if I did not attend to his needs. So I took my leave of Samuel and walked back to the pleasant, light-filled room we had rented in the home of his cousin the glazier, Ephriam Cutter. As I sat by the open casement, feeling the warm summer air caress my breast and lift my babe's silken hair, I felt a drowsy kind of satisfaction. I thought of my father, and how he would have rejoiced to see Caleb and Joel embarked upon such useful and distinguished lives. I thought of Anne, and how that decision, made in the heat of such roiling emotion so many years earlier, had led to such a happy result. I let my fingers play with the soft dark strands of Ammi Ruhama's hair. He was his father's son, though he had some look of my twin brother Zuriel about him, or so I liked to think. I leaned my head down and whispered in his ear: "Soon, very soon, little one, we will make the crossing, home to my island. You will like it there."

IV

I was right about that, at least. Ammi Ruhama loves this island. He was ten years old when we came back here to live, seeking refuge from the dreadful events that then beset the mainland. All through that terrible year of 1675, we would climb the bluffs and look across to the far shore, scanning the distant horizon for rumors of war. Too often, we could descry smoke rising from the latest embattled settlement.

At first, it seemed as if Metacom's rebellious Indians might well prevail. The frontier townships fell, one following the other. The fighting reached even unto Plimouth, where Metacom's father Massasoit had once been a friend to the settlers. News drifted across the water of nightmarish acts: heads on pikes, disemboweled cattle, families burnt alive. Farmers could not bring in the harvest that year unless they assembled in large armed bands to do so. Folk fled frontier villages such as Northfield and Deerfield for the comparative safety of larger towns, but twelve settlements in all, including Providence, were burned and destroyed. It seemed that the English did not know how to fight these foes, who appeared unafraid of death, and who knew their native ground so well that they could melt invisibly into swamp or fen to evade pursuit.

We tried to keep the worst of this from Ammi Ruhama, but Samuel and I held each other at night and prayed that the war would not reach out to us. Our prayer was answered; the native people of this island never did side with Metacom, or King Philip, as the

English styled him. Instead, grandfather put his trust in them, and armed them to defend themselves, and us, should any of Metacom's followers attempt to bring the war across the sound.

For half a year things went ill for the mainland English. Indeed, if the Indians had united behind Metacom, and sunk old tribal enmities, I do believe they would have prevailed, and undone the colonial enterprise on these shores for a generation or more. As it was, the costs were very great. Over six hundred English were killed and the number of Indian deaths much higher. Also dead: the slender hope that our two peoples might live together in any kind of amity.

By the time the fortunes of war reversed themselves—Metacom executed, his followers killed or sold into foreign slavery—Ammi Ruhama had a great dread of the mainland, and begged that we stay upon the island. He had set down his roots, deep into its rich soils, and has never since desired to be in any other place. As it happened, his fear of the world across the water proved well founded, for the end of the war brought the colony no respite from disaster. Every boat that plied hence seemed to bring some news of woe. God's hand lay heavily on his people, and no amount of fast days or prayerful reflection seemed to appease his wrath. Terrible fires scorched the homes and warehouses of Boston in '75 and again in '79, and in between, a smallpox epidemic raged so hot that some thirty English persons a day were laid in their graves by it. The winter of 1680 was bitter cold; the following summer brought shriveling drought. We felt this here, but not with the same battering force as they did upon the mainland. They say the clemency of the ocean's currents moderated the extreme weathers, and kept from us the worst of it.

Even though the news from the mainland continued so bleak, I was surprised that Samuel consented full willingly to stay on the island; I had thought he would yearn too greatly for the society of educated men. But there was no other chirurgeon here, and he deemed he could be of use. So, in time, we built this house. We have lived with great contentment within these walls, and seen those walls expand; a wing added for Ammi Ruhama's family, and now two of his sons have their own cottages nearby. Sometimes, four generations gather here at board. At such times, I look about me, amazed that such a restless girl should have grown old as matriarch to such a settled brood.

While Ammi Ruhama was still very young, I tried to open up his eyes to the world beyond these shores. I would tell him of Padua, where he was conceived—of the city squares and the soaring towers, or the stirring tales from the opera at the great theater there. He would sit with his head on my knee and listen until I had done. Then he would turn his face to me—the face that had his father's dark gravity, even at that young age, but also an elegance that Samuel's ruined profile had obscured.

"Those places," he would say. "Everything there is done and built and finished. I like it here, where we can make and do for ourselves." Although his father and I saw to it that he was an educated boy, he never cared for book learning as we did, and would not hear of leaving the island to attend the college. He grew into a practical man, who liked to use his hands as well as his wits. In this, my friend Noah Merry was like a second father to him, sharing with him the skills that belong to such a man. Noah and Tobia had been blessed with four daughters and no sons. When Ammi Ruhama wed their daughter Elizabeth, it was as if our two families truly became one.

Ammi Ruhama prospered, which is well, since the fruitfulness not granted to Samuel and me has been his lot. (I can boast six living grandchildren and have lived to see three of my great-grandchildren.) Ammi Ruhama is a boatbuilder, and a renowned one. His genius was to study the age-old designs and see how he might adapt them for the particular conditions of our waters and the materials here ready to hand. The design of his craft has proved popular with coasters throughout the colony. One sees his boats often, plying along the shore, their distinctive rig unmistakable, even at a great distance. Whenever I glimpse such a vessel, I think to myself, "My son made that," and I wish fair winds to those who sail it.

Fair winds and foul. Barks and sloops. Schooners and gigs. Waters, wild and wide, shallow and still. How these things have marked out the chapters of my life. I suppose an island dweller should expect it to be so.

V

The boat that brought me home to the island from Cambridge, in June of 1665, was a tired, oakum-patched old lugger, but to me it seemed a blessed craft.

The weather was fair and sparkling. I stood on the foredeck, gripping the stays, yearning to catch the very first sight of the island I had left so reluctantly five years since. Joel was beside me, his own longing even more urgent than my own. My heart flipped in my chest when his keen eyes descried the line in the distance that marked the island. That line soon became a nub, then a vivid cliff, then the vast sweep of beloved shore where I had spent the sweetest days of my girlhood. I cried out to Samuel, who was holding Ammi Ruhama in his arms. He looked up and saw the distant island rising out of the breakers. He smiled with affection in his eyes, happy for me in my joy.

We disembarked to a large welcoming party—grandfather, barely touched by age; Aunt Hannah, frail and wrinkled as a raisin, hobbling with the support of a brace of grandsons. Makepeace, sleek as a hearth cat, his young stepson holding fast to his hand and his wife, Dorcas, at his side, cradling the infant daughter they had named for Solace. A little behind this first press of greeters stood Iacoomis and his wife and all their children, a well-grown, prosperous-looking brood. In the midst of my own family, I looked across at Joel's, smiling to see how the children swarmed all around him, the littlest vying to clamber into his arms, the older ones laying a hand on his back or shoulder, all eager to touch the Harvard laureate on his homecoming. His mother, Grace, circled his slender wrist with her own fleshy hand and clicked her tongue in disapproval at his winnowed condition. There was little sign of the plump boy who had left this place. I could tell she resolved, then and there, to fatten him up in the coming weeks.

I thought of Caleb. There was no one to tend to him in such a manner. With heavy heart, he had determined to stay in Cambridge, even though those who had sat solstices were at liberty for the several weeks until commencement. His only close kinsman, Tequamuck, could not be expected to greet with any cheer his lost apprentice, adopted now into the highest tier of English society. I do not know if Caleb feared his uncle, or, from lingering affection, sought not to confront him with his loss. I do know that this uncommon separation from his friend, and at such a time of celebration, cost both of them a great deal. I also know that Joel had not pressed Caleb to come, understanding better than any other the rend in the fabric of his friend's life.

Now, even as Joel laughed and said kind words to his own kinfolk, I could see his eyes scanning the dock. I supposed he looked for Anne. Their reunion came later, when the Merry family fetched her to the plantation that afternoon. Grandfather presided over their marriage the eve of the following day. Anne had fulfilled her early promise of beauty, her green eyes no longer downcast but flashing, animated at last by a confident and joyous spirit. Joel's dreamy brown gaze rarely left her face. The feasting was prodigious. I would say a good half of the Takemmy band, including the sonquem, came to Great Harbor to join the celebration, bringing with them the pick of their best victuals to add to Iacoomis's ample providence. Only the Aldens and their faction held aloof, though even some one or two of their confederates joined in, once the gaiety of the celebration became apparent.

In the cool of that morning, I had left Samuel to tend to Ammi Ruhama. I went to find Speckle. She looked well for her years, glossy and well cared for. When I threw the bridle over her head, she nuzzled me and did a little dance, anticipating our ride. I did not press her but went slowly, noting the changes the years had brought. These were very great in the lands abutting the settlement. The wilderness of my childhood that had pressed so close upon us had been pushed back, year following year. There were some miles of clear trail cut now, leading out of Great Harbor. Stumps marked out woodlots farther afield, as settlers were obliged to travel greater distances to secure their fuel. Many acres more had been improved for pasture, so that the flocks that grazed now were much enlarged.

I was glad when we came at last to unspoiled, shady groves of tall beech and fragrant sassafras. I breathed greedily the scents of my childhood, watching the familiar play of light through the leaves. I sat for a long time at father's white stone cairn, risen now to twice my own height and sparkling in the sunshine. When we reached the south shore, Speckle broke into a canter of her own accord, and I let her run through the surf until she tired.

In the days that followed, I rode out whenever I could—alone, sometimes; often with Samuel and the babe. I wanted to share my memories insofar as I was able. But some things I did not share, and if at times Samuel caught me, lost in reverie, he did not press me to reveal my every thought.

I think it would have been impossible to find the heart to leave the island, as the summer waxed and the harvest ripened, had we not had the great celebration of Caleb and Joel's commencement calling us back to Cambridge. We had conceived what I thought was a marvelous scheme to enlarge Joel's joy in the day. He had need to return ahead of us, since if he learned he had indeed been honored as valedictorian, he would have to work upon an oration and rehearse his leading role in the many rituals of the day. There was a bark all set to sail on the first favorable tide, laden to the gunwales with island produce—fulled fleeces, barrels of salt cod, bales of sassafras root bound for England, where it was prized as a remedy for the evils of the French pox. The captain had agreed to take Joel as passenger. We said we would see him in Cambridge within the fortnight. We planned in secret to bring Iacoomis, as a surprise.

Anne and I together went to the pier to say farewell. I hung back, to give them a private moment. They stood, heads together, the sunlight gleaming on their sleek black hair, and when Joel went aboard and the sails bellied and stiffened in the fresh breeze, she stayed on the dock, looking after him, until the boat passed around the curve of land and out of sight. Later, when I tried to peer through my grief for any hint of a thing awry, I think that I sensed that the bark sat low in the water. But perhaps that memory is not a true one, just a thought planted in my mind, in the aftermath.

VI

It strikes me now that I have written so little in my various scrawls throughout the years about our sister island, that low crescent, farther out to sea, over the blue horizon beyond the little isle of Chappaquiddick. That grandfather's patent included the other island, I had always known; I recalled his satisfaction in 1659 when he found investors in Salisbury who paid him thirty pounds and two beaver hats—of which he was rather vain—for an interest in it. I also knew that father went there from time to time, with Iacoomis, to evangelize the Indians of that place. But his reports, when he would return, made it out in every way inferior to our own island—smaller, flatter, less various, more windswept—and barely worth braving the treacherous few miles of rock-strewn shoal.

Yet it was thence we went, three days after Joel's departure, my tears lashed from my face by the salt-laden wind and my guts knotted up with sorrow and seasickness, both. There had been high winds, the afternoon of Joel's departure, but not so heavy as to cause any of us great concern. Ships plied the route from the island to Boston in much worse conditions, the mariners thinking little of it. How that bark came to be pushed so far off course and to ground itself on Coatuet, no one has ever been able to explain.

As we approached the island, we saw the bark, lying aslant, washed high up on the sands of the barrier beach just short of a dense cypress forest. It was in no sense a shipwrack, the bark so little damaged it seemed impossible that any aboard could have perished in the grounding. I turned to Samuel, my face lit with hope that the reports which had reached us were false. But he looked down upon me with a sad gravity, laid his hand about my shoulder and shook his head. I realized then that he knew more of this matter than he had yet confided to me.

The skipper of our vessel would not risk a closer approach, so we beat on for the harbor, reefing our sails and tacking slowly up to the dock. Peter Folger met us there, and the four of us—Samuel, the baby, Iacoomis and myself—disembarked and walked the short track to his cottage. Iacoomis was hunched over like an old man, wearing a beaten expression that I had not seen upon him since first he came to our home in my childhood days.

Folger had bread, cheese and beer set out upon the board, and I took a heel of the bread, thinking to quiet my belly, but the crumbs sat like ashes in my mouth and I had to set it by directly. Iacoomis was the first to speak. He addressed Folger in Wampanaontoaonk.

"Where is the body of my son?"

"Friend," Folger replied gravely. "Carry the memory of your son alive."

Iacoomis looked at Folger, his eyes akindle. "I will see my son."

Folger put a hand on his shoulder. "My friend, it shall be as you wish. As you wish. But I would spare you. They were several. They used warclubs. Their frenzy was very great."

I cried out at this, and Iacoomis, who had forged himself into the bravest man I knew, the man who had confronted the pawaaws and put them under his heel, folded in upon himself like a dying leaf and struggled to breathe.

Samuel, who did not understand what had been said, wrapped me in his arms and looked questioningly at Folger.

"We have the murtherers, rest easy on that score. They will hang, be assured of it. They are known to us: wicked troublemakers who for some time now have complained that we choused them from their hunting grounds and let our hogs despoil their clam beds. 'Tis a false claim, for we have the mark of their sonquem on the papers that ceded all their lands to us. They say he did not know what he signed, but how is it a fault in us if they cannot now, as they claim, feed their children? In any case, this was not the first time they turned to theft—for that was their motive, they have confessed it. Seeing the bark run aground they swarmed it, for lucre of the spoil within, and beat any who tried to gainsay them. The first mate, who yet lived when we found him—by God's stern providence, he died thereafter—gave us to understand that Joel confronted them most bravely, making arguments in their own tongue as to why they should forbear, but this only enraged them more against him, seemingly, and at the last all of them together set upon him most cruelly."

When I could speak, I turned to Iacoomis and told him, in Wampanaontoaonk, that it would be my very great honor to be permitted to wash Joel's body and prepare it for Christian burial. Iacoomis would want no other rites for his son.

Samuel tried to turn me from the task. But I looked into his eyes and said I would do it, and it was a measure of how we had become, as a couple, that he simply took Ammi Ruhama from my arms and nodded as I left for the place where they had laid out Joel's shattered corpse. Peter Folger gave me linens from his own store to dress the body. I did my best. Even so, when Iacoomis came to see his son, it was a measure of his courage and his Christian conviction that he was able to refrain from crying out at the sight of him. Thus perished from this world our hopeful young prophet Joel.

We returned with Iacoomis to our island with the heavy tidings that the reports and rumors of wrack and death were true. I was present when Anne learned the news. She wailed and tore at her face and hair, and could not be comforted. I sat up with her that night, and left her the next day in the care of Grace Iacoomis, sitting by their door, her green eyes like brimming pools, staring sightlessly out to sea.

Two days later, Samuel and I disembarked at the Cambridge town landing into a scene of celebration all at odds with our melancholy state. Since the first commencement in 1642, the revels are become the chief summer festival of Cambridge, arriving as they do hand in hand with the earliest of the harvest-time bounty and before the first hint of hardening weather. Since the college's founding even the most sober members of this austere colony have thought learning worthy of celebration, and have sanctioned excesses at commencement that would draw stern punishment on other days. That year was no different, and as always, Cambridge was filling up as the day approached with folk associated with the college and those who came for the festival alone.

I left Samuel and the babe at the Cutters' house and walked directly to the Indian College. It fell to me to carry the news to Caleb. I was his friend: it was right that I should do it. Samuel wanted to go with me, but I said no. Howsoever my friend received this blow, the fewer witnesses the better, as I thought. The worst of it was that his face was all joy when first he caught sight of me. He hurried out into the yard to greet me. He looked as well as I had seen him since my return from Padua, all alight with anticipation of the celebration to come.

I had thought, all through the journey, of what words I could say to him. I had turned and shaped them and spoken them in my mind many times. In the end, all my rehearsals were for nowt. Where one loves another as greatly as Caleb loved Joel, the soul does not need words to bring fell tidings. My face, my body, the heaviness of my step—all these things carried the news to him plain. Before any word passed my lips—"shipwrack" or "murther"—Caleb knew Joel was dead.

He did not cry out. He stood, and the hand that had been extended to greet me fell heavy to his side. His face twitched from the effort of self-control. I was struggling to form words, my throat closed by my own tears. I do not know what I managed to choke out in regard to the events, but after a moment he raised a hand and hushed me.

"Bethia." He took a deep, ragged breath. "I will trouble you to hear this anon. Please leave me now."

"Caleb, if I—"

"Please, Bethia. As you care for me. Go."

So I went. I do not know if he sought the details, some later time, from Samuel or any other. But to me he never spoke of Joel's death again.

VII

I will not say the Harvard commencement of the Year of Our Lord
1665 was joyless. That would be false. There *was* joy, a moment
of sweet festivity, even for those of us who mourned. In this fallen
world, such is our condition. Every happiness is a bright ray between
shadows, every gaiety bracketed by grief. There is no birth that does
not recall a death, no victory but brings to mind a defeat. So was
that commencement a celebration. I believe Joel wanted it so. His
spirit, insofar as I felt its light touch that day, was no unquiet
ghost but a warm and benign companion. I think—I hope—that
Caleb felt this too.

I close my eyes, and I remember that sun-dappled day. The
paths were crowded from early morning with visitors from Boston,
Watertown, Charlestown and every outlying farm or plantation.
Families of the commencers jostled jib by jole with Indians, farmers,
clergymen, and vendors loudly hawking their diverse wares, come to
profit off the throng. It seemed that many folk thirsted not for learning
but for beer and wine, for the taverns did brisk business, and public
drunkenness was evident in some raucous antics among the crowd.

When I had worked in the buttery, the preparations for the
feasting and bevering had consumed us for many weeks prior to the
day itself. By long custom we engaged two Indians from Natick who
were adept at the turnspit to roast beeves, and in the great fireplace
all manner of kettles brimmed with pottages and puddings. We
had rolled out no less than twelve barrels of wine that year, and I

lost count of the amount of cider and beer that was also consumed, and that just within the college precinct. I had thought the fest ill-named that year, for this *inceptio*, or beginning, seemed more apt to be the end of those of us tasked to provision it.

Samuel and I were abroad early, to assure a good vantage point for the academical procession. Even so, many had come before us. I could see the governor, mounted and flanked by his pike-bearing guards, and also the sheriffs providing escort to the Board of Overseers. But the honorable members of the Great and General Court and the reverend clergy of the six leading towns I could not see, since they were on foot. I tugged on Samuel's hand and we wove our way, with some difficulty in that dense throng, until we found a higher vantage point. I was determined to see Caleb marching with his classmates. I glimpsed Chauncy, and Dunster, the former president, in the ermine-trimmed robes and velvet bonnets of their English colleges. And then came our scholars in their plain gowns, their own glowing faces the only adornment they required. They were all grave looks one moment, joyful smiles the next when perhaps they caught the eye of a parent in the crowd. I saw Eliot and Dudley, handsome Hope Atherton and a smiling Jabez Fox. Then Caleb, marching last, taller than the next by a good half a head, stately in his bearing, as one raised to ceremony. He did not look all about him, as some of the others did, but kept his eyes ahead, his gaze intense and focused, as if he truly could see the future towards which he walked.

I could not peel my eyes from him, even as he walked on and past me. The set of his shoulders, the ceremonial cap squarely upon his head—and I thought of turkey feathers and raccoon grease, purple wampum and deer hide. I thought of the hands, dirt engrained, reaching so avidly for the book I held. I had begun this journey following him into the hidden corners of his world and here it ended with him crossed over into the brightest heights of mine.

Samuel touched my arm then and signaled that we needed to make haste into the hall. I had arranged with the Whitbys to spy upon the ceremony from the buttery and had promised to stay well out of their way on this, the busiest day of their year. From my peephole I saw Samuel take his place at the front with the distinguished alumni. The hall was crowded and all abuzz with excited chatter until the minister stood to deliver his invocation. Then Benjamin Eliot was called forth to deliver the Greek oration. He had been named valedictorian. Nothing was said about Joel's untimely and tragic death, and if the honor would have gone to him, no sign of it was given. I do not know why they did not acknowledge him; it seemed to me then a grave misjudgment, so much so that I felt my face burn hot with the injustice of the omission. Surely, had such a tragic fate overtaken an Eliot or a Dudley, we should have heard of it, and offered up a prayer. I expect Chauncy did not wish to darken the merriment of the day, or to belittle young Eliot by making it plain that he was a second choice. Especially since his renowned father sat smiling proudly in the first tier of distinguished guests. Still, it sat ill with me, and it does so even to this day.

I believe Benjamin Eliot had not had much time to prepare his words, for he fell back on the stale and oft-rehearsed theme of salvation by grace, and although it was a competent oration, none would have called it brilliant or memorable. Of course, young

Eliot did not have to use the occasion as others did, to catch the eye of those in the illustrious audience who might have a pulpit or a schoolroom on offer. His path was already set out for him; he would go to assist the work of his father. Later, I learned that a stern providence awaited him. At a young age, he became quite lunatic, unable to govern his tongue or his actions.

Dudley rose next, to take the secondary honor of the Latin oration. This was wittily and prettily done, Dudley taking as his subject the Golden Mean and the desirability of moderation, and then, when he had the audience lulled into acceptance of the proposition, upending the argument by asserting that in truth God allowed of no moderation. Between good and evil, truth and falsehood, there lay no mean, and the least moderate fact of existence was the existence of God himself. When he had done, the approbation voiced in the hall was itself quite immoderate, thus furthering young Dudley's case. I need not write of what became of *him*, his fame—or infamy—depending upon one's faction, having set his name before us oft enough. But when I learned he had penned an account of his adventures in the Great Swamp campaign of King Philip's War, I sent away for it. I read it with dismay, surprised that one who had known Caleb and Joel could gloat upon the murder of Indian women and children as he did.

I felt rather for young Jabez Fox, having to follow on from Dudley with the Hebrew oration. He also resorted to a well-masticated topic: whether goodness manifested itself always in the beautiful. I found my mind drifting to other times when that issue had been probed, and thinking it was a missed chance indeed not to have had Caleb speak to this theme. His might have been a lively exegesis, drawing as it did on a very different experience of what was good and beautiful, and how beauty might be perceived quite differently by foreign souls in unalike times. Although in his work he had been the peer or better of Fox, Samuel had told me that Chauncy thought it unwise to have Caleb and Joel honored with two of the three orations. He said Chauncy had invited Caleb to speak, once the news of Joel's death reached him, but Caleb had declined, saying he was not in heart for it.

While I attempted to keep my concentration upon the speakers, my gaze kept drifting to Caleb, where he sat in the graduates' place of honor upon the dais. He held himself, as ever, very erect. I tried to see him as others in the hall must—this great curiosity, the salvage plucked from the wilderness and tamed so thoroughly into a scholar. In truth, he looked almost indistinguishable from his fellow graduates. His dress mimicked theirs in every particular. If anything, his grooming was even more particular. He was taller, as I have said, but he had shed that breadth of chest and arm that had once marked him out as a different style of man. If his hair was a darker hue than the others', it had lost some of its distinctive thickness and sheen. His skin, though olive tinged, was several shades lighter after the years of indoor life. Only the planes of his face—the high, broad cheekbones—had become more pronounced and foreign the leaner he had become. Caleb's face was tilted towards the speaker's podium, but his expression was very distant. I supposed that he thought of Joel; how could he not?

As the dinner hour approached, Chauncy rose to open the feast, craving a blessing on the young men commencing their roles as leaders of educated society. The governor stood next, and sent around the grace cup, with a warm little speech about the college and the pride that he took in the fact that the universities of Oxford and Cambridge recognized our scholars' first degree as equal with their own.

The feast itself was ample, the beeves succulent, and as the cups were filled and filled again, the noise in the hall became such that folk could not hear the speech at their own tables without leaning in almost to their neighbors' laps. In the end, the clamor and the stifling heat drove me out of the buttery and into the yard, where the air was cooler, if the revels no less raucous. By the time I had recovered sufficiently to go back inside, the disputations were already under way. Although I was keen to hear Caleb, I knew he would do admirably with the hoary old topics of theses *philosophicae* and *philologicae*. Indeed, nothing was said that afternoon that had not already been said a dozen times previous in the same place, the only difference being the occasional interjections from an audience whose spirits had been elevated by a bibulous luncheon. Caleb acquitted himself with distinction; I saw Chauncy beaming every time he spoke, his Latin eloquent and his allusions apt. Once or twice I caught Thomas Danforth, leaning across his fellows to garner agreement from some distinguished person or other as to Caleb's ability.

Well, I thought. You have done it, my friend. It has cost you your home, and your health, and estrangement from your closest kinsman. But after today, no man may say the Indian mind is primitive and ineducable. Here, in this hall, you stand, the incontestible argument, the *negat respondens*.

Finally, Chauncy stood and signaled for quiet. The hall hushed. He adressed himself, in Latin, to the Overseers: "Honorable gentlemen and reverend ministers, I present to you these youths, whom I know to be suffcient in learning and in manners to be raised to the First Degree in Arts according to the custom of the Universities in England. Doth it please you?"

The voices rang out: "*Placet!*"

One by one, the graduates rose up and stood before Chauncy to be handed the book that signified their degree. As Caleb took his from Chauncy's hand, I thought that the old man's voice shook with emotion as he said the rote words, "I hand thee this book, together with the power to lecture on any one of the arts which thou has studied, wheresoever thou shalt have been called to that office."

Later, when all the formal business had been concluded, the graduates stepped down from the dais and into the embrace of their families. The women—mothers, sisters—joined the press now, entering the hall all smiles for their graduates. I moved forward, trying to reach Caleb, to offer him the congratulations the day deserved. But the crowd was so dense and unyielding I could hardly make my way. It parted for him, however, as he made his way directly for the door. I called out, trying to attract his attention. He did not turn, but kept walking. I looked back over my shoulder to where Samuel was similarly encumbered by knots of revelers. He raised his shoulders, to imply that he was pinned, for the moment, in his corner of the hall. I pushed my way through, elbowing honorables and reverends with no regard for mannerliness, and finally attained the door. I looked in all directions, trying to descry Caleb in the crowd.

* * *

Finally, I made him out. He was halfway across the yard, leaning heavily against a tree. His back was to me, but I could see that his shoulders shook. For a moment, I considered whether or not to go to him. If he was in grief, he would not want me, perhaps. But then feeling overwhelmed prudence and I hurried on. As I drew near, I realized that it was not grief that wracked him, but a violent coughing spasm. He had a linen hankin I had sewn for him pressed to his mouth. When he drew it away, I saw that it was speckled with blood.

VIII

I expect that every person alive today has sat with someone dear to them through the rigors of the consumption. So I will not recount the long days and nights, except to say that my friend suffered, and through all of it evinced the stoicism that befit both a sonquem's son and a convinced Christian. Which part of himself he called upon for patience and courage, I do not know.

Thomas Danforth was solicitous. Caleb did not lack for the best food, but it came late to replenish what town and college life had robbed from him. The Charlestown physician attended upon him almost daily and Samuel bled and cupped him as often as he thought good to do it. At first, these ministrations and the chance for gentle walks in Danforth's hayfields seemed to make an improvement in his condition. But as the weather hardened he fell once more into a decline. The day came when he could not rise from his bed.

We were in Cambridge at the Cutters' house through this time, Samuel assisting betimes the new schoolmaster and betimes visiting his chirurgical patients. I went out to Charlestown as often as I could, to sit with Caleb and read to him and encourage him in every way possible. We all of us hoped for an improvement in his condition with the coming of spring, but the gentler air seemed insufficient to arrest his decline. As his state grew grave, Danforth asked me if I would stay at his home and nurse Caleb. Samuel consented, so readily indeed I feared what he did not say; that his experience told him Caleb's end was close. Ephriam Cutter's young wife agreed to take charge of Ammi Ruhama. So I stayed in Charlestown and spent my every waking hour at Caleb's bedside. There, I heard his fevered ravings as his illness worsened and he slipped in and out of consciousness. Sometimes he would murmur passages of scripture, other times, Latin aphorisms and epigrams would tumble forth from his lips. But at night he would ramble in Wampanaontoaonk. Always, at those times, it seemed that he addressed himself to Tequamuck. The rambling took the form of a conversation, or an argument, and often he would become agitated and thrash in his bed, although by day his failing body left him too weak to raise a hand.

After several nights of this, I conceived a plan—call it a fool's errand, or a desperate kind of madness—plucked up my courage and, with Samuel's blessing, bespoke me a passage to the island.

Makepeace and Dorcas were pleased to see me, though I did not give them an honest accounting of the grounds for my visit. That, I confided only to Iacoomis. He waxed wroth, as I had feared he might, and tried every argument to turn me from my purpose. In the end, and sadly, he refused to help me. I cannot say that I was entirely surprised.

This left me with but one place to turn. It took a vast amount of talking on my part to win Makepeace's agreement, but in the end he let me travel to visit the Merrys all alone. My pretext was supplied by the fact that Anne, still in deep mourning for Joel, had returned thence, having decided to honor his memory by walking the path he had planned to walk. She intended to start a school for the Takemmy children, and thereby fertilize the soil for the seeds of Christ's gospel.

I will own it: as heavyhearted as I was, setting out on my errand, the ride out of Great Harbor lifted my spirits. Speckle, as ever, was happy to bear me, and pranced along like a phaeton pony whenever the terrain allowed. When I came over the rise that led to the Merrys' farm, I reined her in and gathered my breath. I had not had an occasion to visit the Merrys when last I was on the island, since they had been all too happy to call upon us in Great Harbor. But now I saw that the industrious family had not wasted a day of the six years since I had last set eyes on their property. They had acquired a pair of calves and trained them up, so that the team of young oxen had cleared the dead trees. The orchard, skillfully pruned and carefully watered, ran in serried rows. I could hear sounds of factory coming from the mill, much enlarged, its great stones turning as the water tumbled brightly through the flume.

There were three fine homes, instead of only one, Jacob and Noah each having built a cottage to shelter their growing broods. It was Noah's littlest girl, Sarah, who saw me first, and ran to tell her mother. Tobia greeted me kindly and sent Sarah to fetch in Noah from the fields. I watched her go, blonde curls bobbing—the very image of her father.

Noah came in, smiling, yet clearly perplexed by my sudden appearance. "I was with your brother, market day last, yet he did not say ought of expecting a visit from you."

"I returned hence unlooked for," I said. Tobia had set out beer and oatcakes, so it was necessary to sit and make inconsequential chatter for some little while. Then Anne came in. She had been giving lessons at her school. She looked well, though without the bloom and gaiety she had worn a year earlier, before her great loss.

We spoke of how she went on with the children, and her looks became more animated as she talked of this child and that one, and how they did.

I could see that Noah regarded me throughout, and when he perceived that I was not about to disclose, before the others, my business in appearing at his door so strangely, he made some excuse about needing to take a message to the mill, and asked if I would like to walk over with him and see the improvements there. I caught the hint of a playful smile about his lips as he said this last; he knew very well I had no interest in grist making.

As soon as we were clear of the dooryard, I spoke. "Once, years since, you proved yourself a friend to me, and took a great risk in behalf of someone I held dear, who was in dire trouble. Noah, I have no right to ask it, but I have come here in the hope that you will come to my aid, as a great friend, once again, for such another in extremis." I told him then of Caleb's grave illness, and made my strange request. "It may be a fool's errand," I concluded, "but our best medicine and most ardent prayers have done nothing for him. If there is anything to be done, perhaps it yet lies in the hands of this other."

Noah looked grave. "I do not know why you should think it, so complete a crossing as Caleb has made into English ways, these many years."

"I have my reasons," I said softly.

"It is not without risk, you know. He is vengeful, so they say who know of him, and filled with spite. He keeps himself alone, these days, since no Christian Indians will suffer his presence among them. He is the last; the only pawaaw who has not renounced Satan and his familiars."

"I know it. But I have to try."

And so we took a mishoon to the Takemmy settlement to seek advice from the sonquem there. He was a prudent man. He made it his business to know where Tequamuck encamped at any given time. Better to give the wizard a wide berth, he reasoned, since he had been rumored to send his demon imps after any who took game that he deemed was his rightful portion.

When the sonquem learned that Noah and I sought conference with Tequamuck, he crossed himself and called on God's protection against the evil one. (He had become a Christian two years since, after long study of the matter.) We set out that same afternoon for the place he named, which was by great good fortune not three miles distant.

I do not know how, but he must have sensed our coming. He was waiting for us, standing, arms folded, behind the blaze of a fire. In its smoke I smelled the sharp tang of burning sage. He was dressed for ceremony. He wore his turkey feather cape and his face was painted in bands of red and yellow ochre.

We reined in Speckle some rods distant from his camp, and dismounted. I was quaking, I own it. My knees buckled when my feet touched the earth. Noah gave me his arm, and I took it right willingly, although when I laid my hand on it I felt that he too was all a-tremble. We willed ourselves forward.

Tequamuck must have cast some charm upon the fire, for as we approached it flared up for an instant. I winced in the sudden blast of heat. His form seemed to waver in the fiery air between us.

"Why does the child of the dead English pawaaw seek Tequamuck?"

That he spoke in English took me aback. I could not think how he might have acquired it, since keeping aloof from us had ever been his way.

"I . . . I come to ask your help." My voice was quavering.

"My help?" He gave a mirthless laugh. "My help? What's this? What of the power of your one god and his tortured son? Have they deserted you at last?"

I switched to Wampanaontoaonk. It had been years since I had spoken it, but the graceful shapes of the long words fell easily into my mouth. "Please, harken to me. Your nephew is sick. He lies close to death. He calls to you in his fit. I have heard him, night following night. I come to you to seek help for my friend in his illness."

"My nephew is sick? You think this comes as news to me? My nephew has been sick—indeed, he has been marked for death—from the day he commenced to walk with you, Storm Eyes."

I felt my breath go out of me. My knees really did buckle then, and Noah had to put out a hand against my fall. Tequamuck smiled. He was, as I supposed, used to having such an effect on people. I tried to fill my mind with prayers—rote words and psalms that were as natural as breath to me. But the fear this man engendered was like a black curtain and I could not summon a single verse. Tequamuck's voice took on the cadence he used in ceremony.

"I have heard Cheeshahteaumauk's cries. I have met his spirit. It is a weak spirit, pulled between two worlds. That is your doing, Storm Eyes. You call him friend. You have called him brother. Your friend and brother is lost now, wandering. He searches. Do you know why?"

I swallowed and I closed my eyes. Perhaps I did know. Or perhaps Tequamuck was bewitching me, putting thoughts into my mind. My mouth was dry as ash and I could not gather breath to speak.

"He searches for the son of Iacoomis. He does not find him, and he grieves. He fears he will never find him. That one never learned the way to the spirit world. He has no familiars to guide him. Cheeshahteaumauk's heart knows this. He knows that if he seeks his friend, he risks abandoning the spirit world of his ancestors, and all his kinfolk there. He will have to go to the house of the English dead."

I let go of Noah's supporting hand then and sank down on my knees. Great sobs rose up out of my chest. Tequamuck looked down at me with disgust. I knew that such a display was a disgraceful show of weakness in his eyes. He turned and began to walk towards his wetu. In his mind, the conference was clearly at a close. But I could not let it end there. I had to know how to help Caleb. I gathered my frayed shred of will, rubbed the tears from my face and forced myself to my feet.

"Wait, please!" I cried. "Please, tell me what I must do. How can I help him?"

Tequamuck did not turn. He had reached the wetu and was lifting the woven mat. I moved forward. Noah reached out a hand to stop me, but I cast it off. I looked back into his eyes. "As you are my friend—let me do this." He turned his hand out in a gesture of helplessness. I ran to the wetu and clasped the wizard by his arm. I felt a shudder pass through him. He stiffened and turned.

His eyes were all black above the lines of red ochre. Intelligent, searching eyes. I felt pinned by his glare.

"What do you want from me? You, who have already taken all. Leave me in peace to mourn my nephew."

"Please." My voice was thin, reedy. "Please show me how to help him."

He drew himself up to his full height and stared down at me for a long time. Though my skin crawled under his searching gaze, I willed myself not to look away. I felt my mind was naked to him, that he probed my every thought. Finally, he gave a great sigh.

"You truly want to help him." I nodded. "Then follow me. I will show you how." He lifted the mat and gestured for me to enter. Noah gave a shout but I turned back to him and shook my head. "Wait for me," I said. Then I followed the wizard into the dark.

I cannot write of what took place in that wetu, because I made a solemn oath, which I have never broken. Some would say it was a pact with the devil, and therefore I am not bound by it. But after that day I was no longer certain that Tequamuck was Satan's servant. To be sure, father and every other minister in my lifetime has warned that Satan is guileful and adept at concealing his true purpose. But since that day I have come to believe that it is not for us to know the subtle mind of God. It may be, as Caleb thought, that Satan is God's angel still, and works in ways that are obscure to us, to do his will. Blasphemy? Heresy? Perhaps. And perhaps I am damned for it. I will know, soon enough.

This much of what took place I will set down. In the dim light of his wetu, Tequamuck spoke to me of what he had foreseen—his people reduced, no longer hunters but hunted. He saw the dead stacked up like cordwood, and long lines of people, all on foot, driven off from their familiar places. These many years later, so much has come to pass as he said, and wheresoever his powers of sight came from, I know him now to be a true prophet.

He told me, also, that he had accepted that the power of our God was a greater power than any he possessed. I asked him then why he did not join his people in the Christian meeting.

"How should I worship your God, no matter how powerful, when I know what he will allow to befall us? Who would follow such a cruel god? And how should I lay aside the spirits by whose aid I have roiled the sea and riven rock, who for long years gifted me the power to cure the sick and to inflame my enemies' blood? To begloom the bright day and set dim night ablaze? All this, my spirits have allowed to me. Your God may be stronger than these; I see that. As I see that he will prevail. But not yet. Not for me. While I live, I will not abandon my familiars and the rites that are due to them."

When I left the wetu, the sun was setting. The sky was gorgeous— all purple and crimson with gold streaks of light giving volume to the billowing clouds. The strange smoke of Tequamuck's fire hung all about me and worked on my senses so that I saw all this with an uncanny vividness, each line and color a distinct and separate thing.

"Bethia, you are white as a parchment." Noah's eyes scanned my face anxiously. He gave me his arm once again. "Did he do aught to harm you? If he did, then I—"

"Noah." I interrupted him. "He did nothing but give me the help I sought." This was not entirely true, although I did not see it clearly then. Only later, when I was face-to-face with Caleb and looked into his eyes, did I understand exactly what kind of help Tequamuck had sent, and that it was both less, and more, than what I had asked of him.

"Let's leave this place now," I said to Noah. "I'm chilled to the bone." It was not a particularly cool evening, but my blood felt like ice, and I wanted to be back in a familiar place, one where ghosts and spirits were not swirling all about me.

IX

When I walked into Caleb's room, in the home of Thomas Danforth, I feared I had come too late. He lay with his face to the wall, and the coverlet barely seemed to rise, so slow and shallow had his breathing become. But I bent down, and whispered to him. The words, in Wampanaontoaonk, were for Caleb's ears, alone. As soon as I began upon the first of the verses, he turned, and stared at me, his eyes wide with surprise. When I had done, he laid a hand—light, hot—on my arm.

"Who?" he rasped.

I gave him the name.

His face smoothed, the lines of pain of a sudden all erased. He closed his eyes. When he opened them again, they were like dark coals aflame in their sockets, great orbs in a skull whose flesh was all wasted away. He gestured me to help him to sit up, so I went to the door and called upon Thomas Danforth, who was hovering, although as soon as I put a hand to Caleb's back I knew I could have easily managed alone. He was spare as a child, by then. Danforth fussed a little about the pillows and bolsters, until I gave him a meaning look. He took the hint and retired again, leaving me alone with Caleb. There was a good fire in the grate; Danforth had insisted that it be kept lit and well fed if the weather was the least bit cool. I walked over to the hearth and held the bundled herbs over the flame until they caught. The scent, clean and sharp, seemed to carry the air of the island into the room. Caleb's eyes followed my gestures as I waved the bundle in a slow arc. He seemed to breathe easier. I came back to his bedside and drew out the wampum belt. The whole history of the Nobnocket band was encoded in its pattern, for any wise enough to read it.

I laid the belt across Caleb's heart, as a sonquem might wear it. His hand closed on the smooth-polished shells. He let his fingers travel across the rows of purple and white. His lips moved, and I knew he was reciting parts of the story, as he had heard it years earlier. At last, when his lips and his hands grew still, I knew it was time. I knelt down beside his bed. His hair had grown long again, since his illness. I lifted a dark strand and smoothed it back from his face. He raised his hand and touched his fingertips to my fingertips. Then I brought my lips to his ear and whispered to him the last of the words that Tequamuck had given me.

Caleb raised his chin, and made a mighty effort to gather his breath. Then his lips parted, and though the sound that uttered forth was strained at first, his voice gained strength until I felt his hymn like a paean, resonant in my soul. He sang out his death song, and died like a hero going home.

Caleb *was* a hero, there is no doubt of it. He ventured forth from one world to another with an explorer's courage, armored by the hope that he could serve his people. He stood shoulder to shoulder with the most learned of his day, ready to take his place with them as a man of affairs. He won the respect of those who had been swiftest to dismiss him.

All that is true and certain. But what I do not know is this: which home welcomed him, at the end. Whichever it was—the celestial English heaven of seraphim, cherubim and ophanim, or Kietan's warm and fertile place away in the southwest, I believe that his song was powerful enough for Joel to hear and to follow him there.

X

They pulled the Indian College down. It was, you could say, a victim of the war. After such bloody fighting, there were few who cared if Indians lived or died, were converted or languished pagan. The building fell into disrepair. And then, in 1698, whatever ambitions had once been lay scattered and broken in the yard, reduced to a pile of rubble and a cloud of dust. They took the bricks, as many as were fit to save, and used them to build another hall. When I heard of it, I was not angry, though once again what was rightfully Indian had been taken for English use. It is an old story to me, by now. And that college had proved itself the greatest thief of all. It was, I now think, a cursed place. How to see it otherwise, since every Indian scholar who stayed within its walls perished untimely. Others came there after Caleb and Joel, but no sooner did word come to us of these young men and their great promise than the black-bordered message followed to tell us they were dead. I know of only one that may yet live: John Wampus, who tarried in the college but a little while, before setting off for healthier climes. He became, they say, a mariner. I hope he prospered.

Often, my mind wanders to that warm day, so very long ago. If I had turned away from that boy, at the edge of the pond, mounted Speckle and ridden back to my own world and left him in peace with his gods and spirits, would it have been better? Would he yet live, an old man now, patriarch of a family, a leader of his tribe? Perhaps so. I cannot see.

He visits me, in my dreams. They say it is a gift his people have. At times, he comes to me as the boy I knew; other times, he lets me see him as he might have been. In one dream, he is a man in his prime, trained in the law, high in the governor's favor, appointed to negotiate with Metacom. He wins for his people a measure of justice, turning hearts from war and the devastation that has flowed from it. It was a good dream. I was sorry, when I awakened.

I grieve, also, for Joel, who might have returned here as the most educated man on the island, to stand between his people and the unscrupulous English who ensnare them into debt peonage. All too often now, one sees a Wampanoag child serving in an English house or upon an English vessel, indentured away from family in payment of some murky obligation.

These are all of them dreams, waking or sleeping, and no one can truly say what might have been. But dreams and memories are all that sustain me now. When, from time to time, I open my heart on these matters to Samuel, he smiles at me patiently. But I know he thinks I am become a fond old woman, my mind wandering, addled, between an unchangeable past and an unfathomable future. I told him not long ago that I dream of a time when the scars of war will heal, and the hearts of our people will soften again, one to the other, and other young Indians like Caleb and Joel will take their places at Harvard, in the society of learned men. He shook his head and said he cannot see such a thing in half a hundred years. And then he touched my face, and kissed me. All this long time we have loved each other, and we love still, even as the ties that bind us to this world have frayed and worn, and are become fragile now as a spider's thread.

He will be here soon. He comes to see to my comfort many times each day, but always at this time, as the light fades. He brings me a draft of laudanum—I am beyond help of his chirurgical skills now—and then we sit together, hand in hand, and watch the last light dance upon the water.

I will put these pages by before he comes. I do not wish to speak to him this night about these matters, things over and done; none of it to be mended. Yet it has eased my heart to make this accounting. I am not a hero. Life has not required it of me. But neither will I go to my grave a coward, silent about what I did, and what it cost. So, let these last pages be *my* death song—even if at the end it is no paean, but as it must be: a dissonant and tragical lament.

Afterword

Caleb's Crossing is inspired by a true story. It is, however, a work of imagination. What follows is the history, insofar as it is documented: the slender scaffolding on which I have rested my imaginative edifice.

The "college at Newtowne," which would be named Harvard, was founded in 1636, just six years after the establishment of the Massachusetts Bay colony. The total number of its graduates in the seventeenth century was only 465. Caleb Cheeshahteaumauk was a member of this elite.

He was born circa 1646 on the island then known to its Wôpanâak inhabitants as Noepe or Capawock, just five years after the arrival of a handful of English settlers. Caleb's father was sonquem, or leader, of one of the smaller Wôpanâak bands whose lands were in Nobnocket, now generally known as West Chop. Since the tiny English settlement was ten miles away, it is reasonable to suppose that Caleb had little contact with the English in his earliest years, and was raised in his people's language and traditions.

The English patent to the island now known as Martha's Vineyard was bought by a Puritan businessman, Thomas Mayhew, from the Earl of Sterling and Sir Fernando Gorges in 1641. His son, Thomas, Jr., then negotiated to buy a parcel of land from a sonquem, Tawanticut, to the east of the island. The sale was opposed by a number of Tawanticut's band but went ahead after the sonquem ceded some of his lands to the dissidents and sold to the Mayhews from what remained under his control. Thomas, Jr., then led a small party of settlers to found Great Harbor (now Edgartown). Thomas, Sr.'s motivation in settling the island appears to have been the creation of an independent manorial estate outside the purview of the Massachusetts Bay colony; Thomas, Jr., by contrast, was a religious man whose life's work became the conversion of the Wôpanâak. To that end, in the winter of 1652, he founded a day school with thirty Indian pupils. It is possible that Caleb was among them, and that he learned to read, write, and speak English there. In 1657, Thomas, Jr., died in a shipwreck en route to England. His father, his son Matthew, and his grandson Experience, among others, continued his missionary and educational work.

Caleb was probably sent off the island to attend Daniel Weld's school in Roxbury. Nine Indian students (including, intriguingly, "Joane the Indian Mayde") were under Weld's instruction there in 1658. In 1659 he and fellow Vineyarder Joel Iacoomis were among five Indian scholars who joined Matthew Mayhew at Elijah Corlett's grammar school in Cambridge, adjacent to Harvard College. Matthew left the grammar school before matriculating and returned to the island.

Harvard's 1650 charter describes its mission as "the education of the English and Indian youth of this country." At least one Indian scholar, John Sassamon, received some education at Harvard before the construction of the Indian College, a two-storey brick building erected in 1656. John Printer, a Nipmuc, ran the printing press housed in the college, where the first Indian bible and many other books in Algonquin were published. Other Native Americans, named Eleazar, Benjamin Larnell, and John Wampus, are known to have been associated with the college.

Caleb and Joel were admitted to Harvard in 1661, where they completed the rigorous, classics-based four-year course of study for a bachelor's degree. On his way back from Martha's Vineyard to Cambridge for the 1665 commencement, Joel Iacoomis was shipwrecked and murdered on Nantucket and never received the degree he had earned. Caleb marched with his English classmates in 1665, received his degree, but died just a year later of consumption. Thomas Danforth, the noted jurist and politician, cared for him during his final illness.

Sources on Caleb's brief, tragic, and remarkable life are sadly scant. Most of the known primary sources are in the writings of Daniel Gookin (c. 1612–87), superintendent of the Indians in Massachusetts, and in those of certain overseers of Harvard College in correspondence with the London-based Society for the Propagation of the Gospel in New England. The New England Company, as it was also sometimes known, raised donations to educate and convert Indians, funds which were vital to the survival of Harvard in its early years.

In a search through the few surviving writings penned by notable classmates of Caleb and Joel, I was able to find no mention of their Indian colleagues. One hypothesis to explain this omission is that the native youths, by the time they reached Harvard, were so assimilated into English society that they were unremarkable to their fellow scholars. Certainly they were as highly educated as any of their colonial peers, having attended the finest prep schools then available. An alternative possibility is that the two

Wôpanâak youths were kept socially and academically isolated by racial prejudice and did not truly share in the college life of their peers. My imagined version of their experience has tried to take account of both theses.

While I am indebted to Wolfgang Hochbruck and Beatrix Dudensing-Reichel for their close analysis of the Latin in the one surviving document from Caleb's hand (in *Early Native American Writing*, Helen Jaskoski, ed., New York: Cambridge University Press, 1996), I take issue with their attempt to cast doubt on its authorship. The errors in the Latin, which they portray as evidence that the text may have been dictated to Caleb, can just as easily be read as evidence of authenticity—the kind of mistakes that any second- or third-year arts student might make in penning a scholarly exegesis. Furthermore, the essayists err in the one piece of evidence they offer in support of the proposition that colonists readily falsified accounts to extort money from England. They conclude that the Iacoomis referenced in an admitted falsification by John Eliot is Caleb's fellow student Joel, when it is certain from the context that Eliot was referring to Joel's father, the first Indian convert to Christianity on Martha's Vineyard, who served for many years as a missionary and ordained minister here.

I found the secondary sources, especially Samuel Eliot Morison's many books on early Harvard, in equal parts indispensable and hair-tearingly aggravating. Morison's reflexive racism makes his choice and use of sources highly unreliable. To give just one glaring example: citing President Dunster's early, failed attempt to prepare two young Indians sent to him by John Eliot in 1646, Morison quotes Dunster: "[T]hey are uncapable of the benefit of such learning as was my desire to impart to them, and therefore they being an hindrance to mee.... I desire they may be somewhere else disposed of with all convenient speed." Perusal of Dunster's actual letter in the Massachusetts Archives discloses that Morison has omitted Dunster's crucial prefatory words: "Whereas the Indians with mee bee so small as that they are uncapable...."

This book grew out of the remarkable environmental and cultural stewardship of the Wampanoag Tribe of Gay Head/Aquinnah. It was in materials prepared by the tribe that I first learned of Caleb, and the many inspiring programs offered to the public by the Aquinnah Cultural Center have helped to inform and shape my thinking. Individual tribal members have been encouraging and generous in sharing information and insights and in reading early drafts. Others have been frank in expressing reservations about an undertaking that fictionalizes the life of a beloved figure and sets down an imagined version of that life that may be misinterpreted as factual. This afterword attempts to address those reservations somewhat by distinguishing scant fact from rampant invention.

For the early colonial history of Martha's Vineyard I am indebted to the late Anne Coleman Allen, whose Short Course on the History of Martha's Vineyard was indispensable for the depth of its research on the Mayhew regime and for its inclusion of insights by June Manning, genealogist of the Wampanoag Tribe of Gay Head/Aquinnah. Jannette Vanderhoop's class on Wampanoag culture at Adult and Community Education of Martha's Vineyard was similarly enlightening. I also relied upon David J. Silverman's 2005 book, *Faith and Boundaries* (Cambridge, UK, and New York:

Cambridge University Press). I am thankful to the Martha's Vineyard Museum for access to its archives; to Chris Henning for his Latin expertise; to early readers, including Graham Thorburn, Clare Reihill, Darleen Bungey and Elinor, Tony and Nathaniel Horwitz. As ever, I am fortunate in my agent, Kris Dahl, and my editors, Molly Stern and Paul Slovak. The students and faculty involved in the Harvard Yard Indian College archaeological dig and the Peabody Museum's remarkable "Digging Veritas" exhibition welcomed me into the material culture of seventeenth-century Harvard.

The fictional exchanges between Bethia and Caleb regarding matters of faith rely heavily upon John Cotton, Jr.'s account of his conversations with native islanders in his 1660s missionary journals, and upon marginalia in religious texts and bibles, written in the Wôpanâak language in the seventeenth and eighteenth centuries.

While the Mayfields in my novel borrow a few biographical facts from the lives of the missionary Mayhews, my characters are all works of fiction, especially Bethia, who is entirely invented. Makepeace Mayfield resembles Matthew Mayhew only in one respect: his failure to matriculate from Elijah Corlett's school. That there may have been tension between Matthew and Caleb was suggested to me by the arresting fact that when Matthew's son, Experience, penned a detailed history of the Christian Indians of Martha's Vineyard, Caleb—certainly among the most illustrious—was not mentioned.

Colonial archives contain no surviving female diaries before seventeen hundred and very few letters. To find Bethia's voice I have relied on such sources as the captivity narratives of Mary Rowlandson, the court testimony of Anne Hutchinson, and the poems of Anne Bradstreet. Her job in the buttery of Harvard College was suggested to me by Laurel Thatcher Ulrich's introductory essay in *Yards and Gates: Gender in Harvard and Radcliffe History* (New York: Palgrave Macmillan, 2004). I have been informed by the work of several scholars of the period, especially Jill Lepore, Arthur Railton, James Axtell, Jane Kamensky, Lisa Brooks, and Mary Beth Norton. I began research for the novel while a fellow at the Radcliffe Institute for Advanced Study, for which opportunity I remain most appreciative.

In recent years, two Vineyard Wôpanâak, Carrie Anne Vanderhoop and Tobias Vanderhoop, successfully completed graduate degrees at Harvard.

I think Bethia Mayfield would be pleased that a woman president of Harvard, Drew Gilpin Faust, now presides at commencement. Among those to whom she will award a BA in 2011 is expected to be Tiffany Smalley, the first Martha's Vineyard Wôpanâak since Caleb Cheeshahteaumauk to complete an undergraduate degree at Harvard College.

Vineyard Haven, November 1, 2010